CAIRO SWAN SONG

CAIRO SWAN SONG

Mekkawi Said

Translated by
Adam Talib

First published in Great Britain in 2009 by

ARABIA BOOKS
70 Cadogan Place
London SW1X 9AH
www.arabia-books.com

Published in agreement with the

AMERICAN UNIVERSITY IN CAIRO PRESS
113 Sharia Kasr el Aini, Cairo, Egypt
420 Fifth Avenue, New York, 10018
www.aucpress.com

Copyright © by Mekkawi Said, 2006
First published in Arabic in 2006 as *Taghridat al-bag'a*
English translation copyright © Adam Talib, 2009

The moral right of the author has been asserted
Protected under the Berne Convention

ISBN 978-1-906697-18-1

Printed in Great Britain by J. F. Print Ltd, Sparkford
Cover design by Arabia Books
Cover image: Sven Hagolani, getty images
Page design by Andrea El-Akshar

To my sister, Fatima, without whose support I could
    never have finished this novel;
To my older brother, Osman, who looked after me
    when I was a child;
And to all the loving hearts that continue to offer me
    their support.

To the warm lightning bolt that I happened upon and
    locked up in my heart never to be released,
For my sake, calm down. Give in.

—Mekkawi

1

It was a little past midnight and the coffeehouse was closing up; only two tables of customers remained, absorbed in their games. They didn't seem to mind the biting cold. They were my only protection against the anxious waiter, who was looking at his watch every five minutes and shaking his head. I was desperate to sit there out of the cold for as long as I could. I was watching the waiter nervously, hoping he wouldn't announce closing time. Every time he went to clear away my empty glass and wipe the table down with his wet rag, I'd order another drink. When he sat down beside me, sighing and rubbing his hands together for warmth, I mumbled an order for a hot chocolate. Head lolling forward, he called to the guy behind the counter who made the drinks. His coworker's curt reply, "The gas tank's empty. No more hot drinks," felt like a push out the door.

Without looking at the waiter, I ordered a bottle of Pepsi. He stood up lazily and brought me a partially frozen Pepsi in a can. He chucked it down on the table in front of me, causing a deep thud. While he was watching a table of customers rising to leave, I asked him to bring me a glass for the Pepsi. He ignored me and went over to tell them how much they owed. After they paid up, he walked back over with his hands in the wide front pockets of his apron. He remembered that I'd asked him for something, and brought me a glass. He sat down beside me again. "You know, pal, cold drinks are the best thing in this kind of weather," he said. I didn't say anything. I was busy watching the remaining three customers; two of them were playing a game and the other was cheering them on. The boy standing next to them was carrying a large ladle of burning coals for the water pipes and shivering almost imperceptibly. He was watching the game and would occasionally lift the coals up beside the table. They'd stop playing and warm their hands over the glowing coals for a few moments before resuming their game. The waiter kept at his mission to get rid of me by counting out the chits I'd accumulated. Every little token he dropped on the table clanged and that, along with my attempts to drink the frozen Pepsi, set my teeth chattering. I was losing my patience so before he could drop another chit I put my hand over the pile. One fell on to the back of my hand.

I faked a smile. "I'm sorry, that noise is bothering me. Count them somewhere else."

He looked at me for a few seconds. "We're closing, sir." Before I could nod in the direction of the other customers, he stood up and said, "Those folks are friends of ours."

I lit a cigarette and waited for him to come back out. As soon as I saw him, I called him over. He refused the cigarette I offered him as I asked how much I owed. Then I paid up, including a tip that was bigger than the total bill. He thanked me coolly a few times before going over to the other table and feigning an interest in their game. I finished my cigarette and sat there loafing while I lit another. I knew he was watching me out of the corner of his eye. He came and sat next to me again as I'd expected he would. He hesitated, but then whispered, "If you're in a bind, there are cheap hotels near the shrine." I turned my head, but he kept on like a broken record. He pointed at the boy carrying the coals and whispered, "Borai lives upstairs, in this building. He's got himself a little spot on the roof. I hope you won't mind me saying, but if you're meeting a hooker, you could take her up there. He'll do anything for a tenner."

That was the decisive moment in our conversation: if I didn't draw the line right then, he'd carry on like that until all his reserves of filth and smut had gone dry. I silenced him with a sharp look and stood up to leave with the other customers, who were filing out. I thought walking in the cold would only make me more anxious. I felt the wide empty square, bathed in pale light, was moving toward me. There were interludes of silence between the flourishes of wind and the echoes of dogs' barking. As I tried to remember where the place was, my mobile shrieked, grating my nerves.

I snapped at her over the phone. "He left me hanging at the coffee-house." I realized that 'left me hanging' might have been too idiomatic for her so I rephrased, "I waited for him there until closing time."

Her response was made up of some phrases that mixed contempt and suspicion. "Call me if there are any developments," she said and ended the conversation.

As usual, my hand missed my jacket pocket and my mobile fell to the ground with an awful clunk. I damned her and I damned the weather; damned love, animal instincts, boredom, and belief as I bent down to pick it up. My scarf slipped forward on my neck, exposing me to the assault of the brutal cold. I stared at my mobile phone: it was like a stiff, mute corpse in my hand, its screen an endless spider web now. I stuffed it into my pocket.

When I got to the square, I became an ideal target for the cold currents blowing from every corner: out of back streets, alleys, avenues, building entrances. The Mosque of Sayyida Zaynab looked captivating and seductive through the heavy mist. I retreated to the corrugated iron door of one of the closed shops and leaned against it. I perched on the cold marble sill of the display window, feeling with my buttocks for the narrow space between the iron spikes, which the sadistic shop owner had installed to keep people from sitting down. I lit a cigarette with the last of my matches to have survived the cold gale. I was waiting for a phantom, not a human; all just so I could tell Marcia that he was going to cooperate with us. If I'd taken him to see her right then, she, having finished her bottle of whiskey and bag of weed, would rocket up to seventh heaven, taking us onboard, paying no mind to the clouds, black holes, or nebulae.

Windows slammed shut, others sprang open violently. The wind was blowing more strongly now, through the bending boughs of trees whose runt branches fell to the ground. I got up and started walking, sheltering under the cover of balconies. Billboards were shaking violently on the roofs of the large buildings bordering the square. My eyes were fixed on the sky, searching for the one that was going to crash down on my head. I walked for a while until the wind died down and I decided I'd see that night through, no matter what the cost. I headed randomly to the right following the imprecise directions Karim had given me. I didn't see any of the signs or landmarks he'd mentioned, but after some careful searching I found a small store, shut up for the night, with an ugly sign that said they mended clothes. Next to it was a somewhat bigger store; it was closed, too, like all the other shops on the street. It looked like a tire shop. There was no sign, but the tire rims hanging on the lamppost out front gave it away.

Across the street, there was a villa with a crumbling façade squatting in the dark, beside shattered streetlights. I examined the villa. There were some irregular lights, glowing faintly and flickering all over the place. I felt like a fighter pilot scoping out a small, disguised target. I crossed over to the front of the villa. Growing more daring, I went through the entrance, which was missing its iron gate, into the court-yard. I stood there a while, unable to advance or retreat. Then, suddenly, the mounds of trash, dirt, and rocks around me were replaced by boys and girls, none older than ten. They surrounded me. The tallest one took a razor blade out from under his tongue and started waving it in my face as I tried to back away. A little girl, his sidekick, was sneaking closer to me under the protection of his razor. The boy's arm came straight down and cut a long slice through my leather jacket. I caught the little girl's hand in my pocket reaching for my mobile. The girl shouted defiantly. They looked even more vicious and angry. I let go of

4

her hand; I didn't even consider following her as she scurried inside the villa. "I want to see Karim!" I shouted.

They immediately fell silent and lowered the small weapons they'd been pointing at me. They looked at one another as if there were some pact between them, and then they ran off in every direction, disappearing completely.

I walked away. I didn't pay the slightest attention to the dogs' barking, or the bracing wind that'd come on stronger than before, or to the falling tree branches along the way. Not even to the billboard that tumbled to the ground and nearly crushed me.

2

I watched the sun set, entertained by the sight of a light-gray pigeon that was shuttling the food and straw she'd hidden in a corner of my balcony up to her nest on the roof of the building opposite, up to crannies in the crumbling concrete just below the eaves. I hadn't seen Marcia for the past three days. My home phone had been cut off for a while and my mobile was busted and stolen. There was no Internet at home, either. Marcia was accustomed to my disappearances, and hiatuses were nothing new to us. I'd pull back when I began to get bored of her and she'd usually drop out when she had work to do. The malaise I was feeling at that moment was almost enough to make me put on my clothes and run out the door in her direction. Instead, I decided I'd spend all night in some club downtown after I'd gone to Essam's studio to drag him along with me, but I was caught off guard by a barrage of knocking and doorbell ringing.

It definitely wasn't Marcia; could've been Essam. I ran to open the door—Zaynab, I hadn't expected. She shoved me back into the apartment and kissed me on the cheeks. She'd already shut the door behind her before I'd been able to get my head around anything. Why didn't I realize it was Zaynab? We were always fighting and giving each other the silent treatment. She was usually the one to end the standoff: she'd either drop by or send a text or else she'd stick a note on my door—she didn't think twice about snooping neighbors or anyone else who might happen to read it.

She was sitting on the couch, focused on taking the Walkman out of her handbag and putting her headphones on. She had a pile of papers in her hand. Her shoes lay overturned on the floor. She was about to start writing again as if I weren't even there or as if we'd never had an argument. When she noticed I was looking at her, she curled her thumb and fingers as if she were holding a glass: a bitchy signal that meant I should make her some tea.

"Go make it yourself."

She didn't get up. I went into the kitchen to make sure there was something for dinner in the refrigerator. Then I went to enjoy a hot shower while she took care of whatever it was she was working on.

I first met her when she came to interview me for a third-rate newspaper that probably no one's ever heard of. That was after I'd come back from the Gulf. I was attracted to her calmness and her beautifully plain face. She wore no makeup and very ordinary clothes. She brought me a copy of the interview after it was published. She called me a few times after that, too, and we ended up going out on a date. I'd become drawn to her in a short period of time. At difficult moments in my life, I often thought it'd be best to put an end to my bachelorhood with her; to be nestled in her hands rather than in Marcia's claws.

She lived in Shubra, in a hostel for girls whose families didn't live in Cairo. Her family was from Minya. I reckoned my apartment downtown was like her idea of paradise. Zaynab lived simply. The silly little gifts I gave her embarrassed her and made her uneasy. Whenever we went to a café, she'd refuse to eat and only ever ordered tea with milk, or the occasional coffee. One night, after we'd known each other for some time, I asked her why. After a little stonewalling, she shyly admitted that her father was a farmer and that he'd had a hard time

7

supporting her, her two sisters, younger brother, and their mother. So that, for many years, all they'd had for dinner was a cup of tea with milk and some scraps of bread. She said she'd never tasted a cup of tea with milk as good as the ones she used to have at home and that she was hoping to rediscover that taste somewhere, either with me or when she went out by herself. And when she said that, a tyrannical wave of emotion overtook me and I decided that Zaynab was the woman for me. In a stupid, irresponsible moment, I decided that as soon as I'd seen her back to her hostel, I'd ask her to set a date for us to go visit her family so I could ask for her hand. I didn't talk to Essam or Awad first, or anyone else for that matter; nor did the thought of Marcia cross my mind. I was like a guy who decides, on the spur of the moment, that he's going to kick alcohol and start leading prayers. I didn't even ask myself why I chose to wait until after I'd seen her back to her hostel.

She surprised me on that wondrous, lovely night after we'd lost track of the time, when she looked anxiously at her watch and told me that her curfew had been hours ago. I volunteered to go back with her to help smooth things over with the matron, but she said that the matron wouldn't be placated by my excuses, and that actually my presence would probably make matters more complicated. She said it wasn't the first time she'd missed curfew. It would've been the third time and she'd already been warned by the management that she wasn't to miss curfew again without prior approval or else she'd be kicked out. I felt radiant and romantic as I watched her, her eyes filling with sparkling, disorienting tears. I couldn't decide whether to embrace her, or cry on her chest, or swear to her that I'd protect her and look after her for the rest of my life, that I'd never let anybody get in the way of her happiness. Zaynab had never been dearer to me than she was at that moment. I settled for circumspectly patting her on the back. We were faced with two problems: one urgent and another for later. Where was she going to sleep that night? That was the question that required an immediate answer. She used my phone to call several of her girlfriends, all of whom made excuses but one. Her friend lived in a suburb called Oseem. Zaynab calmed down after that, even though the commute seemed treacherous at that time of night. There was still the problem postponed so we set a time to meet the next morning to sort out the issue of her hostel.

She stopped outside a coffeehouse and asked me to ask the owner if she could use the restroom to wash her face. I was sitting, waiting for her, when she came back out, drying her neck with a tissue, but she didn't signal to me to get up. She sat down next to me instead. "You're really going to come with me tomorrow to talk to the matron?" she asked with a pleading look. When I nodded, she regained her captivating smile. She waved over the waiter, who'd been watching us from afar, and ordered a tea with milk. When she saw me furrow my brow, she ordered me a coffee and smiled at me. She started telling me about the hostel and her friends there, and about the funny incidents and ups and downs they'd all experienced over the past two years.

I found myself compelled to say, "I love you." She let out a laugh that was straight from the heart and dipped a spoon in her tea. She insisted I taste it. I didn't understand what that had to do with my saying 'I love you,' but I tasted it like she'd asked.

Black clouds loomed once again when she looked at the clock hanging above the counter. She told me that it had got too late for her to go to her friend's place in Oseem. I was exhausted and in no mood to spend the whole night loitering in cafes, captive to her high-velocity mood swings, so when she asked me, "What do we do now?" I said, "Either we hang out on the street till morning or you come spend the night at my place." Her eyes grew wide, but she didn't say anything. I tried to lessen the impact of what I'd said by explaining that I'd take her back to my place, but that I'd go sleep at Essam's.

On our way back, she held my hand and whispered, "You don't have to do that. It's your apartment. I can't make you sleep somewhere else. You only have the one bedroom?"

"Two."

"It's settled then. You sleep in one, and I'll sleep in the other."

I started to forget about the idea of going to visit her family in Minya, but I wasn't going to give in to my wishful imagination.

9

We took a taxi home. The doorman's room was off the foyer, across from the elevator. He usually slept behind his door so he could monitor whoever came into the building late at night. And she was still talking. She talked in the cab. She talked on the sidewalk in front of the building. She was talking as we waited for the elevator, and when the doorman came out from his room, she said, "Good evening." He responded in kind, rubbing his eyes and stepping back into his room while I tried not to look angry.

In the antique elevator, she tapped her long fingers on the worn wood to the tune of a popular song. She wanted to write on the mirror with her lipstick, but then when I scolded her, she just stared at me for a while, puzzled. Once we got inside the apartment, I brought her a gallabiya and changed into one myself. I pointed her in the direction of the refrigerator so she could get something to eat, but she said she wasn't hungry. I gave her the key to the bedroom and she locked the door, but then a few minutes later she popped into my room and handed me back the key, saying I shouldn't let her lock the door because she wasn't used to sleeping alone and she was scared. Then she asked me to stay awake for a bit and talk to her between rooms and when she returned to her room, she left the door ajar. She said I should shut her bedroom door after she'd fallen asleep, but she kept on talking while I was trying to read. I didn't respond until she started whining, but by then I was pissed off and fed up. I was about ready to throw her from the sixth floor. Her voice flagged and it was quiet for a stretch. I figured she'd fallen asleep. A few minutes later, though, I heard her feeble voice, "Aren't you going to go to bed?"

I turned the light off so I could sleep. A few moments later, she called out again, but this time her voice sounded serious and somewhat frightened. "Why'd you turn off all the lights? It's pitch-black in here." I got up from my bed in a huff, this close to throwing her out on the street. Her room was as bright as a movie set. As soon as I walked into the room, she grabbed my hand and whispered, "I'm scared. I'm really scared. Please, sleep in here." She pointed at the bed and before I could even understand what had just taken place, she said, "You can sleep over there," pointing at the farthest edge of the bed, "but please don't move around because then I can't sleep." I did as she asked and lay there for a few minutes like a schoolboy who's sorry to find himself in a room full of the mean teachers he dreads. I was woken by her moist lips nibbling the bottom of my ear. When I opened my eyes, she smiled and whispered, "Thanks for letting me stay the night."

I just played dumb and remained completely silent. She was either playing with my hair or tickling my nose when she spelled it out for me, "Please, don't come any closer." I honored her request, slave to the genes of idiocy that were in control of me that night. I shut my eyes and tried to recall the day's events, which passed by in rainbow colors, as I smilingly crawled toward sleep. Every time our bodies touched, either intentionally on her part or absent-mindedly on mine, I immediately pulled back and a frightening image weighed down on my heart. I could picture her telling her close friends how noble and moral I was, about how I'd shared a bed with her for eight straight hours without once touching her. That really aggravated me. I got on top of her; she looked at me in shock. I kissed her cheeks and her hair and then she rolled me over. I was assailed by kisses all over my body. She was like an unbroken, unbridled mare running out into open country. I kissed her back, and my hands discovered all the visible and hidden treasures of her body, but she didn't let me go all the way. "I'm still a virgin, so don't try anything," she whispered, and yet in spite of that, she used her practiced hand on me. "I don't want you to hurt yourself."

I relaxed for half an hour or more, but she wasn't finished. There were fewer restrictions that time as desire consumed her, and after I'd done what she'd timidly asked of me, lust took over and she asked for more and more. My path was unobstructed and her performance was astonishing: she took me through all my memories of Saudi and Doha and America, sailed me to all the official and underground fun spots. I was exhausted. I'd nearly disappeared in a deep labyrinth where only the echo of her voice could reach me. She told me how her uncle had stolen her innocence when she was a child and that was why she'd left for Cairo and distracted herself with her many newspapers. Maybe I

11

imagined it, or maybe I actually heard her swear I was only the second man she'd ever slept with. Whatever. I was in a totally different universe anyway.

"Are you going to sleep in the bathroom?" Her screechy voice was driving me mad. That lunatic! Did she ever give it a rest? She showed no regard for anyone else on earth. As if I didn't have neighbors who knew me! Her voice was as loud as a field of crickets. It never occurred to her that other people existed, not that she gave a damn about what they thought. She treated me as if she were my wife.

One time, after I'd woken up, I found her standing in the doorway of the apartment, talking to a neighbor as if they were old friends. I was worried she'd introduced herself to the woman as my wife. When they'd finished their conversation, she shut the door and turned to me, but when I let her have it, she was annoyed at me for being angry. "She didn't ask who I was. And anyway we didn't talk about anything. Just 'Good morning' and a little girl talk. That way she won't suspect anything. If I'd hesitated or clammed up, she probably would've reported me to the police. I let her decide who I was. Your wife . . . your sister . . . your daughter . . . your stepmother. The important thing is that you don't bring any trashy types back here anymore and get me in trouble." I laughed, tickled by what she'd done.

I walked in and found her lying on the couch wearing only shorts and a bra. She shifted a little so that I could sit beside her. I leaned back and asked, "Aren't you cold?"

"You know what kind of people get cold in weather like this? Old people like you . . . not me."

"Are you hungry?" I asked as I caressed her thigh.

"Not yet." Then she snapped out of her malaise and gave me a kiss. "I missed you," she said.

The maddening ring of her mobile went off, and she grabbed it before I could reach it, afraid that I'd smash it, since I'd done so once before. She stood up and answered in a whisper.

I couldn't make out a word of what she was saying, nor could I read her lips because she'd turned her back to me. She finished her call quickly and turned the phone off. I was always telling her to turn it off before she came over, but it was a waste of breath. Before I could start giving the speech she was tired of hearing, she attacked my ears with kisses and drenched them in whispers. "He's a real important source. It's great that he called me. This is going to be a knockout scoop."

I slapped her butt and said, "Here's your knockout." That annoyed her so she started punching my chest playfully, babbling about how I didn't trust her and how stupid she was to have given me everything hoping it'd bring us closer, but I was just like any other man: as soon as his lover spreads her legs for him, he begins to wonder if she's spreading them for everyone else. She got up to look for her clothes, pretending to be angry and threatening to leave. My desire for her was inextinguishable so I was ready to put up with everything I hated in order to have her. Like the peasant proverb that goes, "Before you make love, you'll give her an acre, but after you've had her, you pray someone'll take her." I grabbed the blouse out of her hand and pulled the trousers off one of her legs. I was pleading with her as I dragged her to the bedroom. As I laid her down on the bed, I ignored the looks from her glazed, sated eyes, the same look I'd see in her after we had sex. Her body reeked strongly of men, but I ignored even the smell of semen on her breath. Lust propelled me and I didn't stop until it was satisfied.

3

IT WAS A BOISTEROUS PARTY like all the rest. The foreign band was playing like a bunch of madmen and the noise from the speakers was shaking the chairs and the floor. I went out to the balcony and leaned against the wooden door. I stood there smoking, looking out over the beautiful Cairo night. The balcony stretched the length of the two rooms that the partygoers were congregated in and each opened out onto it. I wasn't the only one out on the balcony; other guests were hanging out in corners smoking pot or hash, and couples stood in the dark, one hand on their drinks, the other on each other's bodies. The clamor reverberated through the otherwise serene and lovely neighborhood, even though we were up on the fourteenth floor. The building's tenants were mostly students at the international private universities in the city—most of the foreign students were studying at the American University in Cairo—or else they were consultants or employees of the multinational firms operating in Egypt. The building was extremely well guarded, almost as if it were being kept a secret. Watch out if you've had a plate implanted for a broken bone, or if you've got a silver tooth, or if you're a woman, if you're using an IUD for birth control because the metal detector that's like a second narrower entrance to the building is certain to erupt in an excruciating whistle. You might not even get through without a certificate of quarantine from NAMRU.

I was leaning against the door of the balcony unable to look at the ground below. When I turned my head, I could see Marcia writhing, dancing, absorbed in the music. I could tell she was drunk. She was staring at me with an empty look, warning me against sneaking out unannounced. I wouldn't have been able to dance with her if she'd asked. I was sick with boredom so I tried to keep entertained by checking out the faces of the people there: half of them I'd never seen before, but the other half I knew. Some were students of mine, or I'd met them through Marcia, and there were some Egyptians and foreigners whom I'd met at cultural events. None of my close friends had come. Bloody Essam talked me into coming here and then didn't show up himself. I hadn't seen my German friend, Awad, either. I saw Diana and Evelyn, but I pretended not to, and went to say hello to some losers and exchange idiotic conversation with an idiot. I was drinking steadily and steadily receiving stolen kiss after stolen kiss from the foreign girls I tutored. I was totally out of it by then.

Exhaustion drove me to the study where I found Julia the maid. Clearly drunk at this point, I kicked her out like a tyrant. My mind was wrestling with gelatinous visions, my intestines were near bursting, and I had an awful headache. When I woke up in the morning, I was in Marcia's room and my elbows and feet were painfully sore. Marcia was sleeping at my feet, her legs spread, and her hair looking like tufts of felt. I slowly moved my feet from above her and kissed the part of her hair; my lips felt wet. A plan was just now beginning to crystallize in my mind. I was going to get in the shower and get out of there as soon as possible; no Nescafé, no coffee, no chitchat with Marcia. But as soon as I'd finished my shower and went back into the room to grab my keys from the bedside table, I saw a note written in English under my keys: it said something to the effect of "Wait for me. Don't leave before I wake up. Marcia." Those few lines made me scramble to get dressed so that I could get out of there immediately, hopefully before the maid woke up. I tripped over empty plastic bottles and beer cans causing a racket I couldn't muffle, but, fortunately, no one woke up.

Essam wasn't at home when I went to his apartment-cum-studio. I thought about going home, but it felt unwelcoming so I didn't. I sat in a café nearby and when I thought about Marcia, I got scared. I'd started this cat-and-mouse game with her a little while ago. I was part of her life, but it wasn't like I was her shadow. I came and went as I pleased, but she was a foreigner and our genetic make-ups were totally different. She might've got fed up with the game and grown used to me not being there. Someone else would just fill my place, and I'd met plenty who would've been happy to do so. I decided that I'd take my search for Karim seriously and make some time for the project even if it meant taking a break from teaching or not accepting any new students. If I couldn't find Karim, no matter what the reason, Marcia would probably take that to mean that I'd been stringing her along, especially since it wouldn't be the first time I'd let her down. And if—God forbid—Marcia and I did have a falling out, well then that would've made it impossible for me to maintain those beneficial relationships with foreigners who want to learn Arabic or even with the Arabs who want to live like foreigners.

I went back downtown and hung out in coffeehouses and on the street. I started with the spots I knew Karim frequented. I saw a bunch of kids just like him and I went up to them, and gave them money, and some of them told me that Karim had been carted off to the reformatory. I relaxed a little now that I had some solid information and I was sure he'd be back before long. Karim wouldn't be able to handle it and the teachers and administrators wouldn't be able to tolerate his mischief. My guess was that it would all be over in a few weeks at most; I could convince Marcia to wait patiently until he got out. Even though I'd met a lot of Karim's pals—older ones, younger ones, and ones his age—none of them seemed as reliable as he did. They were all—without exception—blind to any consequences. Karim was unique because he came from a solid background: a working class family. His father was a butcher in the Ezbet al-Nakhl neighborhood. He'd married several times and had a reputation as a bit of a stud. Every one of his wives, the ones he was still married to and the ones he'd divorced, bore him children; Karim was one of sixteen. Like most of his brothers and sisters, he'd never gone to school, but unlike them he hadn't learned a trade either. He'd been mistreated and abused, physically and sexually, from a young age, so he decided—as he told me many times—simply to let the wind blow him away. By that he meant that he'd be under nobody's control, not other people, or the government, or his family. He formed a gang of young kids in his neighborhood and they stole, kidnapped, and vandalized their way through Ezbet al-Nakhl. His father and brothers had beaten him till he'd had enough, so he ran away to downtown where he learned how to get high off glue and rose through the ranks of a big gang of kids who hung out around there, begging and selling tissues.

He'd been arrested more than once and dragged back home where they tried to discipline him with beatings and by burning him on the chest and back with a hot iron, but huffing had made his head more stubborn than rock. It was his intelligence that made it possible for him to lead kids older, bigger, and stronger than he was. He would stagger them out among the alleys and streets after the dawn prayer and then divide up the earnings with them after sunset as they lay down to sleep behind the unending rows of parked cars.

I met him at the Zahrat al-Bustan coffeehouse a year ago or more. He came up to me, covering his torso, with his right hand outstretched, and asked for half a pound so he could buy some food. I looked at him and I could see he was holding something I couldn't make out in his other hand under his tattered jacket. As I was reaching for my wallet, his hand moved a little, revealing the bottle of glue in the palm of his hidden hand. I pointed to it and put my wallet away, telling him I wouldn't give him any money. In fact, I scolded him for huffing and warned him about the danger of it. He smiled innocently, showing his yellowed, decaying teeth and listened closely to everything I said. Then he swore to me that he hadn't eaten a thing all day and I could sense he was telling the truth, so I caved and gave him what he'd asked for. He started avoiding our familiar faces after that even though we were regulars at that coffeehouse. One time, when I offered to buy him a strawberry juice, he just looked at me incredulously, and when he eventually did sit down, smiling, I tried to peek up the sleeve of his jacket. He noticed what I was doing so he brought out the bottle of glue, which had a little palm twig resting inside, and showed it off to us. I asked him what the stick was for, so he stirred the glue up and explained. We became friendly acquaintances after that.

Originally, I was interested in them as a recent phenomenon spreading through downtown Cairo. There was a striking number of these glue huffers, or "street kids" as intellectuals and TV presenters liked to call them, but what really stoked my interest were two events that I saw with my own eyes, and though they were fleeting, they were unforgettable.

The first incident happened around noon on some holiday, those days when downtown Cairo is once again like the downtown of the 1930s that we read about. Everyone had gone to the parks, or the movies, or were sprawled in front of the TV. Downtown was abandoned to calm and silence. I was just one of a handful walking down its streets that day, a hash cigarette in my hand, smoking it with relish, enjoying the quiet and the cracking echoes of children's distant fireworks. I ignored the cops who greet you with a "Good health in the New Year!" hoping for some holiday charity. There were no other pedestrians out to notice the smell of my hash, no shop owners to give me dirty looks.

When I saw a body lying in a heap against the curb up ahead, I stopped in my tracks and peered at it: a boy of about seventeen, dressed in rags. The mud and dirt had done such a number on him that he looked like a miner or someone who made a living carting both coal and garbage. He was alive, lying there smoking the butt of a cigarette. A couple coming from the opposite direction were about the same distance away from the boy as I was. A pretty, giddy girl in a short skirt and a tight blouse, which crept up revealing her abdomen, was walking arm in arm with her boyfriend on a path that would lead them past the body on the ground. They got to it before I did, but they didn't take any notice of it. I didn't know what made the boyfriend look down at the ground as they passed the boy, nor did I know why he immediately turned back and started kicking him all over his body: in the stomach, the face, the arms, the legs, and all the while the boy didn't even defend himself. Nor did I know why the girl joined in, screeching at first, then kicking along with her boyfriend, and then trying, unsuccessfully, to drag him away. I ran over quickly and grabbed the boyfriend from behind to stop him from hitting the tattered pile that was bleeding on the pavement. He struggled against me and slipped out of my grasp. He stared at me in rage as he pointed to the boy, "Do you see what he's doing?"

At that point, I looked down at the rag splayed on the ground. I almost couldn't make him out against the background of the cement sidewalk. He was leaning forward like a puffed-up rooster getting ready to fight, but in the face of the boyfriend's wild-eyed insistence, I pulled the boy upright; he was masturbating, apparently indifferent to his bleeding wounds. He wasn't worried about us or what we might do to him, his red eyes wide open. And as we dragged him along the ground like a dead dog, he didn't struggle or resist. He seemed to enjoy us moving him. The girl was beside us crying and covering her face with her hands so she wouldn't have to watch. There was a coarse rope tied around the boy's wrist and I pointed it out to the boyfriend. I lifted the rope and saw that the boy's wrist was bleeding. It was only about twenty centimeters long; he'd probably cut it and run away from the detective who'd been marching him back to the police station. I told the boyfriend why the boy's wrist was tied. I'd seen it a lot: a group of three or four boys bound like this together, being led like sheep to the police station by a cocky detective. The boyfriend realized there was no point in taking the kid to the closest police station, or the juvenile hall, or even the gallows. So we let go of him and he fell over onto the ground. The weeping girl pressed her head against her boyfriend's shoulder and they walked along slowly, in the opposite direction as I did.

Marcia had listened in complete silence and chain-smoked two cigarettes as I told her what I'd seen. My story made her laugh joyous laughter, but she never explained to me what it was she found so funny.

The second incident happened in Tahrir Square, the biggest and most famous of all the squares in Cairo. It was a cold winter night so I lengthened my stride in hopes of getting home quickly. There was no chance of rescue by cab because the way home was against traffic on a one-way street. It was then that I noticed them from afar, shoving one another. There were three boys chasing another boy their age, pushing him to the ground. They were around ten years old. They started hitting the boy and ended up piling on top of him as he screamed loudly. I thought they were trying to rape him and I was shocked by their audacity. I ran over to them. There was no one out on that cold night, not even any policemen. The boy was still shouting as one of his assailants sat on his lower half and restrained his legs while another, seated on his upper half, held down his chest and one arm. The boy was flailing his free arm up and down until the third boy grabbed it. The third boy held a wet cotton rag in his hand and a bottle lay beside them. At first glance, it occurred to me that they were trying to force him to huff. It was when I'd finally reached them that I was surprised to find the third attacker frantically trying to wipe a tattoo off the forearm of the boy who was lying on the ground, crying out in pain. I started kicking them and pulling them off of him. The boy's arm was bleeding so I tried to cover his wound, while the other boys stood around me, staring in anger. I roared at them, "What the hell are you doing?"

The tallest one replied as he backed away, "We're wiping the cross off his hand 'cause he's a Christian."

I asked them if they were Muslims. When they nodded, I let go of the boy's arm and ran after them. I wasn't able to catch them before they got to the other side of the square. They were too far away. They started hurling rocks, which they got from God knows where, and though I had no problem dodging the rocks, I couldn't stop their taunts: "Dirty Christian!"

What was weird, and surprising, was that I never told Marcia that story, despite the fact that we'd been together a long time, and I usually just told stories to tell stories. I'd told stories that were more pointless. Yet, despite my love for her and our strong connection, or whatever other term described our relationship, I'd never told her; even after we'd begun working together on a project about these kids, I hadn't even used that as a pretext to tell her.

4

I'VE NEVER DONE THE RIGHT THING in my entire life, wasting every chance I've had to change my fate. I always cling, stubbornly and idiotically, to schemes that are guaranteed failures and wastes of time, and frivolous, and thoughtless, and crazy. I ignore disappointing beginnings and watch apathetically as the sails of fiasco draw nearer. I've always been determined to plunge into the bog of shit up to my head. I probably need a battalion of psychiatrists, or to be locked up in a ward of the wildest insane asylum; restraints, too. Some place where I'll be unconnected, out of touch.

I often feel like throwing someone standing beside me off the balcony of some huge building. I avoid cramped spaces and the underground metro, and I'm very wary whenever I have to go down into it. I stand against the cold concrete walls far from the tracks, being very careful not to bump into anyone standing on the platform in case they should fall over onto the tracks and the train turn them into paraplegics. I savor the sight of their blood as it stains the tracks. I enjoy gathering up their scattered body parts like an adolescent girl picking cotton at harvest time. I recoil, sticking to the wall. Everybody waiting there has had the same thought and maybe they'll get to me first and throw me onto the tracks. I tremble, unable to keep up a conversation with anyone until the train appears in front of me and opens its doors, and I squeeze myself into the mass of riders. To me, the metro station is columns and walls, protecting me from harming myself or others. I admit that there was nothing I hated more about Yasmeen than the last few minutes of any meeting with her: when I'd volunteer to walk with her to the metro station. No matter how much I enjoyed our long walks—those moments that reminded me of deeply buried years in the faraway past, of a life that was blissful and filled with something other than the thing that motivates me nowadays—the closer we'd get to the station, the closer I'd get to my phobia and phantoms. All she could do was ask me why I was distracted and talking nonsense and why my eyes were spinning like marbles around a rim. I had no answer and she never stopped asking.

I need a divine reward and some heavenly support. I've been killing myself for a few years now trying to behave like people expect me to: confident, bold, balanced. What a crock of shit! Does anybody really think they're mentally balanced? If they do, then they better get themselves to the asylum double-time. I've traveled to a lot of countries. I've chased a lot of dreams. I came back with a decent amount of money. But the me who came back was not the same me who left. I've been taken over by a monster that entered my body and has yet to leave it. The monster was the one who came back.

The two of us left Egypt for Kuwait. It was the first time Essam and I had traveled together. I spent half the time there correcting the errors of the talentless and brainless, and the other half working the cash register in a colossal grocery store. Essam and I lived in a big room that looked like the lobby of a mini-hospital. At night when we returned home, we'd encounter a modern art installation, what the critics would call post-realist. A heap of twenty pairs of shoes, sandals, and flip-flops in various formations: quartets, sextets, rhomboids, and little pyramids; the reek of fetid socks covering the whole project in a hazy halo. Yet that permeating stench was kinder than the smell inside. Once inside, our noses would fill with the mixed odors of fermented Egyptian cheese, Indian spices, Sri Lankan tea, Yemeni qat, Sudanese chewing tobacco, and sweat. We came home every night hoping to find a cranny between the bodies to bury ourselves in. In the blazing summer, we'd sleep on the floor of the big shared bathroom that looked like the washing room of a mosque. If we'd had any sense, we wouldn't have put up with that place for a moment, let alone the six months we spent there until Essam had some success with his painting: capturing the inner beauty of some of the princely and wealthy. His finances got a little better so we were able to move into a small apartment, and then he helped me get a job editing a cultural journal that was owned by a big newspaper chain. But the constant struggling and the infernal heat, plus contempt and unhappiness, drove us out of that country and we never went back. Essam wanted to go back to Egypt, but I convinced him to come to Saudi Arabia with me. On our first day there, after we'd rented a place in shared accommodation, we sat down to discuss where we'd gone wrong. We concluded that we'd been brought up pampered and that we had to stick it out like the other men who traveled abroad for work so that we could go back to Egypt with skills and with enough money to see our individual plans through. We made a pact. We didn't complain in those first few days, nor in the first few months. We shared, in addition to the apartment, contraband brandy, Afghan hash, lemon-scented cologne, and Filipina women. Essam went on teaching "still life" and "Islamic ornamentation" and put up with it all patiently like a spiritless donkey, while I plodded on like a stubborn mule, demonstrating the art of proper and improper mooching, corresponding with newspapers, and editing theses for university students. I never had the pleasure of reading a good book or an edifying collection of poetry, or of writing a poem myself, and Essam abandoned his dreams of exhibiting his work in Egypt.

We lived with a veteran math teacher named Yahya, who'd been living in the Kingdom for ten years. He had a great talent for earning money and hoarding it. He exchanged currencies. He loan-sharked. He dealt in drugs; mobile phones and laptop computers, too. He was a mass of spreading, gregarious putridity; a marked man on the Day of Resurrection. He was always encouraging us to stay and stick it out, like a little devil, warning us against returning to a country whose citizens were "leaving by the dozens," as he liked to say. I couldn't figure him out. He'd bought the land he'd been hoping to buy in his village near Damietta, he'd bought the mill he wanted to buy, and he'd even built the house he'd dreamed of building. He had sons and daughters, too, who only saw their father from time to time. His spine had curved, his eyes had weakened, and his belly had grown; untamed fat invaded every corner of his body. How long was he planning to stay? He answered me soberly, his face wearing a serious and determined look, saying he'd never leave Saudi Arabia, even if he and King Fahd were the only ones left. King Fahd, with only two riyals left to his name, would scale Mt. Uhud and announce that the Kingdom was bankrupt. Then there'd be nobody but Yahya left to climb up next to him and they'd divide up the two riyals. Only then would Yahya move on. (King Fahd passed into God's embrace and he was succeeded by King Abdullah, but Yahya was still there getting fatter and more savage. In his right hand, he clings to his riyals and in his left, he flips the pages of his Qur'an, and all the while his eyes are fixed on the peak of Mt. Uhud.)

Finally, Essam and I got together and decided to head to the United Arab Emirates, "the Arabian Paradise" as people like to say. Essam helped wrap up my affairs in no time. I was to be gone by the time Ahmad al-Helu arrived; I'd helped get him a job as an engineer in one of the Saudi petroleum companies. When Essam inadvertently found out that I'd begged a student's father to give Ahmad a job, he looked at me with a puzzled expression and said, "You're like a chicken, you go outside and then you come back in tracking shit all through the house."

I didn't say anything. I knew Essam couldn't stand Ahmad, but I liked them both. Essam set about ending our contracts and getting us

25

the money we were due; he accomplished this with unimaginable speed. It was as if he couldn't even stand to be in the same country as Ahmad. He'd also been able to find me a job in the Emirates.

We took our belongings and set out from the Eastern Quarter, the smell of hot wind blowing against us. We were going pretty fast when the traffic came to a sudden halt. We rolled down our windows like everyone else, and as we passed bottles of water and apples back and forth, we wondered to ourselves what was the matter. There was a big backup of cars. An accident on the road up ahead. There were only a few dozen cars between us and the accident. Essam got out two apples and handed one to me.

"I bet you an Indian threw himself under a car," he said in a monotone. That happened a lot. Poor Indians and Pakistanis would commit suicide by getting run over; that way their families would receive blood money, which amounted to about 40,000 riyals. The long wait made us curious, so we got out of the car and walked toward the accident. The road was bordered on either side by the bulges and slopes of mountains and the path was blocked by hundreds of monkeys of various shapes and sizes. There were monkeys at the foot of the mountain, holding stones at the ready, aiming for the cars. The car involved in the accident was dented and the windshield was shattered; some of the passengers were injured and sitting on the side of the road. There were policemen lined up, their arms interlocked, preventing us from going forward. In the middle of everything, the mayor and the police chief, in his official uniform, were trying to calm the monkeys down. The leader of the monkeys came up to them and shook their hands. The police chief nodded toward a policeman carrying a huge bunch of bananas. Another policeman, with a big box of breadsticks at his feet, stood beside him. A large troop of monkeys walked forward and the mayor expressed his sympathies to them while the police chief shook their hands and indicated to his policemen that they should pass out some of the bananas and breadsticks. All the monkeys left their hiding places on the mountain to come claim their portion and then went back up again to eat in peace. Two policemen carried the body of the monkey that had been hit by the car and laid it at the foot of the mountain, each keeping a frightened eye on the monkeys the whole time. Then the small monkeys carried the corpse into the desert. The ambulance drove off carrying the driver, who'd been seriously injured, and the others who'd been riding in the car that hit the monkey. The cars started moving once again and we drove off in shock. We sat silently for a long time and then burst out in nervous laughter at the exact same moment. It wasn't a gag; it wasn't something Hollywood geniuses could have dreamt up. I'll never forget seeing the monkey leader shaking hands with the police chief and receiving his condolences. That's the East for you; now tell me, how can the West with all its rationality and objectivity ever get us to think like them?

5

EVERY ONE OF US KNOWS a "Khalil" who's ruined our lives and made them an unbearable hell. He's belligerent, mischievous, possessed. He's probably older than you by a few months or less. While you're caught up in your new world, he pops in on you like a flea on a blue-black night. He gets you in trouble with the strict teachers and the spinster teachers during Salute the Flag. He's the one who pushes the other kids out the door at the recess bell so they trample you. He stands behind you as you stretch your hand through the tiny opening in the iron gate, which is probably as thick as your arm. You hold a coin out to the sandwich vendor, whose eyes are the only thing you can see through the hole. The vendor hands you back a sandwich, soggy with salad dressing that's turning the falafel to crumbs. You slide the sandwich through the opening and your stomach leaps as you prepare to take a bite. And right then, Khalil grabs it out of your hand and runs off, vegetables and soggy bread falling to the ground behind him. He runs around and suddenly stops right in front of you, glaring at you with angry eyes, so you back away like a humiliated dog, your tail between your legs.

At first, one of your parents waits for you at the school gates. You walk home with them, keeping track of landmarks along your route, because in a few days you'll be making the journey by yourself. In the beginning, you don't understand the value of money; you come back without having touched your pocket money, confused as to why exactly your father gave it to you. That is until you figure out the secret of buying and start asking him for more. Khalil sees you and ridicules you in front of all the other kids because your father still helps you cross the street. After that, you refuse to be escorted to school by either of your parents and you force them to live in fear for those first few days of your independence until they get used to it. At night, you'll dream of your teacher, Firdaws, who's more beautiful than any woman you'll ever meet in the future. In your dream, you kiss her and hug her; you and she have children. Your school, your teacher Firdaws, the walk to school, and the street vendors are like a new, charming, seductive world to you. That is until you meet Khalil, who—like your destiny—will be with you till you die. He'll snatch your pens in plain sight, he'll deface your notebooks, he'll steal your snacks and sweets. Under the table, he'll pinch your thigh so hard that it bleeds and you cry, but then he'll play the teary innocent when the teacher comes over. As soon as you lose sight of him and begin to relax, to think that he was just a figment of your imagination, that he's forgotten all about you, he'll surprise you with another torment. Maybe he'll lift up the back of your smock to expose the patches on your shorts, while you stand there, subject to the laughter of mocking girls and boys and their taunting gazes, hoping that the earth will open up to swallow you. He'll chase you around with his water gun, refilling it till you're completely soaked, and you'll see first-hand the glory of his pellet gun. He'll become the voice of anxiety in your head, filling your imagination with devilish schemes to get rid of him, none of which you'll ever carry out, and he'll have made you frightened and skittish for the rest of your life. And even after he's left your world for good, you'll still remember him in your nightmares and, even in your greatest achievements, you'll be haunted by him. He murdered you when you were just a child, stabbed you with a knife from which your blood forever drips. You'll never be happy, not even when you see him tumbling down the ancient marble staircase from a great height. He won't be able to speak, lying in a pool of blood as your classmates gather around him, and for the first time ever an ambulance will drive through the school gates. You'll be happy when you hear the words you've always wanted to hear: "Khalil is dead." You'll tell this story, in all your childish innocence, to your family gathered around the dining table. But you'll be too worried to ask about him in the days to follow. You'll think you've forgotten all about him and that your life will return to normal. But Khalil will come back. He'll come back with his arm in a cast, resting in a sling. The female teachers will kiss him and the male teachers will pat him on the back. The principal will visit your classroom and congratulate him on his speedy recovery. He'll become the school's lucky charm. Your teacher will sign his cast and all the students will imitate her, using the letters they've only recently learned. You'll stand there hesitantly till you see Khalil smile, and in a moment of boldness, you might go ahead and do like the other kids are doing. Khalil's smile will grow as you write the letters and when you're almost done . . . he'll scream out in pain and say your pen went through his cast. The teacher will scold you without bothering to look for any evidence of a hole. The other students will look at you in disgust. After a few days, you'll be the first to get whacked by Khalil's cast, or shoved by it during your perpetual games of soccer, or else he'll pelt you in the head with the rock-hard fruit of the doum palm. For God's sake! How'd you manage to spend six years with Khalil without killing yourself? Or killing him? And why is it that Khalil appears in your dreams and nightmares at regular intervals over the years? You see him in everyone who hates you and you hear his devilish, hysterical laughter your whole life, even when you've grown old and senile.

I couldn't find you, Essam. The studio was locked with the big padlock, which meant you were out of town. Did you go to al-Wadi al-Gideed? Or maybe to Fayoum? You weren't answering your phone. Maybe you found a new "model" to draw and adore? Last time we spoke you said you wanted to tell me something I wouldn't believe. Marcia was taking up all my time, so we never made plans; plus I wasn't exactly burning with curiosity, so I didn't make an effort. You know what she's like. You were the one who introduced me to her and her little world after we'd come back from Dubai, where we'd stayed for four unreal years. We finally left once we'd realized we were living in a fantasy city straight out of a video game. There, everything was available, possible. It was clean and shiny, but there was no sign of anything human. We were like puppets or robots. I didn't smell any wood there, didn't run my fingers over any rust, didn't once smell urine on the wall of a building. I never saw piles of garbage and dirt. I didn't stumble over broken pavement. We hung around in all the nightclubs, the hotels, in the streets, in lobbies and hallways, even in the casinos, but we never saw human beings. It was as if we'd all plugged up our ears, focused our eyes on the screen, put our fingers on the keypad. . . . And the next thing you know you're having sex with the most beautiful women on earth. But I dreamt of smelling the khamaseen winds, of splashing through the mud in alleys during a downpour, of stepping in excrement, of watching the little branches hanging on in the storm. I didn't have to convince you to leave that space-town and its people of many nations, Essam. Laughing and smoking a never-ending joint, you said you agreed with me. Without a moment's thought, you said, "Alright, we'll get out of here. Enough talk. You look like you're about to write a poem about shit in the streets."

You introduced me to Marcia at the Mashrabiya Gallery and you told her all about me as we discussed some of the paintings. You took me to her apartment. I started going there by myself to give her lessons in Egyptian Arabic and how to play the oud, which I used to be quite good at. I'd play the oud and sing my poems for lyrics. She insisted on paying me extra for my hard work in teaching her the oud. After that, I decided to make the oud lessons more structured, using books and a CD. She introduced me to her group of friends and arranged a lot of work for me with them. Essam, you never warned me about her. You would just laugh occasionally and say, "Dump her as soon as you're bored. There are a lot more just like her."

You never warned me. You didn't tell me she was like quicksand; the harder you push down trying to climb out, the closer you come to certain death.

6

I OWN A 9MM BERETTA PISTOL. The nine rounds are still there in the magazine. I've had it for a long time. Many years pass that I never think about it. Other years, I take it out every couple of months. I feel the muzzle and I rub it down with a wool cloth dipped in alcohol. I trace the etching on the handle with my fingers. I daydream a lot about a bad guy; I aim the gun at him and put a bullet right between his eyes. I don't lower my weapon until I see his skull crushed and blown away, blood pouring from his head. No one on earth knows I have a gun. Not my siblings, my friends, my sweethearts, my lovers. I hid it in our house near Haram Street, in a locked suitcase in the bedroom. I don't have a receipt for it or a permit to carry it. I love the idea that I could kill or be killed with a traceless gun.

When the days are depressing, the treacherous corner of my mind doesn't remind me about the gun, and when I'm feeling myself again, I realize it isn't time yet. I have a foreboding sense that this miserable part of my mind is preparing me for an even more miserable end. I'm going through a psychological convalescence.

I'd emptied the bullets out and cleaned the magazine, and then put the bullets back in. After I'd put the gun back in its hiding place,

I drifted off into memories of tall tales from the past. The happy hours spent sitting on the sidewalk of Qasr al-Aini Street with Yusuf Hilmi, the old movie producer. Listening to his wonderful stories about the artistic community, its funny moments, and its scandals. I was footloose, young; it had only been a few months since I'd graduated from university and I was already seeking refuge from the headaches of teaching in dreams of becoming a journalist. One of my friends, who owned a bakery on Qasr al-Aini Street, introduced me to him. Yusuf Hilmi was one of his customers and they got along well. Whenever he saw him coming in, the bakery owner would bring him a chair and order him a coffee. And whenever there was a lull in business, he'd go over and chat with him. After I'd sat with him a few times, he began to relax around me and he asked me about my plans for the future. I told him I was an aspiring journalist and that I wanted him to tell me all about the years he'd spent on the arts scene so I could publish an article about it in some Egyptian or Beiruti arts journal, and then my career would take off.

He hesitated at first so I didn't bring it up again, but as far as I was concerned, I never gave up the idea. I started listening to him closely. The other people sitting with us were bored of his oft-recounted stories and his elderly digressions since they'd already heard all the scandalous details. I was the only one left to tell. I used to walk him back to his apartment, which wasn't far from the bakery, after I got out of work; I was an unhappy schoolteacher at the time. He invited me up a few times, but I always declined until finally one time I said yes. I'd make him tea and coffee and help him heat up some food or whip up something that didn't require any skill. He grew to trust me and agreed to tell me his reminiscences under one condition: that I didn't publish a word of them until he'd finished telling me everything. I used to use his big, antique double-reel recorder to capture everything he said until he'd get bored and I'd switch it off. Then he'd turn to his albums and his rare pictures of old movie stars. When he saw how interested I was, he'd start talking about events in the past, but when I'd run over to the recorder to start it up again, he'd stop talking and start cursing me. I'd pout silently like a child and he had to spend a lot of time apologizing.

I wasn't allowed to look around his big, cold apartment except for in the living room, where the walls were covered with oil paintings and two photographs: one of his son, Sharif the accountant, and the other of his martyred son, Said, dressed in his fighter pilot uniform. He didn't talk much about his children. He only rarely, and bitterly, spoke about his son, Sharif, who worked as an accountant for an oil company and who'd married and moved away. They didn't see each other much; the only thing that connected them was a thin telephone wire. I was allowed to use the small bathroom that was intended for guests, or the help, or relatives who weren't that close.

In essence, I was like a priest for Yusuf Hilmi to confess to. He told me about his numerous infidelities, which his lifelong companion had borne with a patience that eventually turned to despair. He told me how he'd been caught up in his little universe. Money, women, fame. He told me he didn't remember where his wife had given birth to his oldest son, Said. At home or in the hospital? Who'd helped her with the delivery? Who'd been by her side? When had the boy been circumcised? He'd gone to Lebanon, Syria, and Jordan on business, you see, and by the time he returned home the boy was nearly a year old. His second son, Sharif, had better luck: Yusuf Hilmi went to see him two days after he was born. Even though he'd been working in Cairo at the time, he was in charge of producing a big-budget movie, which didn't leave him a spare moment. So he left his wife in her sister's care, and he went to see her as soon as he could after she'd given birth.

Most of the time, Yusuf Hilmi spent all day sitting in his rocking chair facing the picture of his wife on the bedroom wall and declaring his love for her; words he'd never said while she'd been alive. He'd ask her to forgive him almost every day. Whenever we'd meet, especially in the mornings, I could tell what had happened the night before. If she'd forgiven him, he'd drag his feeble seventy-something body all over the apartment, jabbering with the energy of a twenty-year-old. But if she hadn't forgiven him, I'd be able to hear his clumsy, heavy steps from outside the apartment; his throaty sobs, too. He would struggle to open the door, barely wide enough for me to get through, and shut it listlessly behind me. On days like that, my role was to come in and greet him and get no response.

He didn't let me keep any of the pictures from his albums of priceless photos and he always insisted on keeping the filled reels of recordings in his antique chest, its wooden face decorated with an English lion in copper. It was as if, subconsciously, he couldn't allow his memories to leave his hermit's cell. At the beginning of every month, though, our interactions were very different. He used to call me up early in the morning to come take him, by taxi, to the Film Guild so he could pick up his pension check, and then to Banque Misr so he could pick up his other pension check from the production company. I never let on to him about the trouble he caused me: making excuses to the school and having to wait for him outside the Film Guild, or in the hallways, or in the infernally hot, claustrophobic lobby of the bank, which wasn't cooled by its ancient fans in the summer and wasn't warmed by its central heating in the winter either. He wouldn't even let me go outside to smoke a cigarette or get some air. I had to stare at a numbered copper marker until his turn was called and then help him up, hand the marker to the cashier, hold his hand as he signed the slip, and count his money for him.

He always insisted on going to the famous sweetshop beside the bank to buy a kilo of fancy chocolates, plus a couple extra, which he'd stick in my hand. I had absolutely no idea where he hid the chocolates or who he was buying them for every month. For as long as I'd known him, I'd never seen a single piece of chocolate in his apartment, not even an empty one of those embossed tins that the chocolates came in; never saw any shiny wrapping paper or colored ribbon either.

I recorded his authorized reminiscences on tape, but as for the unauthorized, he would just tell them to me, carefully watching to make sure I didn't reach for pen and paper. And yet, despite the Wailing Wall he'd made of his departed wife's picture—begging at it every day for forgiveness in an obligatory rite that purified him, as they say—thinking about his son Sharif made him crazy. Sharif had become very religious and his wife had started wearing a veil in public. Sharif had a long, matted beard and he insisted on wearing a short white robe over ankle-length, loose white pants whenever he visited his father. Sharif was the only family Yusuf Hilmi had left and he was awfully worried about him. He constantly imagined the worst possible fates for Sharif, the least horrific of which was that Sharif would give up his job at the oil company—which his father had only managed to get for him by calling in favors, and even then it had been nearly impossible—in order to devote himself to proselytizing. Sharif was always threatening to do just that, but back then I didn't know as much, so I told Yusuf Hilmi not to be silly, that it was just an idle threat.

I was introduced to his other moods, too, those that didn't depend on whether his wife was mad at him or not. Sharif had started interfering in his life during his brief, infrequent visits. At first, he decided to take the pictures of artists and actors down off the walls of the apartment. Then he forced his father to get rid of the posters of his successful films and dismantled the old-fashioned bar that stood in the living room and poured out the bottles of alcohol, in spite of the fact that Yusuf Hilmi had stopped drinking since he'd got older; the bar was there merely as decoration. Yusuf Hilmi stopped leaving his mementos strewn around the apartment and started locking them up in his antique chest.

Six months hadn't passed before Yusuf Hilmi fell into a bottomless depression, immersed in a transparent sadness unlike any I'd ever seen. His sullenness and violent mood swings began to wear on me, but because I liked him, I put up with it. I think he liked me too, and he gradually opened up to me and told me what was bothering him. Sharif had turned into a heaven-sent prophet; he'd been transformed into an angel that hides its wings from mortals. He blamed his father for having worked in the arts (for shame!) and for having raised and provided for his son with dirty money. The son kept it up and demanded his father purify himself of this corruption. He burned his father's money along with the photographs of movie stars and jesters, and the old movie scripts that had corrupted a generation of young people. As for Sharif's wife—whom Yusuf Hilmi himself had chosen out of all the other girls from the top families, with great hopes for her as a wife for his son and a mother to his grandchildren—she told him he should go visit the tomb of the Prophet (peace and blessings be upon him) and pray for forgiveness; maybe God would grant him that before he died.

The man who once had only to raise his voice on any movie set for the crew to stop in their tracks, the cameras cut, and the cast freeze as if birds had landed on their heads; the man who used to make movie stars tremble in his presence; the man whom the newspapers used to write about to boost their sales; the man who'd risked his entire fortune for art's sake more than once, and lost it all several times only to rise again, iron-willed, earning more than he'd ever lost—all it took was a few trivial, cruel words from his son and daughter-in-law to send him to the intensive care unit at the Qasr al-Aini Hospital.

He survived this time, too, though, and came back, with the same dilapidated skeleton, the same curly white hair, the same sunken eyes, and the same unceasing breaths. All of that came back, but there was none of the old Yusuf Hilmi left.

When I visited him at home after having heard about his illness from the doorman, his surging tears were like a glass wall between us. He wasn't embarrassed or timid anymore; he no longer measured his words before speaking them. He didn't pay any attention to the nurse either as she monitored us, warning him periodically of the danger of getting too excited. He didn't stop talking except to catch his halting breath, worry settling over the nurse's face. She asked me to make him stop, but I couldn't. He told me everything his son and daughter-in-law had done to him. I pleaded with him to take it easy. He did, finally, after telling me to come every day for the next few days so we could finish his memoirs. He also promised me that as soon as he felt a little better, he'd round up all his rare photographs, the receipts bearing movie stars' signatures, the scripts with their notes scribbled in the margins, the detailed budgets of movies and the stars' salaries, all the documents pertaining to his work, and that he'd give it all to me with the recordings of the interviews we'd done. As the nurse walked me to the door, she told me to give him a break for a few days and to check in with him by phone. When I left him that day, I was certain I'd never see him again.

7

ESSAM AL-SHARIF IS UNIQUE. I don't say that because he's been my close friend for years or because we went to work abroad together, but because when we got back to Egypt, I realized that he was more than extraordinary. He is widely adored and respected, and a great number of the young, old, and multi-cultured are fans of his art. He introduced me to the fine arts scene, even though I couldn't decipher the symbols or appreciate the aesthetic. He also showed me around downtown Cairo where I'd lived for many years. He showed me its bars and notable coffeehouses; its exhibition halls and galleries; its clubs and special apartments that served as meeting places for Gulf Arabs, Westerners, and the Egyptian cultural elite. Essam was like a bee, never sticking with one clique and constantly heading in multiple directions. He might suddenly be taken with film and do nothing else for months, or be taken with the theater and start designing experimental, abstract sets, or else he'd do nothing but make handmade furniture—the kind that connoisseurs snatch up. He introduced me to Marcia, but I'd only ever seen him at her place a handful of times for parties. I'd met many members of this velvet class (as the Beiruti magazines would put it) on my own or through Marcia, but Essam played no part, except that he guided me through any problems I had with that group. He knew that unemployment was going to drive me insane. I hadn't had any luck with the newspapers in Egypt: they couldn't put up with my mood swings and I couldn't put up with their feeble salaries. Nor did I have any desire to teach school again. My entrance into that world was thanks to Essam; he set me up with jobs with them, with good connections that earned me decent money or, at least, money enough. And yet, he was always warning me about getting involved in entangling romances and about getting used unwittingly. I wouldn't pretend that I really understood him at the time; I was immersed in it all then, intoxicated, and plus I knew that our desires and dispositions were a lot alike. He had no business giving me advice when he was even more of a playboy, always seeing multiple women at the same time. He never once gave himself over to just one woman. That was how women got to know him and that was how they fell in love with him. I used to envy him. I never understood why others adored him so much. Did his face give off the aura of a dashing artist while mine displayed nothing of the sort? Or was it because he never thought through today or ahead to tomorrow? Or did it have something to do with the look of wisdom and spirituality that his features would occasionally take on? Essam grew up in a household that was imbued with the ambiance of Sufism. His great-grandfather was a sheikh of one of the Sufiorders and his father had soaked it all up, too. Essam had read and understood books on psychology, metaphysics, art, Sufism, Buddhism, and Taoism. He frequently re-read al-Ghazali's *Deliverance from Error* and the writings of Ibn al-Arabi, and he brought them along with him when he went abroad for work. He was equally avid about going to the Indian Cultural Center—Abu al-Kalam Azad Hall—to do yoga. He had his morning walk, too, that he started at six a.m., heading out from his studio in Abdeen, passing through the streets of Garden City and then downtown before heading home. He always went for his walk, even in the peak of winter, wearing his training suit with his hair tied up in a ponytail that swung back and forth as he walked. They made fun of him: the boys from the workshops, the street vendors selling socks, and

39

the people loitering around. They threw cans and burning cigarettes at him. Their insults and hand gestures accusing him of being gay followed after him. He didn't pay any attention to them, though, and never changed his route. He never even looked in their direction. Finally, they got used to seeing him and they started smiling at him; a few of them would offer him tea. I often thought that the person who went for a walk every morning, whom people saw and talked to me about, wasn't Essam, but his secret twin. How could you picture the guy who'd stayed up with you, dancing and drinking at the Greek Club till it closed at three a.m., going for a walk at six in the morning while you sleep in till the afternoon?

If someone had said to me, "I saw Essam floating in the air," or "lying naked on a bed of nails," or "pulling snakes out of his nose," I'd have believed it. But when Awad told me Essam was madly in love and planning to get married soon, well that was a slice of impossible. If it were true, I'd have been the first to know. If it were true—and it was highly unlikely—it would've taken Essam ten years to be certain of his feelings and get married. I hadn't seen him for a few months, but I was certain that if I'd left him for four centuries he'd stay the same. Finding the one that could make him fall in love with her and propose to her in such a short time would've been no easy feat. Essam's whole life has been filled with ecstatic romantic experiences, but none of them ever lasted as long as the lifespan of a housefly. Like me, he'd never been married, so how could he possibly have made a decision like that so hastily?

I knocked on his door in the afternoon. After a little while, he opened it, yawning, having just woken up from a nap. He didn't say anything. He let me in and headed toward the bathroom. I had to clear off papers, frames, color palettes, scissors, and glue sticks to make room to sit. He came back smiling and, as if he knew what I was going to ask, he said, "I haven't been able to get in touch with you since Marcia the Siren got her hands on you. What can I say?"

"So it's true?"

His smile grew and he said, "Do I look like a spinster to you?" He took a plastic envelope out of the pocket of his training suit and opened it carefully. He pulled out a photograph and brought it up to his face. Then he kissed it gently before handing it to me. I grabbed it angrily and examined it. It was a picture of a pale young woman with sharp Asian features. There didn't appear to be anything striking about her; the kind of woman who if you'd proposed to her in the midst of a grazing flock, you might've mistakenly come away with a she-goat instead. Sensing my disappointment, he said, "Not everyone has to be as pretty as Marcia," under his breath. But he was the one who'd introduced me to Marcia! I owed him an apology. I said I was sorry and kissed him on the forehead, but before I could reel off pointless justifications, he cut me off, "By the way, you're invited to dinner tonight at a Chinese restaurant in Tawfiqiya. I want you to meet her. You'll like her a lot."

I went home feeling a bit depressed. The heavy feeling you get when your friend, or a close colleague at work, tells you he's leaving for the Gulf the next day, or when instead of finding your favorite newspaper vendor, you find his son, who tells you he's died. Of course, it was possible for me not to see Essam for months or years. He'd gone to Russia for two years; I hadn't been with him. I'd gone to America for six months; he hadn't come with me. He'd disappeared for stretches in Egypt, too, and I hadn't missed him that much. But I was overcome with a stupid feeling that day, that Marcia wasn't the siren that was going to take me away from him. That pale picture of a plain face, she was the siren: the siren who hides in the trees near a stream and waits for the victims she'll drag to the water's depths. My shower didn't pull me out of my melancholy; neither did a call to Marcia. I took a book from the bookshelf. Essam had given it to me for my birthday one year. It was a difficult book and I hadn't been able to understand certain parts of it so I'd given it back to Essam, who returned it to me with some handwritten notes explaining the concepts I'd struggled with. It was a book on Sufism. It dealt with the relationship between Man and the Self, Man and Creation, and Man and Truth. It detailed the sources of knowledge, or as the Sufis say 'ilm, which are three: first, knowledge of perception, which is what you know when you look at something and can verify it. Second, knowledge of states and it includes valuable knowledge that can only be transmitted through appreciation of a thing and experience; it usually deals with the kind of knowledge that can't be translated, like the sweetness of honey, or the pleasure of sex, or love. And finally, knowledge of secrets: part of which comes from the testimony of a trusted person, for example the reports of the prophets that there is a heaven and a hell; this is like knowledge of perception. The second part of it resembles knowledge of states, like the knowledge that there is a river in heaven whose water tastes sweeter than honey. I fell asleep more than once reading that book and when I'd wake up, one question dominated my thoughts: Did you fall in love with her and experience her through knowledge of perception, Essam, or was it knowledge of states?

I was there right on time. I put a smile on my face and tried hard to keep it on. I met her. My description was spot on; the she-goat would've been better. Young, slight build, lacking in charm, stern face. Her long black hair was about the only thing noteworthy about her. Her English was shrill and rapid and her voice had a metallic tone. *After being visited by women from every corner of the globe, you've docked at this desolate shore, Essam?* What was weird was that I started treating her like a first wife treats a second wife. I'd get angry if she touched his hand while we were eating, or when he fed her a piece of meat off his fork and she grabbed it with her mouth like a frog, or when he wiped her mouth with a warm towel and massaged her hand after the meal, or when she, quite drunk after finishing a whole bottle of booze, plopped down on his lap on her way to the restroom; of course, she didn't get up right away, but took her time and turned what appeared to be her neck and kissed him on the mouth, bits of shrimp on her tongue and calamari in the corners of her mouth. I was embarrassed and angered by her inappropriate behavior even if most of the customers were foreigners and the staff were grinning as they looked at us.

Essam was on a different planet. I was deeply worried that I might lose him if I spoke ill of her while she was in the restroom. He could tell I had something on mind so he asked me what was the matter. I was scared he'd connect my annoyance to the presence of his girlfriend so

I pretended that Marcia and I were having problems and that it was keeping me up at night. He smirked. "Marcia's like a black-widow. She won't let go of you until she kills you." I grabbed my words by the reins before they shot out toward his ears, nearly saying, "Marcia is one of the manifestations of divine beauty, unlike this little lizard you're proudly carrying around under your arm." I got up to leave as soon as she came back. I shook hands with Essam and kissed him on the cheeks. My fingers touched her fingers, but she was unsteady, totally gone. I left. I learned afterward that they'd left for a resort in al-Gouna the next day for a short vacation in order to rekindle the memory of their first meeting. He'd been commissioned to do paintings and small sculptures to decorate the guestrooms and lobby of the resort, and Samantha—that was her name and I had no idea what it meant, maybe it meant "wasteland" in her language—was traveling with a group of fellow Singaporeans who'd come to the resort for some relaxation and a little business. I also discovered that that feeble body— lacking in planes, angles, and corners—called Samantha was a business woman, who, they said, was exceptional and gifted and in charge of marketing seafood, caviar, and tuna to the Middle East. She was a discriminating art lover too, they said. She liked the execution in Essam's traditional pieces and she was blown away by hisental work, which she got to see in pictures on his laptop. So they had something in common, and then they became friends. And then—against my will—she landed in my world. I might've been a bit relaxed before I met her, but after I'd seen her—and in spite of all the ugliness I found in her features, her waifish figure, her severity, her tinny laughter— I was certain that she was the only one who could throw Essam down to the mat and pin him. Everything he'd learned about Sufism, Taoism, yoga, the pantheon of metaphysical sciences, was a prelude to her coming, a premonition of her arrival, a cosmic proof of her advent. Essam had summoned her, but it would've taken more than a thousand Essams, or a thousand stronger than Essam, to drive her away. All the women in my life were just passing through; Essam was my true friend. I needed him then, in my loneliness, so we could lean on each other till death came to take us.

Essam was a die-hard romantic deep down to his genes, and so was I, or maybe I just pretended to be. On our best nights, we'd stay up in my apartment or in his studio drinking rum. I'd improvise verses of poetry and songs on the oud and, inspired by the moment, Essam would pencil sketches. We'd drink to the point of insanity and then, on a whim, head out to a third-rate nightclub and return home with a couple of prostitutes. Once we'd accomplished our goal—or sometimes without so much as that—we'd bundle them off quickly. Occasionally, they'd offer us a discount if we let them spend the night, but we—either because we were scared of being robbed, or had had our fill of sex, or were just sick of them—would throw them out of the apartment. We'd drink more and weep because romance was dead. I had a wound that wouldn't scar over and he yearned for a true love story. Old poems—some were mine, some belonged to others—would pour from my mouth then and Essam would retell the life story of one great artist after another. He'd point at the walls of his apartment as he told the story of an internationally acclaimed artist from Mexico, Diego Rivera. Diego Rivera was madly in love with his wife, the artist Frida Kahlo, and when she was bedridden with a serious condition and unable to go outdoors and interact with the world, he worked tirelessly in his apartment, painting the floors, ceilings, columns, and furniture. He drew all the people Frida loved and all the places she missed. He drew fields, the sky, the plants she loved, and the daily life of Mexicans she treasured. He was always creating new drawings so that she wouldn't feel powerless for a moment. She had only to look in front of her to see the person or place she missed. I carried that image of extraordinary love with me for a long time: to put my life on hold for someone I loved. To give her back what life had taken away, or what the cruel hand of fate had struck down. I didn't do that for Hind, who left me prematurely, and I'd never loved another woman as much as that artist loved his wife. I didn't do that for my mother, who was shut up in the apartment for two years after she'd been beset by all manner of illness, not to mention the problems of my two sisters. I used to leave her for the neighbors to look after. I used to come home at night, staggering drunk, and before collapsing into bed I'd look in on her from far away, never daring to move close enough to give her a kiss. I watched for the rhythm of her breathing to see whether she'd live another day. In the mornings, I'd hear the screech of her wheelchair as she went into the kitchen to get the teapot. She'd make tea on the sibirtaya and toast strips of bread for me if we were out of breadsticks while she waited for me to get out of the shower. She'd ask about my work and ask me to tutor the neighbor's son for free or she'd talk to me about my two sisters and ask me to back them up against their husbands' greed. I never asked myself: How does my mother spend her day within the cold walls of this house? How does she brace herself on the bedpost to climb into bed when she goes to sleep?

Why hadn't I insisted on getting her a professional aide? How could I have played along while she pretended not to need any help? I was in my own world of fog, absorbed in its interconnected alleys; that was at least until she woke me up one morning, with the usual difficulty, and looked at me reproachfully. She poured me a cup of tea as I lay in bed and told me to buy an alarm clock because she wouldn't be waking me up the following day; she was tired of coddling me. Then she turned and wheeled off.

After my first class of the day, the principal sent for me and offered her condolences. I realized my mother had passed and that she really wasn't going to wake me up the next day. I lifted up the sheet that she was lying peacefully under and embraced her. I kissed her as the neighbors fought me, pushing me off, screaming, "It's forbidden! It's forbidden!" in my face.

I often wish I could give my whole life to have her back, even if it were only for one night. I'd carry her on my shoulders and take her round the world.

8

I'D BEEN CALLING YUSUF HILMI for three days straight. The nurse would keep me up-to-date about his health in a worried voice until, on the third day, she told me that his son and daughter-in-law were with him and asked me whether I wanted to speak to them. I begged her not to mention my name in front of them and to pretend that the person calling was just some old acquaintance. After that, I got busy preparing for mid-year exams and the private tutoring I was doing so I didn't have time to stop by the bakery.

One day the baker sent the boy who worked for him over to the school to ask me to come over immediately. It gave me an awful feeling so I made my excuses to the principal and went over right away. I was surprised when the baker told me that Yusuf Hilmi wanted to see me urgently and that he'd already had his nurse call the bakery several times for that reason. I hadn't been expecting to hear that, and I was so relieved to hear he was still alive. I didn't know why I'd doubted it; every fiber of that stubborn man's body was living proof of his great capacity for fighting back.

The nurse took me into his room. He looked like a worn-out ghost, his face bloodless. His voice was strong, though, as he spoke uninhibitedly about his memories, never pausing, not even when he took his medicine, or when the nurse stuck a needle into his veins, or when I changed the reels. This time around his stories were fantastic, seductive. He told me hilarious stories about extraordinary events, all of them true. The nurse asked me to tell him to take it easy, but he snarled at her, telling her to mind her own business. When I asked him if I could take the recordings with me, he smiled and told me that he'd gather them all up, along with the albums of rare photos and his signed authorization for publication, and send them with the nurse to the bakery the next day. All I had to do was stop by there after I finished teaching and pick them up. We'd recorded a lot of reels and from what I'd seen of the photo albums and posters, I didn't think it'd all fit in even a large suitcase. I was worried that I might never get my hands on it all, but even more worried that I'd slip up and say, "I should take them with me today," and that he'd get violently angry as usual. Then I'd be to blame for his death from overexertion. I held my tongue and didn't say anything, though a look of disappointment may have crossed my face because he looked at me and smiled, and then gestured for me to come closer. He pulled me toward his mouth by the ear so the nurse wouldn't hear him. And he promised me that I'd find everything I wanted and wished for tomorrow at the bakery, even the pairs of sexy panties that had belonged to famous actresses, who'd written on them the date of the rendezvous and the initials YH beside their own initials. I laughed, but he gave me a grave look and furrowed his brow. "You don't believe me?"

I shook my head and kept laughing. He smiled. "Tomorrow, you'll see." I excused myself to leave, but he was dead set against it. He said that he was going to nap for an hour and then he'd tell me the little that remained of his memoirs. He told the nurse to shut the door, and not to wake him up for an hour. She was not to let me leave before he'd woken up.

I had no choice but to wait for him, and the whole time I felt that it was going to be our final session. Sadness and despair came over me; mysterious, desperate emotions smothered my breathing. I still hadn't got over the tragedy of Hind's departure when I'd met that man. Hind had left me three years earlier, but it was as if she were sitting next to me at that moment, whispering in my ear that nothing's safe from fickle fate. *Will I lose him? Will I miss his exuberant stories, which he imbues with life, making them seem fresh and exciting no matter how old they are?*

I'd miss his smiles and tears. Most of the time, the last story he'd tell at the end of our sessions would make him cry until his eyes nearly bled so that I'd have to leave. I'd feel like I never wanted to go back, but pity would take over and I'd forget about it and go back to listen to him and keep him company. He used to bring his wife up a lot, and even though his tired, septuagenarian mind used to confuse some points about his craft, or movie stars' names, or movie production dates, that wasn't the case with memories of his wife. He used to tell those stories very carefully, accurately, with great detail, even when he told them more than once.

One time, he'd been busy producing a big film, which went on to become famous, and the crane in the studio had broken down right as they were about to start shooting the scene. He sent someone off to get a replacement, and he pleaded with the director to shoot the ordinary scenes in the meantime so as not to derail the schedule and get him and his family thrown out onto the street. Right then that very same family showed up. His wife—who'd been barred from visiting him at work—came to the set, with Sharif sitting on her shoulders and holding Said by the hand. She retreated to a distant corner of the studio to watch the filming. During the tenth take, right before the end of the scene, Sharif started crying loudly. The director stopped filming and yelled for everyone who wasn't supposed to be there to be removed from the studio. Yusuf Hilmi, restraining his anger, hurried over to her. He didn't hear a word she said and he didn't ask why she'd come. He didn't kiss Sharif. He didn't hug Said. He manhandled them into his car and ordered the driver to take them back home. He turned his back on them and headed toward the studio, ignoring the trembling and loud crying of the young ones, and the blood-red tears that filled his wife's eyes. When the driver got back to the studio, Yusuf Hilmi asked him why they'd come, but he was no help. That only made

Yusuf Hilmi more upset so after they were done filming the scene he called to ask the reason for her surprise visit. At the time, he thought her answer frivolous. "The kids miss you and they were dying to see you." He berated her for her ignorance and stupidity, which prevented her from appreciating the concentration required by his art, and threatened to send her back to her mother's house again (he'd often send her there when he got angry and wouldn't speak to her until she returned of her own volition). His wife apologized in a voice choked by tears. Yet I can certify that however much his wife cried that day, and in the days that followed, it wasn't as much as Yusuf Hilmi cried every time he told that story.

Yusuf Hilmi was expected to die at any moment, and it wasn't unlikely that it'd happen in front of me. After the nurse had made me a nice cup of tea, I gestured to her to go in and wake him up, but she looked at her watch before going in. She gave him his medicine and an injection, and cut up an apple and fed it to him. Then the doorbell rang. I watched intently as she opened the door and in walked a pretty girl carrying a Samsonite briefcase like the one I used to carry my students' workbooks. The nurse let her in to see him and came out wearing a bemused smile as she went into the kitchen to get some fruit juice for the girl. I was bored, but I was also curious. The nurse took the juice through to the girl, and when she came back, she sat down beside me. I didn't say anything, but she smiled and moved closer to me, whispering in my ear, "That's the hairdresser. She cuts his nails, gives him a pedicure. She comes every four days." I smiled. I should have known.

I whispered back, "Did he forget about me?"

"No," she said, "as soon as he woke up he asked about you and told me not to let you leave."

I decided to see that day through to the end. My younger sister was at home, preparing food for the week as part of the schedule she shared with my older sister: taking turns cooking and doing the tidying and the laundry. As soon as one of them saw me coming through the door, she'd hand my mother over as if she were a ledger passed from one shift to the next and fly off before her loser husband could make a mess of her life. So my younger sister could indulge me for a day, even if her husband would divorce her for it. Otherwise she'd have to leave my mother for the neighbors to look after, which happened pretty often.

The hairstylist walked out of the room and Yusuf Hilmi finally called me in. He apologized for keeping me waiting and then feebly asked the nurse, as he handed her a large bill, to buy him some imported cheese, French pastries, and a kilo of chocolates from Tseppas. The nurse seemed a little annoyed, but he smiled pathetically and told her that she was like a daughter to him, that he was craving that type of cheese; he pointed to me and said I'd be there to look after him while she was out. She gave in reluctantly and after she'd gone, the blood returned to his body and his face glowed as if he'd been waiting for years for her to leave. The man who'd lain in bed, almost immobile, as he talked to his nurse now sat straight up. He turned around and lifted up the pillow he'd laid his head against. He grabbed a keychain, which he'd hidden under the cushion, and handed it to me.

"What's this for?"

Looking stern, he barked at me, "Take it before she gets back!" I took it and he pointed to the old chest to the right of his bed and said, "Open the chest, I want something out of it." I hesitated again, but by then he was yelling, "Don't screw around, I thought she'd never leave!" I did as he asked, clutching the key with the tips of my fingers. I backed away quickly as I opened the chest. "Come on already! We don't have time for this!" I didn't move. He shouted, "I didn't tell you to open it so you could take a picture. I need something from it. Now!"

As if the vibrations of his raised voice had sedated my nerves, as if I were now under hypnosis, I walked to the chest and opened it. Inside the chest, there were three wide shelves and at the bottom, a large, locked drawer. On the top shelf, there was some foreign money. The second shelf was empty. There were bundles of twenty-pound notes on the third shelf. My apprehension was cresting and I was ready to curse him, damn him, and drop him forever if he were planning to offer me money, no matter what the pretense. I steeled myself and asked, as if I knew what was coming, "Well, I'm here and I've opened it. What is it you want?" The anger in my voice surprised him; he pointed to the large, locked drawer.

"There's a small key for the drawer on the keychain."

I unlocked the drawer and pulled it open. It was full of folders and documents. I relaxed a bit, figuring he was going to give me some important papers having to do with his memoirs. "Which file do you want?"

He smiled. "Lift up all the folders." When I did, my fingers were startled by something solid and cold. I trembled. I put the files on the bed and went back to get the thing that was still lying there. It was a goddamn revolver.

His voice made me tremble. "Hand me the gun, please." This was early on in my life when bad things were always happening to me, but this was the worst thing to date. Did that nutcase think I was going to hand him the gun so that he could kill himself and leave me with hell to pay?

"I'm not giving you the gun."

He looked at me for a while and then he smiled as if it all made sense. "You idiot. You think I want to kill myself? I'm an artist, son. That means I want to live a hundred times over. Now stop being a jerk and give it to me."

I don't know why I took him at his word, and even though I was certain that people like him never committed suicide, I still hesitated a bit as I passed it to him. He took it and kissed it. He pointed at the files and whispered, "Hurry up and put those back." I put the documents back and stood there, wavering. He gestured to me to close the chest so I shut it. When he asked me for the keys, I grabbed the edge of the bedsheet and wiped the key off, afraid that my fingerprints would show. He laughed and said, "If I was still in the business, I'd get you to write me a detective movie."

He asked me to sit down next to him. I took the revolver back, nervously, after he kissed it one last time. "Give me the key so I can put it back."

He smiled. "I want you to have it."

51

"Are you crazy!? It's not a bloody candy bar! You have to have a license for these. Anyway, I don't want it," I shouted and stood up. He sat me back down with a nod. I sat on the very edge of the bed. As he started talking, I sat back and listened intently as he told me an incredible story that he'd never mentioned in the months prior. He told me that the revolver wasn't his. It was the military firearm issued to his martyred son, Said, who was suddenly called up one morning during the October War in 1973. He forgot his gun when he left the house, but he never came back. He flew and fought for four straight days and then he burned up with his plane. No one ever asked Yusuf Hilmi about the gun and he never mentioned it to anyone other than his wife. Ever since his wife, the martyr's mother, had passed away, he was the only one keeping the secret.

"Sharif doesn't even know?"

He shook his head. "Of course not. How would he?"

"Why didn't you turn it over to the military?"

He stared at me. "I couldn't exactly tell them that my son went to war without his gun. And anyway, I think God left it for me to remember him by."

He started to sink back into his old sadness and despair, so I tried to change the subject. "Anyway, I really appreciate it, but I can't take it. I don't even know why you want me to have it."

He gave me a lot of preposterous garbage that I didn't believe then and I don't believe now. He told me that he'd got very close to the people of the afterlife recently; that he was there with them more than he was here with us. I said something to get his mind off it, but he silenced me with a gesture. He told me a day didn't pass that he wasn't visited by the mother of his children or his son, Said. Said apologized for what he'd had to go through with Sharif and asked him to forgive him. His wife swore that she'd forgiven him and that she couldn't wait to for them to be together so she could show him how much she'd missed him. He said he'd once asked Said, the martyr, what he should do with the gun but Said hadn't given him an answer at first. He'd visited him last night, though, and specifically told him to give it to me.

I didn't understand the nature of Yusuf Hilmi's illness, but I was sure that it would end in madness. The guy had really gone off the deep end. I refused to take it, but when he started to cry and swore it was his son Said's wish, there was nothing I could do. I surrendered completely in the face of his earnest tears, his oaths, his cryptic quotations from his son, the martyr. He told me to put it in my bag quickly before the nurse came back.

I started to leave, but he insisted I sit back down. He winked at me so I leaned forward to hear him whisper, "We've got to work a little so she doesn't say anything to Sharif. In the end, she's going to sell her conscience to the highest bidder." The nurse, whose loyalty he doubted, had returned and gone into the kitchen to put the purchases away. I asked if I could call home to check on my mother. I was told that she was asleep and the neighbor was enjoying herself watching television. I told her I had to work late that night and she said she was happy to help and that she'd check in on my mother periodically. Most of the neighbor women treated my mother as if she were their mother. They all had keys to our apartment and could come in whenever they wanted. The nurse brought me some bread and cheese like Yusuf Bey had asked her to. I ate a little and then I went out on the balcony to smoke a cigarette.

When I went back in, he started telling me about his lovers and how he used to spend more time with them than he did at his own house. He seemed proud as he told me how every time one of his lovers got angry, she'd go to his house and out him in front of his wife and tell her about the others. But his wife never once dared to talk to him about it. The nurse brought the tape recorder in and he began to recount details of his artistic life that he considered important, but I was satisfied with what we'd already recorded. I felt like yawning and my eyelids were heavy, but he was brimming with energy as he spoke.

The doorbell gave no warning. I didn't hear the elevator stop at our floor. I didn't even hear the key turning in the lock. Out of nowhere, I was suddenly attacked by a giant demon phantom in a short, white gallabiya. He stood in front of me and beside him there was the specter of a small woman, completely covered except for her eyes. When she saw me, she stepped back and hid behind her husband. I watched Yusuf Hilmi shiver and gasp, his eyes roll back in his head and the blood drain from his face, turning it yellow. The giant didn't utter a word. He simply stared at Yusuf Hilmi and it was as if his sharp gaze had run him through, like a laser beam in a science fiction movie. In an instant, it'd turned him into a wasted old man who'd forgotten all about years past. The man advanced slowly, his face cruel and full of hate. He bent down and ripped my notes and the rare photographs of Yusuf Hilmi's lovers, those actresses he'd been talking to me about, out of my hands. He tore them to pieces in mere seconds. The veiled woman, meanwhile, was busy taking the reels out of the recorder, clutching them as she asked the nurse to bring her the tapes lying beside the bed. I looked over at Yusuf Hilmi for help. The rattle in his throat grew louder and the veins in his neck were bulging. His glasses were fogged over, the sweat almost dripping off. He pointed at the man and said, "My son, Sharif."

That mule, Sharif, didn't give me a chance to hug his father or say goodbye. He grabbed me by the collar like a housewife grabbing a tame rabbit and I knocked his hand away with a violence I could barely control. He flew into a rage and started accusing me of being a thief and taking advantage of a senile old man, of trying to cash in on his salacious stories. Then he started making all manner of threats. Yusuf Hilmi was hollering weakly: maybe he was trying to stop us from fighting, or maybe he had some final word to say. The veiled woman threw my bag at me. The nurse fled to the safety of the kitchen. And Yusuf Hilmi died.

He didn't leave this life, though. He came back in the intensive care unit, where he lived another two days before the doctors declared him dead. When Yusuf Hilmi died, there was no obituary in Egypt's leading newspaper, *al-Ahram*, no big tent for receiving condolences outside Umar Makram Mosque like they had for his friends when they died. A few days later, the doorman told me that Yusuf Hilmi's son had refused to bury him in the plot he'd bought for himself from the Actors' Union and buried him in his veiled wife's family plot instead; separating him from his wife, whom Yusuf Hilmi had had buried in his plot so that he could lie beside her. To this day, no one has ever offered their condolences for the death of Yusuf Hilmi. Maybe I needed to be consoled; I didn't know what to do with my fragmentary memories of him. I did own a 9mm Beretta pistol, though. I didn't know what to do with that either, but Said the martyr knew.

9

THE NEWS WAS UNSURPRISING; it didn't really upset me. Karim was actually in jail for slashing his wife Warda's face with a razor blade. Warda came by the coffeehouse that night as part of her usual nightly rounds. The gallabiya she was wearing was thin and you could see her tattered underwear. Her face was completely covered with gauze and bandages except for her big, black eyes, her thick eyelashes, and her wide mouth. The way she was staggering it was obvious she'd huffed three bottles of glue and drunk a whole thing of Codiphan. She could barely stand up straight as she stood in the middle of the narrow street in front of the coffeehouse, our usual hangout, where the customers had raucously celebrated the night she and Karim got married. She stood there defiantly in front of the customers, most of whom had given gifts of money and bought rounds of soft drinks and mango and strawberry juice to celebrate the loss of her honor. Her head was lolling backward, and she was teetering wildly now as she taunted us. No one went near her; everyone was watching just as we were. She was shouting, boasting gleefully about how she was proud she'd sent Karim to jail and that he was never getting out. As she accused us of being stuck-up, she almost fell over and some of our female friends felt sorry for her and went over to help. In the past, they'd helped her out, had her sit with them, ordered drinks for her, shared their food with her, but this time she refused to sit with them and slapped their hands away. The whole scene was a farce: Warda, dressed in a filthy gallabiya that looked like mud, her calloused toes sticking out of her torn sandals, our friends recoiling from her face like the flies, repelled by the fumes of her huffing. The workers at the coffeehouse moved her along roughly, but she came back a little later with a huffing buddy. She put her arm around him and hugged him and stood close to him, moaning as if to goad us. I didn't dare go up to her even though I needed to find out everything I could about Karim. The workers chased after them that time so they ran off, shouting insults we could still hear. She was throwing whatever trash she could find at us, but the workers ran after them till they were out of sight.

Warda had sat with us more than once in the past, when she used to come here with Karim. She used to look at us like we were freaks. She'd stare dumbfounded at our female friends as they smoked apple-flavored tobacco from water pipes and drank from straws they held like cigarettes in their mouths. She'd order a mixed fruit juice, and then a soft drink, and then a water pipe, Karim watching her proudly the whole time. You could tell from the way he looked at her that, to him, she was a thousand times more important than those so-called intellectual ladies. She, being naturally clever, realized that not everyone sitting around her found the discussion of her domestic life with Karim all that interesting. They wanted to hear about their sex life; every last one of them, men and women. And that was why she told a different story each time: about how one time she was raped by seventeen boys . . . or another time it was twenty street sweepers . . . or fifteen policemen and three detectives, followed by the station chief, who'd had her for dessert, in the Qasr al-Nil police station . . . or how the guards got angry with her once at the Kotska station and threw her in the men's cell and every inmate took his turn. She didn't mind if we scoffed at her made-up stories or gave her sarcastic looks. She kept on telling her lies as Karim sat beside her, having probably huffed away all his brain cells, nothing but a stupid smile on his face; cocky and proud that she would be his wife. He wasn't happy until we drew up a common-law marriage contract with his full name and hers, though it was probably made up since she didn't have a certificate of anything. At the coffeehouse, we pronounced them man and wife and we got them a fancy dinner from Manaeesh, a Levantine restaurant. Karim had his fun with her for an entire week, during which nobody saw her; it was as if she'd disappeared from the downtown streets. Karim, on the other hand, started coming out at night, puffed up and macho-like, telling us how he'd left her back at the hideaway while he went out to clear his head. He caught the bragging bug from her and started to boast to all of us about his sexual performance, each time mentioning a different number of times they'd done it. According to him, she couldn't handle more than a week's worth of his virility. She refused to be cooped up waiting for him instead of being out, working, so she started to work on her own. She washed windshields whether the driver wanted her to or not. She offered herself to the kind of man who went for her type. She slept with many of Karim's friends, with the guys he'd appointed himself leader over. He chewed her out at first, then he threatened her, and then he went at her with a razor blade.

That skinny, filthy girl, who used to bolt at the sound of a police car's siren, took herself down to the Abdeen precinct and filed a complaint—complete with medical examination—against Karim. And then she asked him to meet her. She goaded him until he attacked her; the ambush was set and the cops caught him red-handed. The shoeshiner, who saw what had happened, told me that Karim had sworn he'd kill her as soon as he got out of jail. I didn't think he'd ever go through with it because, in spite of all the violence he'd committed, it didn't seem like he'd ever kill her or seriously hurt her. He was a street kid by circumstance, not by nature. That's why I always thought that he and Warda would never make it. He was actually bright, not thuggish; even though his friends were all lowlifes.

Karim and his friends used to sleep in front of the locked entrance of the big car dealership on Huda Shaarawi Street in the summer. Once, when the owner came to open the dealership in the morning and found them crowded together in front of the door, he flew into a rage. But when the owner and his employees chased Karim and his friends away, Karim would just run off and keep his distance. He put up with their shouts and insults and avoided walking down Huda Shaarawi Street in the daytime. When he'd stop by the coffeehouse to see us, he was cautious, constantly looking over his shoulder. Eventually the situation got serious: the man and his employees had finally caught Karim. They savaged him with hoses and cables, and made him think they were going to electrocute him and blow him up with an air pump. When they let him go, Karim just cried and walked away downcast. I thought Karim and his friends were going to set the dealership on fire one night, or break in and smash up the cars and the furniture, but nothing like that happened. Essam and I—in our capacity as familiar faces at the coffeehouse and having earned the respect of the shop-owners in the neighborhood—were invited to a summit at the dealership between Karim and his crew and the owner. We went purely out of curiosity. The owner had ordered a bunch of boxes of Kentucky Fried Chicken and some kebabs and was sitting there, waiting nervously for Karim and his friends. When Karim appeared in the entrance of the dealership, the man's face lit up and he bolted toward him. He kissed Karim on the cheeks and hugged him warmly before shaking the others' dirty hands. He passed out the boxes of chicken and all different types of fruit juice himself. We recited the Fatiha to bless the deal and congratulated them on the peace. Then we said our goodbyes and Essam and I left along with the owner of the coffeehouse and some of the regulars who'd come along.

We left the reconciliation just as we'd entered it: not knowing anything for certain. I told Essam that Karim must've done something awful to get that guy, who was so proud of his cars and the different suit he wore every day, to give in and agree to a rapprochement. "What do you think Karim did to him?" Essam asked.

I racked my brain. "I bet he got some kerosene and poured it under the door of the dealership without setting it on fire. The owner was probably scared that Karim might go overboard and burn the whole place down."

Essam laughed. "I bet Karim threatened to kidnap one of his kids."

The really crazy thing was that Essam and I were way off the mark. Now, we can say that Karim didn't do anything of the sort. He and his friends just started eating constantly all day long and at night, when the street was totally dark, they squatted down in rows in front of the dealership, directly in front of the entrance, looking like the Avenue of Rams at Karnak. Twenty human beings defecating thick excrement in unison, trying to shape it into pyramids and spheres, and then walking away. All it took was two nights of that before the owner of the dealership gave up and flew the white flag. Ever since then, he'd been friendly toward Karim. The thought of that vile-smelling protest thought up by street kids facing injustice always cheered me up.

As happy as I was about the news of Karim's imprisonment, since it would postpone work on our ill-defined project, I was scared of how Marcia would take the news. She was coming to meet me at the coffeehouse after she got out of class at the American University. I didn't know whether to cancel our meeting or change the location to one of the cafés next to the university. In the end, I did neither; I was worried it would only make her suspicious of how I'd been acting the past few days. *Fine, let her come to the coffeehouse and we'll see what happens. She's not going to find Karim. Was I supposed to tie a leash around his neck so I could drag him wherever I wanted?*

When Marcia came, I told her the short version of what'd happened to Karim and the waiter filled in the rest. I hadn't been expecting her to laugh about what Warda had done and beg me to introduce them. It wasn't an impossible request. It wasn't even difficult. What point was there in putting it off? We bought some food and crossed Huda Shaarawi Street over to the street parallel to the Middle East News Agency. Karim had told me this was one of their downtown hangouts. They'd meet there and then they'd spread out through the downtown streets and alleys, and then after their tramping and roving, they'd meet back there to chill out. The street wasn't very big and, after four p.m., it was quiet. There were no office workers, no government vehicles; there were only a few pedestrians out. Even the apartment buildings opened out onto either Huda Shaarawi Street or Sabry Abu Alam Street; none had entrances on that street. There were just some parked cars, private and official, in rows on either side. Karim and his crew set up camp on the wide sidewalk behind the cars. They spread out tattered carpets—most likely stolen from some mosque—and just piled up on top of one another, rolling around, passing around their loot of cigarettes, tickling one another's hands and feet. Marcia and I went up to them, but we didn't see Warda. They watched us suspiciously and two of the kids walked up to us to ask for money. I spotted Warda at the end of the street, balancing boisterously on top of one of the cars. I pointed her out to Marcia and whispered excitedly, "There's Warda."

When the two kids heard me say her name, they quit begging. Warda was inventing dance moves while some dark hands surrounding the car playfully tried to grab her gallabiya. She was dodging coquettishly. They didn't seem too keen on getting a hold of her; it was just a game they were playing. There was another group of them next to the car, stoned, sorting packets of tissues. Marcia held me tightly by the arm as we moved toward them and I could tell she was afraid. "Do you want to turn back?" I whispered sarcastically.

"Of course not," she answered in English, bold once more. I shouted across to Warda. She turned her head, but she didn't say anything. We stood there directly in front of them. The hands that had been playing with her feet and the hem of her gallabiya froze and the children turned to look at us. I called her name again and she quit her unsteady dancing. She stretched her hand out toward her friends and jumped down on top of them. They fell over onto their backs and she punched their chests, laughing loudly. I called out her name, angrily this time, and she glared at me, like a student who's fed up with this one teacher and is determined to ridicule him in front of the entire school.

I put on a smile and motioned for her to come closer. She shook her head: "I put Karim in jail, mister. He's not getting out. And I'm not going to change my story for money."

Marcia spoke to her in that accent of hers, pleading with her to come with us and not to be afraid. The kids were looking at us warily, but when I threw them the containers of food we'd bought, they pounced on them. Warda left us and went to wrestle with them over the food, but I pulled her back by her hair. She kicked me. Her friends noticed what was going on and they stopped squabbling, looking to butt in, but Marcia hugged Warda and kissed her without any sign of distaste. Marcia continued to soothe her until she calmed down and came with us. Her friends started fighting over the food again and forgot all about me. Before we got to the main street, Warda stopped a few steps behind us. When we looked back at her, she mumbled, surprised and sarcastic, "Both of you?"

Marcia was oblivious, but I knew what she meant. Pointing at Marcia, I told Warda, "This lady's going to look after you and give you some money."

She looked at me scornfully. "You're going to turn me over to the foreign lady?"

If it hadn't been for Marcia, I'd have knocked her head off, but I remained calm and bit my tongue. Rather than getting into a stupid argument with her, I hailed a taxi. When we got to Marcia's building, the security guards stopped us with cloying smiles and searched Warda buffoonishly, despite Marcia's obvious annoyance. She finally told them off when, after they'd finished searching Warda, they started asking her for her ID card. Marcia cursed them in English and then started threatening them and calling them idiots and hicks in Arabic. What were they thinking asking a young girl for her ID card? Her reaction caught them by surprise and they seemed chastened. Their pathetic apologies followed us all the way to the elevator.

Julia was shocked when she saw us come in; she was only a little older than Warda, but much more petite. Warda sat between us, terrified, as Julia came in and out, casting a confused look at her each time. When Marcia had finished making some phone calls, she called for Julia who hurried over to her and stood awaiting her orders. Warda was intrigued by Julia's dark copper face and her hair, done up in dozens of small braids, and she watched her curiously. Marcia told me, in English, that she was going to have Warda take a shower. I said I'd go visit my French student, Sophie, who lived on the third floor of the same building. Marcia insisted I come back after the lesson to see what could be done about our project.

As usual, Marcia was the one who'd introduced me to Sophie. Sophie had never once talked to me about payment. What really pissed me off was that they were all—every last one of them, without exception—intensely careful around me, as if they considered me Marcia's personal property; that made me anxious. It made me fear Marcia, who could obviously influence them, even if she'd only known them a few months, or weeks, as she claimed. It always made me feel like some talented knight, who turns every head when he's on horseback, but no matter how good he is at riding he's constantly worried his mount will betray him.

I finished my lesson and returned to Marcia's as I'd said I would. Warda was lying on the sofa wearing Marcia's pajamas, which hung on her so loosely you could almost see the slight curves of her body. Julia was busy with Warda's feet, trimming her toenails and painting them with pretty, simple patterns. Warda looked confused and astonished, like a sparrow when you hold it in your hand and don't let go. She'd yielded to her destiny. She didn't even look in my direction. Marcia, shell-shocked, came over and explained to me in English that the girl was completely wild, and that she thought we'd brought her back there so Marcia could have sex with her. Marcia told me that when Warda was in the bath, she'd leaped on her and tried to knock her down and rape her. "If Julia hadn't come in, she wouldn't have let me go."

I hid a wicked smile, but she glared at me and said, "Don't you start blaming this on me. Explain to her that I'm going to give her some money to help get her integrated into society."

Anyone else would know better, I said to myself.

Warda was staring back and forth at each of us, as if we were making her nervous by talking in a foreign language. The filth had been completely washed off her body and the bandages had been taken off her face so that the wounds, which she'd used against Karim, appeared quite trivial. If the investigator had seen them as I saw them then, he'd have let Karim off in an instant.

Marcia went to her room, and I was left to talk to Warda about getting re-integrated into society. The horrors Julia had faced getting Warda cleaned up were like the horrors she'd suffered through during the civil war in Southern Sudan. I dismissed Julia, who was afraid of me. She considered me the man of the house as long as I was sleeping with the lady of the house. There was a mutual unease between us. Her constant timidity embarrassed me, and there were a hundred reasons she'd never relax around me, the least of which was that she was afraid I'd cause her to lose her job.

Boulos the Copt, who owned the pharmacy located on the ground floor of Marcia's building, was the one who'd brought Julia to Marcia; that's what Marcia told me. She also said that Sibt Loka, a Southern Sudanese who worked in Boulos' pharmacy, was another victim of the war. The Evangelical church in Qasr al-Dobara Square entrusted him to Boulos so he could apprentice to him and make some money while he waited to immigrate to the United States or Canada. That was what they'd been promised by the United Nations High Commission for Refugees. Egypt had been selected as a temporary residence for Southern Sudanese fleeing the civil war. Marcia said that Julia and her cousin, Sibt Loka, had plans to marry, but they insisted they'd only get married on American or Canadian soil. Marcia told me she hadn't asked for Julia specifically. She'd only asked Boulos the pharmacist to find her someone trustworthy to help her. He came back two days later with Julia. As soon as Marcia saw her, she was moved by how frail and emaciated she looked. Marcia thought back to the slaughterhouses of Rwanda and Somalia and vowed she'd protect this girl against a similar fate.

What Marcia hadn't told me, but which I later inadvertently found out from Boulos the pharmacist, was that Sibt Loka's trustworthiness had made Marcia comfortable about dealing with the pharmacy. She liked his passable English, so she asked Boulos about him. He filled her in on the details of his story and when he saw how touched she was and how much she wanted to help, he asked her to help Sibt Loka immigrate to America. She told him, non-committally, that there was nothing she could do about that, but she was happy to help in some other way. That buoyed the pharmacist so he told her about Julia, who was living at the Evangelical church in Qasr al-Dobara awaiting some hope. Sibt Loka loved her very much in spite of their close kinship. Marcia got excited about hosting her and was kind enough to offer her a job as a maid. She eagerly went with Boulos the pharmacist to the church and made an official request. The church accepted and allowed her to take Julia Mawal Daniq home.

Julia was energetic, smiling, and tireless in front of Marcia's Western guests, but she was anxious, doltish, apprehensive, and gloomy with Egyptians and Arabs. I detected her animosity not two days after she'd arrived: how she never did what I asked her to do, pretending it'd slipped her mind or that she hadn't understood my English pronunciation; or else she'd bring me the opposite of what I'd asked for, or she'd barge in on us when we were being intimate. Whenever Marcia wasn't around, I treated her roughly but it made no difference. So then I took her to task, reprimanding her in front of Marcia, and though she stood stock-still and pretended to be meek, imploring Marcia with her eyes, Marcia completely ignored her and took my hand, embracing me and kissing me to calm me down. I didn't enjoy Marcia's kisses nearly as much as I enjoyed hearing Julia crying in the kitchen. Things changed completely after that, as she realized what I represented in that household, my true strength. Julia started doing what I asked and anticipating my requests before the words even left my mouth.

I looked at Warda like a cowboy looks at a wild horse he's just roped and saddled; standing there, staring at it, asking himself whether he ought to tame it like any other broken horse. Or would it be better to release it into the wild only to spend the rest of his life chasing after it?

"So can I leave already? Or do you two need me for something?" she asked pitifully.

I was silent. I didn't speak. The decision wasn't mine to make.

10

I LOVE MANY PARTS of this city, but the neighborhood dearest to my heart is al-Talabiya off Haram Street. Not because I lived out my childhood, my adolescence, and my dreams there, as the romantic poets say, but because of the hidden links that bind me to it even when I can't grasp what they are. I just know that I fill up with the feeling of it, so that whenever I pass through it, or find myself there—even when I pass by it on my way to some other place—I can feel the grass, dry straw, and twigs crunching under my feet as I walk through its vast fields. I still feel the grass pricking my legs to this day. None of my childhood friends live there anymore except for Ahmad al-Helu's family. The name of the street we used to live on—where our little house still stands—is different now: it used to be Tutankhamen Street, but now it's Good Works Street. The exteriors of the houses are still the same, but their corners and facades are crumbling now. New houses built on the same plan as the old houses have filled the street: four-story houses built garishly by a rough neighborhood contractor without a conscience. The ground floors have all disappeared behind the asphalt that rises year after year, so that now the windows look out onto the shoes of passersby and the bare legs of little girls. My father was one of the first to own a house in that neighborhood. We used to live exclusively on the second floor and use the ground floor for entertaining and storage. There was no third floor, only a few pillars that my father was planning to roof over in order to make a suitable apartment for when I or one of my sisters got married. But, of course, he never did, and the pillars remain, imploring the heavens to this day.

Our street is five meters wide and, nowadays, the distance between balconies on either side of the street is no more than a meter and a half. When my father built the house, there was a big, green field across from it, planted with corn. We never had any problems in that house when we were little, except for the flies and the beastly mosquitoes, but we got used to them. Most of the homeowners left the street because of difficult economic conditions. Once they'd removed the apartment doors and knocked down some of the walls, they rented the buildings out by the room to students from Cairo University or to villagers who came to work in Giza.

I lived in that house until my first couple of years at university. Most of my friends in the neighborhood had finished their schooling, be it secondary, trade, or technical, and had gone to work in Libya or Iraq. Ahmad al-Helu, whom we used to call the neighborhood genius, and I were the only ones to have completed secondary school. I studied literature and he studied engineering at Cairo University. Essam, our friend from secondary school, didn't much like Ahmad al-Helu. Essam didn't live on our street; he lived on Haram Street, the main drag. A while later Ahmad al-Helu succeeded—because of the extraordinary influence he'd had on me since secondary school and because of his structured, prolific reading and organized mind—in getting me to join one of the Egyptian leftist cells. Our relationship grew stronger than my relationship with Essam, which had cooled off a little since Essam was going to college in Zamalek. Ahmad al-Helu, on the other hand, used to spend his free time with me on campus, recruiting new students for his cell. He and I used to study together in secondary school and he would still come by the house to study even after he'd started his engineering degree. My father was really taken with his towering height, his athletic physique, and his clean-cut look, as opposed to Essam the Hippie, as my father liked to call him. He used to criticize me, too, for my long hair and tight trousers, and when Essam started studying at the College of Fine Arts, my father said it suited a pansy like him. But in spite of everything he said, he was always very polite. He never scowled at Essam, or teased him when he saw us together or found him drawing in my room. He'd reserve his mockery and rib me at dinnertime when the whole family was together. The girls would laugh, but my mother was too embarrassed to laugh at one of my friends. My father was friends with Ahmad al-Helu's father, too, so that endeared Ahmad to him even more.

That all changed later. My father would come to despise Ahmad al-Helu and refuse to speak to Ahmad's father until he died. That was after we were arrested one dusty night and accused of establishing a cell to agitate against the government. We'd been ratted out by a nobody informant, one of the many people that Ahmad al-Helu had indiscriminately taken into his confidence, announcing the cell's principles the same way his father hawked oranges, watermelons, and fresh dates. (That informant later went on to become minister of one of the most important ministries in Egypt.)

Those days were tough for me and my family, but it wasn't as bad as when Hind suddenly disappeared from my life. My father cheated certain death after we were arrested, but his grave cardiac crisis left him a shell of his former self. As I was his only son, he'd hoped he could be confident of my future before he left this world, but instead he'd been ambushed by the worst imaginable news: I'd become a guerilla fighter, an enemy of the state, a jailbird. His reaction was the opposite of the country peasant Hamid al-Helu, Ahmad's father, who bore the news with the timeless patience of Egyptian fellahin, who never complain or chafe under oppression. Later, I heard that he'd boasted about his son's imprisonment, proud that he'd grown up to become an intellectual feared by the government.

I was released after three months on account of the triviality of a cell led by a recent college graduate (that was what the sardonic prosecutor had told me at the time). My father treated me as if I were a slave after that; like a father who locks his daughter up in the house because he's discovered she's been working as a prostitute. He refused to allow Ahmad al-Helu in our house for as long as he lived and he forced me to cut all ties with him, just as he'd ended his relationship with Ahmad's father before my release. Figuring that art was less trouble than politics, my father started treating Essam warmly, with genuine affection. He took to Essam's drawings and started discussing them with him. He promised Essam that, after he graduated, he'd put him in charge of decorating the Misr Insurance Company's apartments, which my father was responsible for marketing. That promise was never fulfilled, for reasons outside my father's control: he'd died by then.

I finished the school year as if I'd been serving an extension of my prison sentence under house arrest. Those difficult times, which had altered my view of life, got me thinking about Hind again and I was drowning in crushing feelings of defeat, injustice, and anger. I failed that year, too. I was becoming a real professional at it: failing one year because Hind abandoned me and another because the government summoned me. My father didn't yell at me because he didn't have any energy left for yelling. His solution was to move us all, over the summer, to an apartment downtown—my mother told me he'd spent his whole savings to rent it—in order to get me far away from al-Talabiya and Ahmad al-Helu, who'd ruined my prospects by making me cross the government. The apartment was spacious, taking up almost half of the sixth floor of a building on Qasr al-Nil Street. It was one of the things that'd been left behind by the wealthy from Egypt's royal era, co-opted by the revolutionary government who left it to Misr Insurance to administer. The apartment was a lucky find and I was very happy there. I didn't stop seeing Ahmad al-Helu on campus though, even if I no longer shared his political views, which had only grown more revolutionary and extremist after our arrest. My father didn't sell our house in al-Talabiya or rent it out to anyone, but he did leave me the upper floor, which we used to use for my two sisters, and the skeleton of the top floor for when I got married.

My father left the keys to the old house with my mother and insisted she not give them to anyone without telling him. He made her responsible for anyone who used it without his permission (meaning specifically me). After I passed my exams with distinction the following year, my father relaxed his surveillance a little, confident that Ahmad al-Helu was safely in the past. My sweet, loving mother would always give into my pleading and hand over the keys for a variety of excuses: to check up on the house, to go there to study because I was sick of my father watching me all the time. She'd conspire with me, too, sometimes lying to my father. I made a copy of the key and our old house became the setting of my sex and hashish adventures. The first thing I did after returning from overseas with some money was to buy out my sisters' shares in the house, and I still own it.

Whenever I enter the house, I breathe in my mother's scent, may she rest in peace. I remember her frailty, her fragility, her support. I can imagine the family gathered around the dining table and the smell of cooking coming from the kitchen. My memories are hidden in its corners and crannies; my poems and experiences are locked up tightly in the ground floor. Our childhood scampering has worn away the paint on the cheap tiles in the living room. I can almost hear the water sloshing on the tiles from Fatheya's bucket. She used to come, all forty years of her, to clean the apartment every Saturday. I was always sure to stick around on those days. I'd come in, reading out loud from a book I was carrying, pretending to memorize what I was repeating. I snuck looks at whatever I could see under the gallabiya, which stuck to her body. Like most poor maids, she used to roll up the bottom of her gallabiya and tuck it into the front of her panties so that it wouldn't get in her way. I watched her, the water flowing between her bare feet, her legs completely exposed, showing even the prominent blue veins. I'd stare at her round backside as she bent over to polish the floors with a steel wool brush. My heart would speed up and my eyes would almost jump out of their sockets when her panties would slip down and I could see half of her sexy, creamy ass and some chestnut down, which got thicker as it neared her anus. Then I'd break out in a sweat; my knees wouldn't be able to support me; I'd tremble as my voice trailed off. And at that moment my mother would notice and call to me from the kitchen, so that Fatheya would suddenly turn around and see me, stifling with her hand the loud laughter that made her breasts shake alluringly, as I retreated, embarrassed and damp.

Ahmad al-Helu laughed hysterically when I told him how Fatheya was fond of what I used to do, and one time, he said I should try talking to her. I saved up my entire allowance until Saturday came around and when, almost as soon as I'd started speaking to her, I began to stammer, she instantly caught on and whispered to me to wait for her downstairs in the sitting room beside the pantry. She followed soon after me. I don't know what excuse she gave my mother. She didn't even give me time to take my trousers off, pulling me toward her and putting me inside of her, raping me. Was it so wild, fun, and delightful that I didn't notice how dirty she was, how she smelled of sweat, how rough her skin was, how threadbare her underwear? I used to pine for her all week long as if my life were on pause except on Saturdays; as if I were waiting for Madonna.

My study was on the ground floor of our old house. My father set it up for me when I started university so that I could hang out with my friends far away from my sisters. I still keep a bunch of Essam's finished and unfinished paintings there because he used to prefer to stay with me at the house when he was preparing for an exhibition: that was before he'd rented the studio in Abdeen. I even used to leave it to him for long stretches so he could entertain his girlfriends and models.

The street's changed. Maestra Fakeeha, who lives at the head of the street, runs the show now. New houses have replaced the plant shops that stretched alongside it. Fakeeha runs the business for her husband, Maestro Fawzy, while he's gracing the penitentiary with his presence on charges of dealing in narcotics. Fakeeha has since added pills and Maxitone Forte syringes to the menu.

Halfway down the street, if we can still call it a street, lives Maestra Nasra, who specializes in pimping minors and advertises her skills as a disciplinarian to anyone who needs help with an annoying family member or neighbor.

I like this part of summer and the pleasant weather in the late afternoon when the women come out carrying buckets to sprinkle water in front of their houses. Each group lays out a modest rug or country mat near the others to sit on. A sibirtaya for boiling the water for tea or a pan for roasting dried watermelon seeds sits in the center of each group, and occasionally they buy sunflower seeds, one of the cheapest types of seed. They smoke, passing around a gouza, which is a glass jar filled two-thirds of the way with water and covered with a rubber stopper, with a hole just wide enough for a reed to pass through. The women usually spend the majority of their time gossiping and quarreling with God's creation. If you happen to walk by carrying a bag of fruit, or anything else you've bought, you won't be safe from their tongues: they'll start out by asking you what's in the bag and end up asking to have a taste. That's if you live on the street or if they know you. But if you're a stranger, God protect us, they'll send a young child after you to snatch some of what you're carrying, or stick a finger in your ass, or throw a rock or a handful of dirt at you. At the very least, they'll hurl obscenities at you to drag you into a fight that only you can lose.

I thanked God that they knew me and respected me because my father had been one of the first homeowners on the block and had always helped everybody. He was known for having a good heart and a steady mind. People used to ask him for advice and they'd listen to what he said, submitting to his wisdom. That respect for our family was passed down to this sad generation, descended from the original inhabitants of the street. They respected me and they knew who my friends and guests were so they never overstepped their bounds. They never made fun of Essam and his ponytail or the models that came to pose for him and when I took Marcia to visit the house, the female neighbors greeted her warmly and treated her like a porcelain doll. No one even asked how long we'd been together. Your wife? Girlfriend?

In the end, those women are pitiful. Most of their daughters are captivatingly beautiful, even if it's hidden under filth, and when one of the girls turns sixteen, she starts taking an interest in her appearance and adorning herself with plastic rings and worthless necklaces. She starts going out to Haram Street nearby and coming back a different person. As for the boys, they try to outdo one another with their busted mobile phones or toy dart-guns, and when they get a little older, most of them start out as lookouts before they start dealing in pills and pot like big boys.

Ahmad al-Helu got addicted to jail; he got locked up another five times after our first imprisonment. He'd accuse me of being a coward and I'd accuse him of being a braggart. He was always coming up against the police at demonstrations; it was as if he were shouting, "Arrest me!" Ahmad al-Helu had his followers and disciples: students and workers, who thought he was a great leader and thinker. He fell behind in his studies for a few years and I didn't see him much after I graduated, except by accident. He used to like my political poems. He was the one who turned me on to that type of poetry, just as Hind had been the one who got me to write poetry in the first place. He used to tease me a lot, accusing me of being a decadent poet because I ran away like a healthy person running from a leper after my first taste of adversity. He used to reel off the names of resistance poets to me: "Nazim Hikmet, Muzaffar al-Nawab, Mahmoud Darwish, Pablo Neruda, Amal Donqol." But what are you going to do? I've only got one soul and I've got to preserve it.

One of our accidental meetings took place downtown at the Cosmopolitan Hotel after the big earthquake that struck Cairo in 1992. I'd been with Essam, who'd asked me to go to the Indian Cultural Center with him and wait for him there until his yoga class ended. I told him I hated green tea so I'd go have a beer at the Cosmo instead.

It was daytime, but the bar was dark except for a sliver of sunlight that struggled to reach us through the window. I went in and was surprised to see Ahmad al-Helu sitting with Shahinaz. There was a big bottle of Brandy 84 in front of them and they were sitting with two guys who looked like students. I sat far away from them because I had no interest in listening to deep thoughts and futile arguments. I planned to drink my beer quickly and leave before Essam could catch up with me and see Ahmad and get annoyed. I was gulping my beer and nibbling on cucumber sticks while stealing occasional glances at them. Their gestures and facial expressions indicated that they were absorbed in a tempestuous guerilla gathering, as if they were expecting the revolution to take place that very day. Maybe it was going to start in Tahrir Square and they'd hear its echo from their spot in the bar. Then they'd head toward it to throw themselves into the heat of it.

Shahinaz appeared thinner than she'd been during our days at university. I expected Ahmad al-Helu was starving her. Meanwhile, he'd grown a double chin and his shoulders looked wider. Two guys came into the bar and sat down at the table next to theirs. They ceased talking and looked at one another anxiously. The atmosphere was tense and the two young guys they were with seemed less able to hold it together. I was an old hand at these meetings, which are convened in order to make important revolutionary decisions and whose participants are all convinced that everyone around them is an informant. Fortunately, two young prostitutes walked in and headed for the table where the two young men were sitting. They greeted them with kisses and sat down. I could see the relief on Ahmad al-Helu and Shahinaz's faces and how the two students were reinfected with courage as they picked up their discussion once more; with more whispering and less gesticulation this time. Ahmad spotted me during one of his lost-in-thought moments, which were rare because he was always holding the microphone and he never gave anyone else a chance to talk. He peered at me and waved. I finished my beer, put some money down on the table, and headed toward him. I stood in front of their table and waved hello. Shahinaz replied dully, whereas Ahmad raised his glass, saying, "To your health." The young men looked at me and smiled. I mechanically asked him how he was doing and he answered mechanically. I couldn't think of anything to talk to him about so I decided to be boring and ask him the question all of Cairo was asking at the time: "What did you do after the earthquake? Pray or get drunk?" He stared at me like an intellectual who's just been asked what he thinks about actresses who repent and start wearing headscarves by an idiot television host.

"Drink! What else could I do in the face of the brute, supernatural force's rage?" he asked sarcastically.

I couldn't think of anything else to say so I said goodbye and left the Cosmo.

I'm in al-Talabiya now because of him. His father, Hamid al-Helu, called me and asked me to meet him. He said it was extremely important.

11

IT'S AS IF YOU'RE LOOKING at your life through a keyhole: you see nothing but cold walls and furniture covered in dust and insects crawling about everywhere. No sign of people and not one indication that air was ever breathed in or out. And no fragrance, no stench, just emptiness.

Essam went to Singapore. He left without telling me, but he called me after he got back to tell me about his trip. He told me breathlessly about everything he saw while he was there: how clean and safe it was, how polite the people were, the gripping beauty of it all; like a gift from above, not the work of man. I was surprised when he told me that he'd turned down a fantastic offer to work as an appraiser and design supervisor for the biggest center for the arts in Singapore. Samantha was really beginning to upset me: she took him out of the country without him even telling me, not even through Marcia or Awad or any of our friends, and she was planning on keeping him there. It was a fully thought-out plan she'd sketched with practiced skill, with intent and malice. Disappointment came through in my voice. "You think I should've taken it?" he asked.

"Of course not," I said, weakly adding, "I just think she's going to keep at you until she gets you to stay there for good."

Then he said, "Drop what you're doing now and come over. I've got something important I want to tell you." (At that point my pessimism started to creep up over the horizon.) I suggested to him we meet that evening in some low-key place for dinner. He agreed, but he made it clear that there would be no backing out because he was expecting Samantha the following week and he was planning to take her to Luxor and Aswan.

Essam didn't come back his normal self as I'd expected he would. He wasn't going to be that free bird endlessly roaming the sky of his native Egypt anymore. From now on he'd always be with that migrant crow who'd never be happy until she dragged him to her habitat in a net, not even allowing him to fly alongside.

I didn't taste the dinner. I was in such a bad mood that, in a moment of lunacy, I decided I'd marry Marcia and live the kind of life she wanted to live, whether in Egypt or America or even in Israel! Essam put my mind at ease a little that night with his sincere talk of how he was tired of traveling so much and how he was better suited to Egypt because of the people here, the Nile, the protection of God's virtuous saints. How even though he'd been blown away by Singapore and its many material temptations, he felt it was like a ghost city, frozen at its apex, the ice failing to have preserved a soul.

His candid feelings were enough for me and I had no interest in delving any deeper. I left in a hurry because I wasn't up to dealing with Essam's constant surprises. I hadn't forgotten that Samantha was coming the following week so that he could take her to Luxor and Aswan to reciprocate for her having shown him around Singapore. I was content with the intimate conversation we'd had up to that point; it was enough to settle my nerves.

Three weeks later, Essam told me he had a surprise for me and invited me and Marcia to dinner at al-Umam. Samantha was with him and he whispered to me as we greeted each other, hugging and kissing, that she was leaving in the morning. I told myself it was a going away party for Samantha and that I had to do my part to make sure she had a nice evening. Essam was dunking his seafood in the spicy sauce and gobbling it up exactly like she was. Marcia and I watched them both as we ate. Whether she was speaking in her unintelligible tongue or in English, Samantha sounded so much like Essam that, as I approached drunkenness, I got confused and couldn't tell which one of them was talking. That was a worrying sign. This clone of a clone of a clone of a clone had succeeded in getting Essam to love her, in getting him to submerge himself in her. My reserves of political sense told me that it was imperative that I get on her good side so I talked to her about Egypt and about the good investment opportunities for foreigners these days so that maybe she'd take the bait and stay here with Essam. She was looking at me, dumbfounded by all the bullshit I was spewing. Marcia was listening to me talk about the free market and smiling. Samantha's tinny laughter shut me up. She was laughing as if I'd told her I'd just seen a dragon. I quickly shut my mouth, fearing that the drink would let out the worst in me. I said goodnight and Marcia and I left.

Marcia picked up on my animosity toward Samantha and did me one better. As we lay in bed, she told me, whispering as if she were letting me in on a secret, that this woman came from a deformed Eastern society that'd lost its authenticity, that its people aspired to be Western in everything they did. This woman didn't appreciate art or artists, though she skillfully pretended the opposite. She was like a mangy dog, the kind that if you feed it just once, it'll rub up against you and chase after you forever. Her meager beauty (even Marcia could see that!) made her cleave to Essam. When her fun with him had run its course, she'd throw him in some Singaporean jail. I didn't respond. She went on to say that the woman had been attracted to Essam's virility. I was taken aback for a moment and I pushed her off me reflexively. She understood why. She came closer and held me, whispering, "It's not what you think." It was just something people said about Egyptian and Arab men and they liked to hear it. They were proud to be singled out for it. I turned my back on her and said I was tired. She slept fretfully, but I couldn't. Samantha was circling the ceiling, sticking her tongue out at me. When I closed my eyes, I saw her holding Khalil the Nightmare like a mother holds her nursing baby. They were both laughing at me.

I smoked a cigarette, thinking about what Marcia had blurted out in apology a few hours before, about Essam's virility. I couldn't think straight, but I knew Essam wouldn't do that to me. Maybe what Marcia had said was a projection of our relationship onto Essam and Samantha. In that case, she was stroking my virility. What a good feeling it had given me; I hoped it was true.

I didn't call Essam for a few days, didn't see him out at night, didn't think about him, didn't look for him. He found me. He didn't find me at the coffeehouse when he went by there, so he called Marcia and she told him that I was at home going over some of my writing; that was the excuse I usually gave whenever I wanted to get away from Marcia. He called the house. I didn't know it was him calling, but I didn't answer because I wasn't in the mood for human interaction. My mobile was off and I sat there waiting, not for Godot, but for nothing at all. The doorbell rang and when I opened it he was standing there. I let him in. He took out two cigarettes, handed me one, and asked for some tea. I poured water and scooped tea into the big kanaka and went back to him.

We smoked our cigarettes as we watched the steam rise from the kanaka that was resting on the gentle flame of the sibirtaya beside us and made mindless small talk. It seemed we both had a common desire to avoid the main issue. I finished my cigarette so he handed me another and took one for himself. "Do you want a drink?" I asked. He shook his head. I felt it was only polite that I ask after the chameleon. As I pulled on the wick of the sibirtaya and cut off the burnt bits, I asked him, "Is Samantha gone?"

I didn't see his expression, but I heard him say cheerfully, "Yeah, and she arrived safely, thank God." He told me that he chatted with her every day online. We sat silently for a while. I'd put out the sibirtaya and got rid of the burnt end of the wick. I tried it again. The color of the flame had gone from glowing green to orange and the flame reached higher. When the tea boiled, I put the metal cover on the sibirtaya, extinguishing it. "You should've made it on the primus," he said, with a half-smile.

"You know I don't have a primus," I said. (Essam used to really like the sound of the primus stove on cold winter nights. I'd put the primus in my study room on the bottom floor of the al-Talabiya house for him so that he could sleep with the warmth and sound of it in the background on nights when we studied together, but Ahmad al-Helu would always make a fuss and warn us about the risk of suffocating. He used to bring us clippings of newspaper stories about primus stoves going out while people slept and suffocating them, but I always ignored him and left the primus there on the nights Essam slept over.)

I was lost in my memories. I was brought out of it by a monotonous sound like raindrops falling on the asbestos-cement roof. Essam was getting ready to say something. He told me he loved Samantha, that she was different from all the other women on earth, that the few days he'd spent without her were like an unbearable lifelessness. I cut him off with an annoyed sigh. "And?"

He said he'd decided to marry her and that he was going to see her the following week to sign the marriage contract. I asked him with an edge in my voice I couldn't control, "Why don't you sign it here?" He said they were planning to get married in her country because he didn't have any relatives left here to celebrate the marriage. Plus she insisted on keeping her faith. "But she's a Buddhist!" I said sarcastically.

He didn't say anything.

"You're going to marry a heretic?"

He stood up and put his hands on my shoulders, fixed his gaze on mine. "Mustafa, you're not being serious."

Even I was surprised by what I'd said, so I hid behind a smile. He seemed a little confused at first, then irritated. As he was walking out the door, he said, "You're better off going back to Saudi and feeding breadsticks to the monkeys." I sat there depressed, but then after a while, I decided I'd go out and commit suicide on Marcia's chest.

Gloomy days passed sluggishly as if they'd never end. I bet Awad that Essam wouldn't come back and Marcia was of the same opinion. Every few weeks, chatting online, Essam would tell Awad that he was coming back soon, but six months had passed and my prediction had nearly come true. As was typical of Essam, he returned to lose me my bet. He came back a different person. He was like his eighteen-year-old self again, painting and creating extraordinary pieces. I attended the exhibition that he put on shortly after his return. His work was lively; the paintings almost leaped from the canvas and ran around in their exuberant colors. That wasn't just my opinion. Most of the critics said the same thing. He told me that he could never stay away from Egypt again after his long absence and that he and Samantha had agreed that she'd come visit him every three months. After he'd turned down all the temptations she'd offered him, Samantha understood that he was committed to remaining in Egypt and she respected that. She got over being irritated and went back to being normal. I started to like Samantha then. It made me happy every time Essam mentioned her, because he was revitalized. He came back engaged with life and so in love with her that I worried that he was too attached. I was struck with the fear of superstitious villagers who, frightened to discover that a small child is brilliant, start calling him "Son of Death" and wait for him to die. I'd been feeling the way they feel, that I was on the verge of losing Essam. That's why I came to love the person who'd given him the kiss of life. I began waiting for a divine gift that would make my relationship with Yasmeen as strong as Essam and Samantha's.

That delicate wildflower Yasmeen, a gift from Heaven. An old friend had sent her to me so I could read her poems, give her some comments, and publish whatever was good enough. When we first met, I was surprised more by her youth than I was by her headscarf and the long skirt that almost completely hid her feet. She was a nineteen-year-old child. I never once pictured myself having a son or daughter, or leaving any offspring in the world, but, deep down, I felt like a father toward her after only two meetings. More meetings followed, and I helped her publish a poem or two. I was happier to see her name in print than I'd been when my first poem was published. I got into the habit of calling her frequently and we saw each other as often as possible. Yasmeen took me back to years deep in the past that I thought I'd forgotten. She reminded me of Hind. The first love in my life; my only love.

That beautiful, slender girl that I fell in love with the first time I saw her, the first day of university for us both. Every day as we went from the university to Khayrat Street downtown where she lived, we'd sketch our dreams and live out the details of our nuptials on the covers of our notebooks and on bus and ferry tickets. She'd think of something and ask to use my pen for a moment so that she could write down whatever we'd missed: a silver cabinet, a shoe rack, a record player, a bookcase. I still have some bus tickets scribbled over with our lists.

The taste of that icy-cold Coca-Cola, which the boy used to pull out of his rusted bucket as he weaved through the ferry, is still stuck in my throat. I can still feel the tremor in my hand every time it accidentally brushed against her palm. Whenever there's a rerun on television of a play we'd seen together, my ears prick up to catch the sound of her unique laughter among that of the entire audience. My friends' snickering and mockery of my romantic side still rings in my ears. The romantic side that made me think ridiculous things, like that Hind didn't defecate or belch or sweat or breathe like the rest of us. She was almost the only girl—with the exception of my sisters and my female relatives, out of propriety—that didn't bring out any animal lust in me. I used to dream about us being married, living in a big apartment with two separate bedrooms, one for each of us. I'd be sure to wake up before her and I'd go in and spread apart the halo that surrounded her and kiss the air above her, without touching her lips. I'd wipe her face and arms with a damp towel and feed her with my hands. (My feelings toward her were impotent, and no psychoanalyst will ever be able to decode the symbols.) Yet I'd had a full-blown sexual relationship at an early age with the maid, Fatheya, and toward the end of secondary school, Ahmad al-Helu, Essam, our friend, Farid, and I used to sleep with prostitutes. During my father's long absences on Insurance Company business, we'd bring anyone we wanted back to the ground floor, which my mother and sisters never went near. My mother feared for my sisters so she used to lock them up upstairs, leaving me to study with my friends on the ground floor and regularly bringing us provisions so I wouldn't have to go up and down the stairs and interrupt my studying. I remember one time when I'd had a fit of piety brought on by approaching exams, I hadn't allowed Ahmad, and the two prostitutes he was with, to come in. He got the message so he sent the prostitutes away and hurried back to ask me the real reason for my refusal. "We shouldn't do that kind of thing right before exams," I said.

He smiled broadly and put his hand on my shoulder. He pointed at a passing ant and said, with the air of a know-it-all, "Tell me, would it bother you if this ant got screwed by her boyfriend?"

"Of course not."

He squeezed my shoulder. "Well, dumbass, God is the greatest thing in the universe and we're a hundred times smaller than this ant to him, so do you really think His Magnificence is going to give a damn about us having a little fun?"

That godless sophist hypnotized me. At that hour and in my state of mind, what he'd said seemed reasonable. I found myself saying, "Well, it's too late now, I guess, but next time tell me ahead of time." He chuckled and went out for a few minutes, and then came back with the two girls and oh my, what a night we had!

With Hind, I was entirely different: proper and respectful. I treated her almost like a higher life form from another world. Once when we were on a university trip to the Nile Barrages, she fell off her bike and her skirt rode up, exposing her thighs. In a split second, I'd jumped off my bike, which went off crashing into a tree, and ran back to Hind to hide her from the gaze of the other students. I startled her as I covered her with my hands and used my body to block their view. The girls in our class treated her scrapes with alcoholic perfumes. The guys were all laughing, but I was standing apart from them so they wouldn't see me blush. Hind looked for me, but she couldn't find me. She always asked me why I'd disappeared in the middle of helping her. I don't think I've shared that story with anyone till now. Ahmad al-Helu was the only one who had an inkling of the fundamental problem in our

84

relationship. "If you marry her," he said, "you won't be able to get it up for her and then you'll be screwed."

I got really mad at Ahmad and so Essam tried to calm me down. "Ignore him. He's saving himself for a female comrade from the Soviet High Council."

Yasmeen knew about my story with Hind. I had to tell her so that my platonic treatment wouldn't confuse her and so she wouldn't think there was something wrong with me. I took her for a child, but she was brighter and more aware than some of the adult women I knew. I was longing for love, and my heart, which had laid dormant for years, had woken up. Samantha and Essam probably had something to do with that. Yet I wasn't able to confront the truth of that love. I could feel it as if it were real and I was worried that my delusions would take form, or that they'd be taken from me, that they'd abandon me, naked in a terrible confrontation with a love that shook me. Yasmeen was too small to contain that kind of love. She'd get scared and tremble frantically like a sparrow standing between the paws of a feral cat. I could've been her cruel, wild fate. I saw you with my heart, Yasmeen. I didn't see you with a headscarf or without it. I didn't need to touch the fingers you'd hide behind your back when we greeted each other. I didn't care about the contours of your body, whether they showed as you walked or not. I was just confused: Why now, Hind? Why did you come back now? Was it such a long trip that it took you decades to return?

My psychiatrist was as confused as I was. Delusions. Schizophrenia. Paranoia. Delusions with religious content. It was as if he were unloading everything he'd learned at university on me. None of it mattered, because Hind had returned. With the same slender body, similar features, and in clothes that covered every inch of her because she knew I had no need of her transitory form. She came back with her old soul. With her crooked smile. With the glimmer she had in her eyes when she'd look at me. *Up yours, Doctor! Do you know that sometimes I finish conversations with Yasmeen that Hind and I started twenty years ago?* Yasmeen was never surprised. She wouldn't blink. Sometimes she'd finish the conversation as she wanted. Other times she didn't say anything, she'd just smile indulgently. My meetings with the two of them would last until God knows when, even if she'd started out by saying that she had to leave at a specific time. She didn't give a damn about her curfew. She'd listen to me. She wouldn't leave until the silence stretched between us and the conversation was over.

My fate began to reveal itself to me and I moved closer toward insanity. I was relieved because it meant that I'd be done with the exhausting restraints of the brain, its complicated calculations, its worldly interests. I'd escape them all and leave the reins to my mind so it could abandon this galaxy and ride toward the black hole.

12

THE DOCTOR CHARGED ME with having "variations on a condition of schizophrenia." It was something I constantly thought about; I was always trying to determine the reasons for it. Once the Wahhabi invasion of Egypt—waged by teachers, doctors, white collars, and even some blue collars who'd worked for long stretches in Saudi Arabia—was complete, a lot of things about Egyptian life changed. We pretty much abandoned the beautiful Qur'an recitations of Abd al-Baset, Muhammad Rifaat, Muhammad Sadiq al-Menshawy, and others, and instead people have generally started favoring the nasal voices of al-Huzaifi, al-Sudaisi, al-Thumayni, and the like. Nowadays, we listen to Gulf shrilling and we ignore Abdel-Halim Hafez and Umm Kulthum and Nagat. Our kitchens have been overrun by kibba, tabboula, and maqlouba, and all that remains is for us to start eating locusts and lizards.

Schizophrenia struck my society before it struck me, Doctor. I'm just a symptom. Suddenly we went from the age of the miniskirt and hot pants to head-scarves and black tents, which have to lift up the front of their veils every time they bring a spoon of koshari or an ice cream bar to their lips. I tried to analyze these phenomena, relying on what I'd read in specialist books, or even the help of a friend, but I failed completely.

Sometimes when I wake up in the morning, I turn on the radio to listen to old classics or, if I'm anxious, to Radio Qur'an. The lovely recitation ends and the host welcomes an honorable sheikh from al-Azhar to answer questions from listeners. That's when the ridiculous questions that transport us back to prehistoric times begin. The honorable sheikh never ignores the questions or criticizes the questioners; instead he always answers them with the wisdom of an exceptionally pious religious scholar. One time a listener asked a peculiar question: "Did the companions of the Prophet, peace and blessings be upon him, walk beside him or behind him?" At a time when America is destroying us with smart bombs, trying to exterminate us, the righteous listener was worrying about a question like that? And instead of gently chastising him, or even explaining his mistake, the honorable sheikh said, "In the name of God, the most Merciful, the most Compassionate. There is no power or strength but God. I seek God's refuge from the accursed devil." He cleared his throat, "When the Prophet's companions walked with him they did so in accordance with the rays of the sun, so that if the sun shone from behind the Prophet or in front of him, the companions walked beside him so that his noble shadow would fall in front of him or behind him and so that none of them would step on his noble shadow. But if the sun shone from his left, his shadow would fall to his right and the companions would walk to his left so that they would not step on it, and so forth."

I shut off the radio and sat thinking. The most reverend Prophet used to eat with his companions from one large bowl and share dried bread with them, and consult with them, but I've never once heard of him busying them with issues in the science of optics.

I was at the headquarters of the independent weekly newspaper correcting the proofs before the issue went to press. My colleague William asked to use my mobile phone and I was busy with revisions so I left him to talk. After talking for a few minutes, he gave it back and thanked me. I finished my work and left the newspaper offices. As I was walking, my mobile rang. I didn't recognize the number and I hesitated before answering. I heard a tender voice asking, "May I speak to Mr. William?" I told her that I'd left him back at the newspaper office.

"Do you two work together?" I told her we did. "So what's your name?"

"Mustafa."

"Named Mustafa and friends with William. That's a good one."

"What about it?"

"No, nothing. Why're you so touchy?"

"I'm not touchy. You can call him at the newspaper."

"Are you bored of me already?"

That stupid conversation went on for a while, meandering through delicate territory, starting with, "Are you seeing anyone?" "Do you know somewhere we can meet?" "What color lingerie do you like?" It ended with a date for the next day.

Curiosity was my only motive for meeting her even though I did feel bad about answering the phone. It seemed like a betrayal of William. I didn't feel right about it, so I called him at the newspaper office and told him exactly what'd happened. He laughed loudly and said, "It's all good."

"You're not mad?"

He laughed. "Man, give it a rest. It's not like I'm married to her. She's just one of many sources."

She described herself as pretty, not too fat, not too skinny, divorced, mother of three—although it didn't show. Anyone who saw her would think she was still a virgin. I bet myself that no more than ten percent of what she'd said was true. At eleven o'clock on the dot, my mobile rang. It was her. She said she was waiting for the elevator downstairs so I told her how to find the apartment. I said that if the doorman asked, she should say she was going to Dr. Zihni's clinic on the fifth floor and that she should actually get out on the fifth floor and then take the stairs the rest of the way up to my apartment on the sixth floor. I usually only asked professional working girls, whose appearance betrays their defilement, to do that. The doorbell rang in soft bursts.

I opened the door to a surprise that made me blush. A woman, dressed in a long, loose black cloak, her face veiled, was standing in front of me. Before I could even think to shut the door in her face, she whispered, "Are you Mr. Mustafa?"

All I had to do was nod and she shoved me back inside. She shut the door behind her and whispered like a hissing snake, "I'm Hiba." I pointed toward the bedroom. I was still numb with shock. Less than thirty seconds later, after I'd locked the front door with the key and turned out the lights in the living room, I walked to the bedroom and this time my surprise was even greater. I found madam lying stark naked on the bed, her clothes piled up on the headboard. I thought my hallucinations had started back up again, but she grinned and started talking to me. When she noticed my discomfort, she got up and embraced me. She took me by the hand like a mother leading a young child to preschool for the first time, and laid me down beside her as she whispered in my ear, "Are you alright?" Then she sat up and stretched her hand out, mechanically grabbing her scarlet bra and panties and putting them back on quickly. She was looking at me the whole time. "What do you think?" I watched her, wordlessly. Frustrated, she stood up on the bed and picked up the rest of her clothes. "You're really something else. Alright, I'm going to put all my clothes back on and you can take 'em off just like you want."

I grabbed her calf. "Sit down." She lay down and turned to look at me. She seemed confused. I wasn't going to get through to this idiot. From veiled to stark naked in a matter of seconds? I couldn't believe it.

"Are you just going to stare at me? Don't you want to get the show on the road?"

I put my hand on her lumpy flank and touched her flabby belly. "I've got a body like Asar al-Hakim," I mimicked her sarcastically.

"Yeah, just like it. Haven't you ever seen Asar's body?"

After that, conversation was beyond me, so I got down to business, serious and single-minded until I finished. We sat around eating fruit afterward. "You want to go again? I'm free till two o'clock," she said, dropping grape seeds in the ashtray. I told her I had to be somewhere and she asked me when we should meet again.

"I'll give you a call." She let it go and asked if she could take a shower. When she came back in, she got dressed in front of me and then politely asked, "Have you got a prayer rug?" I blushed a little, but I didn't say anything. I pointed to the wardrobe. She opened it and took the prayer rug from the lower shelf and then asked me which way was the direction of prayer. I pointed her toward Mecca. She took the rug out to the living room and dimmed the lights. When she was done praying she came back in. As she lazily snacked on grapes, I handed her the money, which she stuck in her small purse without counting. We had nothing to say to each other. She adjusted her clothes in front of the mirror beside the armoire and then walked over to me and slapped me on the thigh.

"Can I ask you something? Promise you won't get mad."

I was determined not to give her any more money no matter what reason she cooked up. "Go ahead," I grumbled.

"Is your name really Mustafa? Or are you a Copt like William and just pretending?"

I didn't grasp what she meant at first, but my curiosity forced me to ask, "Why?"

"It's just I don't really like to do this kind of stuff with Christians. It's not right."

"You little liar! I met you through a Copt in the first place!"

"Once I found out he was a Copt I wouldn't even let him touch one of my fingernails. I swear to God. We're just friends."

After Hiba left my apartment that day, she never came back.

There was still something I didn't get. Which one of us is schizophrenic? Me or society? Why is it that I love my society, but can't live in it or get along with it? A society I hate. A society I cling to. My story with Marcia ought to have ended a long time ago. Why was I still holding on to her? I was in orbit around her. Her gravity pulled on me wherever I was. No matter how far away I got, I went back to her. My condition was bad and getting worse every day. And I didn't know what my end would be. Was I going to remain stuck between heaven and earth; my opinions, my values, my talents, and my relationships in limbo?

I needed Yasmeen right then, I needed to wash my sins on her doorstep. Should I have asked her to come over? And continued to circle around the issue? Unable to confess directly. Unable to connect my feelings to details. And the young girl would've gone home and asked herself over and over about the strange man that had suddenly entered her life. How she didn't know what exactly he wanted from her.

13

I NODDED OFF for a bit, floating on the wings of a mythical flying creature through layers of clouds so magical you couldn't even remember them. As if you'd smoked a ton of raw hashish, or bathed in a rainbow at the top of the Andes. I'd fallen asleep after the Friday prayers. I'd forgotten I was in al-Talabiya waiting to see Hagg Hamid al-Helu until I heard him calling for me loudly. He was standing outside, leaning on a young man in his twenties. He refused to come upstairs and told me to hurry up and come down.

The young guy was his driver. God had smiled down on Hagg Hamid and now he owned a huge fruit and vegetable store in the neighborhood. I got into the back seat of the car beside him. The way he was patting my leg made me nervous. He told me about his long friendship with my father, God rest his soul, without touching on their falling-out, which had lasted until my father's death, as if I'd been in a coma or couldn't remember. Then, he talked to me about my friendship with his son, Ahmad, and he made me swear on that memory that I'd do something. My father had always believed that Ahmad was the reason for my misfortune and me getting thrown in prison. He died believing that. Uncle Hamid, in spite of his idiotic pride in his son's rebellion against the government, thought that I was the source of evil that drew Ahmad toward the morass of Communism. He would scowl at me every time I walked past the wooden cart he used to sell watermelons and honeydews from. He almost wouldn't return my greeting, and sometimes it seemed like he'd spat at me. To be honest, he and my father succeeded in ruining a friendship that could've lasted to this day. Essam also had a part to play in stifling that relationship. When he heard that I'd helped Ahmad get a job in Saudi Arabia, he bolted, taking me with him because he didn't want Ahmad and me together in the same place. I didn't know what had become of Ahmad or what had made his father ask for my help.

I asked him to fill me in on the details. Ahmad al-Helu's apartment was on the main street that led to the Academy of Arts. It used to be called Khufu Street, but the name was changed to Seal of the Prophets Street. Hagg Hamid made the driver circle around several times so he could finish briefing me. Ahmad al-Helu, the engineer, had been quickly promoted owing to his distinction and skill until he reached the post of head engineer at the machine shop of one of the Egyptian oil companies. Then he traveled, at his own expense, to work in Saudi (Uncle Hamid didn't mention that I was the reason he'd gone there; maybe he didn't know) where he'd worked for an international oil company for four years. At some point, he got into a political argument with one of the foreign consultants about the Middle East and the superpowers' battle for hegemony in the region, especially after the fall of the Soviet Union, engineered as it was by CIA agents who were planning to do the same thing in the Middle East, using Islam to scare the West in order to facilitate their takeover. That kind of talk worried the foreign consultant, so he reported Ahmad and the company sent him— essentially deporting him—back to Egypt. (I knew the story up to that point and had received updates from some of my students, but I hadn't told Essam because I didn't want to hear him crow about it.)

Hagg Hamid went on: Ahmad came back from Saudi devout, mindful of his prayers and religious duties, praise be to God, and traded shirts and trousers for a short gallabiya. He started leading his co-workers in prayer in the courtyard and giving religious lessons after the afternoon prayer every day. (This was all very unexpected. I stared wide-eyed at Hagg Hamid as he related these developments to me.) Company security summoned him and asked him to stop the religious lessons, but he refused. Matters escalated and he was summoned by a State Security officer, who sternly told him to cease any and all religious activism. After all he had a long record from back when he was a Marxist and there was no need to go opening new files. He ignored them, instead citing a fatwa from some sheikh that condemned government money as unlawful because it doesn't come from certified licit sources. It comes from tourism revenue based on amusements for infidels, selling alcohol, gambling, and displaying the three-dimensional idols, which God has forbidden. And it comes, as well, in the form of aid from nations whose godlessness was indisputable and whose only goal was the eradication of Muslims and Islam. And in order for Ahmad al-Helu to be an upright example for those who listened to him and prayed behind him and followed his advice—the people he instructed in religious matters—he decided to resign from his job with the infidel government and to seek his livelihood in accordance with the sharia. He started selling sweets, basboussa and kunafa, by the slice from trays that his wife, Shahinaz (formerly Comrade Shahinaz), prepared at home. He sold them in front of the workshop to the workers, employees, and engineers who used to work under him. The members of the company board, who knew he was highly skilled and had a model employment history, met to discuss the case of Ahmad al-Helu. They were reluctant to accept his resignation and declined it several times, but, after he'd cursed them and accused them of being infidels and heretics, they finally relented.

The security forces weren't able to drive Ahmad al-Helu from his chosen spot in front of the workshop. They were blindsided by the situation because his records, filled as they were with his rotation through all the leftist cells, didn't contain a single scrap of paper testifying to any similar activity as a religious extremist. He wasn't involved with any overt or underground Islamist groups. They ignored the complaints they received about him; perhaps they were reluctant to put him in jail where he could've been drafted into an extremist group since that would've meant the end of their ever profiting from his masterful intelligence again. State Security left him to the local police, who harassed him and generally made his life hell. But, as usual, with his silver tongue and deep-rooted faith, Ahmad was able to scare them off in the name of religion. He warned them of their black fate come the Day of Resurrection if they prevented a peaceful Muslim from earning his living. The local police lost interest, and some of them would even pray behind Ahmad on occasion. The board took one last step to save Ahmad al-Helu and summoned his father, Hagg Hamid al-Helu. They explained to him what had happened and what his son stood to lose if he kept it up and didn't withdraw his resignation within the sixty-day period prescribed by law. When Hagg Hamid wept, they embraced him and patted him on the shoulder, and beseeched him to do whatever he could to get Eng. Ahmad to back down. Especially, they said, since he was on the verge of being promoted to general manager of the workshop. He could become general manager of the company in a few years, and you never know, maybe he could be a minister one day; Ahmad is competent and the government values competence.

Those dreams filled Uncle Hamid's head, but his son, Ahmad, dashed them by refusing to back down from his resignation and told his father not to bring it up again. That was why Hagg Hamid turned to me. He thought there was still a strong bond between Ahmad and me and that I had the same influence over him that he imagined I'd had in the past. Faced with the man's advanced age and obvious frailty, I couldn't tell him no. I was curious, too. I wanted to see Ahmad al-Helu after his 180-degree transformation. I couldn't tell his father that Ahmad's head was harder than iron, that he'd been my leader, never my follower, that he could direct me and not the other way around. It's worth a try, I said to myself.

We went up the cement steps, the driver and I supporting Hagg Hamid on either side. His cane tapped the cement like the beating of a nervous heart. I'd never visited Ahmad at that apartment. I hadn't visited him at all after he'd married Shahinaz. I'd known her as Ahmad's classmate from the Engineering Department and our comrade in the cell. She was thoughtless and impetuous, parroting everything Ahmad said without understanding its importance or realizing its scope. We never cared for each other. We all lost the chemical formula for harmony. She may have been one of the reasons my friendship with Ahmad disintegrated. I never saw what was so special or eye-catching about her. She was prettier than average and came from a wealthy family—wealthy in the way that families who'd returned from working in the Gulf were: new money. Even though Ahmad had had numerous relationships, I was certain that he'd marry her in the end; she was a sticky scrap of blotting paper that would cling to him forever. And so it was. Ahmad al-Helu was transformed and Shahinaz was transformed in turn, changing her colors just as he had. Never in my entire life had I been more eager to see someone than I was to see Shahinaz at that moment.

Because of Essam's cautionary advice, I'd never allowed anyone from the cell to come to the al-Talabiya house and I stood firm in the face of Ahmad al-Helu's insistence. I told him I'd meet them anywhere but my house or else I'd have to drop out of the cell. I didn't fall for it when they said that the place where we met had been compromised or was liable to be searched. Essam, who tried time and time again to get me to stay away from them, told me that if I ever had them over, I'd be implicating my family, who weren't at all political, and getting us all into big trouble.

An exasperated Ahmad gave up once I'd refused categorically. It bothered me that he was trying to score points with the cell at my expense, trying to convince me to host the meetings at my house since his apartment down the street was too small. Anyway, we turned the page on that and Ahmad remained one of my closest friends. He was still part of the group that I studied with even though we were doing different subjects. He retained his control over me in the cell, too. And Ahmad, Essam, and I still shared the prostitutes we or our friends would bring over to the house. During my father's long absences for work, the ground floor was like a brothel. My mother had completely washed her hands of that floor and left the task of cleaning it to Fatheya. I never knew whether she was suspicious about what we were up to down there. She loved me very much (after all I was the only boy in the family) and if she ever wanted to punish me, the most she'd do was to threaten to ask my father to lock up the entire ground floor and make me study upstairs; to stop me from hanging out with my friends downstairs and to spare her the cost of the tea, sugar, coffee, cheese and tomato sandwiches, and the halva sandwiches we consumed. I realized that my mother was really only worried about the expense, so I started collecting money from my friends to buy fuul and falafel or occasionally rumi cheese. My mother noticed that I was only asking for quarter-kilo boxes of tea and coffee so she asked me about it. "Weren't you charging me by the bite before?" I said.

My mother relented and smiled a gentle smile of reproach. Tapping me lovingly on the chest, she said, "You little jerk. You're going to end up quick-tempered just like your father. I was just joking." And after that she might've even outdone her old self. Whenever I'd go upstairs, I'd find a tray brimming with French-bread sandwiches.

I'd see Shahinaz at meetings and campus occasionally when she was with Ahmad. I was never comfortable around her. I found her ideas a bit extreme. Her loud, gloomy tone and the way she'd contort her face whenever she discussed an issue with one of us only made it worse. She was more extreme than any of us, including Ahmad. She was provocative. She'd go from cafeteria to cafeteria on campus, carrying Marx's *Das Kapital* under her arm. Because the Engineering Department was located outside the main campus, her being there in the first place was cause for worry, but she walked around caring about nothing in the world but Ahmad al-Helu. It worried me so much that I suspected her of being a State Security agent who'd infiltrated us, and, in a moment of foolishness, I told Ahmad that. He leaped to his feet, wildly angry, pounding his chest and shouting, "Shahinaz!? Shahinaz!? The beating heart of the revolution!? Shahinaz, the blossom of hope!?

You think she's a rat?" He was like a poet who recites a rousing verse and expects to be applauded for it, so I stood up and hugged him and apologized, whispering in his ear that it was only an impression I'd had and I could've been mistaken. He shouted at me, "You call accusing comrades of duplicity an impression? Well, then, please keep your impressions to yourself!" He refused to speak to me for a while, but he was forced to make up with me so he could tell me about his never-ending flow of revolutionary ideas. Things cooled between me and Shahinaz, and I was certain he'd told her what I'd said.

"Of course he told her," Essam said. "I bet he's told her everything about us. Even about what Farid does before he has sex." (Farid was obsessed with cleanliness so after he'd chosen the prostitute he was going to sleep with, he'd insist on taking her into the bathroom and bathing her with his own two hands, even though he had to put up with our merciless teasing, and pay twice the price for the woman's efforts.)

Confidently, I told Essam, "There's no way he tells her. He's in as deep as we are. And anyway, don't buy the sweet act she puts on when she's with him. She'd eat him for lunch."

Ahmad and Shahinaz's relationship entered a new phase. He wouldn't go anywhere without her and he stopped going by himself to remote locations on campus with other girls in order to recruit them. There was a noticeable intimacy between them then, which they openly displayed, even during our meetings. He'd sit in the front row and wrap his right arm around her, paying no attention to us or to the leader. She'd push her fingers through his short hair and toy with his earlobe or run her palm over the hair on his arm. If they'd been overtaken by passion and made love right in front of us while we were discussing how we should advertise our tiny group to the struggling masses without alerting the State Security forces, well, I wouldn't have put it past them.

What followed next was weirder than the wondrous. Ahmad al-Helu came over one night and, after making sure that Essam and Farid weren't there, tried to talk to me about something. He kept getting caught up in his nerves and hesitation, though, and that got me worried in turn. *He's going to tell me about some catastrophe that's happened or else he's going to draft me into one.* I tried to get him to spit it out, but then he started toying with me and I got fed up. "It's the end of the month and I'm out of money. Just wait till my father gives me my allowance," I said.

He looked surprised and smiled. "Who said anything about money, Moneybags? If you need a loan, just tell me."

When he said that, I was certain my fears weren't unfounded. He was going to say "The cell's been exposed" or "We're being watched." I started to worry about my mother, my sisters, my father. "I told you I wasn't cut out for this political stuff. I'm weak. I don't want to get my ass kicked. And anyway what's wrong with wanting to write love poetry? To hell with this revolutionary poetry; it's only going to get us into trouble." His soft laughter soothed me. "Ahmad, spit it out. My mind is racing and Essam or Farid or Mohi could come in any minute."

That was the magic phrase that got him to start talking. It uncorked a bottle, releasing a genie of a topic that would never have occurred to an idiot like me. His request was simple and banal: that I clear out and leave him my room for just two hours. I couldn't help but tease him, "And who are you planning to bring over, huh? Sophie Marceau? Bring her over when we're all here, and if we like her, we'll be in on it whether you like it or not." He seemed nervous. His face went pale as he whispered in my ear, "Please, I don't want anyone to be here. I'm going to bring Shahinaz over." That sent a chill down my spine. There was a straightforward, implicit agreement between us all that none of our female classmates would ever be brought back to the apartment. I stuck to that rule as if it weren't my apartment and so did all the others. I said no and nervously reminded him about our agreement. His words sounded like background music played by an orchestra of the deaf and dumb; off-the-mark, out-of-sync, disjointed, unbalanced. It was all about the great love that connected the two of them. About their intense desire to be alone together. About how I'd be rescuing them from rendezvous in stairwells, and dimmed movie theaters, and by the fences around abandoned buildings. I stared for a long time at that agitated revolutionary who'd been conquered by lust. That was one of the only times I'd seen him so miserable. I shook my head deliberately, indicating my absolute refusal. His head drooped as he collected his thoughts. Then he stood up and headed toward the door. He turned back and begged me not to tell any of our friends about our conversation. I promised him I wouldn't and I stood up and hugged him and patted him on the back. I asked him to forgive me; there was nothing I could do. I tried to explain to him, whispering in his ear that we could still share women, just not our classmates. I grinned. He didn't smile, instead he held my hand and earnestly told me that he wasn't going to come over and share prostitutes with us or go near other women anymore. He'd been cleansed by his love for Shahinaz, just as he'd been cleansed by the writings of Karl Marx, which had rid him of the instinct to exploit human suffering as a means of attaining the profits of scum. I laughed for a long time after he left. I admired his perseverance in the face of defeat and the farewell speech he gave as we stood at the door of the apartment.

I, myself, was confused by what I'd done. I knew I was lying. It was true we all had an agreement, but I was prepared to violate it however I pleased. If the roles were changed and it'd been Essam coming to me with his classmate, I wouldn't have used our agreement as an excuse to say no. Maybe even if Ahmad al-Helu had wanted to bring a classmate other than Shahinaz, I wouldn't have objected. But Shahinaz, specifically, was a no-go because I knew her, she and I were in the same cell, and I could never win an argument with her. In that moment, I'd emerged the victor and I had a crazy, uncontrollable desire to tell everyone I knew and everyone who knew her. I didn't, though. I never told anyone what Ahmad al-Helu and I had discussed that day.

A few days later, we met on campus and he whispered in my ear that, sooner or later, Shahinaz would be his wife. I smiled and told him that was why I couldn't give in to his request. My relationship with Ahmad al-Helu didn't change after what happened, but I started avoiding conversations with Shahinaz, who didn't seem to know what Ahmad had asked of me. I was worried that a trace of my inner feelings toward her would come through if I couldn't out-debate her about a dogmatic opinion or a provocative theory about third world issues, which, according to her, I was always suggesting sentimental fixes for. I cut back on reciting my revolutionary poetry even though the leader of the cell would ask me to at the end of every meeting.

Almost all our meetings took place at our cell leader's house. He was a recent engineering graduate from a leftist family. The apartment would be empty when we had our meetings, or else the family would withdraw to the inner rooms. We never saw them or heard a sound except for a few knocks on the door when the little sister, with the help of the even littler brother, brought us drinks, or sandwiches if the meeting dragged on. I used to hear rumors about his father, the great communist, who'd been in prison in the fifties and sixties, and about his uncles, the great fighters, but I was never sure if any of it was true. His house was at the end of Haram Street in a sparsely populated area. Ahmad would whisper the meeting time to me and I'd go on my own. I went home alone, too, except occasionally when Ahmad would insist that I go with him in Shahinaz's car. She'd drop us off right outside al-Talabiya and then she'd continue on to Murad Street where she lived. They'd usually give me a ride if I'd impressed them with a rousing poem or if I hadn't got into an argument with Shahinaz during the meeting. After what'd happened between Ahmad and me, I planned on making my exit before they did or waiting around a little so that they'd be gone by the time I left. They left a few minutes before I did that day, and the leader had instructed us to leave one-by-one so as not to attract attention. There weren't more than twenty of us in the cell and it was rare for us all to show up at a meeting. As soon as I stepped out of the entryway, I saw Ahmad al-Helu bent over, swapping out the tire on the right side of the car. Shahinaz was handing him a tool from the small kit. I had too much momentum coming out the door to pull back when I saw Shahinaz right in front of me. Our eyes met so I couldn't pretend I hadn't seen her. I had to offer to help. Without a moment's hesitation, she pointed to the flat tire. I put it in the trunk and cursed her under my breath, furiously brushing at my clothes. Ahmad al-Helu finished changing the tire and signaled for me to get in the car. Shahinaz cut my wavering short: "Get in. Do you need an invitation? People are watching us," she said with a smile. Faced with no alternative, I jumped into my chosen spot in the back seat. The car traveled in the usual direction with the same monotonous conversation that always accompanied us on our trips home. We suddenly came to a stop in front of a huge building. Even Ahmad looked confused. He shot Shahinaz a reproachful, sidelong look. That was one of the only times I saw Shahinaz stare Ahmad down. She made him look like a scared rabbit.

"You're not going to go up?"

"Let's drop Mustafa off first."

"If you told him you were coming, you should just go."

If I'd had something sharp with me then, I'd have run her through the back and danced for joy. To save Ahmad the embarrassment, I said, "Ahmad, go ahead. I can catch a bus or something." I didn't hide the resentment in my voice.

"It's not a big deal. I just have to ask him a question. I'll be back in two minutes," he said and insisted I stay in the car.

Shahinaz turned to me. "Ahmad won't be long," she said, and faked a smile. "But he'd better not come back empty-handed."

Ahmad got out off the car quickly as if he couldn't face her or her sarcasm, and ran into the building. He actually came back just two minutes later. His expression wasn't the same as the one he'd gone in wearing. She didn't start the engine right away. She turned her whole body toward him and stared inquisitively. "Everything alright?" she asked abruptly. He kept looking forward, avoiding her gaze.

The words came out with difficulty, "Samih says he's sorry he can't help." Shahinaz took the key off the dashboard and stuck it in the ignition. She sighed, snarling and grimacing. She didn't say a word, she just drove as fast as she could. It all made a huge racket: the friction of rubber on asphalt, the choked exhaust pipe, her high-pitched horn, the squeal of her brakes, the echoes of the obscenities the other drivers shouted, and the pleas of pedestrians who'd miraculously avoided being mowed down. I felt like I wasn't going to survive that night. And I didn't even know who Samih was, or what he was sorry about.

In any case, I somehow survived. The car finally stopped at the edge of al-Talabiya. Ahmad stepped out so I could get out of the back seat and before he could go back to her side, she slammed the door in his face and drove off without a goodbye. The whole walk back to our street, he didn't say a single word.

It all struck me as pretty shocking, but I didn't say anything about her behavior. I didn't ask him to explain either; I wasn't even curious. Her contempt was directed entirely at him so I respected his silence and kept quiet. We parted with nods, not with words or even a handshake.

I expected Ahmad would come by the next morning to explain what had happened. I was afraid that my leader would go to pieces in front of me even more so than he had the night before. I hid the schadenfreude I felt creeping through my body, but I could hardly keep it down. He didn't come by that morning. In fact, I didn't see him for three more days and I was too embarrassed to go find him at the Engineering Department to ask him when the next meeting would be in case he took it the wrong way.

Shahinaz had to ask several classmates before she found me in the Cultural Committee room. Just seeing her made me uneasy and I couldn't return her terse greeting. We went and sat in the cafeteria, but my patience was running out. She didn't let me call the waiter over. She said she wanted to talk to me about something important, but right then we were joined by two of our classmates. She looked put out. Standing up, she said, "Come on. I need to talk to you." I excused myself and followed her past the rows of tables, past the groups of students on the stairs, and through the courtyard until we got to the main gate of the university. I was confused, curious, quiet. We went to the empty lot between the Engineering Department and the main campus, where she parked her car. The only thing I could come up with as we walked to her car was that something important had transpired between her and Ahmad and she wanted to know my opinion. Or something like that. Although I didn't think Shahinaz ever cared about what I thought or gave a damn about my wisdom, perspective, or opinions. She drove to a café by the Nile where Hind and I used to go and I was sure that Ahmad and Shahinaz went there together, too. That was the first time I'd ever gone to the café without knowing why.

Shahinaz sat down and quickly sent the waiter away with an order for two beers. I hadn't even asked for one. It was as if she was trying to get rid of him. She pointed at me with her index finger and set two conditions: "First, I'm treating you so don't try to pay. Period. Second, what I'm about to tell you doesn't go past us, not ever, not till we die. Don't even dream about it." Then she placed both her hands on mine. "Swear on your precious Hind that you agree to these conditions."

I got goosebumps when she mentioned Hind's name. But then I figured she had the weight of a mountain on her shoulders and that she needed my help. She took out her pack of Belmont cigarettes—the kind Ahmad al-Helu smoked to show his solidarity with the proletariat—and handed me one. The waiter had poured our beers for us. She picked up her glass and took a long sip. I copied her reflexively. Shahinaz, completely hidden behind cigarette smoke, began to speak. "You know I'm still mad at Ahmad from that day we gave you a ride."

"Really?" I asked just to be polite.

"By the way, you're sworn to secrecy. Ahmad didn't say anything to you?" I swore that he hadn't said a single word to me about what had happened. She sighed a sigh of relief and took a bigger swig than before. She puffed out thicker smoke and started talking like a student who's failed once too often and no longer cares what her family, friends, or critics say. *Yeah, I failed again this year. Anyone got something they want to say to me?*

"Samih is the fourth friend to turn Ahmad down. I'm sure you heard our conversation last time when we were all together." I didn't say anything. She went on, "He arranged with each of them to borrow their apartments for the day, but then they all come up with these pathetic excuses. I don't know what's going on anymore. Why do we have such bad luck?"

I didn't understand a word of what she was saying even though she sounded like she was making sense. I was totally confused; I felt like I was on another planet. What was happening in front of me, what she was talking to me about, was something out of a fantasy. She stopped talking, so I asked stupidly, "What do you two want to borrow an apartment for?"

She glared at me, "Don't pretend you don't know. Ahmad told me you were the first one he asked."

Then it all fell into place. What I hadn't seen coming, what I'd thought was impossible, what I could hardly believe was really happening: Shahinaz had come to ask me for the same thing. I didn't know how I was supposed to deal with the young woman sitting in front of me. As a political intellectual? As the outstanding student that Ahmad claimed she was? As an engineer with a bright future? Or as a whore looking for some place where she could extinguish the flame that burned inside of her? We were both silent for a long time. I was lost in thought, turning the issue over in my head. No way was I going to tell her yes after I'd already told Ahmad no; plus, her boldness frightened me. That young woman never thought twice about doing anything. There was no limit to what she'd do.

"How long does it take you to think?"

"Yeah, Ahmad did ask me about that. And I assume he told you the reason I said no. Does he know you're seeing me today?"

Nervously, she drained her glass. "If he knew, I wouldn't have made you swear to keep this between us." Her defeat thrilled me, but in a whisper—convinced that everyone in the café could hear our conversation—I told her how much I liked Ahmad and appreciated our friendship and the vow of brotherhood we'd taken in the cell. But still, I wasn't going to let them borrow my apartment because I didn't want that image in my head; I didn't want it to affect our friendship. Then I told her that my mother and father had been getting suspicious about my recent behavior. (That wasn't true.)

She cut me off, her expression frustrated, but when I got up to leave, she asked me to sit down and have another beer. I refused, but she kept pleading and unpursed her lips, trying desperately to crack half a smile. Softly, her voice overcome with disappointment, she told me she understood my position and respected it, but that she needed another beer and someone to drink with. I gave in and sat down; I almost gave her what she wanted, but something inside me urged me to stand my ground. Two bottles came and she talked to me about Hind to the limited extent of what she knew about her. She'd only met Hind a handful of times, plus she knew whatever Ahmad had told her about our relationship. I was going soft again, but I held it together. The beer had emboldened me a little. I sprung a direct question on her, "Be honest. Why do you want this? I figured Ahmad was the one who wanted it bad, not the other way around."

She stopped me with her hand again as if she were afraid that I was going to say something hurtful. "I can't imagine living without Ahmad. I think about him when I go to sleep and when I wake up. I'd never been in love before him and I don't think I'll ever be able to love anyone else. We agree on everything: ideas, emotions, politics. You know, Mustafa, I went to his apartment and met his family. Really nice people, regular folks, but I didn't go to meet them. I went to see the bed he sleeps in. The books he reads. The first thing he sees in the street when he wakes up. His dirty clothes in the hamper. You know, Mustafa, when I went into the bathroom, all I did was pick up his clothes that were soaking in the wash, smelling them, trying to make out the smell of his sweat through the detergent. Recently, I've noticed that he wants to touch me and hold my hand. At the movies. In the car. Standing close to me on the bus. He was wearing me down, and I didn't know what to do. So then I started to worry. What does he want from me exactly? Eternal love or physical love? Does he just want to get on top of me and then dump me? Or does he want to live with me and inside me forever? It was like I was dying and coming back to life every day because I didn't know which one of those two guys he was. You know, Mustafa, I don't care if you think I'm crazy but I can't think of any other solution than to give him what he wants: the desire that fills his eyes when he holds me. If he wants me for my love, I can't hope for anything more out of life. And if he wants me just so he can get a taste of my honey and leave, well then I'd rather be burned early, then maybe I can save myself before I get completely lost in him." There were tears in her eyes.

107

I didn't say anything. I couldn't make a sound. I was thunderstruck by her stormy love. I couldn't tell right from wrong; truth from forgery. I was watching her closely as she spoke, trying to remember things I could use against her in the future, but she unleashed a gushing flood of torrential emotions on my ears, washing away my entire being. When I left her car that day, I'd already made up a beautiful corner for her in my heart, and I go there whenever I feel down.

14

THE DRIVER WAS KNOCKING persistently, but Hagg Hamid told him to give it a rest because they needed time to make themselves presentable. After a little while, the door opened and a giant dressed in a white gallabiya, with a bushy beard but no mustache, appeared before us. He hugged his father and kissed him on the shoulders as he usually did. He put his hand out and tried to get a good look at me. It took him a moment to recognize me, but then suddenly he was hugging me and kissing the air by my cheeks and over my shoulders. "Mustafa, God bless you, man! May God provide for you and grant you the mercy of the righteous," he said, patting me on the shoulder with unintended violence. I thanked him as we walked through the living room. There was a low wooden table in the center of the room; there weren't any dishes on it, but there were crumbs. It looked like they'd cleared it off in a hurry. Ahmad led us to a small sitting room and excused himself for a few minutes. The driver hadn't come in, so it was just me and Hagg Hamid. I sat there, wondering how I was going to face Ahmad. *What am I going to say to him? Am I going to be able to change his mind?*

Ahmad al-Helu, who'd out-read me in almost every subject; who'd taken others on, whether he'd been standing at the podium or sitting in the audience; who'd led others in protest; who'd endured the cruelty of jails and jailers; who'd dealt with the wretched as well as the elite. Could I get him to listen to me? Could I get him to back down? Of course not. *You're in for a disappointment, Hagg Hamid.* I began to feel like my presence was only going to end up making him dig in his heels. It made me nervous that he was being so quiet since it seemed so unlike his old self. He never used to be so physically imposing. He'd filled out and you could see the bulging veins on his hands. That was the thing that stood out most about these people. I don't know what they feed them in those fundamentalist cells, but they're all giant, clean, and brooding, and though they try to hide behind insincere smiles, it always gives them away; no matter what mask they wear.

One of the main reasons I'd gone was because I was curious to see Shahinaz, but as soon as I got there, I realized that was an impossible dream. Ahmad brought a tray of teacups in and handed one to his father and one to me. He slapped my thigh and said, "God willing, you will join us for dinner."

I said I was sorry, but I had to be somewhere, and promised that I'd come back some other time. I knew full well I'd never go back there again. Hagg Hamid started to approach the subject with extreme caution. He told Ahmad I'd become a journalist. Ahmad scowled when he heard the word 'journalist,' and said, "May God have mercy on him," under his breath.

I didn't say anything. I let father and son dance around each other. The father started up again: he lied and said I'd asked him how Ahmad was doing. Ahmad chimed in, saying he was fine and everything was going well, thanks be to God, and then he asked how I was doing and whether I'd got married yet. I said that I hadn't, but before he could throw out some cliché about the importance of marriage, how it was "half of one's religion," I quickly added that I was planning to. He smiled and wished me well. He asked me who she was so I said the first name that came into my head, Marcia, but as soon as he heard her foreign-sounding name, he started squirming in his seat as if he'd been bitten by a scorpion. He told me to think twice about it, because Imam Ahmad ibn Hanbal had ruled, in his verdict on the permissibility of burying a Christian woman in a Muslim cemetery, that she should not be buried there so that the Muslims would not suffer from her punishment, but that if she were carrying a Muslim fetus in her womb, she should not be buried in an infidel cemetery so that the child would not suffer from their punishment. Rather, she should be buried by herself. And all the scholars of the Muslim nation agreed that when you die, you're either in God's grace or in torment, even if it only affects the soul, and therefore Muslim cemeteries must be kept separate from those of non-Muslims. His father seemed proud of what he was hearing out of his son. I decided to stay out of pointless arguments and waited quietly as his father tried to guide the conversation back to the reason we'd come. He pretended that the news of Ahmad's resignation had upset me, but Ahmad cut him off, "Why should that upset you, Brother Mustafa? Do you not want what is best for me? Or have you come here to convince me that I should go to work with you and your lot so that I may fool people into believing that the lies and propaganda you peddle are the truth?"

I love the Arabic language, it's how I make my living. But I've never liked people who use it that way; people who want take us back thousands of years. I ignored his sarcasm; I was determined not to get pulled in. "You're a good engineer, Ahmad, why do you want to sell bassbousa?"

I could tell from the look on his father's face that he wished I hadn't said that. Ahmad flew off the handle and practically screamed at me, "I am free to choose how I earn my living and I do not give a damn about your unlawful money or your despicable ignorance!"

I told myself there was no point in arguing with him, and that I'd just say what I wanted to say and leave the rest up to God. I patted him on the thigh and started talking; I ignored his interruptions. I told him to think about his family's future because they were his burden to bear till the Day of Resurrection (he was yelling at me then: "What do you know about religion?"). I told him it'd be better for him and everybody

111

else if he opened a store or a workshop where he could put his skills and talent to use rather than selling bassbousa and kunafa, which he did more for show than to earn a living. At that point he stopped interrupting and listened to me contemptuously. I went on, "That's right, you want to remind them at every turn that they're the reason a successful engineer is living hand to mouth. Some sort of silent, passive protest that doesn't do anything for society; it just adds to the burden."

He smirked. "You still remember all that bullshit? I wonder who taught you that stuff?" In spite of his goading, I wasn't going to stoop to his level. I was ecstatic that he'd reverted to speaking in dialect and dropped the mask of phony high-mindedness he'd been wearing. Suddenly, his daughter, who couldn't have been older than four, came into the room. I'd never seen her before, nor any of her sisters. The little girl was wearing a lovely, long cloak and a headscarf, which pinched her soft neck. She leaped into her grandfather's lap, and then she turned to look at me. I smiled at her and put my hand out. She stretched hers out toward mine, but when Ahmad saw her moving closer to me, he snapped. "Fatima! Where is God?" he shouted at her. "Where is God, Fatima?"

The little girl froze and sat back, trembling, staring up at the ceiling. When I tickled her fingertips, she scurried from the room, and I felt I'd seen enough. As far as I was concerned, Ahmad had fallen into an abyss so deep I wasn't going to be able to reach him. He was worried about his little daughter being around men. I stood up and asked Hagg Hamid to excuse me. I said a tepid goodbye to Ahmad and waited for a few seconds as he went to make sure that the path to the door was clear, and then I raced down the small flight of stairs. Before I'd gone over to Ahmad's apartment, I'd sketched out a romantic scene in my mind: that I'd see Shahinaz, in a headscarf, or veiled, or however she was, opening her bedroom door a crack to catch a glimpse of me as I left the apartment. I wiped that scene from my mind because I didn't care anymore whether she saw me or not, or remembered me or not, or whether there was any connection left between us; be it in the past or in the future.

15

I LOVED THAT COFFEEHOUSE where I was sitting then in Bayn al-Sarayat. I had fond memories of the chairs and tables, the corners, and the pillars, which appeared taller than they were because of the sooty cloud that buffeted the ceiling. I used to go there as a student. It wasn't as spacious or as polished back then; but some of the old character still remained. It was located in a bank of buildings in the Bayn al-Sarayat district, directly across from the university. From the university gate I'd go past the Department of Economics and Political Science, and then on to the School of Humanities. There was no upstairs to the coffeehouse back then. There were no girls sitting on the sidewalk smoking water-pipes either.

I went there that day on purpose. After I'd left Ahmad al-Helu's place, I just wanted to be alone. After I had a great kebab at a restaurant on Haram Street, I suddenly remembered the coffeehouse. Nostalgia led the way. I looked around, trying to remember which corners my classmates and friends once favored, which spot Hind and I used to withdraw to. Our friends would let us talk, just the two of us, without any care for the time. They wouldn't even try to drag us off to lectures because they understood what we had. I owed her so much. I met her on my first day at university, watching her from a distance even though there wasn't anything particularly eye-catching about her. I followed her as she went around, looking at the schedule of classes. She wasn't pretty enough to stand out and she didn't have the kind of body that leads men into temptation. She was very plain. But my destiny was catching up with me. At our first lecture, I was standing by the bench where she was sitting, looking for a seat, and when I asked if the seat next to her was free, she smiled. *That smile's going to hold me captive till I die.* She was so easy to talk to, we chatted right through the lecture. We walked out of that lecture hall together. We met other students together. A few months later, we were inseparable. She was uncomplicated in every way: in talking about her problems; in voicing her opinion, no matter how shocking it was. Four days after we met, she gave me her number and told me to call her.

Occasionally, I'd skip class to go visit Essam at his college or drop in on Ahmad al-Helu. One time, when she told me I'd missed an important class, I asked her if she could catch me up on it later.

"Why later?" she asked, smiling. "Come by my house tonight and I'll explain it to you."

I figured she was joking and I was determined not to mention it the next day. I'd pretty much forgotten all about it, but several days later, when I reminded her that she'd promised to fill me in on what I'd missed, she snapped at me and told me I'd stood her up and embarrassed her in front of her parents. I was taken completely by surprise; I didn't think she'd meant it. I didn't get why her family would've been expecting me, but she said they wanted to meet me since she'd told them so much about me. There wasn't anything anyone could say about me: I'd only just started university. I didn't say that though. I made another date with her and that time, I went.

Her father greeted me with a smile and sat me down and the two of us talked about life for a bit. Her mother welcomed me, smiling affectionately, and kept bringing out sweets for me to sample. I played with her younger brother, Hossam, who was in middle school. We played a board game, which was set up like a soccer pitch with two teams and a wooden ball the size of a large chickpea; you had to draw the player back with your finger and when you released him, he'd kick the ball, which was resting in a shallow hole. While Hind was getting her room ready for us, I chatted with her older sister, Sawsan, who worked at the Ministry of Finance, about her time studying commerce at university. When Hind had finished, she took my hand and pulled me away from my game with Hossam and I asked Sawsan to excuse me as we had a lot of studying to get through. She led me to her modest room where she'd laid out our books and notebooks on the desk and beside those, she'd placed two cups of tea opposite each other. I looked over the walls that were decorated with simple drawings and well-known sayings. She smiled as she watched me. When I turned to examine the wall behind me, I saw a sheet of poster-board with some verses from Amal Donqol's poem, "No Reconciliation!" written on it in marker. It caught my eye and I went closer to get a better look. Then we took turns reading the verses aloud:

No Reconciliation!
Not even if they crown you a prince,
How could you shake their hands
And not see the blood that stains every palm?
—The arrow that struck me from behind
Will strike you a thousand times—
For blood's become a badge of honor now.

No Reconciliation!
And if they tell you reconciliation is but a ruse,
It is vengeance!
As the seasons pass,
Its flame fades in every breast,
But the hand of shame, with its five fingers,
is forever branded
On all the abject brows . . .

When we got to the end of the poem, she said, "Do you like it?"

"Of course, I know it by heart," I said, and I could see how happy that made her. That intimate setting, the poem, some mysterious feelings making their way toward the light: it all filled me with a spiritual energy and I lost any interest I'd had in studying. There was a child's swing out on the balcony off her bedroom rocking softly in the wind. "Is that yours?" I asked, "Or Hossam's?"

She laughed. "It used to belong to Sawsan, then it belonged to me, and now it belongs to Hossam." Then she whispered, "Do you want to get on and I'll push you?"

"I wish," I said and smiled. She thought I was being serious and started heading toward the balcony, but I grabbed her by the hand and sat her down. Then she flipped open the book and was all business as she started explaining the lesson. But none of it was making any sense to me. All of a sudden, she stood up and opened the balcony door part way.

"Go ahead, smoke your cigarette. I know you can't focus without it," she whispered.

"No, I shouldn't."

She laughed softly. "Don't worry, no one's going to walk in on us while we're studying."

I smoked a hurried cigarette as she stood by the balcony door fanning the smoke out of the room with a towel. She went to wash out the teacups since I'd used mine as an ashtray. After that, Hossam would knock from time to time and bring us fruit, or sandwiches, or more tea. The time flew, but Hind didn't want me to leave. When I said goodbye to her father, who'd been doing the crossword in his favorite newspaper, he stood up and shook my hand and asked me to look after Hind on campus. He said I should come over to study more often but, in reality, days like that were few. I only went to her place every once in a while because her family's unusual interest in me made me nervous. I was young. I was green. I didn't understand how the world worked. But, to this day, the thought of that humble family is one of my happiest memories.

Hind and I became friends and then sweethearts, without ever discussing our feelings. There was nothing in the world but her glance, her gorgeous, thick eyelashes, her slender body, her smile like a pearl when an oyster is first opened, her black eyes, her unique nose. I even loved the birthmark above her right temple, halfway between her eyebrow and her ear, which looked like a lotus blossom.

Even though Essam and, after him, Ahmad al-Helu were the first to read my poems, Hind was the first to appreciate them. When she opened my notebook and found one of my poems by accident, she devoured it with her eyes as I looked on bashfully. She ran off exuberantly with it in her hand and showed it to all our friends. It was as embarrassing as being caught naked. Our friends all said nice things about it, but I wasn't convinced: they never read a word that wasn't in their textbooks. She started asking me every day to see what I'd written and she insisted on looking through my notebooks until she found my newest poem, which would fill her with the joy of a mother for her newborn child. I started to insert messages to her in my poems. If I were annoyed with her for something she'd done, I'd write a verse about it and then I'd watch her as she smiled, surprised at first, and then remembering what had set me off. And if she'd done something to make me happy, my poem would be full of joy. (At that point in my life, I wasn't writing poems per se; they were more like vignettes.)

Hind was a lively flame. She was involved in loads of activities. She was an active member of the Expedition Club, the Friends of the Theater Society, the Journalism Club, and she was secretary of the We Love Egypt Club. She worked tirelessly to put together an exhibition, which paired my poems with the photography of a third-year art student. I was cocky: proud that she'd gone to so much effort for me. There I was, a first-year who'd been at university for less than four months, sharing the stage with a senior student. She'd picked out the poems for the exhibition herself. She showed up bright and early and took me to greet the guests against my will. She'd bought a fancy guestbook so they could sign their names and write down their impressions of the poems. (I still have that guestbook and I wouldn't trade a single page of it for all the money in the world.) Every time I open it, I'm overwhelmed by the amount of spontaneous praise for my poetry, which—up until the day before the exhibition—I'd always considered to be trite. Hind had made it into something valuable.

I was like a tourist who'd just touched down in a city he'd never been to before. Hind introduced me to all kinds of student activities: concerts, student theatricals, and some of the Expedition Club trips.

Hind lived on Khayrat Street near Lazoghli Square and I lived in al-Talabiya. We had an unspoken arrangement, and while I don't remember exactly when it started, I know when it ended. She used to take the bus to Giza Square where we'd meet and then walk to campus together. On the way back, we'd part ways at Giza Square where she'd take the bus back to Lazoghli Square. I often insisted on escorting her home and, after a moment's hesitation, she'd give in. When we were about halfway there, she'd suggest we get off the bus and walk the rest of the way.

She began urging me to publish my poems in newspapers and magazines, but I wasn't confident about the level of my poetry. *Was it good enough to publish?* I always refused until one day she took an envelope and a stamp out of her bag. She took the new poem that I'd been showing her, and stuck it in the envelope. Then she wrote out the address of a newspaper she'd been carrying around with her, stuck the stamp on, and licked the envelope closed (I'd give my life to be that envelope now). She ignored my angry protest, and took me by the hand to the mailbox on campus and dropped it inside. A week or two later, when we met up in Giza Square, she was carrying an extra plastic bag that looked like it had clothes in it. I asked her what was inside. "I bought you some pajamas so when you come to study at my house you'll be comfortable." She was smiling and I believed her because I knew better than anyone how crazy she could be. We sat in the cafeteria and talked until all our friends, plus some of hers from the Expedition Club, showed up. There were more than twelve of us there, guys and girls. I figured it was someone's birthday and that she was planning to give the birthday girl her gift while I sat there looking like an idiot. I was planning to chew her out for embarrassing me. She took a large stack of newspapers out of the plastic bag. My poem was on page eight along with my full name printed in thick, black letters. My eyes darted over the lines of the poem, which I'd never believed was any good until I saw the effect it had in Hind's proud smile. For me, it was the first, and most beautiful, display of love from a girl to a boy; I don't think anyone will ever do anything like that for me again, not even in another life. We ordered a bunch of drinks to celebrate and she insisted on footing the bill. Our friends said they wanted copies of the poem, but they didn't care about the rest of the newspaper, so Hind leaned over the table and, with a small ruler in her hand, started tearing the pages out of the newspapers and handing them to me to sign before giving them to the friends who'd asked for them. The pen in my hand was shaking and my friends were rushing me, but, at the same time, I was flooded with happiness. I watched her with a mixture of apprehension and love that I'd never felt before as she carefully straightened the pages she tore out and looked for my name one more time before handing them to me and smiling as if she'd been afraid that it might've been missing from some of the issues. We skipped our lectures that day in celebration, though she did go off for a few minutes to take copies to some of the professors we were close to. She told me I had to go back home with her that evening and give signed copies to her whole family. She'd held back a copy for me and five more for Hossam, Sawsan, her mother, her father, and herself.

We left campus to go have lunch and catch a movie, but we went back later to see a play that some of our friends from the Friends of the Theater Society were performing in. After the play, I went to the restroom because it was a long trip back to Hind's house. It was the end of the day and the restroom looked awful: water dripping from the open faucets on the urinals mixed with urine, clean water from the sinks and from making ablutions, and the dirt from all the students' shoes and sandals had made an ugly paste across the floor; add to that the pervasive stink of accumulated excrement. I went into the last stall, thinking it'd be the cleanest, but I was met by the same squalor, the same stench. Someone had covered the toilet seat with newspaper to protect his backside from the filth. The sheet was so wet it'd almost dissolved, but it did look familiar. I lifted it up with my fingertips and found myself looking at a copy of the poem I'd spent half the morning signing for my classmates. I searched like a lunatic for the dedication so I could find the guy who'd done it and make him pay, but the dedication had been torn off. I knew, whoever he was, he'd done it on purpose, not because he was stuck for a sheet of paper to protect his ass and the asses of those who came after him. I didn't need to use the restroom anymore. When I came out looking like a ghost, the whole day's joy drained from my face, she was alarmed. She thought I'd suddenly taken ill, so she marched me to the cafeteria and ordered a lemonade from the server just as they were about to close. I sat there, lifeless, and then I downed the lemonade. She let me sit there in silence; she didn't demand to know what was wrong. She just watched me anxiously. She tried to get me to lean on her as we walked out of the university, but I pulled myself together and told her I was fine. She wanted to get a cab to take me home, but then she saw a friend of ours who was just getting into his car, so she waved to him. I grabbed her hand before he could spot us. "I'm fine!" I said. She flinched. It was the first time I'd ever raised my voice to her. She shrunk away from me. I felt bad, so I squeezed her hand and she smiled wanly. "Let's walk to Giza Square," I said.

She hesitated. "You're still not feeling well?" I shook my head. When we were halfway there we stopped to rest by the fence outside the School of Agriculture. She said she could tell something was bothering me. There was a giant weight on my chest and I was afraid I'd suffocate. At the time, I felt that what had happened was a deliberate insult, an intensely disdainful act of mockery that could never be forgiven. I started to tell her as we walked on. The more she heard, the more the veins on her neck stood out. I pulled out the wet sheet, which I'd balled up and stuffed in my pocket, unfolding it so she could look at it without dirtying her hands. She took it from me and examined it in disbelief and then she began to sob. She blamed herself for ruining my excitement about having my first poem published. I tried so hard to stop her from thinking that, but there you go. I forgot all about my pain and began to pity her. It took a lot of effort to calm her down. My anger, my nerves, my sense of hurt all disappeared; worry for her, worry about what she might do to herself because she thought she was the reason for what'd happened took their place. When we got to the bus stop, she looked at me, her eyes still full of tears, and begged me in earnest never to write a dedication to anyone ever again, no matter how dear they might be, or how close, or how important, because as time went on they might turn against you and defile your dedication. She placed her hand on mine and asked me to swear to it. I smiled, my mind ablaze. *What are all these lovely dreams, Hind? Am I going to have books and collections of poetry to dedicate? Will people actually ask for my dedication? Why are you talking about my books as if they already exist, as if you can stare straight into the future without a crystal ball?* I swore to it.

"Except for you, of course."

She shot me a look. "Especially me. What you write doesn't belong to you or me. It belongs to the reader who appreciates it."

I didn't know what to say to all that big talk. She saw the bus pulling up and said goodbye. "Wasn't I supposed to come home with you and give the copies to your family?"

"I'll do it," she said, "Without a single word from you to any of them. You just promised me you weren't going to dedicate anything to anybody."

She left that day. And later, after she'd left me for good, I never dedicated any of my books to anyone; big or small, important or insignificant. That is, with the exception of my first book of poems, which was published in Beirut. That was printed with a dedication to her, and a plea for her not to be angry about it.

Most of that first year, we studied for exams together; she insisted on it. Just to screw with her, I tried to get other classmates of ours to study with us, but she wouldn't have it: "You know how they are. You think they're going to understand any of it? They're just going to hold us back with their talking." That was how I knew that we'd been made for each other and that she was as in love with me as I was with her.

During the summer vacation, which she divided between camping trips with the Expedition Club and trips to the seaside with her family,

I went to great lengths just to see her for a few hours. I had to take humiliating loans from my sisters or from my father to whom I had to lie about why I was taking a trip or why I needed the money. She used to say I should join the Expedition Club, but I didn't think much of it. I wanted to be with her forever, but the idea of climbing a mountain, or wasting my energy driving in tent stakes, or sitting around a fire belting out "Shooma lak booma lak" struck me as silly. She had the admirable dream of visiting every province in Egypt so for her, joining the Expedition Club was the first step toward her goal. Back then I was living as two different people. With her, I was one person, devoted and loving; but the other person liked to party with Essam, Ahmad al-Helu, and Farid.

At the beginning of our second year, our friends convinced her to run for a spot on the Arts Committee. I was neutral: I didn't object, I didn't encourage. Her popularity worried me mostly because I didn't want anything but me to intrude on her life. I never imagined that Hind would sweep a university election, that she'd beat the students from the Islamic groups who were pros at it. Beyond making a few banners, I wasn't involved in her victory. I didn't write any fiery poetry in support of her like Ahmad al-Helu had tried to get me to do. For the record, Ahmad al-Helu played a crucial role in the two days leading up to the election. He talked to students from our class about why they should vote for her; she'd get things done and serve them well. I was there with her, but it was as if I were from another planet. Her slightest movement drove me wild, but my only contribution was the lone vote I gave her. I displayed no signs of being affected by her temporary preoccupation with being on the committee and organizing arts activities throughout the school year. I ignored my classmates' gossiping about how I'd sit by myself; or how I'd sit with them, but taciturn; or how I'd sit beside her as she signed permits to hold events or to post ads for various arts programs.

Essam was busy experimenting with one of his models. He'd started having a lot of relationships because according to him he was an artist, a bohemian, a nihilist. He was too busy for me, so the only person left was Ahmad al-Helu, who began influencing me politically.

122

I went to various protests and discussion groups, on the main campus and at the Engineering Department. I kept Hind away from it all, since it might've created a scandal for her as an elected member of a committee, but word got around and she found out what I'd been up to. Once, when we were studying at her house, she told me she thought that what I was doing was great and she wished she could join me, but I told her that using her position to serve students was probably more useful than anything I was doing. She smiled and looked at me lovingly. "I doubt it," she said and we never discussed it again.

How I loved it when she'd find time to hang out with me, or when she'd shyly invite me over to her house to study. Her attempts to make up for the time we weren't able to spend together made me love her even more, so much so that I didn't even need her to actually be there. She completely took me over; while I was asleep, while I was awake, while I moved, while I stood still. When I was with her, I experienced all those exact same symptoms of romance I later read about.

One time when we were walking to Giza Square, we met one of her friends from the Expedition Club. She wasn't in our department so I'd never met her before. I said hello and stepped away while they finished their conversation, but I could still hear Hind as she whispered to the other girl about me: that I was her fiancé and that we were going to make our engagement official at the end of the year. I could hear the echo of their celebratory kisses through my dizzying confusion. *What made her so sure?*

I had actually been planning for us to get engaged at the end of the year, even though my father was going through a rough patch. He was preparing for my older sister Mahasin's wedding, and since her fiancé had exhausted our patience with his shiftlessness, my father had to bear the brunt of the costs just to get the whole thing over with. Rida, my other sister, was engaged as well and her fiancé was certain to be as opportunistically impoverished as the first, so my father was—most likely—also going to have to cover the cost of their wedding. My objections to these two matches had fallen on deaf ears. They still considered me the little brother, the one who couldn't see what they all saw: that marriage protected girls. It was an idea my mother had embraced and she'd convinced my father of it. If I'd so much as asked to get engaged while I was only in my second year of university, there was a high likelihood that I'd have been refused and, on top of that, I would've had to face a storm of ridicule from my father. After all, Mahasin and Rida were girls and they hadn't got engaged until they'd finished secondary school. My engagement to Hind wouldn't have cost much and I wasn't planning to get married until after graduation, but all the same, I chose to have my mother break the news to my father and get him to agree. After a lot of begging, my mother promised that she'd tell my father about it after I passed my exams at the end of the year, so I put it on hold, confident she'd keep her word.

"That's good news," said Ahmad al-Helu. "But why are you in such a hurry? Anyway, isn't getting engaged going to distract you from what's going on in the country right now?"

Even though he hadn't seen much of her, Essam was happy for me. "It's for the best. She's a good girl and she loves you. It's better than being like me and going from relationship to relationship, ending up a bachelor because you can't tell who's good for you in the long run."

The weather was gloomy; the sky over the university gray and depressing. From time to time, small raindrops fell from the sky, sending us running for the protection of the cafeteria's ceiling and glass walls. Then beams of sun would sneak through and we'd go outside again and sit at the umbrella-shaded tables. My thin winter clothes weren't up to those conditions; all I could do was zip or unzip my jacket depending on the temperature, and nurse a cup of hot cocoa in my hands. There was a steady rotation of friends at my table as some went off to lectures or appointments, and others arrived. I was waiting for Hind; she was at a meeting of the Expedition Club, drawing up a schedule for the upcoming mid-year break. We'd met up that morning when the weather was beautiful and gone to al-Munasara, an area that specialized in furniture, because she wanted to pick out a desk for her room. She said she was going to keep a corner of the desk clear to house my future writing. Hind used to love going to furniture shops with me. She used to look through the bedroom sets, the children's furniture, the chandeliers, the kitchens. She'd pick things out and haggle over the price, and after she'd extracted a discount from the salesman, she'd ask him to lower the price even more because we were newlyweds just starting out in life. The salesman would walk over and shake my hand, congratulating me, and he'd give her an even larger discount, which she still wouldn't accept. She'd leave, promising to come back if she couldn't find anything cheaper at the other stores. (At that point, we'd never spoken a word to each other about love or marriage.) I didn't like how she negotiated with the salespeople at all, but I never once hinted to her that it bothered me. For even though I was tickled by the things she was saying about us, every time we left a disappointed salesman, I, too, walked away disappointed.

The sky was a gray, thundering mass. There was fleeting lightning followed by torrents of rain. I ran back into the cafeteria and weighed my options: I could either dart across the quad and go upstairs, soaking wet, to find her; or wait it out with my friends in some lecture until Hind was done with whatever was keeping her from me; or stay put until she remembered I was waiting and came down. There was zero visibility; our bodies were enveloped by a gloomy, gray-black fog. The people running through the quad looked like ghosts trying to escape the rain. One of them stopped a little ways away from me and stared, ignoring the rain that poured down on him. Then he started making insulting gestures at me and sticking his tongue out. By the time I'd realized it was Khalil, he'd disappeared. I'd stopped shivering when the rain let up a little, but then it started to come down again, with a sound like an explosion.

The howling screams reached us in the safety of the cafeteria and I saw all the students look to the sky. We streamed out of the cafeteria and looked up at the university building. The windows on the second floor were all open, framing the faces of stunned girls looking out and guys calling for help. A few of us ran over to the entrance of the building where we found terrorized faces and a crowd on the ground floor. I squeezed past the students coming down the stairs and headed up to the Expedition Club office on the second floor. I saw pools of blood and the wounded bleeding out. I couldn't tell who was who, and then, suddenly, I fainted.

I came to on a wooden bench just outside the building, beside a girl who'd woken up right before me. She was sobbing, but I couldn't understand a word she was saying. The student union president spotted me and took me under his arm to the union's car. The passengers were all squeezing my hand and patting me on the shoulder, but I was too terrified to ask them what had happened. The student union president turned to me when we got near Haram Hospital and said, "It's minor, God willing. Our friend Hind's going to be just fine. I saw her with my own eyes after the explosion helping her friends."

The hospital where the casualties were taken was full of students and a few administrators. The only thing they let us do was wait in the lobby. They told us not to worry; they were just performing some basic procedures and that we shouldn't worry. I was passing in and out of consciousness, returning to find faces different from the ones that had been sitting next to me. At dusk, Ahmad al-Helu and Shahinaz were beside me; the news had reached them at the Engineering Department. In the evening, the hospital administrators made us leave so we wouldn't disturb the patients, but I didn't go home. Ahmad took me back to his modest apartment. I didn't sleep. Ahmad came and went a lot, once to tell my father where I was, once to get food, once to call Shahinaz from a payphone. I didn't sleep. I didn't cry. What I was feeling went beyond sadness and pain. I'd close my eyes every few minutes and imagine that when I woke up, it'd be as if none of it had ever happened.

In the early morning, Ahmad and I were sitting in the lobby of the hospital. He left and when he came back, he was holding back tears and telling me that Hind had passed. But I didn't believe those lies. I didn't let anyone say it to my face. It took months for me to return to a somewhat normal state, but something inside me had changed. I went to her funeral and I did everything that, according to theologians, the sharia and Islam have forbidden. I cried. I wailed. I punched walls. I rubbed my face in the dirt. I paid no attention to her friends, her classmates, her relatives. I didn't pay my respects to her family at all. If anyone had been hurt, it was me. I was the one who needed to receive condolences from the masses. I never went back to her house after that. I never had news of her family and they never heard about me; it was as if I'd died with Hind. I didn't want any of them to see me. I didn't want to remind them of her, didn't want to re-open their wounds. For a whole month or more, I went every evening, right before sunset, carrying a notebook filled with my poems, and waited for the sun to set at a coffeehouse on Bab al-Wadaa Street next to the Bab al-Wazir cemetery. Once it was dark, I'd sneak down long dirt paths past the tombstones until I reached her grave. A group of stray dogs would always follow me, barking at me and trying to tear my clothes the whole way there. I didn't care about them or about any human being on the face of the earth. The dogs got used to me after a while, and some of them would wag their tails, running ahead of me, accompanying me silently to her graveside. I used to read my poems out to her; ones she hadn't read while she'd been alive. The ones I used to hide from her because I was embarrassed by my love. Then I'd read a few long chapters to her from the Qur'an in my hand until it was time for the evening prayer. Then I'd leave. I used to tell her everything that had upset me that day. One time, I told her how I'd gone to the al-Munasara district and haggled with the salesman until I got him to give us the bedroom set for a good price; I was just waiting for her to come pick it up with me. I yelled at her for leaving me and going to the Expedition Club meeting, for leaving me out in the icy cold that has become my life.

Her classmates told me she'd been overjoyed at the end of their meeting because they'd agreed to all her proposals for how best to spend the vacation. And that they'd started goofing off—as they usually did at the end of their meetings—and throwing whatever was lying around at one another. One of them threw her the souvenir grenade, which had been there in the same spot for fifteen years. The grenade hit the floor before Hind could catch it and blew up. Her fragile body bore the impact of a kilogram's worth of highly explosive material. During the investigation, it was established that past members of the Expedition Club had picked up the grenade at an exhibition on landmines after the October War in 1973, and that they used to throw it around all the time, that it had fallen on the floor dozens of times without anything ever happening. Hind died from an enemy grenade that'd followed her all the way to her scholastic headquarters, as if it'd had her name on it, as if it'd been set to detonate and "H-I-N-D" was the code.

The gravedigger surprised me one night and told me that he often watched me, that he'd cry when I recited the Qur'an. We went to a coffeehouse nearby and he listened to my story and told me some amazing tales about martyred lovers and the departed. He patted me on the back and told me to swear to God that I'd never go back there again. "It's a sin," he said. "God doesn't approve of what you're doing to yourself. You're only weighing her down with sins this way." He asked me to promise, but I didn't respond. He hugged me to his chest for a long time and then he left. I tried desperately to hold it together and not to cry. He'd planted a frightening thought inside me: that I was burdening the most precious thing I'd ever loved down with sins. Because of that, I stopped visiting for three days, but on the third night I decided I'd go visit her the next day no matter what. That night, I was woken by a dazzling light that pierced my eyelids, but when I opened my eyes, my bedroom was completely dark. She was sitting on the chair in front of my bed, wearing the same clothes she'd been wearing on her last day. There was no halo around her head—contrary to my psychiatrist's mockery—but her face was radiant and she wore her usual loving smile. I was disoriented and when I tried to sit up, she stopped me with a gesture. I stayed where I was, looking at her in disbelief. I closed my eyes and opened them again. Her smile grew. "Have you forgotten about me yet, Mustafa?" I couldn't speak. She was giggling. "Don't be mad, I'm just joking. I know exactly how much you love me. But please don't visit me again. I'm doing fine and when I want to see you, I'll come to you." She could tell I was stunned. "Not like this. I'll visit you in the flesh. And we'll finish the life we started. Forget about me for a little while, do everything we dreamed of doing, and one day, suddenly, I'll be right there beside you. I'll give you signs. You know what I mean, Mustafa, signs . . . ."

The lovely phantom left and I sank into my bed and wept and the sound of it woke my mother. The whole household was already worried about what'd come over me after the accident. My mother held me, but I cried harder and I didn't stop until her own hot tears fell onto my face. She recited the Qur'an over me till I fell asleep.

A few days later, I went to a psychiatrist for the first time. I didn't tell anyone I was going. He seemed to be listening closely as I told him what'd happened, but then he told me he liked my fanciful stories and that I'd be better off writing movies than poetry. Ahmad al-Helu and Essam were the ones who supported me during that time; they stuck by me until I could pull it together.

16

I WAITED FOR KARIM while he went to the paint shop. The owner was sitting behind the wooden counter, which ran the length of his small storefront; a boy inside the shop handed him whatever the customers asked for. As soon as the owner spotted Karim standing in front of the store with the other customers, he frowned and shooed him away. I stepped off to the side so that Karim wouldn't come over to me because I didn't want the owner to think we were together. But Karim didn't go very far. He just leaned against a parked car, watching the shopkeeper serve the customers one by one until there were none left. The man looked over at the stock-boy, who ran to grab him a can of quick-dry glue. The owner wrapped it up in newspaper and glared at Karim as he walked toward him. The owner whistled. "Why don't you hurry up, you piece of crap! You think you're walking down the aisle?"

Karim laughed that laugh of his that teetered between brilliance and idiocy and held out some small bills he'd had balled up in his pocket. The owner glanced at the money and threw it in the drawer. I walked on ahead of Karim and he followed, keeping his distance. When I stopped on the corner of a secluded street, he walked right past me. The glue had blinded him and he'd forgotten about our deal. I called out to him, softly at first, then loudly until he turned around. "You idiot! Didn't I give you the money for that crap? 'Twenty pounds, boss, so I can get high.' And then you go and give him the change in your pocket and keep the twenty pounds?"

He laughed for a long time. "I lost your twenty pounds."

"How'd you lose it, dummy? I was with you the whole time except when you went to go buy that trash. And just now you walked off like I wasn't even there."

"I figured you didn't need me for anything."

"No, I do need you, you motherf— "

"Leave my mother out of it, Mr. Mustafa."

"Okay, Karim Bey. Now you're going to get all proper on me. So are you going to come with me tonight or not?"

"I'm free right now, but I don't know what I'll be doing tonight."

"Busy, you son of a bitch! Since when do you have anything to do?" I said under my breath. *I've got only myself to blame.*

He started pouring the glue into small plastic bags. I looked to see if anyone was around and shouted at him, "Put that away! You can do it after I leave."

He stopped and said, "No guarantees about tonight. I might forget."

I ignored him. "I'll be waiting for you at the coffeehouse."

Zaynab had been calling my mobile for three days straight. I was depressed and anxious, but I was too busy to wonder why. I had neither the time nor the peace of mind to put up with Zaynab for an entire night. I'd been debating for a while whether to break up with her, to give up those intimate moments that calmed my nerves—or to let her keep her place in my life, repaying her with fake emotions—but I was finally ready to put an end to things. I was going to level with her and sever the thread that connected us. First, I called Marcia and told her I was going to spend the night at her place.

I was on my way to Essam's when an unknown number popped up on my mobile. It was Zaynab calling me from a payphone. Before she could lay into me for ignoring her, I asked her to meet me at the bar in the Hotel Cosmopolitan. She wanted to know why. I didn't elaborate. I told her I was in a hurry and said I'd see her at eight o'clock that evening. With that, I'd only left myself four hours to spend with Essam. He was happier than I'd ever seen him. As he'd just returned from Singapore two days earlier, his mind was completely at peace; you couldn't say the same thing about mine. I didn't let on that anything was bothering me and listened as he told me all about the fairytale wedding they'd put on for Samantha and Essam, about how her family had treated him like a son, about how her employees and clients had tried to outdo one another in offering to help. He told me about his trips around Singapore, about the restaurants and bars, the landscapes that looked like something out of a dream. The clean streets. The pristine air: dustless as if you were living in an oxygen tent like Michael Jackson, the deformed singer.

I was absorbed in his tales and travels. I was seeing through his eyes, smelling with his nose, tasting with his mouth, feeling the breeze and the raindrops on my face. I forgot all about Ahmad al-Helu and Marcia and Yasmeen and Karim and Zaynab and saw Samantha and Essam against the backdrop of a high-tech world.

The troublemaker in me, tireless in disrupting my own life, asked him about his art. Did he put on any new exhibitions while he was there? Did he make any new pieces to show in Egypt? Essam started as if he were coming out of anesthesia. The question seemed to take him by surprise, and he mumbled almost inaudibly, "I made some sketches and I'm going to finish them here." When he asked me what was new, I told him all about Ahmad al-Helu and he seemed amused. He wasn't surprised, though, and he didn't have anything to say about it.

"Did you hear me?"

"I heard you," he said as he poured me a glass, "and I'm saying, 'no comment.'" I swore at him playfully, but I was sick of how he always acted like nothing ever surprised him.

"How come you didn't predict he'd turn into a fundamentalist?" I asked.

"Thank God he's not claiming to be a prophet!"

"Well, what about Shahinaz?"

He laughed out loud. "I didn't see the bassbousa thing coming, I'll give you that, but you know Shahinaz better than I do, and you know that if Ahmad became a Druze, so would she. It's the same old story." I didn't want to tell him that Ahmad had said Jews and Christians weren't allowed to be buried in Muslim cemeteries because Essam's situation was worse than mine. Samantha was a Buddhist and—according to Ahmad's interpretation—she didn't have the right to be buried in the first place. But if I'd said it, even as a joke, Essam would've been angry.

He swished the wine around in his mouth and then said, "Yeah, so you weren't expecting it, but what's the big deal? Isn't what happened to Ahmad a lot better than how some of our brothers on the left have changed? At least he's not stealing, or covering up corruption, or sucking the blood of downtrodden workers. Ahmad al-Helu's been chasing after lost ideals his entire life. Let him think he's found one. It doesn't matter what flag he's marching under, he thinks it'll keep him safe." What he'd said had got me thinking about it in a new light, but before I could ask him another question, he said, "What's new with you and Marcia?"

"Nothing."

He spoke softly as he poured out another glass, "Could you be more specific?"

I needed that glass and I drained it in one go. Then I stood up, and he looked at me. "I'll come over tomorrow and explain everything, but right now there's somewhere I've got to be." When he insisted I sit back down, I told him to show me the sketches he'd drawn in Singapore.

He looked at me a while and smiled as he pointed to the door, "You're free to go. I'll show them to you tomorrow after you've told me everything."

As I was leaving, I wondered what had stopped me from opening up to him. Essam was the last person I had in the world. He was the only person I could confide in, even if it were something embarrassing or taboo. Why didn't I want to tell him? Was it because I didn't have

133

anything interesting left to say? Or was it because I was scared he'd admonish me or that all he'd do was smile sarcastically? I didn't know. The only thing I felt at that moment was that I was drowning in a bog of shit, too proud to call for help. I'd have sooner died than been mocked for having to be rescued.

Zaynab was munching on peanuts and pushing the mezzes around with her fork; there were two bottles of beer in front of her, one empty and the other nearly so. I was only a half an hour late, so she should've waited rather than start drinking without me. She smiled as she lit her cigarette and said, "I got here half an hour early and I thought my head was going to explode. I thought a beer would calm me down." The waiter brought us two more bottles. I filled my glass and downed it quickly. I didn't care whether the beer would mix badly with the wine. There were things I needed to say. I had to end it, to get over this mental burden that was weighing down my conscience for no good reason. She laughed and whispered, "You're not being very romantic. Wouldn't it've been better if we'd just had a drink back at our place?" She said *our place* for my apartment and *our dresser* for my dresser, as if she were determined to share my life. As if she weren't the passing shadow I'd taken her for. I didn't say anything so she brought it up again, ending each word with a whimper. I couldn't help but smile and think, *This woman's just a vagina with legs.*

"It won't work. I'm really busy and I've got lots to do. I don't have time." She popped a peanut in my mouth to shut me up.

She took a sip from her glass and studied me. "I guess you've found somebody else," she said. I didn't respond. "Maybe not just one. Maybe there's several." I didn't feel like playing her feminine game. I ignored her and focused on the mezzes. She drank from her glass and then let out a sigh that got my attention in spite of myself. She nodded her head knowingly and then, grinning, she said, "What's the deal? Say whatever you brought me here to say. I'm listening."

I didn't know what to make of her smile, but it was taunting me so I started to speak. I talked a lot about love, friendship, and marriage, about how we might work as friends, but we wouldn't make it as husband and wife because we were both so different. She suddenly stood up so I stopped talking, thinking I'd offended her, but she surprised me by kissing me on the lips and brow, and sitting back down. I didn't understand why she'd done that and I was about to start talking again, but she put her finger to my lips and told me not to go on.

She poured me a glass from her bottle and whispered, "Ever since we met I've liked a lot of things about you: you're a real man, you're kind, you're intelligent, you're confident. But there's one thing that's always bothered me: you think you're smarter than everyone else. I used to hate how condescending you can be. Whenever I asked you about something, I'd get a smirk and a patronizing explanation. I've never loved anyone. You're the closest I ever got to the kind of love I'd hoped for. I've got a lot of problems. I love everyone. I see the good in all of them and whenever someone does right by me, I reward them for it. Maybe I give him my body. You know lots of people would probably call that whoring, but you know me. I don't do it for money, or for a promotion, or for work, or to see my name written in lights. I do it like a child, who gives you a kiss when you give her a piece of chocolate. My honor was sacrificed a long time ago and I'm not going to sit beside it and slap my face in mourning. You were the most important person in my life. You listened to me. You cared about my problems. I feel like you'd do the impossible to help me. When you had my back and let me stay the night, I was rewarding you, Mr. Genius. You think you're so much smarter than a little country girl come to be chewed up in your cruel city. I could've lied to you and not let you touch an inch of my body, got you to marry me. I could see in your eyes that you were aching to have me. But I had to show you what I am. And do you know why? Because I love you; I respect you. I gave you my body because you were crazy about me. But if you'd looked into my eyes and asked me to marry you, I could never have let you have my tainted body."

As she spoke, I could feel the sincerity rising up from deep inside her as if she were carving the words, letter by letter, on my heart. I stood up and held her for a long time, caressing her back, kissing her cheeks. I didn't care about any of the customers there, or the bartender or the hotel manager. I sat back down and leaned back in my chair, shutting my eyes. My embrace had brought tears to her eyes. She left me to drown in a long silence while I tried to make sense of my life. Even Zaynab, who hadn't cared how she fit into my life, had shown me things I'd never considered before. I remembered our times together. How quick-tempered I was, cruel for no reason, how she bore it all so patiently. How I'd mocked her; how she'd take it with a smile and jump on me, kissing me and holding my hands behind my back so I couldn't get at her. How many times had I slapped her and shouted at her and thrown her off the bed? But she never got angry. She'd simply wipe the dust off her clothes and climb back up. She'd curl herself up, but then after a little while she'd wiggle herself into my arms. I never had any reason to be so cruel. Once, I got angry because she'd woken me up by kissing me all over so I got up like a madman and smacked her. Sometimes, she'd pretend to be angry and leave the bedroom, heading for the kitchen. She'd come back carrying a cup of tea and stand a safe distance away, drinking it and ignoring me. After I'd kissed up to her a little, she'd smile and say, "Do you want some tea?"

"It's not like you made me any," I'd say, but before I could finish my sentence, she'd run out of the room and come back in with a cup of tea she'd made and left in the kitchen just to screw with me.

I was in a pitiful state. If the choice were mine, and I'd had the ability to make sound decisions, I'd have married her straightaway, escaping from Marcia, my destiny, and Yasmeen, my fantasy, and Hind, my memory. I was pathetic; I'd come to end a relationship, but it was all wrapped up in veins and arteries, and if even a part of it were cut, I'd bleed to death.

I woke up to a sympathetic hand on my own and Zaynab whispering, "Hey, where'd you go?" I was drinking in silence and watching her, but then she said, "I thought you said you had somewhere you had to be right now."

I'd completely forgotten, but, thank God, the coffeehouse was near the hotel where I'd lost track of time with Zaynab. That whole neighborhood followed Karim's orders. I decided I'd go meet him and then spend the night with Marcia, but something told me not to leave Zaynab that night. I grabbed her hand and stood up. She laughed and whispered in my ear, "I knew before I got here we were going to spend the night together."

Zaynab left early in the morning to go collect her assignment from the newspaper; I woke up five hours later. I tore up the note she'd left for me on the nightstand and threw it in the toilet. My ugly mood returned. I cursed her for constantly trying to force herself into my life. What did I care about her assignment? If there even was an assignment or a newspaper to begin with! The stories published under her byline that she showed me from time to time could have been written by any moderately educated person while they were moving their bowels or waiting for their turn at the barber shop.

Marcia didn't call me at home or on my mobile. It was as if we hadn't made plans and I hadn't stood her up; as if it didn't bother her that I was too rude to apologize. I'd decided a bunch of times to call her and chickened out, but my evil side didn't let up until I called. Yet in the end it was all for nothing. I sent her a short text message asking her to forgive me and telling her that I was bringing her a surprise. I left her to guess about the surprise; I myself didn't know what it was going to be.

I went to give a lesson to one of my foreign students who lived downtown. My body was still drunk and sluggish from all the alcohol and a few hash cigarettes I'd had the night before. The world seemed narrower than the eye of a needle and I couldn't find any friends to take refuge with. I ruled out Essam because I'd been at his house the night before; Zaynab I was sick of; Marcia I was going to see that night; and Yasmeen would've been busy studying, or writing papers, or sitting with her grandmother, who got depressed whenever she was left alone for a long time.

A brief text message cleared the fog from my head. Sender: Marcia. Text of message: "I'm in the Fayoum with Diana. I'll be back in a week. Try to use the time to work hard so we can get a move on." I was worried so I tried calling her again, but she didn't respond; that made it worse. Essam wasn't at his studio and he wasn't answering his mobile, which was usual if he was busy with his work. I called Ewald, Awad. He said he hadn't seen Essam and hadn't heard he was back from Singapore until I told him. Awad said he was busy planning his wedding and handling the paperwork it entailed.

What was this wedding fever everyone had? Marriage . . . marriage . . . as if it were feline mating season. Awad the German was going to marry an Egyptian, and Essam had married a Singaporean. Maybe I was destined to marry Marcia the American.

Marcia was going to stay in the Fayoum for a week as a guest of Swiss-born Evelyn. It was lovely there and Evelyn had a beautiful country house. And even though it was small, it felt like the village elder's house; always full of people of various nationalities, "the cosmopolitans," who came to stay with Evelyn. In the 1960s and 1970s, she'd been married to a famous colloquial poet-turned-literary critic. Evelyn used to divide her time between Switzerland and Egypt until she finally settled down to supervise her pet project: raising a generation of Egyptian potters and weavers of carpets and gallabiyas, which the people of Kardasa were known for. Evelyn went to Europe every year to market her products and meet Oriental travel enthusiasts, people taken with the ambiance of *The Thousand and One Nights.* She'd bring them to the Fayoum. A few of them would be shocked by what they saw and hurry back to their own countries, but most of them would stay and intermingle and get what they came for, in peaceful surroundings. Marcia loved Evelyn. To be more precise, Marcia loved Evelyn's lifestyle and her capacity for putting up with life in Egypt; she'd essentially immigrated. She was good at both Cairene Arabic and country Arabic, which was what the people of Fayoum spoke. She even thought in Arabic.

Marcia told me that whenever she felt down, she'd rush off to the Fayoum to enjoy the simple life: raising chickens, pumping water up from the well, taking a few dance lessons with the Russian dancers taught by the coach and professional dancer Evelyn had hired. Marcia would come alive again in the midst of the zaar ceremonies, the zikrs, and the dance parties that Evelyn was so good at throwing. I met Evelyn years before Marcia, but I wasn't the one who introduced them. Marcia knew Evelyn the way she knew a lot of people like her; people from all the minorities in Cairo: the Armenian community, the Greeks, even the Knights of Malta, and there weren't more than a handful of them.

Going to see Evelyn was a message directed at me, the contents of which were: she was disappointed about something and I was probably the cause. She hadn't invited me to go with her and I'd have looked desperate if I'd followed her. She needed something to make her happy and that was what I was going to try to give her when she got back. But to make her completely happy would've meant my demise. The idea was probably Diana's, her close friend who was head of educational exchanges at the U.S. embassy in Cairo. Marcia had known her for years and they had many things in common, but I didn't know what they were. Diana scared me; she had an organized mind and high standing among the American expats. I met her a few times and we were always friendly. Essam and Awad often warned me about her, but they never explained why. Even though Diana and Marcia lived in the same building, I wasn't in on the visits to her apartment and I very rarely attended the parties she hosted. Diana was big on metaphysics and had a lot of diplomas from online courses. She claimed to be proficient in Chinese acupuncture and shortwave treatment. I used to make fun of Diana about that to Marcia, but she'd get mad at me until finally she decided never to discuss the topic with me again. Diana was married and had two daughters. Her husband lived in America and had never visited Egypt. I didn't know how long she'd been married, or whether they were separated or not. I did know that she was in love with a singer from Upper Egypt named Sharif, who'd been blessed with more sex appeal than fame. Sharif's specialty was singing in the Upper Egyptian style, which I loved. I loved his voice, and I'd gone to several of his concerts at the Cairo Jazz Club with Marcia and Essam, where we'd see Diana. Marcia told me Diana was madly in love with him and that she'd tried to use all of her various connections to put him on the map of Egyptian music.

I stayed home that night, smoking what remained of the hash cigarettes, drinking what was left over, waiting for whatever wasn't coming. I got bored of reading books that I instantly forgot about. I got tired of begging at poetry's door and receiving only a pittance. Constantly dwelling on the past was pulling me toward the worst type of psychotic mania, if the doctors' warnings were true. The state of the nation, in all its decrepitude: that was my refuge, my asylum. When Marcia returned, I'd protest and sit-in and strike and sign petitions. I'd be active and vibrant once more.

I loved Marcia and all the mystery that surrounded her. Maybe it was that mystery that kept our relationship going. She was of Polish descent, American by nationality. Her grandparents had immigrated to America during the Second World War. Marcia had all the hallmarks of beauty that a Middle Eastern man craves: green eyes, blonde hair, slender build, medium height. She was bright and methodical and had an extensive knowledge of Arab culture. Marcia had never finished any of the PhD dissertations she'd worked so hard on. She changed the topic of her dissertation more than once, from "Leftist Cells in Egypt" to "Marginal Movements and their Influence on Mainstream Egyptian Politics" to "The Fundamentalist Movement and its Connections to Arab Regimes." She changed supervisors and universities in America more than once, too. For her latest attempt, she settled on "Moderate Islam and Extremist Islam among the Lower Classes in Egypt: A Sociological Survey." I was hoping she'd finish it while I was still alive. Marcia had lived in Jordan for a year where she learned the basics of Arabic, and then six years ago she settled in Egypt. She got good at written Arabic, really good at colloquial Arabic, and learned Nubian, but she could only understand it, not speak it. She claimed it was all to help her with her dissertation. Her mother was a rhythmic gymnastics coach in Washington, D.C. and had been separated from her husband for years. Marcia's father was a professor at a research center attached to Columbia University. Marcia was an only child, but she had lots of relatives on both sides. She'd never visited Poland, never thought to. She was hoping to visit Saudi Arabia, Iraq, Qatar, and Kuwait. Why? I don't know.

After I was visited by the specter of Hind, I visited America. I was working for an advertising firm at the time, but she'd made it clear that she wasn't happy about that. So I quit my job and decided to try my luck by going to America; I even considered moving there. I'd started attending rehab sessions in Egypt and I'd been somewhat successful in beating addiction.

The things that surprised me about America weren't the things most people remark on. I was astonished by how they subject everything to calculation, even emotions and ideas. They transform moral values into material values to make them easier to deal with. Technology has ultimate control over their lives so that if a person wants to interact with a machine, he has to format the raw material first. A bag of potato chips, for example, starts out as batter and gets poured into molds that give the desired shapes and sizes, and then it's fried in oil. Everything in America, even natural substances, has to be formatted and leveled and squared off, so it can interact with the machines. Humans have to be flattened and cut at right angles so they can fit in with the machines' gears. Machines are incompatible with humankind. It's a well-known fact that the human body doesn't have a single sharp corner.

Americans live with binary code, made up of ones and zeros. The advantage of this system is that things have only two possibilities. At one, it goes, at zero, it stops. The U.S. government gives you just two options: Are you for democracy or against it? Are you with the terrorists or against them? Are you part of the Axis of Good or the Axis of Evil? The U.S. government thinks they're making the choice easy for their people by simplifying things, and when they got their hegemony over the world, they started dealing with all other countries the same way.

I was living in Manhattan, a borough divided by streets laid out in a grid pattern. The cross streets are numbered, not named, and the north-south streets, called avenues, are named, not numbered. The convenience of the system is clear: 77th Street definitely comes after 76th Street, whereas here, Safiya Zaghloul Street doesn't necessarily come after Saad Zaghloul Street. There, numbers store information; no more, no less. Our street names store memories, emotions.

There, it's easy to get around; there's order. But human emotions are subjugated to data. And, after all the technological advancements and the spectacular leap into the world of the Internet, Americans are surprised to find they've become slaves to technology. An American can't write his novel till he's turned on his computer, because it's all saved in files inside. All his ideas are recorded on the hard disk, and if for some reason it should break, they will all disappear.

Once when I was visiting the University of Connecticut, in the northeast, about four hours away from New York, the power went out. It was only for less than half an hour, but, in that short span of time, you couldn't buy gum or food, or pay your school fees, or take an exam, or find out your grades—because all the grades were recorded in the computer. The electricity went out in the daytime, but humans were still slaves to technology. Humans don't have any sharp corners and colors have their own colors: there's black in the white and white in the black. Our country is a civilization with history, and it's not easy to subject it to a binary system like that because it's a complex, emotionless system. Colors go on forever; there's nothing separating one color from another. A rainbow goes on forever. American civilization seems opposed to human nature and lacks great human creativity; it's mostly the creation of robots, which do everything with precision and reject all error. Yet, human error is beautiful. You can see it in the works of ancient civilizations and it adds to their splendor. Zaki Naguib Mahmoud, the great Egyptian intellectual, had an idea about American civilization: "It is a civilization that can be explained by chewing gum, skyscrapers, and jazz." It's a very precise description, because the same unit gets repeated an infinite number of times: chewing gum is the same action repeated an infinite number of times, jazz is made up of a group of repeated segments of harmony, and skyscrapers are a single unit that can be multiplied as many times as you like.

The problems America faces in administering any of the nations it conquers goes back to the fact that it's incapable of coexisting with the randomness of creative human thought.

The way I felt about American culture was the way I dealt with Marcia. I understood her and her expectations. I appreciated her reasoned decision-making; I fully understood that I was just a number in it. I even tried to be obedient when she wanted me to be, and when I wanted to be rebellious, I'd treat her with the randomness of creative thought.

I came back from America a year later a failure, a joke to my relatives and neighbors. But when I told Essam everything I've just said, he listened, slack-jawed. When I finished, he laughed hysterically and told me not to bottle it up and to get myself to a psychiatrist right away.

17

I WATCHED SCENE after scene of repulsive violence against children, trying as hard as I could to hide my discomfort. Marcia's face was flushed and excited, even when she pretended to be moved, as she played certain scenes in slow motion and went zooming past others. She was taking notes with her right hand and controlling the remote on her thigh with the fingertips of her left, and at the same time she was giving me some background on what had happened there. I'd never seen footage of it before. The kids looked just like Karim, Warda, Maryam, and their friends.

There isn't a big difference between us Arabs and Brazilians. We're both third-world, backward, on our way to extinction. The scenes playing on the screen were genuine documentary footage of how the phenomenon of street kids spread in Brazil and how the Brazilian mafia worked together with the police to stamp it out once and for all. Peeling them off the streets, crucifying them on lampposts, chasing them down at night in armored cars, sniping them like dogs. The last scene showed some officials with stars on their shoulders boasting about how a problem like that could be successfully wiped out in just a few months' time.

She was very quick that Marcia; organized, too. She thought systematically. While I'd been busy goofing around, she'd corresponded with major international production companies; first to introduce herself, and then to get her hands on whatever documentary footage there was on the issue. Marcia had sent away for tapes, watched them by herself, selected the best ones, and bought the archival footage from a British TV channel along with the rights to use it in our forthcoming film, all without checking with me, the "consultant." I was alarmed; throughout our months-long discussions about the film, she'd never told me she was going to buy archival material from international TV channels to back up her story. All she'd asked me to do was to contact the family of the Nubian musician Hamza Alaa al-Din, who lived in America, and ask them—because I used to know them—for permission to use his music in the film. I put off dealing with that request, just as I was deliberately trying to slow down production of the film. I was using the carrot and stick on her. I'd read her everything that was written in the newspapers about the phenomenon, I'd take her to documentaries that dealt with it, I'd even collect news clippings about novels or TV serials that portrayed street kids. I introduced her to some of those kids and told her their secrets. I told her about where they lived and where they hid out. I told her about what they ate, what they wore, how they ran away from ordinary people and the police. I'd act like I was really hard at work until she turned her attention elsewhere. It was as if I were the security guard manning the gate at the entrance to the world of those kids; the only one who could allow her in or keep her out. Now she was giving me back twice as good as I'd given. Without having to say it, she'd shown me, with that famous Western self-importance, that she was going ahead with the project even if I wasn't with her and that my stalling and procrastination weren't going to hold her back. Khalil, the midget, was jumping up in front of me. I could almost see him. I imagined him telling all the other kids that she didn't need me anymore and that she'd already found my replacement. Someone she could use to get the censors' okay and permits to film in the street. And that she was getting her bed ready for someone else, too.

I had something like a fever. Even though I'd dunked my head in water a few times, the embers were still roaring in my head. When I came in from the bathroom, Marcia looked at me with concern, and as she stroked my head she said, "You're ill. You need a doctor." I shook my head and tried to pull it together. She brought me a double whisky and I calmed down a bit. Seeing that I was feeling better, she relaxed and kissed me lightly on the cheek. Then she went to get some papers out of her bag. I moved my eyes over the documents, faxes, and letters without pausing to read any of them. Like a magician who's failed to dazzle and has to resort to her best trick, Marcia pulled the budget for our movie out of a big folder and showed me where my name was written under creator/screenwriter and production supervisor; beside each position, there was a big number in U.S. dollars. All I could think about was that the film was going to be made with or without me. Meanwhile Marcia was spreading out her carpet of temptations, showing me correspondence with some international festivals that offered funding. Other festivals congratulated her on the project and invited her to participate when the film was finished. Others still offered to buy the film after screening and evaluation, and a big Swiss festival offered to contribute forty thousand dollars (part of the amount to be delivered after submission of the final shooting script for their approval). Another festival offered a symbolic grant of fifteen thousand dollars to support the project in return for being acknowledged in the titles.

Marcia accepted the Swiss offer, which I suspected Evelyn had been directly involved in. She hadn't declined the offer from the last festival either, the one that wanted to put its name down as one of the sponsors. It had all taken place behind my back, while I'd been busy fooling around with my ideas, my paranoid delusions, my sexual stimulants, and the pharmaceuticals the doctor had prescribed to balance me out. Marcia had been busy with mailing, negotiating, putting up money to get remarkable archival footage, soliciting support to cover the initial costs as she took care of the costs of production.

Marcia looked at me as I sat thinking about all the footage we'd just seen. She was staring with her piercing gaze. She was looking at me expectantly, like a controlling woman who's given herself to her husband, but as he's failed to get it up, she looms over him and demands he give her a gold necklace, or a snake bracelet, or else she'll expose him to ridicule. "What do you think?" she asked. If I'd tried to make a noise, I'd have given myself away. All I could do was embrace her. I kissed her cheeks, and the part of her hair, settling finally on her lips. She patted me on the back. "I didn't think the news would make you so happy, love."

So that my tongue couldn't betray me, I swallowed what was left in my glass and made an excuse about having to meet Karim. I had to fight against myself to keep Marcia happy. She was holding one end of the string, which was as taut as could be and beginning to fray, so I had to give some slack at my end to keep the relationship from splitting in two. I had to move the project forward to keep Marcia from flipping out. I had to find Karim. It took a little effort, but after looking for him in every place he might've been, I found him on the corner by an abandoned building behind the Diplomatic Club downtown. That abandoned building was just one of the places he controlled. I had to give him quite a bit of money to get him to come with me. He caused me a lot of trouble: first, with the policeman who wanted to know why I was chasing him when I'd been trying to get him to come with me, and then with the taxi driver, who eyed me as I was bundling Karim into the taxi and who looked in his rearview mirror apprehensively as I tried to get Karim to stop pouring the glue into little plastic bags. The sound of crinkling plastic was making both me and the driver nervous. Perhaps the only thing that saved me was that the driver couldn't be sure I wasn't a plain-clothes policeman or some other official. He appeared to have settled on that interpretation of things and lost his interest in us. Karim was talking to me and the driver about things that were completely unrelated to what we were talking about, trying his hardest to stretch his flexible grammar around everything he wanted to say. Every time we stopped, I thought about throwing him out of the car and returning to Marcia empty-handed. By the time we got to her building, my patience had completely run out.

Karim went through the metal detector, no problem. Thank God he hadn't had a razor-blade hidden under his tongue. The security guards didn't search him. When they saw he was with me, all they did was smirk. I'd stuffed all but one of the bags of glue in his waistband under his shirt. He kept one up his sleeve for topping up his high. I watched in amazement as he checked himself out in the elevator mirror and used the bag of glue in his hand to smooth his hair down like young guys do with gel. Then he messed his hair up. He looked horrendous, but he was grinning as he contemplated himself vainly. He turned to me and said, "Is she hot?" I didn't understand so he rephrased his question as if he were talking to an idiot, "The American lady." I understood him that time and he could instantly tell I wasn't happy about it. "I didn't mean it that way, boss," he said. "I know she belongs to you and you're my friend. I don't double-cross my friends." I laughed abruptly and hoped he wouldn't torment Marcia like Warda had.

As she opened the door, Julia froze like a surprised imbecile; the terror of her unpleasant experience with Warda renewed. I shooed her away and took Karim into the sitting room. He was staring at Julia's ebony skin and her tight braids. Marcia beamed when she saw Karim and told Julia to bring us some juice. Marcia sat down and watched, mesmerized, as Karim pulled bags of glue out of every corner of his body. He was like a goldsmith spreading his gold and pearls before an Arab princess. He leaned over to me and whispered, "Ask her if she wants to try it." I elbowed him and told Marcia what he'd said. She laughed, her eyes shining, and winked at me.

"Will you try it with me?" she asked me.

Karim answered all her questions and watched as she wrote down what he'd said. He'd remember things he'd forgotten and go back to them. He was proud that a foreigner found his life interesting. Marcia was chatty with him, almost hand-feeding him a croissant as he sat there across from her, his legs crossed, not noticing the dirty toes that stuck out from his sandals. Marcia asked him about the glue and its effects. She filmed him with the digital camera as he stirred it up and huffed. And as it took effect, it dulled his mind so that he started taking a long time to process the questions; answering the part of the question he'd remembered, however it made sense in his head. Whenever she asked him a question he considered dodgy, he'd turn to me, as if silently asking, "Should I answer that?" and I'd nod my head and he'd answer. The whole time we were there, he made it clear to her that he was loyal to me no matter how nicely she treated him. I was happy about that. Karim was no Warda. She'd have sold you to Satan for a fistful of cash or maybe even for free. Karim was shoring up my standing with Marcia and I was actually starting to like him.

When we were in the kitchen, Marcia told me she wanted to have Karim stay with her for a few days so she could film some interviews with him. Interviews she'd then send to some of the production companies to show she was making progress on the project. I told her it was a stupid idea, that Karim wasn't one to be controlled. You couldn't anticipate his reactions. In my opinion, he was more dangerous than Warda, who'd already terrorized Marcia for an entire night. After Marcia had gone to bed, she'd attacked Julia in the office and tried to rape her, and Marcia hadn't been able to get her under control until I got there at six in the morning and kicked her out. I told her that even though Karim liked me and did as I said, I wasn't sure what he'd be like when I wasn't around. I assured her that I'd be able to bring him to her whenever she wanted. That way we wouldn't be putting too much pressure on him. We both knew how important he was. He was the one who could unlock the world of the street kids for us. Marcia was still looking at me. Now that she was filled with the fear of repeating her experience with Warda and a renewed confidence in my control over the situation, she was reluctant to disagree with me. Whispering, I told her to give him some dollars since they always had a magical effect. That way if she ever asked to see him again, he'd rush right over. She did as I asked and gave him some fruit and groceries, as well.

Marcia wanted to go out to dinner and then to a concert at Townhouse Gallery with a bunch of her friends, but I told her I was exhausted. I said I didn't feel like waiting around at her place until she came back either. I needed to be alone. I'd recently started to notice the crowds of foreigners downtown, even though I'd been knee deep in them for the past two years. For the past few days, especially, I'd felt like they were surrounding me everywhere I went. I'd started seeing them in my dreams. As I walk through the downtown streets I know by heart and the Haram neighborhood where I was born and my beloved al-Hussein district, I see only foreigners. My ears pick up different languages, but Arabic isn't one of them. I see fair and ruddy faces, green eyes and blond hair. Dwarfs and giants, fat ones and thin ones walking in military formation, always coming at me head-on. No one stands beside me, no one behind me. There are thick rows of them for as far as the eye can see. They smile at me like grinning sharks and politely make room for me to pass, but when I pass through them, I become no one.

The dreams and nightmares kept coming. Another hideous nightmare: I'm guarding the lion cage, responsible for feeding and cleaning up excrement. They're flying all over the place and then they hover over me. They're throwing children of all ages down at me from their warplanes; their bodies intact, their necks butchered, their heads smashed. I throw them to the ferocious, caged-up lions. The children's faces aren't clearly defined, but if I focus a little, they might resemble Karim, Warda, Maryam . . . .

Zaynab never lacked for surprises. She walked around carrying a big bag full of them and handed them out all over the place. I was at Groppi, having a coffee and waiting for Essam to finish his yoga class. She was walking down Qasr al-Nil Street when she spotted me through the window. She knocked giddily on the glass and then she came in and sat down. She took a cigarette from my pack and lit it. "Who are you waiting for? Should I go? I don't want to embarrass you 'cause, you know, maybe you've got a date?" she asked, smiling mischievously.

I smiled. "You can stay. I'm waiting for Essam and I'm bored."

"Good, 'cause I was going to come see you tonight anyway. I've been wanting to tell you about something you'll never believe. It happens once in a million."

"Talk till Essam gets here, but please make it something funny."

"You know what? If you can't sit still, you can at least talk right. Do I look like I'm running a puppet show? You think I've got nothing better to do than to entertain you? Next you'll want me to dance for you, too!" She acted angry, grabbing her handbag and standing up.

"Sit down and stop acting like a child." She stared at me and then she sat back down like a frustrated mother obeying her spoiled son. Leaning back, she stretched her hands all the way out in front of her. Then she rested them on the table and played with my lighter and cigarettes. She picked up my demitasse and brought it close to her face. Using her finger, she spooned the grounds into her mouth. She dropped a drop of water in the cup and turned it over onto the saucer. I'd never seen her like that before. I watched in silence and when she was done, I said, "Are you going to read my fortune?"

She sighed and said, "I'm the one who needs my fortune told. And a lucky charm. This spell I've been cursed with can only be passed onto an orphan crocodile." The waiter came over and she ordered her usual tea with milk. He'd only just turned around, when she asked me, "Is it true they stopped serving alcohol here?"

I nodded. "Why? Could you use a drink or two?"

She looked away. She took a cigarette from her handbag and played with it in her fingers for a while before putting it to her lips. I lit it for her and then she told me what had been keeping her up at night, what had taken her breath away. It took mine away, too.

She'd been covering the judges' protest at the High Court for the newspaper. It was an assignment from the editor-in-chief. She followed all the tedious goings-on, but as far as she could tell, it was a pretty ordinary affair: flat drama, no crescendo. The building was surrounded by security forces, who stood behind barricades, facing the people protesting in support of the judges across an empty space. The protesters were shouting and holding banners. Under the pretext of security, the judges, dressed in their official uniforms, their chests covered with medals and sashes, were shielded behind the protesters. Imagine tuning in and having to watch that scene all day long. Zaynab left her photographer colleague who was taking pictures, and went to copy down the protesters' signs and the slogans they were shouting. She watched them protesting in place, their numbers steadily waxing and waning. Zaynab had to be always on the move so she quickly got fed up and decided she'd seen enough. She figured if she'd gone back to see them on the Day of Resurrection, nothing would've changed. All of a sudden—that's how she put it—she saw me on the edge of the demonstration. She walked toward me through the protesters, but at the last minute she saw that I was standing next to a foreign chick who was filming the protest with a digital camera, and then she saw her take my hand as we walked around to the other side. (Everything Zaynab was describing had actually happened, but I hadn't seen her that day.) She said she'd watched us until she'd memorized the way the other woman looked and what she was wearing. She said she saw me talking to her, said she saw us walking off together, said there was no point in pretending I didn't know her.

"You thought I was going tell you I don't know her?"

"I know you're shameless," she answered quickly and continued her story, "After 'I Saw You Two Together' like the Nagat al-Sagheera song."

"You mean the Kamil al-Shennawi poem, stupid."

"Fine, I won't tell you."

I was uncomfortable. I could sense some worry, some malice. She was talking as if she were jealous, as if she felt like she had the right to grill me about who I was with. It was a twist I hadn't been expecting. Maybe she'd thought about it and decided I was her best investment. She seemed to know what was swirling around in my mind because she decided to go on with the story. She'd gone walking on Talaat Harb Street to look at the clothes and shoes she'd never dream of buying (Zaynab bought her clothes from the barrows in Wikalat al-Balah and her handbags and shoes from the shops in Sayyida Zaynab). Then she headed toward the last stretch of Qasr al-Nil Street. The pavement was crowded with street vendors and people window-shopping just like she was. As she squeezed through the crowds on the pavement, she nearly crashed into him. Their eyes met for a split second, for a femtosecond to be exact, and then they set off, each in a different direction. A young man, a foreigner, dressed in shabby clothes, an acoustic guitar slung over his back. He had a thin beard and his hair was drawn back in a ponytail. His wan, pockmarked, freckled face gave him a saintly air. According to Zaynab, he looked like a cross between Che Guevara and Charles Manson. "I couldn't stop thinking about him that whole night," she said. "I went to the newspaper office the next morning and chucked what I'd written at them. I didn't even wait for the photographer so I could back up my story with some pictures. Then I went to go look for him over every inch of downtown for three straight days." (I pictured her, as she spoke, as a lioness in the brush sniffing the scent of her prey and following him until she got what she'd come for.)

"I found him behind the wooden screen at the Halijian Bar, drinking from a bottle of Brandy 84. His guitar was on the chair next to him. I ran in and headed straight for his table. I didn't ask for permission, I just sat down right in front of him. He was confused at first, but then he remembered me. I didn't ask him to offer me a glass. I didn't wait for the waiter to bring me an empty one. I took a couple of swigs straight from the bottle. I started talking to him in my broken English and I could understand the simple phrases he was saying back to me. We could understand what the other was saying. We agreed on some things and disagreed on others." (You've got to imagine for yourself, to the degree you choose to imagine, how much English this guy knew at all.) His name was Julio Andrenas. He was a musician from Mexico. He had a folk music band and they played concerts all over Mexico and Latin America. He'd ditched his tour group and the organized sightseeing and gone around to the Pyramids, to Old Cairo, to monuments, Coptic and Islamic, all on his own. He'd observed the humble Egyptian people and dreamed of taking a beautiful Egyptian woman back with him to Mexico. When he saw Zaynab, he'd felt she was a sign from heaven, but she was a sign that had only lasted for a few seconds and disappeared. And when she saw him, she knew that she'd come face to face with her destiny and, although he'd vanished, she was determined not to let it slip away. She'd searched for him and she'd found him. And when he found her, real and in-person, sitting in front of him after three nights of pining, he swore to himself he wouldn't leave Egypt unless she came with him. They spent the night together at a small hotel downtown, far from where his tour group was staying. The hotel manager and the desk clerk had been obliging, and they spent another two nights together. Julio's departure was drawing near, but it was only after an exhausting effort that Zaynab had been able to convince him to return to Mexico without his Egyptian girlfriend. She'd been the cause of the endless bureaucratic paperwork that came between them and their dream of leaving together. It had delayed her getting a passport and exit visa because, as the excuse goes, these things take time. He said goodbye to her and left, vowing to write to his country's embassy in Egypt until they gave her a visa. Zaynab, for her part, promised that she'd finish all the unforeseen paperwork. That was the end of Zaynab's story. I didn't know whether to believe her or laugh at her, or whether to worry that she, too, was going to abandon me. All the same, I shocked her by asking what she was going to do about her mother and father, her sisters and her disabled brother.

She didn't say a word. She just looked at me, her expression colored by hope and sadness. She was interrupted by Essam, who came up to our table and greeted her with reserve. I introduced them. She looked at him and then said, "This is your friend Essam? Really?" Essam didn't know what to think.

"Who else would he be? Does the devil have a tail?"

She laughed and said, "Well this one's got a ponytail."

I could see Essam was mad, his veins sticking out, so I had no choice but to yell at her. "Get out of here, you trash! Your time's up." She was surprised that I'd chewed her out in front of Essam and she started to apologize.

"I'm sorry. I didn't mean it. Mustafa knows I like to tease, especially when I get upset."

She could see that neither of us was going to ask her what she was upset about, so she got up and left without saying goodbye. "I'll come see you soon," she said, trying to make it seem that she wasn't angry.

After she left, Essam quietly said, "Aren't you ever going to stop screwing around?"

I laughed and pointed at him. "You're a pot calling the kettle—"

"Yeah, but I went straight after I got married. Now, it's your turn. Why don't you just marry Marcia and get it over with?" I didn't say anything. "I swear I'm being serious. You're going to chase after phantoms and in the end you're still going to crawl back to Marcia. Is it really worth the trouble? Get it over with already."

"What's new?"

He gave the answer I'd been expecting: he was leaving for Singapore in two weeks. Samantha had booked him the most important gallery in the country so he could show his paintings. He said that he was going to spend an entire month there: one week to catch up with Samantha and three weeks for the exhibition.

I didn't know how to respond. To me, he and Samantha were like zombies crawling out of the grave, lurching toward their prey. She'd sucked his blood and he'd become one of her followers. "Let's go to my house and I can tell you about it over some wine," he said.

I was seized by the image of him drinking red wine through fangs, so I blurted out "No." He patted me on the back and tried to calm me down, but I remained in its grip.

18

AFTER HIND, I was selfish in all my relationships. As relieved as I was to be rid of Zaynab—if my behavior was an accurate reflection of my state of mind—I was equally distraught and jealous and irate and I wished she were here so I could abuse her, verbally and physically. Deep down, I already knew for certain that she'd been with that foreigner she'd met and that it was perfectly ordinary; it was something she did almost every day. But what really made me mad was that she'd told me about it. That it became undeniable fact, rather than a notion I'd only guessed at. Stupid Zaynab had fallen in love with a foreigner who was passing through. She'd met him by chance among the tens of thousands of people downtown every day. She saw Che Guevara, the leader of the twentieth century, in him and Charles Manson, the leader of the hippies, and maybe Nelson Mandela, the liberator of South Africa, too. She fell for him and his acoustic guitar, and he, for his part, had got her fallow imagination dreaming again: she was currently waiting for him to sponsor her visa to Mexico. She was dumb enough to believe it all, dumb enough to have started dreaming about her life there with him.

As if my thoughts had summoned her, she called me at home. Before she could say anything, I told her I wasn't going to be at home and I was going to sleep over at Essam's. She said she was busy, too, and she wasn't calling because she wanted to spend the night with me. She wanted to apologize for how she'd reacted when she saw Essam. She swore that she'd been startled because, at first, she'd taken him for Julio's brother. Apparently, they looked a lot alike, except Julio was skinny and relatively pale and his cheeks were sunken from smoking so much marijuana. I told her to keep away from Essam and not to catch him in her net, or else. She laughed and said she didn't know whether I was jealous of Essam or of her. She asked me to tell Essam that she was sorry and that she was happy to tell him in person if only I would arrange it. I told her not to worry about it since I'd already explained to Essam that she was crazy. She laughed out loud and as she ended the call, she said, "The day'll come when you'll be wishing you'd had one extra day with Zaynab."

The world was setting all around me and I was bobbing on a scrap of cork in the wide-open ocean. I didn't know where Marcia was going to let me off, or where Karim and Warda and their pals were going to take me, or where my path with Yasmeen would lead, or when Essam was going to abandon me and shack up with Samantha for good, or what was true and what was false in the story Zaynab had told me.

I've recently given up trying to balance between evil and good. Everything good I want turns into utter evil. I feel like my guardian angels are asleep on the job. I've always been a fan of the old school of drama that says there's a good side and an evil side. That there's a struggle between them, and that one side triumphs. I've always believed the entire world is built upon this struggle and that without evil the world would've never come into being. Our survival depends on this struggle. And we struggle in order to survive. Thus we revolve in a vicious circle.

I'd scribbled that down before falling into a deep sleep. I'd clearly been drunk and had figured that all I needed to do was wake up and I'd have been able turn those thoughts into a poem. But I didn't write a poem. No inspiration came. I read the sheet a few times and threw it down the drain in the bathroom. Poetry had deserted me for the past few years. Not that I was sorry about it; I was no Mutanabbi and Hind wasn't around to read whatever I wrote, regardless of how good or bad it was. I was definitely going through a bad case of depression. A melancholy that the psychiatrist couldn't get me out of; neither could the antidepressants or the ones that had "to restore psychiatric balance" written on them. Usually, all it took was for me to get caught up in some new event, positive or negative, to make my depression go away.

Outwardly, it may seem like I look down on Karim and his gang, and Marcia and the ghetto she inhabits, and Zaynab (who, if Darwin had known her, he'd have said man originated as a vagina), but on unconscious and subconscious levels, as psychiatrists say, I was certain that the lot of them were my only salvation from the depression that could only end with me withdrawing from the world. Whenever I saw Essam, he'd make like he'd already heard about my latest screw-up and give me a lecture about it. What was Essam criticizing me for? Was it because my memories pulled on me, or because I searched for things that had passed, or because I was preoccupied with longing? Or nostalgia, as Marcia calls it. Was that what he was hung up about? Or were Awad and the others feeding him lies? I didn't argue with him much because I didn't really care anymore. Neither of us had anything the other wanted. Essam was an accomplished painter and sculptor. He was at peace with himself and with others; life had given him his missing half. As for me, life had never given me anything, just taken. Took Hind and left me this stupid, stubborn body, which clung to the trash of the earth. Hind hadn't come back to me like she promised. It'd been years and she'd yet to return. She hadn't sent me a sign. There was no way Yasmeen could take her place, no matter how much she resembled her in however many ways. Hind was celestial, unique. Yasmeen was of the earth like all the rest.

I needed to go back to my psychiatrist. He was arrogant, proud of his doctorate in hypnotism from Russia. He claimed that if he hypnotized a bald man and ordered the follicles trapped under his scalp to grow and multiply, the man would have hair down to his shoulders when he came to. I never saw a single bald man go into his office for him to prove it, but I pretended like I believed him because my condition couldn't stand to lose another healer.

The latest diagnosis from my Russian-doctorate-holding psychiatrist was that I had bipolar anxiety disorder. He said many ignorant psychiatrists would've inaccurately diagnosed my condition as schizo-phrenia. I was actually comfortable with that diagnosis since it was close to how I felt: some of the time I was absolutely ecstatic and, at other times, I couldn't bear the world around me or life itself. Thinking he was reducing the impact of the diagnosis, my doctor went on to say that the most famous sufferers of the disease were among the greats: Ernest Hemingway, the world-famous novelist, suffered from it and committed suicide during a bout of acute depression; the eminent British leader Winston Churchill commanded the critical battles of the Second World War while riding a wave of mania; and our own genius, the poet Salah Jahin, was one, too—he wrote the operetta, *The Great Night*, while manic and committed suicide while depressed. May God put your mind at rest, Doctor. I know my destiny now. I'll either kill myself, or else I'll get so happy I become a maniac and they stick me in the lifer ward at the insane asylum.

I wasn't feeling myself: I'd fallen in love with Zaynab and I couldn't stop thinking about her body. I was hoping she'd call so I could convince her to come spend the night with me, hoping that she'd disregard my story about being out of the house and come through the door at any moment. Or that she'd just come over no matter what the reason: to pick up her panties, to write up an urgent story because she couldn't afford to write it in a café or in the subsidized canteen at the Journalists' Syndicate. I could see our relationship was ending and it made me want to hold on tighter.

I remembered the good bits. I stored every part of her body in fortified cells in the recesses of my mind. I remembered how horny she was. How her body smelled. How she'd smile when she was happy and how she'd gasp over and over as she climaxed. I could taste her slapdash but delicious cooking. The sweet-smelling laundry she'd wash by hand so she wouldn't have to deal with the washing machine. How she'd hastily iron all of my clothes, including my gallabiya and underwear. How she'd clean the rooms in the morning, the ones that were used and the ones that never were. How she'd take the place over. I could almost feel her small touches, almost see her hair in the sink and on the soap. I could still smell her breath on my bath towel, which had grown used to her scent. In the olive she'd taken a bite of and hadn't finished. In the tea with milk left over in the cup in the sink.

I was traveling down a long, dangerous path. Attached to many worlds without any true love. Yasmeen was no Hind and Marcia wasn't satisfied with me. The other women weren't satisfying me either. Zaynab wouldn't have stayed with me, even if her fancy for the Mexican sputtered out and she returned. All my mental models of women were distorted; except for Hind, who'd become purely a soul. She wasn't limited to a physical form or defined by any details. My life was rusty and ruined and there was no hope of redemption. I never even became a great poet or a mediocre lyricist. Being in limbo is the worst place for a man to be. Our teacher at primary school used to tell us that he never remembered any of his students except for the uncommonly outstanding and the rebellious, trouble-making good-for-nothings. When one of the students in our class did really well in a subject like oratory, or gave a good answer in front of the school inspector, or was clever in front of some official, they'd tell the principal that someone from Khalil's class had done such and such. Eventually, Khalil, that destructive menace, became the hallmark of our class, and then of our entire school!

After I'd graduated, but before I'd started working for the Ministry of Education, I was put in touch with an advertising firm and started doing short, inspired ads for them. I was making a lot of money and becoming something of a star in the ad world. Other agencies started asking for me and offering me even more money, but then Hind appeared to me once when I was on a bad weed and Maxitone Forte high. I was stunned to see her sitting on the chaise longue in front of me. She stared at me for a long time in a revelatory silence. She turned me into a child facing his mother's rebuke; the kind that's silent, just a look, something like suppressed sadness, the pupils taking on the color of parched earth when it's sprinkled with water.

"I promise I won't do it anymore," I said. She said she'd never visit me again unless I went back to the way I'd been when she left me. The studio owners, my composer friends, and even the other poets, who were my competition, tried to stop me, but I left them all without any regret. I abandoned the business of writing about bug killer and insect repellent. I stopped peddling inane products, menstrual pads, diapers. My co-workers, competitors, and bosses all considered it a rash decision— something they saw a lot of in that industry. They thought I'd come to my senses in time, but I never went back. Later, after I'd gone into teaching, which I all but fell in love with, my hallucinations suddenly got worse and I started imagining all my students were Khalil. With the help of the doctor from my health plan, I moved to a writing job in the ministry for a year. They exempted me from teaching, but after they received the report from my doctor advising them that I was no longer fit for the job, they suggested I submit my resignation. The good thing about that phase was that I beat my addiction to prescription and intravenous drugs, which had intensified alongside my delusions. It's true that I went back to drinking and drugs after a number of years, but only a moderate amount, nowhere close to addiction. But I wasn't in demand anymore, not as a lyricist or as a good ad man, like they used to say. I didn't write rousing political poems any more either, or the revolutionary poetry that Ahmad al-Helu had turned me on to. I'd changed just as my leaders and intellectual role models had changed. The only slight difference was that they started pouncing on profits, and the effects of the good life started to show on them. They still go on all the satellite channels, though, and talk about helping the poor and securing civil rights. And as for me, the spotlight, which hadn't been all that bright to begin with, started to pull away. I came to live

161

off of the savings I'd inherited from my father, salaries from countries I no longer liked, and from teaching Arabic to foreigners, which will make it easier for them to control us for a great many years to come. You didn't leave me Hind and disappear, but you didn't take me with you either. I'm the child you left behind without any protection; what did you expect?

19

"DON'T GET ATTACHED to anything. You'll just lose it in the end."
That was one of my psychiatrist's favorite lines and he was always
saying it to me. Everything I'd ever done ran counter to that advice.
I always got attached to whatever I was bound to lose. There was a
picture of Hind under the glass on my desk. Some of my poems and a
few quotations covered it up, but I'd often take it out and sit admiring
her and talking to her. Then I'd stick it back under my clippings.
Zaynab sat at the desk once or twice, but she never found it. She never
bothered to read my scribblings, which were right there under the
glass. She was more interested in getting her reporting, or her fabri-
cating, over with.

I had lots of time before I had to get ready for the bachelor party
for Ewald the German. He'd changed his name to Awad after
converting to Islam the month before, in preparation for his marriage
to Aisha the Egyptian. She worked at the Egyptian-German Friendship
Association. I'd been friends with Awad for two years. Essam, who was
better friends with him, introduced us. I took to him instantly. He was
good-natured and an all around stand-up guy, and I didn't know what

to think at first since I always thought Germans were exactly the opposite of that. Awad was from East Germany and he still leaned to the left, philosophically, even though the wall that had divided his country in two had fallen and they'd united under the banner of the West. The Mercedes Corporation had sent him to Egypt to teach at the German University in Cairo and train future engineers. Awad was the only Westerner I'd taught Arabic to for free, because I considered him a friend and because we had similar tastes in wine and politics, which were different from the views of most Westerners. Marcia was against me not taking anything in return and often remarked on it. "I don't care if your brother asks you to tutor him, you still have to get something out of it," she said. Awad was smart. He soaked up the dialect easily so we dropped our common English and spoke Egyptian Arabic together. He preferred it that way, insisted on it, just like all the foreigners, who scribble a new word down in their notebooks as soon as they hear it and start using it right away.

I couldn't deal with pen and paper. I was dying to be taken up in some exhausting physical labor. I went over to the al-Talabiya house and shellacked Essam's frames, repaired the shelves, organized the sketches, and swept the floor until I was completely worn out and had to take a nap. As soon as I got back to my apartment and showered, Essam showed up, on time as usual, and we went to the party at Awad's house in Maadi.

Bachelor parties originated in America, I think. The Europeans took the idea from them. The groom's close friends get together to have a good time with strange women and new friends and all sorts of booze. That's how the groom celebrates the last day of his bachelorhood. Marcia, who knew a little about bachelor parties, whispered in my ear, giggling, that I shouldn't drink too much or get too rowdy, or else she'd be celebrating the end of her bachelorhood pretty soon. We made plans to meet the next morning.

Essam hadn't been expecting me to say that I'd shellacked his frames and organized his sketches. I guess he'd forgotten about them because he looked at me blankly at first, but then he said he'd go to the house in al-Talabiya soon to look through some of his old work; he wanted to get some inspiration for his upcoming exhibition in Cairo.

We could hear the roar of the party from the street. The doorman greeted us warmly, but I couldn't believe the neighbors were going to put up with all that noise without complaining. Awad set me up with some hash cigarettes and then whisky, and I drank and danced a lot until the people dancing around me turned into jelly shapes and Essam started nagging me about leaving. I got angry with him and turned to Awad for help. I was swallowed up by the groove I was in and I lost track of Essam. I guess he left after his conversation with Awad.

I woke up with a frightful headache, slightly nauseated. A nude black woman was sleeping soundly against my chest; I pushed her off and ran to the bathroom to throw up. Then I went into the kitchen and made myself a big cup of Nescafé, black. The fog cleared and I could focus. I smiled when I saw all those naked bodies lying in the hallway, in the bedrooms, in every corner of the apartment, and wondered how I'd managed to get across without bumping into any of them. The noise I made in the kitchen woke Awad up and I made him a Nescafé. He drank it in one go. After he got out of the bathroom, he started yelling at everyone to wake up. As they got dressed, they devoured whatever they could find in the kitchen: fruit, juice, bread-sticks, and then they left one by one. The black woman came over to me and kissed me and asked for my phone number. Awad watched her and smiled. I made some excuse so I wouldn't have to give it to her. When I asked Awad about her, he laughed and said she was Eritrean and that I'd proposed to her the night before. She'd left by then so I never did get the chance to size her up well enough to see whether I'd have gone through with the wedding plans. Awad's apartment was in total chaos, it looked like a battlefield. I offered to help him clean up, but he said he had someone who took care of it.

I waited for Marcia in a café next to the Catacomb Gallery, not far from Awad's. Catacomb was owned by three sculptors; one was British and the other two were Egyptians, friends of Essam. Catacomb is a fairly gruesome Latin word that means "collective grave." Even though the gallery was in the basement of a big building in Maadi, the décor, the rooms, and the cavernous lobby all gave it a gothic air. Essam sold most of his paintings, handmade wood furniture, and artisanal pieces out of the gallery. You could have spent a whole day just examining the intricate touches on the walls and ceilings, not to mention the artwork, which represented all the styles on earth, from the primitive to the postmodern. It wasn't me who turned Marcia on to the gallery: Evelyn took care of that. And all it took was one visit for Marcia to fall under its spell. She took every opportunity, along with all the sales staff's flattery, to buy pieces for her friends and acquaintances from there. She mostly bought the handmade rugs and ceramics that Evelyn had made. The place was always full of foreigners: expats and passers-through, Arabs and Westerners from the diplomatic corps and their wives, and some businessmen's wives. As you walk inside, it's like stepping into a painting of various styles. You're among furs, minks, coattails, Arab headgear, jeans and denim jackets, and smart-casual outfits and your nose is met by the smell of strange tobacco smoke mixed with the scents of Chanel and Christian Dior and Arabian musk and Sudanese and African sandalwood dilka.

Marcia pulled her car up in front of the café and signaled for me to get in beside her. We went to park the car in the garage together. She looked me over, fussing with my appearance, sniffing me and then, taking out a small bottle of breath freshener, she asked me to open my mouth and sprayed inside. The spray was for getting rid of bad breath and the smell of alcohol and tobacco. She normally used it on me on our nights out, not in the morning, but I didn't say anything.

Marcia picked out an expertly woven, handmade tapestry and I chose a small desk that I knew was one of Essam's pieces. Marcia laughed in a hushed voice and picked out a jewelry box that we both knew was also one of Essam's. The gallery manager wrote down Ewald's address so he could send the stuff over and we wrote both of our names on the card.

Marcia didn't ask me about the bachelor party the night before; she didn't seem to be interested. She wanted to talk about what clothes and which cologne I should wear to the wedding that night. As she was leaving, she said she was going to skip the ceremony at the Noor Mosque after the sunset prayer and asked me where and when the reception was going to be. She said she'd meet me there.

When I saw Essam, who was surlier than I'd ever seen him before, he told me I'd been rude to him and nearly threw him out of the party. He said he could tell I was in a bad state, but I hadn't listened to him when he pleaded with me to stop drinking. He said I'd been acting like I wanted to commit suicide. I didn't remember any of it, so I apologized and kept my mouth shut. He mellowed out and asked me to tell him what he'd missed. I couldn't remember anything but the Eritrean woman so I told him about her and the wedding plans. He laughed hysterically. "Maybe you did marry her last night. Maybe, in nine months, she's going to dump a son on you," he said.

"I wish." Essam peered at me. I blushed.

The marriage ceremony at the Noor Mosque was almost moot: Awad and Aisha had already had their marriage certified by the Notary Office and the German Embassy, but a ceremony with a cleric in front of the bride's parents and friends was non-negotiable. When the ceremony was over, all but for the signing of the marriage contract, the bride's family and most of the guests, except for a few people who were very close to the bride, went on ahead to the small reception thrown by the groom to celebrate his marriage. Marcia met up with me there and sat with me and Essam and some sculptors. I danced with Marcia and Essam danced with a sculptress friend of his. The evening was lovely; nothing could've ruined it, nothing but Essam's moment of idiocy. When I was saying to him what a lovely evening it was, he said, "I'm looking forward to your wedding, if you ever have one. Why don't you get married already? Are you planning to be single forever?"

I could see Marcia grimace, but I didn't understand why she was upset at first. She should've been happy about what Essam had said: he was trying to get me to marry her. Essam could also tell that Marcia hadn't cared for what he'd said so he changed the subject and started joking around with her in English.

Awad and Aisha came over and sat with us for a little while before thanking each of us for the presents and going over to another table. I'd silenced my mobile and every time I took it out to see what time it was or who was calling me, I saw calls from Zaynab or unknown numbers. She'd sent me five texts in a row, so I went to the bathroom to read the messages in peace. They were essentially all variations of the same message: "I need to talk to you. Pick up."

It wouldn't have been very polite of me not to escort Marcia back to her house. As we danced, the signaling scents of her body filled my nose and she rubbed against me. I laughed and asked her why she'd been upset about what Essam had said. She said she thought he had some devious plan, that he wanted me to marry some Singaporean who looked like his wife, Samantha; or maybe it was Samantha herself who'd told him she had the right woman for me. Whenever I think back on that, I laugh and the scent of my virility makes me feel light-headed.

This had happened before with Marcia back when we were first going out. She'd asked me to define our relationship. Sheepishly, I told her we were close friends. I'd been expecting her to get angry or upset, but she surprised me by smiling and giving me a kiss. Then she said she felt the same way. And when she got pregnant, she just said, "What are we going to do?"

Just as simple as that, as if she were asking me what I thought about the color of some bra. And when I asked her timidly and carefully to get rid of it, she hugged me and said okay. Then she whispered in my ear that she'd always do whatever I wanted so long as we were both in agreement. The same thing happened to me then—I got drunk off my manliness. After that episode, she started taking birth control pills. I refused to wear condoms; they seem like an unnatural barrier to me.

On the subject of the Pill, it's originally a German invention. Adolf Hitler ordered his scientists to invent a treatment for sterilizing the peoples soon to be occupied, so that they wouldn't breed and mix their blood in with holy Aryan blood, to preserve the purity of Aryan blood forever. But Hitler lost the war and committed suicide and his scientists fled to other countries in Europe and to America with the formula for their new invention. The Americans gave them equipment and money, but the treatment didn't work when they used it on Puerto Rican and African-American women. It only prevented pregnancy in the short term. That was how they got the idea to use it for population control and thus a military invention became civilianized, and it's widely considered the most scientific important breakthrough on behalf of women. It even became the symbol of women's liberation in the 1960s.

Marcia was using the Pill that was supposed to have made us extinct, to have purified us out of the human species. I guess I was wrong to keep her from getting pregnant after that. I should've polluted her with a drop of African sperm.

I wasn't up to tutoring or going around to apartments where they put out independent newspapers, so I went back home, wrecked, and I immediately fell asleep in the living room. But then I was woken up by the incessant ringing of the doorbell. I dragged myself to my feet and met her, silently and angrily. I almost slammed the door in her face. It was Zaynab in the flesh. She came in, brushing past me carelessly, and knocking me to the floor; I was still half-asleep and off-balance. My temper flared and I started yelling at her. I didn't care about my neighbors or the other people in the building, or anything else in the whole universe. She looked at me as if she'd come in from a different planet; she didn't understand my kind and we didn't understand her. She flashed me her usual moronic smile and then held out her hand for me to grab onto. But when I pushed her hand away, she didn't move, she didn't back off, she simply bent down and grabbed me under my arms and picked me up. I was shouting at her. I nearly went crazy, being carried like a baby. I started kicking like a stubborn little boy, raging against her fierce strength until she dropped me on my bed. She ignored me completely. It was as if she'd merely righted a garbage can that had tipped over. I calmed down as I lay there, soothed by the sound of her moving around in the other room. Only Satan could've defeated that woman. She was standing at the foot of the bed in her underwear, adjusting her bra, asking me why I'd been ignoring her, why I hadn't answered her phone calls or replied to her texts. She didn't wait for an answer. She walked out of the room and returned with a bottle of whiskey. She poured a glass for herself and one for me and she left the room again, taking her glass with her.

I lost all track of time. Was it before midnight or after? I could hear Zaynab in the other room—she was constantly coming in to fill her glass and top up mine—and there were my intertwining, entangling imaginings, and then I started seeing two of her and four, then there were gelatinous phantoms, and then I passed out. Hundreds of nightmares and disheartening dreams bounced around in my mind against a giant roar. When I woke up, it took me a while to realize it was the sound of the washing machine. I knew Zaynab hadn't left. Frowning, I walked to the bathroom and found her there, wearing my gallabiya, busy running the wash. She heard my footsteps and turned, smiling like a naughty child. "Good morning," she said. I couldn't hear her over the din the washing machine was making and the absurd headache I'd had since waking up, but the movement of her lips sucked me in; not sure why.

"Laundry first thing in the morning?" I shouted.

She nodded toward the bathroom window, full of sunlight. "I think you mean 'Laundry first thing at noon.' You can wash up in the sink till I'm finished." Ignoring her, I walked into the bathroom and sat down, fully clothed, expecting she'd get up and leave, but no: she just looked at me defiantly. As soon as I made to lunge at her, though, she ran out and shut the door behind her.

When I was done showering, I sat in the living room and waited for her to finish what she was doing. I could smell eggs frying. *How could I have given into her so easily? How can I put up with the racket she makes and not want to kill her? How could I have accepted the role of the put-upon husband without striking back?* She was making breakfast, but she hadn't asked me what I wanted to eat, or whether I wanted coffee first or breakfast. On that day in particular, she was acting like a high-handed wife, acting like I was the husband who wouldn't dare open his mouth.

170

I accepted everything submissively. I ate the eggs, cheese, and nibbles she put in front of me and drank my warm milk. And then I realized something I'd missed: where had Zaynab slept the night before? I hadn't felt her body shifting or smelled her unique scent. My leg hadn't bumped into her behind; my hand hadn't grazed her chest. I hadn't found her kneeling over me kissing me wherever she could. My nose hadn't filled with the smell of her excitement. I hadn't found any of her clothes hanging from the bedpost or thrown beside me or tangled up in my feet when I got out of bed. I asked her where she'd slept and she laughed, really laughed, as she pointed to the other bedroom. I was surprised. "Weren't you scared sleeping by yourself?" I said. She laughed and stuck her tongue out. That turned me on so I got up and went over to her. I held her and kissed her cheeks, but I could feel the coldness with my lips. It was as if the life had drained out of her face as soon as I touched her. I moved devilishly toward her earlobes, her erogenous zone, but she shuddered and, for the first time in our relationship, she pushed me away. My instincts were right, my fears confirmed. I took her by the hand and headed for the bedroom. Her hand felt like ice. She was shaking her head.

"Mustafa, let's not. Please."

I sat down far away from her in a funk. I didn't need to have sex with her: I'd exhausted myself the day before with Marcia. But I knew that her period, an earthquake, volcanoes wouldn't have stopped Zaynab from having sex; it was love that stopped her. It was something I knew, something I could feel in a woman. Zaynab had slipped away from me and my defeats were beginning to pile up.

She looked at me pityingly, confused, maybe even doubtful that I cared about her so much. She was worried she'd give in or that she'd put her foot down too hard and ruin the image of her I had in my already muddled mind. I held out the pack of cigarettes and she took one and put it to her mouth. She lit it and then she stood up and set it between my lips. She usually did that. Then she lit one for herself. I tried to take her mind off it by asking about her trip. She leaped from her seat as if she'd been waiting for that very question and dragged her suitcase in.

She was gone and back in a couple of seconds. She took out the paper she wanted me to see with a flourish. Papers: stamped, certified, in English. The one I was reading said that the sponsor, Julio Andrenas, leader of the band "Dreams of the Peoples" has offered to host Miss Zaynab Hussein during her visit to Mexico. I tossed the papers at her, pretending not to care. She opened her passport and pointed to the Embassy-stamped entry visa. Her trip was just a big joke to me and I was skeptical, as usual (I plan on being buried skeptical), that it would ever actually come to anything. But the impossible had happened.

I didn't ask her how she got her employer to agree to it, if she'd ever actually been employed, or got permission from the Journalists' Syndicate, if she were even a reporter to begin with, let alone how she'd managed to get her father to say yes. I didn't ask how she got around all the pointless government bureaucracy. How she got it all taken care of in only a few months. Or why stupid, foolish Julio trusted her enough to sponsor her for a visa even though he'd only ever seen her in the street, and in bars and restaurants. He hadn't met any of her family or her friends. He couldn't have known whether she was insane or not, or whether she was an idiot. I couldn't imagine what she'd do there, either, with no money, no Spanish, and no real talent, except for being a slut.

Zaynab was still, but for her eyes, which stared at me. It was as if I was out walking with a girl I'd just met and she suddenly jumps up onto the railing of the Qasr al-Nil Bridge. She balances on the narrow iron rail, and taking a deep breath, stretches her arms out to the side to hug the air that fills her chest. She's about to jump down into the Nile. What could I do? Let her jump off and drown? Watch the dance of death until the finale? Could I have got her to think twice about her trip, even if it meant having her clinging to me like a leech from then on? Or should I have kept quiet and looked the other way?

She was still looking at me, silent. She stood up and started undressing as she walked toward the bathroom. Then came the sound of her singing. I got up quietly to see if the bathroom door was open. It was ajar as usual. I waited for the moment after the song when she'd call for me to come loofah her back. When excitement would come over her as she watched me watching her; the showerhead dripping gleaming, silvery crystals onto her body. I waited, but she didn't call my name. When she came out, she could see I was upset. She came up to me, leading with her lips, and kissed me from under my chin up to either temple. "Ouch, your beard's scratching me." She ran to the bathroom and a few minutes later, she came back in and took me by the hand. My shaving set was laid out on the counter by the sink and next to it was a dish for cooling the water and cleaning hair off the brush. She dragged a chair over and sat me down. Then she laid a towel over my chest and started shaving me. She loved shaving me. I don't know why; I never asked while we were together. When she saw she'd nicked me, she went to lick the cut like she used to do, but she stopped midway. She scurried over to her bag and brought back a cotton swab she'd wet with perfume and wiped my face. She pointed at our clothes hanging on the line. "When they're dry, fold them and leave them for me. I'll iron them next time."

She got dressed and put on some perfume, looking like she was getting ready to leave. I walked past her into my bedroom. I came back out and when she kissed me goodbye, I slipped a thousand dollars into her pocket. She'd felt my hand and when she touched the money, she went ballistic and threw it on the floor. "What's that for?" she asked, almost in tears.

I was speechless for a few seconds, but then I pulled it together and gave her a lot of talk about friendship and partnership. I said that if I'd been in her shoes, I'd have asked her for the same. She said Julio had already sent her plenty of money, plus a plane ticket, and that she'd already bought what she needed. She was planning to give the extra to her family to tide them over until she had the chance to send them money from Mexico.

The bills were strewn on the ground; she was heading for the door. She stopped and turned to face me. "You want me to give you a proper good-bye before I leave? Or did you do that shitty thing so I'd never come back?"

I was mortified, but I'm certain a few words like "Come see me before you leave" escaped my lips.

20

I'D ESSENTIALLY CUT MYSELF OFF from the world in order to prepare for filming and to make Marcia happy. Fortunately, after a lot of work, I'd convinced her to shoot the script for "The Danger Ahead" in two stages: the first stage during the dog days of July and August and the second in December and January when it's bitterly cold. Before each stage, I'd pretty much move in with Karim and his crew so I could monitor them up close. I told Marcia that I'd be able to watch them open up like little flower buds, leave their chrysalises like butterflies in the spring, that I'd observe them in the scorching heat and frosty cold. She loved the idea, but she was worried about the length of the timeline I'd laid out. She suggested bringing in a Western film crew, at her expense, or an Egyptian crew if I preferred, but I wasdead set against it: if the kids felt like they were being watched, they'd alter their behavior, and we'd be asking for State Security to get involved. Plus the censors would never have given us permission to do a project like that. She gave in, eventually. I needed all that time so I could gather my scattered thoughts and make the right decision for the first time in my life.

I figured that Marcia would be happy to follow my progress from a distance and that rather than getting involved in the details, she'd leave me to work, or not work, in peace, but that was wishful thinking. A week later, she asked me over and gave me an imported professional-quality digital camera (most likely from America, but manufactured in Germany). She was going to hold me to the strict work schedule that she'd drawn up; it included my teaching schedule, the occasional work I did for the newspaper, personal time we could spend together, and time I could spend on the film. She also gave me a large sum of money for the script. I couldn't believe it when she took me to see a lawyer who specialized in copyright law, and had him draw up a contract that granted me all the legal rights against distortion of my idea; Marcia was listed only as the director and producer. I made her agree to an explicit clause that prevented the removal or insertion of any scenes without my written approval. I spoke to the lawyer, treating her as if we were in court, as if we weren't on speaking terms. I was certain she was going to be upset and say no, but she agreed to it, no big deal. "It's perfectly normal," she said "It's your work as much as it is mine. What makes you think I'd edit things out without your permission?"

It was the first time we'd interacted that way in front of strangers and made agreements we hadn't discussed beforehand. We were playing out in the open and I thought I was winning. But she'd agreed to everything and signed with such confidence and goodwill that I began to feel better about her and my paranoia diminished slightly.

I was completely caught up in it now. I'd entered the swamp of uncertainty. I was openly collaborating with foreigners on issues that could damage the State or tarnish its image, that could turn everyone, friend and foe, against me.

Once I was alone with my thoughts, worry took over. I could sense the devil sticking his tongue out at me and laughing. I'd fled from America, yet here I was serving its interests. Marcia had lived in Egypt for a long time and changed the topic of her PhD dissertation like it was underwear, but now all of a sudden she wanted to be a filmmaker simply because she'd studied filmmaking in America before coming to the Middle East. I knew how you got a filmmaking degree over there. For three three-month-long semesters, you take classes from out of work, or long since idle Hollywood film people and then you get a diploma to hang up in your house, not to direct with. I'd seen her very short film (running time: eight minutes), her final project at the Institute; it was sub-par. I saw another film of hers that was thirty minutes long, but it was all talking and overacting. What had got her thinking about directing again? Who had got her thinking about it again? Was it my fretting about street kids? Or was it her uncanny ability to root out the ticking time bombs in Egyptian society? Or was she receiving direction from over there?

I was being held captive by my body and by an undying passion and I knew that this illness was going to lead to my destruction. I knew I wouldn't survive, but I didn't want to save myself. I didn't even want to try. My doctors' diagnoses may've been right. Maybe it was all a delusion, or a perfectly ordinary thing I exaggerated because I was ill. I wasn't going to stick up for any nation, or any society. I was a nobody. I didn't deserve notice.

I began to draw the broad outlines of the script. I swore I wasn't going to make those kids into a tourist attraction. I wasn't going to use them to shock and entice the West. Nor was I going to make it look like those kids had chosen to live on the street. I was going to condemn the families and the government and society as a whole; and the international community, too. It keeps governments busy with agencies and benchmarks and conflicts, and meanwhile people around the world are becoming worse off. I was looking at frightening statistics from the World Health Organization—copied down by Marcia—which estimated the number of homeless children in Egypt at a million. That number could've been an exaggeration, but if the real figure were even half of what they estimated, it'd still be a nightmare. We needed a hundred documentary films to examine the issue, to wake people up to the danger, to propose solutions.

The street has an unspoken code, and it has its bosses, thugs, followers, weaklings. The sidewalk is taken over by people selling fruit, vegetables, packets of shampoo, counterfeit cosmetics, socks, and sneakers; they don't care about the laws against blocking pedestrian traffic. They solve their problems with the powers that be with bribes, which they factor into the price of their products.

When a street kid wakes up, there's nothing to eat so he nicks an orange or a guava or a peach or an apricot, driving the fruit vendor mad. He'll chase after him, but he won't catch him. The street kids bother the customers, too, especially the women. They harass them and grope them and then they run off. At nighttime, they amuse themselves by cutting open the tarps that the vendors use to wrap up their wooden carts at the end of the day and stealing whatever they can grab. The conflict escalates when the vendors pay policemen to chase the street kids away, or rough them up, or throw them into jail cells with hardened criminals; or when they make a deal with the gangs and the mafia to have the kids killed or buried alive, which is what happens in Chile and Brazil and other Third World countries. The danger ahead won't come from the kids killed in clashes with the police and gangs. The danger ahead will come from the kids who survive; the ones who cheat death. The terrible violence they suffer will lead them to chase after us in the streets, to rob us and rape our daughters. They won't hesitate to break into our houses. I felt like it was my duty to draw attention to the problem. Me, the one who hadn't left a single fingerprint on the world, I wanted to state my case. I wanted to warn about the danger.

My vision for the film grew out of that premonition and I was earning my keep, as the saying goes. The dollars were still warm in my desk drawer. The next day, I took Marcia to the building Karim and his crew used as a headquarters. I knew what she was going to see would upset her and that it'd be a one-time thing. That was why I took her. Karim was waiting for us inside the house. We crossed over to it as the passersby watched us curiously: an Egyptian man leading a blonde

177

foreign woman, who was stumbling over pebbles and stones, toward an old house, most of which had collapsed. Karim was standing in the entrance and he welcomed us as if he were the man of the house, the host. Dozens of surprised and wondering eyes looked us over. We walked through the ruins and corridors of the ground floor, or what was left of it. Marcia didn't dare go into the dark, dingy rooms; she was content to peer in from the doorway. They'd given up watching us. They were reassured by Karim's presence so they went back to what they'd been doing. Karim smiled and looked at Marcia, who was staring up at the floor above, at the children who were watching us. Marcia asked me to take her upstairs. It was impossible as the staircase was completely demolished; there was nothing left of it. When I asked Karim how they got upstairs, he giggled and yelled to his followers and, suddenly, we could see a big group of children looking down on us from the floor above, three meters up. The children were carrying a smooth plank and they slid it down until it reached the floor where we were standing. They set it at an angle to make it climbable. Marcia balked. "There's no way I can go up like that," she said. Karim figured she'd say it was too difficult to go up so he was forced to demonstrate it for us. He ran up the plank, his arms outstretched like Leonardo DiCaprio in *Titanic*, and, a second later, he was looking down at us triumphantly. It turned into a game. Kids on either floor started imitating him, going up and down. Their aping of Karim's movements, their guffawing like Tarzan in the jungle, their mocking of our obvious inability: it all worried Marcia so Karim told them to stop. A girl who was carrying a baby came over to us. Marcia took an interest in the baby, examining it and tickling it while the mother, herself not yet sixteen, was feeling Marcia's blonde hair and the cheap necklaces she usually wore. All of a sudden, a boy upstairs spotted the girl and leaped down the plank and started beating her. The girl threw the baby to Marcia and shielded her face with her hands. When Karim stepped in, the girl grabbed the baby out of Marcia's hands and, carrying it apelike, climbed to the floor above. Then she pulled the plank up to keep the boy from following after her.

Marcia and I were blown away by the speed at which things were taking place; it was as if we'd fast-forwarded through an entire film. Marcia felt faint, but she couldn't find anything to lean against; the walls were filthy and dust had turned the cobwebs that covered them into disgusting black threads. Weasels and rats were colliding with our feet. She leaned on me and I whispered to her that we ought to leave. She almost agreed, but her stubborn spirit returned in the nick of time and she said she wanted to go upstairs to see how they lived. I told her neither one of us was acrobatic enough to be able to climb up like them. She nodded toward Karim and told me to tell him what she wanted. Karim gave it some thought and told me he had a solution. He yelled at the kids to bring a thick palm-cord rope and slide the plank down. He smiled and said he was going to train us to climb up just as he did with the kids who came there for the first time. Karim went up in front of me. With one hand I grabbed him around the waist and with the other I held onto the tightly braided rope; the kids on the floor above were holding the other end. I climbed up slowly until I reached them; pleased to have made it. Marcia was able to climb up the same way.

Something Marcia said to Karim made him bust up laughing, but it wasn't the reaction she'd been expecting. I asked her why he was laughing. "I don't know," she said. After a violent coughing fit had put an end to his laughter, Karim told me Marcia had said she'd give him the money to build a cement staircase. I smiled, but she was even more confused so I had to explain the wisdom of those illiterate children to her. They'd knocked out the staircase on purpose when their leadership had decided to settle in the crumbling villa. After being chased numerous times by the police and older bums, they decided to destroy the means of getting upstairs so they'd be out of the reach of the police or whoever else. The police wouldn't go to the trouble of bringing in a ladder and climbing up to chase after them, and even if they did, the kids would've had enough time to climb down the pipes and escape behind the house through the alleys of Sayyida Zaynab.

The rooms upstairs were bathed in the sunlight that was pouring in through the windows, which were mostly broken or had had their glass removed. The setup was orderly and it looked like it'd been planned out: each group of approximately the same age had chosen one of the rooms upstairs. Girls under the age of ten shared a room. The girls over fourteen had taken the most welcoming room and their boyfriends at the villa had made a big dresser out of dry wood and some wooden boxes for them to store their belongings and their clothes, which were considered the tools of the trade they plied in the allies and streets of Cairo. The girls could be picked up at any moment by donkey-cart drivers, gas station workers, coffeehouse errand boys, and then they'd return with a few pounds and bags of fuul and falafel; that is, if there were any money left after they'd bought glue and pills.

Theirs was the only room that still had a door; the door was ajar. Maybe it was their ability to bring in money that had helped them gain that independence. Karim nudged the door open and there, we could see them. They didn't look annoyed; there was just a little flash of curiosity on their faces. I watched them as I stood in front of the door and Marcia stood behind me. Marcia pushed me forward and we went in together. She ignored the other girls, who were playing and quarreling, and moved toward a thin girl with a protruding belly, who was leaning against the wall. Marcia patted her on the back and rubbed the astonished girl's belly. Karim whispered, "She's five months pregnant." Marcia's interest in that girl was making another girl jealous: Rabeea was obviously a close friend of Safiya, the girl Marcia was fussing over, and she walked over to Marcia and pushed her out of the way. She hugged Safiya and stroked her hair; I had to stop Karim from hitting her. I could see that Rabeea was very protective of Safiya and we weren't going to get involved in a squabble. Marcia came over to me and held my arm as she watched them. Then Rabeea barked an order to another girl, who immediately ran over to the dresser and brought over a carton of milk. Rabeea opened it with her fingernails and gave it to Safiya lovingly. She drank some, and gave it back to Rabeea, and they took turns drinking until they finished it.

As Karim took us into the other rooms, Marcia was bursting with excitement. She couldn't hide her glee, her pain, her disgust at what she was seeing. Before we'd visited, I'd suggested other shooting locations, which she'd liked. But, that day, she said that all we needed was there in that magical, mythical place; a place that would've been a rare find on any of the five continents. She told me to examine every brick of that place since most of the film would be shot there. Our visit did a lot to help me regain control over Marcia and prove to her I was capable of handling the project and providing amazing details. I had only one worry, which I kept to myself. Was I going to be able to live with them and observe them up close and film them like I planned? Was I going to be able to put up with them? To put up with their fits of anger; the anger that doesn't make allowances for my fits of depression? Was I going to be able to protect myself and get out of there unscathed even though they're fickle, even though they're constantly brandishing weapons at one another while they're in the fog of drugs? The experiment was frightening, but I had to go through with it. Time was the only thing I had left to fear and this was an opportunity to hide from it. There, with them, I could hide from unforeseen sadnesses.

21

A RECORD WORTHY of the *Guinness Book of World Records* had just been set: Zaynab had been over at my apartment for two hours and was still wearing the clothes she'd come in with. I asked her to make something for dinner; she told me to call a restaurant. She used to run to the kitchen—without asking first—and whip up whatever she could find and then she'd insist on feeding me her inexpert cooking. I miss it. I can still taste how delicious it was. Now she was just sitting there, statue-like, with half a smile on her lips.

She didn't wake me up with her incessant doorbelling and knocking this time. It was faint ringing that had stirred me so I was surprised when I opened the door and found her there. She hugged me weakly and took a seat. In a lifeless voice, she told me her plane was leaving Cairo after midnight. When I asked about her luggage, she shrugged and said, "Back at the hostel." She'd already arranged with a taxi driver to pick her up from the hostel and take her to the airport, as if I were a ghost or just plain invisible, as if I wouldn't have wanted to take her to the airport and see her off.

I was in a bad mood and she was only making it worse. I didn't respond to her. I just watched her eat the rice and fish I'd ordered.

I don't think she ever ate; it was like she'd been put in charge of filling a bucket halfway up. She threw back a piece of fish then a half-spoonful of rice, and then either a spoonful of salad or tahini in that order. She didn't bother to debone my fish this time, or cut it up and feed me by hand. I think if I'd actually died in front of her, she wouldn't have noticed. And when she took her clothes down off the line, she left mine hanging up. She didn't do the ironing for us both like she'd promised she would the time before. She was busy packing her things into a plastic bag; she'd refused to borrow a suitcase from me. She didn't even leave me a pair of panties, autographed in red lipstick, like the starlets used to do for Yusuf Hilmi. I'd been hoping she would.

I wanted nothing more than to stand behind her and put my arms around her, to kiss her hair and down her neck. I felt like she was expecting it, hoping for it, that she couldn't wait. But then I worried that her reaction, reflected in her miserable mood, would only make me angry. I got on her case about not spending the night before her departure with me like she'd promised. The half-smile she was wearing disappeared and she gave me a startled look and retreated in on herself. She was so excessively gloomy that my own gloom started to recede, and a deep, distressing sense that I was losing her for good settled over me. I wouldn't see her again. She wouldn't throw open her arms to me again. Her hair would never cover my face again. Her breath wouldn't invade my nose again. I'd never be covered in the intoxicating scent of her sweat again as we slept. She wouldn't wake me up ever again by kissing me on the forehead, or violently shaking my shoulders as she lay on my stomach. Zaynab would leave me like all the others had left, never to return. She'd slip out of my life after having stirred it up. Wasn't that what I'd wanted on more than one occasion? What was this mysterious sense of loss, then, that had me worked up?

When Zaynab left, so did all the warmth in the place. I couldn't stand my apartment anymore, but I certainly wasn't going to move in with Marcia. I wouldn't have been able to stand her and she wouldn't have been able to put up with me. When we were apart, the attraction was mutual, but when we got too close to each other, the faults were magnified. Anyway, I needed to get away from everything and everyone, not just from myself.

Karim made up a place for me on the upper floor, far away from the bathrooms, which the boys and girls chose to use not as they were intended: they preferred to urinate in the general vicinity of the toilets as a form of rebellion or corner-cutting. They didn't care about passersby like me, who might be curious enough to look in and disapprove. Karim seemed really happy I was there. He hadn't believed I was going to spend the night with them, let alone many nights, and he stood in front of me and watched incredulously as I set up the tent Marcia had bought me. He prevented the gape-mouthed boys and girls from bothering me with their antics and questions. I was cut off from the world. I enjoyed watching their amazed, giddy reactions as they felt the outside of the tent and stretched their hands out to touch the sponge mattress, the zipper that shut it, the vents along the side. Karim gave me a nightstand, which the kids had found in the mess of leftover furniture in the house, so I could store my tent and effects when I wasn't there. He'd bought me a new lock, too, with some of the money I'd given him, so I could lock it up. He laughed as he whispered to me that even though they were all thieves with rap sheets, none of them would dare break the lock. When I asked him why, in that case, it was necessary to lock it at all, he squinted his eyes as if he were explaining an important equation in mathematics and said, "So we don't leave it out in the open. 'Cause if they see it, they'll steal it."

I spent a sleepless first night there because of a girl, who couldn't have been older than fifteen. She'd managed to slip through the cordon Karim had imposed around me. At some point after midnight, she was circling my tent like a feral cat. I was frightened at first because I couldn't make her out in the dim moonlight that filtered through the broken windows, but when she came closer and her little hand scratched at the oilcloth over the tent, I ignored her. She could see that I'd sat up and pulled away the thin cover so I could look at her. She felt for the double-door of the tent, which opened from the outside and from within. I held onto the zipper from inside to keep her from undoing it.

184

Thinking I was playing with her, she grew bolder. She moved her tiny body closer to the tent and pushed on it until she came up against my body. I had no choice but to open the tent and have a word with her, but when I opened it, she propelled herself with all her might, nearly ending up in my lap. She begged me in a whisper to let her sleep in the tent with me because she was trying to escape the wicked boys, who wanted—she claimed—to have their way with her. But I shoved her off and threw her out. I didn't know her name and I wouldn't have been able to pick her out among the other girls. But she didn't give up. I cursed myself for not listening to Karim and not setting my tent up beside him. I'd picked that far-off room, thinking I'd be a safe distance away from them as I slept. When she renewed her boring attempts to sleep in there with me, I lost my temper. Her stupid behavior could've ruined my stay with them, ruined the project, and damaged my relationship with Marcia. She pretended to cry in a hoarse, hollow voice and sat in a pile in front of my tent. She lifted her head, from time to time, to see if it were having any effect. She was like a stubborn child, thinking up new ways to infuriate her mother. I smiled and climbed out of the tent. I invited her to go inside, saying I was going to sleep on the floor in the parlor. She hadn't been expecting my stratagem. Her eyes followed me as I pulled the comforter out and laid it on the floor, and then she stood up from where she'd been slouching, her tears having dried in those few moments, and walked away nervously, hurling curses at me, questioning my manhood. I got back into my tent and slept a little. I didn't tell Karim about it the next morning, but I told him I'd rather sleep on the roof from then on. He didn't object; he seemed to understand. I filmed them, asleep and awake, eating, fighting and bickering. I was happy with what I'd got that day so I sneaked off. I walked once around the villa, but no one, on the inside or the outside, noticed me, and that made me happy: I was being careful not to screw up the project from the start. I was getting into it. I wanted to capture as much as I could in sound and image because I was certain my stay with them wasn't going to remain a secret for very long. Many of the neighbors, ordinary citizens, would find out about it and then the officials, the police and the like, would hear about it, and I wanted to delay that for as long as possible. I had no business discussing what I was trying to do with those kids—even if I pretended to understand it—or trying to convince other people of the purity of my intentions. I visited them once a week, on different days, so no one could keep tabs on me and also so I wouldn't get used to them and abandon the project out of boredom. I filmed fantastic scenes of them high on glue, and pharmaceuticals, and narcotics; of them fooling around with one another: boys and girls, boys with boys, lesbian girls. They were used to me so they didn't care about me or the camera I was pointing at them anymore. When they were finished, they'd rub against me like a cat waiting for a treat. I kept written notes on them, too: observations, concerns, impressions. My shock faded as I hung out with them. Faces were always coming and going, and when one of the faces disappeared, I'd ask after him and someone would say, "He died in an accident," or "He's in jail," or "His family found him," or "He joined a gang."

I worried more and more about my fundamental reliance on Karim and it made me get as much done as I could. There was no guarantee he'd always be there: he could've been killed in a fight, or gone to jail, or started missing his wife, Warda, whom he'd driven out of the neighborhood (she'd taken refuge in the Mohandiseen district out of fear.) He might have gone after her; after all, he still loved her. Maybe he'd get into a fight over her and get killed on his way to reclaiming her. Or maybe I was imagining things; maybe he never thought about her.

I started working on a study of the kids that I was planning to publish when the film was completed. The book was going to reflect my views; no one else would be involved—not Marcia, not the film's funders. And that did a lot to soothe me, to keep the anxieties that almost made me want to quit the film at bay. I wasn't moved by the kids' stories about evil fathers and prostitute mothers and incestuous-rapist uncles. I was only interested in the extremely complicated stories of how, and why, they'd run away. Those were almost too good to be true. I made them tell me their stories on different occasions so I could separate out the facts, or pseudo-facts.

Marcia didn't watch everything I'd recorded with me. She was smart never to have asked to see my progress or quizzed me about details, and she bore my absences with patience. She never got angry, except once when she inadvertently found out that I'd cancelled lessons with two of my students and passed them off on a friend of mine. "How could you make such an important decision without consulting me?" Her question had surprised me more than her anger had worried me.

"What important decision? It was just some tutoring I had to cancel because I've got more important things to do." I thought it would have some effect if I added, "Because of our project." The film was the more important thing.

She didn't take the bait. "They're foreigners. I know them better than you do. To them, a job means an agreement between two parties and you can't get out of it unless you've got extenuating circumstances and even then you've got to ask for permission first. They're going to tell the rest of your students and you're going to have a hard time getting other jobs from now on."

On the inside, I was cursing foreigners and their contracts and their money and Marcia, who'd introduced me to them and who was now acting like she depended on me financially, but I said nothing. She could tell I wasn't happy so she cooled down and patted my thigh. "I'll call them and explain why you had to cancel. They'll understand." Then she whispered, "Please don't keep things from me anymore." It was a threat wrapped in a request, precisely the sort of thing I couldn't stomach, but, to my chagrin, I found myself driven to please her. I said our work on the movie was the most important thing, the more enduring thing, and that I'd finally found my passion in screenwriting and when we were done with the film, we'd pursue a whole host of other movie projects together. I was lying through my teeth and she had no choice but to believe me. We hugged without another word, which could have only damaged our relationship or led to a huge fight. After that temporary détente, I thought it wise to show her some of the scenes I'd shot. Her heart soared after every scene or conversation she liked, and then she asked me, shyly and haltingly, if she could use a few of the scenes as samples to drum up support for the film. I consented without the slightest reluctance. I wasn't going to let her see most of what I'd filmed—that I'd stored in my apartment—and I'd shown her those scenes just so she'd see I was still making progress. What was weird was that that little taste I'd given her, which I'd considered pretty meager, got us even more funding and invitations from organizations and festivals that went on and on trying to outbid one another.

Months passed and Zaynab still hadn't got in touch as she'd promised she would. I knew nothing about where she was staying in Mexico; I'd forgotten to ask. But I missed her. Or maybe it was because there was nothing in the world around me that moved me; all I had left was a memory of her. I'd reserved a ticket to Minya and I was to leave depressing Cairo that evening. I was planning to stay in Minya for a day or two if I could find a decent hotel, and then I'd hire a car to take me to her village, Beni Hassan. There, someone would be able to point me in the direction of her house. I needed to clear my polluted vision with the sight of the virginal Nile. I needed to hear the sounds of open country, of crickets in the fields, of howling jackals and barking dogs. I needed to cleanse my sight in the greenery and wash my nose in its sweet scent.

Yasmeen called me on my mobile and asked me to meet her. For the first time since we'd met, I wasn't looking forward to it. I felt like she'd thrown a bucketful of cold water over me and killed my desire to be alone. My mind was muddled and my spirit was topsy-turvy; hurling my emotions up to the heavens, up to Hind and her exalted soul, and then swinging me low to get tangled up in Zaynab and Marcia and their earthly delights. In my state, I couldn't afford the luxury of negotiating with Yasmeen. I had no choice but to go meet her.

I picked a secluded restaurant downtown that I knew served beer. She showed up after I'd finished my first bottle and was getting started on a second. She scowled as she watched me drink, but I ignored her. She didn't want to eat in a restaurant that served alcohol and she didn't want to drink a Coke, or anything else, because she was boycotting American goods. She even refused a hot drink as she was trying to get me to go elsewhere. I paid her no mind and when I'd finished my second bottle, I ordered another. She grumbled, she tried her hardest to conceal her irritation, but I didn't give a damn. *Even if you were a child, Yasmeen, like you pretend to be, I wouldn't be your father, or even a stand-in. And I won't be blackmailed by childish behavior. Why don't you just play down at my feet? Or just go away already.*

I think she figured it out, either by intellect or instinct or ESP, by reading lips, or telepathy, or the sixth sense. She stood up. "I'm leaving." I smiled; the playing field had been laid bare.

"Who told you to come in the first place?"

She looked at me as if she were looking at a junky-alcoholic. "You must be very proud of yourself."

I'd had enough of being foolish so I said, "Sit down, you're making a scene. Why don't you tell me what you called me for?" She seemed mortified, as embarrassed as she'd have been if I'd walked in on her waxing her pubic hair. She turned and walked away, but I stood up and put my hand on her shoulder. She shuddered, retreating in case I tried to touch her again. Everyone in the restaurant was watching us; they were probably laughing at us: the man-child begging the little girl to sit with him. She gave in because she saw I was so distraught and sat down, trembling. I was about to let her have it, but I quickly composed myself and forced a smile. I tried to get back on her good side, but she was implacable. I wanted to scream at her: *When will you realize, little girl, that I don't give a damn about your prepubescent body or your barely pubescent charms? I don't want to touch you. As a woman, you mean nothing to me. No, you're just a hypothetical woman. I'm sick of watching you play the Virgin Mary. I hate it. Hind I used to touch, and she used to touch me, but she used to enter into me like a spirit. She used to wash me clean of all beastly and human instincts. That's the gaping difference between your soul and hers.* I realized then that they weren't one and the same and I lost any interest I'd had in taking things further with Yasmeen.

She must've said something, though I didn't hear it, because she looked irritated. "First, you make me sit down, and now you're not even listening to me." I felt bad for her so I said I was sorry, but I had

189

a lot on my mind. She didn't care to ask what was bothering me, but she did ask that the next time we got together we not meet at that restaurant, or any other place that served alcohol. I had nothing to say about that. I told her I was going to Upper Egypt to visit relatives and spend some time alone so I could get writing again. She surprised me by telling me she was planning to go to Hurghada, Sharm al-Sheikh, and Northern Sinai with some of her classmates during the mid-year break. I asked her why those places specifically. "Because we owe it to ourselves to see every corner of our country," she said, running me through with her gaze. She said her grandmother had agreed to it and when she'd told her father, who was busy with his other wife and his other kids, he didn't object.

She was ready to leave so I paid and we left together. We walked to the Metro station in silence. She didn't invite me to come along on their trip and I didn't want to impose; I understood. She might've been embarrassed about the difference in our ages if her friends were around. Plus it was an indulgence I didn't have time for. Even if she had looked like she was waiting for me to say I wanted to go, I wasn't going to. My mind started to warn me of evil: if I'd gone down into the Metro station with her, I definitely would've thrown someone in front of a train. I stopped at the entrance and held out my hand. She was confused for a moment, but then she whispered, "Goodbye," and, as usual, she didn't shake my hand.

That little habit of hers really pissed me off and I was swearing at her as she descended and disappeared. The passersby gave me and my rage plenty of room to get by.

22

I READ AN AMUSING STORY on my way to Minya about a nine-article decree on government publications from around the end of the reign of Sultan Abd al-Hamid II. The most important rule forbade discussion of the protests and revolutions that were taking place abroad because it wasn't considered good politics for the loyal flock to hear about what was going on.

Perhaps the strangest application of this rule resulted when an Ottoman newspaper gave the censor a long piece of reporting on the Russian Revolution, which ended with the coming to power of the communists under Lenin's leadership in 1917. Among the words the censors deleted were words like "revolution," "constitution," "civil rights," "oppression," and anything having to do with attacks against the Tsar, or about the People's Revolution. The only thing left of the report was one line, which was published in the newspaper the day after the Revolution, as follows: "A fight broke out in Russia yesterday."

I arrived in Minya, but I didn't stay there as I'd planned. I decided to go straight to the village of Beni Hassan to get what I'd come to do out of the way. I took an ancient microbus to the village and when I got there, I asked the first person I saw where I could find Uncle Hussein al-Dab, Zaynab's father. The man was riding a donkey and he gestured for me to get on behind him. Then he took me to the ferry crossing where he told the boatman to take me across to the East bank. I tried to give him some money, but he refused clucking, "Tsk, tsk."

Her father greeted me with a mix of hospitality and the kind of surprised and suspicious reaction an Upper Egyptian has when approached by a stranger asking about his daughter. Her mother was all the more welcoming, if only to make up for any embarrassment. Safiya, Zaynab's younger sister, was at her middle school and Ahmad, the disabled child, was at home.

Our meeting started off awkwardly; the only opening I could think of was to tell them some funny stories about Cairo. I gained their affection by eating with them from the same low wooden table. I didn't grumble. I wasn't put out by the setting or the smell, mostly of dung from the small paddock up against the side of the house. I looked like I was enjoying the food and I asked for seconds. I wasn't acting; I'd missed the intimacy of a family gathering.

I told them I worked with Zaynab at the newspaper and that I'd been assigned to write a report on the issues facing Upper Egyptian families as a prelude to the government's initiative on their behalf. Her father wasn't convinced there was any point in newspaper coverage. Her clever mother seemed extra-careful not to let her husband get me into a one-on-one discussion on topics that might've soured the atmosphere. She interjected and interrupted, ignoring her husband's rebuking looks and gestures. I had no idea what Zaynab had told them before she left, what lies she might've told to get them to allow her to go abroad. Was she on an education exchange? Or on a job assignment? To hell with her! It was her fault that I had to try to dodge the traps of their questions like an acrobat. She was the reason I had to pretend that I'd been on assignment in Algeria and that I hadn't heard she'd gone abroad until I got back. Her mother intervened tidily. "God grant you success, son! Does your news-paper have offices all over the place? Even halfway around the world?"

I got what she was driving at. "Mexico? That's one of our biggest bureaus. But don't worry about it, Hagga, Zaynab'll be back soon enough."

Her mother was surprised to hear me say that. "But she told us she was going to be heading up the office there for two years." Grateful to her mother for setting me on the right track, I took off, eloquently listing the benefits of working overseas in terms of salary and promotion. I told them Zaynab was as tough as any man, that you didn't have to worry about her, and that if she didn't like it there, she'd come right back. Working in Europe and America was better than working in Arab countries, I said, because of the money and the quality of society and the opportunity to learn a foreign language. The company only chose the best of us to represent it in those special locations. Zaynab's mother looked satisfied and her father more relaxed, or—at least—that was how I saw it.

Her mother insisted I stay with them for at least a couple of days, and her husband echoed her grudgingly. My spirit needed those two days so I said I'd stay. Later when I was alone, I could smell Zaynab's scent all around me. I breathed in deeply through my nose and held it in, savoring it, exhaling only when I had to. Her father made the guest room up for me. Zaynab was always trying to get me to visit Beni Hassan with her: I could stay in the guest bedroom there and she'd look after me. Her father took the television out of his room and put it in mine, but I told him I didn't want it because it would distract me from my work. Her father sat with me a while to keep me company, but when he saw that I wanted to get writing, he left me alone. As if Zaynab had given her instructions, her mother kept bringing me tea and coffee and whatever I asked for. I turned in early because her father had promised to take me fishing in the morning.

I'd gone into town with him and we'd sat at one of the coffee-houses. He'd seemed embarrassed at first as he introduced me to the people he knew. He hadn't mentioned that I was his daughter's co-worker; he'd just said I was a journalist. That had caused some headache as everyone smothered me with their questions, requests, and suggestions. I couldn't take sitting with them for more than an hour so I made an excuse about being exhausted. We'd walked back through the fields that ran parallel to the long, boring road. As I tried to catch up with him and stumbled in the darkness that surrounded us, I said, "Uncle, I work with your daughter, who we value very highly. I'd be honored if you introduced me to people as her co-worker." He didn't say anything; it was as if he'd been listening to a language he didn't understand. He lengthened his stride so that he was almost running and I had a hard time keeping up. I thought maybe he was hoping I'd get lost in the pitch-dark and lose my way back to his house. But at dinner, I was determined to bring the issue up again, this time in front of the mother. She heard me out, and then, smiling, she said, "This is Upper Egypt, son. Leave it to your uncle the Hagg, he's the one who does the talking. He understands how things work around here." Ahmad was staring at me lovingly. He'd look at the toy I brought him, which lay on the floor, and then he'd say a few unintelligible words, which he didn't tire of repeating. When I finished eating, I wiped my mouth on the towel and stood up and walked over to Ahmad. I kissed him on the forehead and cheeks, not minding the drool that hung from his mouth. They were all behind me, watching me: the stern father, the tender mother, the happy daughter, and I was overcome by warmth and affection.

The main reason I'd gone on that trip was to give Zaynab's family some money to make up, in part, for everything she'd done for me, and because I was worried she wouldn't be able to give them any of the money from her Mexico trip and that they'd run into problems. I lay down a bit and thought about how I should handle the conversation with her father so that he didn't feel like there was something untoward about the money. I also wanted to forget Cairo. But it was them I couldn't forget. I'd brought them all with me: Essam, Samantha, Yasmeen—who'd have been better off wrapped in cellophane with "Don't Touch" written on it—Marcia, Karim. Then I remembered the trip Yasmeen was going on and I realized that if I'd been in a more peaceful state of mind, I might've taken that as a message from Hind. Hind had had the same idea. She and her club had traveled to most of the provinces in Egypt; the reason she'd joined the Expedition Club was so she could see every patch of the country. She was always trying to get me to do the same, but, as much as I loved her, I hadn't been anywhere except for Cairo, the seaside resorts, and now, finally, Minya. I'd worked in the Gulf countries and I'd visited America, but I hadn't seen my own country.

Yasmeen and Hind shared a love for Egypt, but I didn't take her trip as a sign; it was just a coincidence. I wasn't going to transform my desire to be with Hind into a bridge for Yasmeen to walk across— Yasmeen, whom I could no longer stand. I didn't want to talk to a soul; I had enough, what with the troubles of the souls that clung to me. I had enough of the delusions they'd made incarnate; incarnations that never held up for long in the face of time. I wasn't going to attribute any of Hind's qualities to Yasmeen anymore, no matter how similar their long eyelashes were, or their thick eyebrows that they never trimmed, or their fine fingernails, dirty with pen-ink, or any of the other insignificant details. Hind was a celestial being, unique, and the chance of finding someone like her once every five hundred years was less than one in a million. This era certainly wasn't going to see another one like her.

Karim wasn't like all the other street kids. The world had swept him away so he swept up everything he had and everything he could get his hands on. As his world grew darker, he drowned himself in oceans of glue and checked out of reality. He looked like an insignificant, mangy dwarf when you saw him begging in the street, but, back in his lair, he'd puff out his chest, his arm would unfold, his voice would boom. He could control a group of professional criminals all on his own. A state of humanity grew between us the more I visited and stayed with them. Karim was like my fixer. If one of them started making stuff up, for example, a glare from Karim was all it took to get him to take it back and start telling his story straight again. But Warda was his cruel wound. Even though she'd had him locked up and even though he'd taken revenge by exiling her from downtown, when I'd talk to him about it, it was as if I were picking at his scabs; it brought him nearly to tears. He didn't care who she slept with, whether there was one of them or a hundred; he only kept constant tabs on her—though she didn't know it—because he was afraid someone was going to hurt her and he wanted to save her. Street kids have hearts, too, and when they fall in love they don't hide behind the symbolism of poetry. They don't pretend like they're going to abandon their families for their beloved; street kids don't have anything to abandon. And if, having fallen in love, they should fail in love, their bleeding wounds will eat away at them up until the very end.

I hadn't been sleeping well and, to add to that, Zaynab's father woke me up early after he'd finished working in the field. I didn't normally take my tea with milk, but I drank it like that in Zaynab's memory, and I enjoyed it as much as she used to enjoy it when we went out together. I walked around the house and everything seemed familiar. It was as if I'd been there before. I knew almost every brick in the place. Did Zaynab's sleep-talking have anything to do with that? I wasn't sure.

I went fishing, a few steps away from the house, but I came back empty-handed. That pleased her father, but I didn't see why: I was happy to eat what he'd caught. I helped her sister, Safiya, with her schoolwork in the afternoon and I spent a lot of time playing with Ahmad. Ahmad was ten years old and both his arms were crippled as a result of the meningitis he'd had when he was still nursing. He was hard of hearing, spoke with a stutter, and was frightened by any sudden noise. I avoided bringing Zaynab up because I didn't want to slip up and tell them something that could've got her in trouble, but her mother was always ready with a question about her daughter. She started out with small talk and then she surprised me: "Does Zaynab call you?"

"No," I answered hesitantly.

Her mother shook her head. "She called us when she first got there, but she hasn't called since." The devil on my shoulder sprung to life and said that Zaynab had run away and that she'd never be able to come back to face that wretched poverty, which I'd seen with my own eyes, and her family's great hopes, which must've felt like an anchor around her neck. That she felt she could never live up to all those demands, not even if she became a professional prostitute. That she'd been driven to the logical solution: escape.

I realized I was on a failed mission, as usual, to force myself into their lives, and that they, in turn, would force themselves into my life as the days passed and no news came from Zaynab. Maybe they knew there was no news agency that had sent their daughter overseas, and it didn't bother them that there was no bureau there, no plane ticket. Maybe they'd accuse me of covering for her or maybe they'd kill me. It didn't matter. I'd been sinking into a lake of flowing shit for years and I wasn't going to survive it. My only problem was that it seemed to be taking me a long time to drown.

When I snapped out of my reverie, her mother was looking at me. I faked a smile and said, "I was thinking about all this work I'm behind on." When she stood up to leave, I took an envelope out of my pocket and handed it to her.

Her expression turned surly. "What's in the envelope?" I quickly said it was money I'd borrowed from Zaynab before I'd gone to Algeria. When I got back, I found out that Zaynab had gone abroad and I didn't know who to give it to, so I asked the newspaper for her address and took the opportunity of this assignment to bring it to you.

She didn't seem convinced. "Where's my daughter going to get all that money?" she asked as she looked inside the envelope. I hadn't expected that reaction: there was only two thousand pounds in the envelope. You couldn't really call that a lot. I told her everything I'd planned to say: that Zaynab had joined in on a savings pool with all of us at the office and that it'd been her turn to win the money. She'd used it to help me pay for my trip and I was supposed to have paid her back when I got there, but I ran into some money trouble. And then when I called her to ask her to give me a little longer, Zaynab had sworn by everything that was holy that she wouldn't accept any money from me until after I got back to Egypt because she didn't need it.

Her mother turned the envelope over in her hands and then she tossed it onto the sofa next to me. "I'll go get Abu Ahmad."

That was what I'd been dreading. Zaynab's father was a stern, stonefaced man. His brother used to tease him for having only one son, a cripple. When we were out fishing, I'd been too scared to give him the money so I rethought my plan. I figured it was better to give it to her mother, but then she'd gone and ruined everything. Now she was calling for the guy I'd been afraid of! As soon as her father walked in, I was hit by the daggers shooting out of his eyes. He sat beside me, but he didn't say anything. The silence only made me more nervous. He and the mother were exchanging meaningful glances that I couldn't decipher. All of a sudden, he said, "Did you finish the report you were writing?"

"I finished most of it, and I'll finish the rest of it tomorrow in Minya."

He asked a troubling question next: "Did you really come down here for your newspaper work?" I nodded. "So then what's all this about money?"

I had to fight hard to keep the tone of my voice from betraying me. "As I explained to Umm Ahmad, it's a debt I have to repay. I just figured it made sense to stop by here on my way to Minya."

Her mother whispered in a hoarse voice, "Aren't you ashamed, son, to give us charity like that? Even if you don't care about us, you should think of your co-worker."

I realized, then, the knot of the issue and untied it in an instant. "I'm ashamed that you'd think I'd do such a thing. How could I give you charity when my family's poorer than you all? Sure, we live in Cairo, but our lifestyle isn't that different from yours. If me paying the money I owe is going to bother you, I'll just leave it at the newspaper until Zaynab gets back, or I can leave it with you and you can ask her about it when she calls. When I accepted your invitation to stay here, I thought Zaynab had told you all about me, about how we're friends, but it's obvious she didn't mention it. Anyway, I'm sorry for the misunderstanding. I'm sorry that's what you thought I was trying to do."

With that little speech, I gave it back to them twice as good as I'd got. They were inclined to believe me, and her mother, her words dripping with joy, reassured me that Zaynab had told her all about me. Her father shook my hand and picked up the envelope. "If you need some money, just take it and you can give it back later," he said. I thanked him.

Her mother started treating me more intimately after that. Perhaps she'd got the message I'd been sending: she thought I was going to marry Zaynab, so she went on and on about what good habits Zaynab had, how pleasant and loving she was, and how she worried about her family. I didn't want to sever the string her mother was clinging to so I shrewdly encouraged it by suggesting that as soon as Zaynab got back we'd come for a visit together. Her mother was so happy she almost flew off the ground—anyone with a daughter like Zaynab was certain to be plagued by constant worry. I put her mind at rest, but I didn't make any straightforward promises. I relied on my intuition that Zaynab would never come back; even if she did, the chances of me being alive were slim. But if I were still alive, I wouldn't have had any problem about marrying her. After all, what harm does it do a ewe to be flayed after it's been slaughtered? I decided I'd leave early in the morning even though her mother wanted me to stay. They sat with me for a long time after dinner. Her father didn't go beyond being hospitable, even if he did seem slightly affectionate. We sat around watching local TV, following the Israeli armed forces' invasion of Gaza. The anchor was summing up the latest news.

When I got to Cairo, I sat watching the satellite channels for hours, nervous, fearful, aggravated, furious. I could see that the old Ottoman censorship was still weighing down on our chests and the censors were still living among us. They presented the news of Israel's aggression against Gaza just as they'd done with the Bolshevik Revolution in 1917: "A fight broke out in Russia yesterday."

23

ESSAM OPENED HIS BRIEFCASE. He wrote down the combination and stuck little handwritten labels on the keys for his apartment, the cabinets, his office, and his studio. He told me to shut off the gas and the water and close up the windows. Then he wrote it all down for me because he didn't trust my poor memory and he told me to pay the rent if he chose to stay in Singapore for good. I'd gone by his place to take him over to the al-Talabiya house to pick up the paintings he was going to use in his upcoming Cairo exhibition, but instead he took me to some unknown sector of the universe: he'd decided to move to Singapore. He paid no attention to me as I reminded him that in the past, he'd said that would never happen. He simply repeated some old Sufi-mantras and verses, and finished it all off with, "It's God's will." He hid behind that rather than coming out and saying it was Samantha's will. I couldn't get him to reconsider. I couldn't sway him an ant's breadth. I couldn't even get him to delay his trip until after the exhibition. The sadness, despair, and longing all started mixing, in unequal amounts, in his eyes and I was moved by the look of them; shining and bright at one moment, dark and depressed at the next. He'd decided he was going to go and the impossible itself wouldn't have been able to stop him.

Awad was too giddy about his wife Aisha's protruding belly to listen to what I had to say. He rubbed it the whole time we were sitting there. He swooned with joy and knelt down lovingly to listen to what was happening inside. He told me to come have a listen; I was extremely embarrassed, as was Aisha. I was losing my patience and Aisha could either sense it or else she realized that I needed to be alone with Awad. She stood up, excusing herself, and left the living room. Awad, at his most ecstatic, leaped to his feet and walked beside her, rubbing her back. He touched her belly and hugged her, careful not to press against her stomach. Then he stepped backward and put his hand on her back to support her. Aisha giggled, but my irritation was boiling over; I was an inch away from storming out of that lunatic's house. Aisha walked as fast as she could out of the room and pointed back at me as she tried to keep him from following her. He remembered himself, and me, and came to sit beside me, thank God. My doctor had remarked that I suffered from depression and mania. I knew what depression was, but I had no idea about mania. That was until I saw Awad. He was whistling and slapping his thigh rhythmically, to European and Arabic beats. I caught his hand. He could see I was anxious so he kept quiet. As soon as I mentioned Essam, he nodded, raising his hand, and started talking. I was surprised that he knew all about Essam's decision to move to Singapore. But he also knew something worse, something more bitter: Essam tried to call her, but she wouldn't answer. She'd let her friends answer instead. She ignored his texts and emails, and when he saw her online, she'd sign off as soon as he tried to talk to her. All that had happened in the past three months, but I hadn't heard a word about it from Awad, who'd been busy with his marriage, or Essam, who'd been trying to look strong in front of me. He hoped to emerge victorious so he blamed Samantha for a decision he'd made. But she'd pinned him by using a few little feminine tricks that I hadn't expected Essam to fall for. Awad said she started off by making a big fuss about how bitterly lonely she was without him in Singapore and then she reneged on their agreement that he'd stay in Egypt and visit her frequently. She'd crassly asked him to give up his art and go into business with her and then she stopped responding to him altogether. Awad said that he'd talked to Essam about it a lot and that he'd told him not to give in to her, but even though Essam had listened to Awad some of the time, in the end, he took off his trousers.

Marcia liked hearing everything I was telling her about Essam, and she especially liked it when I cursed Samantha. For my sake, she almost entirely hid her smile. I'd never been angrier than I was when both she and Awad laughed me down for insisting that Essam would never give in to Samantha and settle there permanently. Once again, he'd performed the duties of his loyalty and betrayed me. I got away from Marcia as quickly as I could so that my rage wouldn't get out of control.

I sat drinking, trying to clear my mind, but what do you expect? After I'd come to trust Samantha, after I'd come to adore her passion for Essam, hoping to find someone like her for myself, she reverted to the image I'd had of her at the beginning. She took off the veil to show us her hideous face. She hadn't actually revealed anything, though; it was still ugly even when it was covered up. All she'd done was throw a handful of dirt in our faces to hide her ugliness. And when the sky cleared, we could see her for what she really was. And now she was dropping my poor friend just because he couldn't stand to stay in her country for very long. Does the idiot think she's ever going to find someone as talented, good-natured, classy, and generous as Essam? Is she going to replace him with one of her monkey brain-eating countrymen, or one of the visionless foreign investors there? If it's her vagina that's causing her distress, then let her fill it up with cement while she waits for him to return. Our grandmothers in Upper Egypt used to do that. Their husbands left them to work as forced labor excavating the canal or as builders in the oil states for years and years. They didn't complain about having to wait. Just receiving a letter, or a cassette tape he'd recorded, or some cheap fabric, or a promise he was coming back delivered by a co-worker was more than enough for them. They'd fondle his belongings in the dark of night for years while he was away. Not one of them asked for a divorce, or even thought about asking. There were no affairs; none of them had to have sex with a human, mineral, or animal to quench any desire. As far as that filthy woman was concerned, Essam could either be a millstone between her legs, grinding her flour, or else she'd mow his head off with a sickle. The schmuck really loved her and she was the only one who could set him free.

24

MARCIA WAS SITTING between her friends, resting her head against Diana's chest, as they watched one of the satellite news channels. She gave me a kiss and hugged me and sat me down next to her. Diana was holding the remote and Marcia was trying to act like she wasn't worried that one of them was going to say something that would upset me. She let me watch for a little while and then she squeezed my hand, meaning we should go off together. When we were alone, she asked if I'd made any progress with the project. I gave her a curt answer. Then she asked if I minded if her friends stayed for a while, and I could go on the Internet for a bit until she sent them away. I said I wasn't going to stay even though I'd originally planned on spending the night there. Something was bothering me so I changed my mind. She couldn't understand why I had to leave so I told her Karim had called me on my mobile a few minutes before I came up and said he wanted to see me about something important. That was true and the surprise of it distracted her from guessing about my early exit. She seemed concerned. "You don't think it has anything to do with us, do you?" she asked.

"Nothing ordinary or out of the ordinary happens to Karim, it's all the same to him. Most likely, he just wants some money."

Marcia sighed. "Do you want some money to give him?"

"I have cash," I said. "And anyway, don't let them get used to it. I know them better than you do." She nodded and took my hand and asked me to come back later, whispering that she'd have got rid of them by then. I kissed her and left.

I'd arranged to meet Karim downtown and as soon as I sat down, I saw him coming from some distance away, leaning over as he walked, barefoot, his left hand folded up. He'd huff some glue and then he'd try to focus until he could pick out his mark among the foreigners. He'd go up to their table and beg for money until the waiter or one of the tourist-spongers they were with chased him off. I was smoking, exhaling angrily as I watched him, like a swing at a mulid festival: sometimes coming close, sometimes at the other end of the street. Boredom . . . boredom . . . boredom. I was fed up with waiting for the Amazing Huffing Kid. Finally, he saw me and came over. I gestured to the waiter to keep away and had Karim sit down in front of me. I didn't care if the other patrons were nosy. Karim didn't start talking until he got his hands on a glass of mango juice; he tossed the straw to the ground and drank it blissfully. He took a cigarette out of his pocket and offered it to me, but I shook my head. Then he moved closer to me and whispered, "Are you coming over to our place today?" I cursed him for an idiot, clenching my teeth to keep my voice down. I'd told him time and time again that the two of us would agree beforehand whenever I was going to stay the night, and it was all conditional on him not telling anyone about it; not the girl he was hot for or the boy he was mounting. A donkey would've understood. Karim was shaping up to be worse than a jackass. Everything I'd said about his brilliance was bullshit. He was looking at me; he seemed happy that I was frustrated. Then, with gleaming eyes, he lowered his voice and came so close that his breath offended me and I had to lean back. "It's just that the pasha asked to see me this morning," he said.

"Who's the pasha?"

He smiled. "The pasha of this area here, of Abdeen not Say-yida Zaynab."

I enunciated clearly so he'd understand, "What the hell are you talking about? Abdeen? Sayyida? Slow down."

He winked. "The pasha's the station chief."

He had my attention, but I didn't want to swallow the bait. "And what does the Abdeen station chief want from you? Did that girl Warda make another complaint?"

His thoughts drifted for a moment and then he shook his head. "Not because of Warda. Because of you two."

Now, the silliness starts. Karim was trying to manipulate me and if he detected any weakness, the blackmail would never end. I resigned myself to being patient. "I'm sure he asked you what I was doing with you all at night?"

Karim was indignant. "He doesn't know you spend the night with us. He's the station chief for Abdeen, not Sayyida."

Go to hell, you dog! You're going to start playing word games with me!

The anxiety I'd been feeling ever since he'd called almost made me pummel him, but I held it together so that I still appeared relaxed. It was quiet for a stretch, but he must've thought I'd said something because he said, "Not you. Not the foreign lady."

"What does the foreign lady have to do with it? Haven't I told you, you sixtieth-generation son-of-a-bitch, that none of you are to mention her? Ever?"

"I didn't say anything about her! Just hear me out, Boss. The point is . . . ." At that point, he lost his train of thought. I gave him a cigarette to calm him down and get him talking sensibly. He lit it. "It's just that, no offense, there's a protest tomorrow at Talaat Harb. I don't know what for. And the pasha—I don't have to tell you—knows that this here's our area. He knows I call the shots so when I went to see him, he told me to bring five or six good kids from my crew with me and then he sent us to this sweet, humongous house and the people there gave us money and soda."

Where's the story, you bore?

He seemed to realize I wasn't keeping up so he winked his dingy eye and, looking over either shoulder, he said, "The truth is, the pasha said that as soon as we saw anyone taking pictures or carrying a bag and handing out leaflets or any of the stuck-up girls who like to shout and scream, we should steal the cameras and bags and feel the girls up."

I listened intently, intrigued by what he was saying, but I didn't understand how it affected me. "What does any of this have to do with me?"

"Don't you and that lady go and film with them? I've seen you. Drop her a hint, tell her to forget about it and skip the protest tomorrow."

My ears perked up, and despite feeling sincerely grateful for his concern, I challenged him: "Why should I?"

"Those guys are no good, Boss. Take it from me. And the foreign lady doesn't need the roughing up," he whispered. I took out some money to send him on his way, but he refused to take it and drifted off.

My yearning for Essam took me to the Indian Cultural Center, where I loitered in the Mawlana Abu Kalam Azad Hall, flipping through books on yoga and spiritual control over the self, watching the people who'd just finished their classes, looking at the sculpture exhibition that was on display. The receptionist knew me from all the times I went there with Essam and waited for him out in the hall. She didn't ask me if I wanted to join in. She didn't hand me a form. She didn't say, "Essam's not here." She didn't tell me about the membership benefits. She just smiled and brought me a cup of green tea with the utmost grace. She wasn't Indian or foreign, she was Egyptian, but just being in that place gave her a very Indian quality.

Boredom . . . boredom . . . boredom . . . crushing boredom, and my feet took me to Marcia once again, bringing what Karim had said along with me as a funny anecdote. I already knew everything he'd told me. It wasn't news to me, or to Marcia, or to the protesters, but I felt like I should tell her anyway so that she'd feel as grateful toward me as I'd felt toward Karim. The surprising thing, though, was that Marcia was speechless for a few moments after she heard my story. She was thinking, her head drifting backward, her fingers twirling at the ends of her hair. Finally, after some hesitation, she said, "If you don't feel like coming with me, it's no big deal, but I'm going to go take pictures."

It was beyond infuriating that she thought I was worried about whether I should go to the protest. Protests were all I had left. I wasn't part of any official political groups anymore, any secret cells; shouting at the top of my lungs, getting riled up, watching a few old friends who'd become capitalists or informants or Muslim Brotherhood or spectators, that was all I had left.

It was a demonstration against the despicable treatment of Iraqi prisoners of war by the Americans at the Abu Ghraib prison. Marcia was keen on covering the protest and I guess she figured my fervor for protesting against Zionist activity in Palestine was stronger than it was for protesting against the crime of putting prisoners on display. What else could she have meant when she said she was going to go without me? Maybe she was taunting me? She just watched me silently, worried, waiting for me to speak as my thoughts drifted for a while. Since I was captive to a state of mind that was deteriorating—because Essam had left, because of what I'd seen on the satellite channels, because of Marcia's presence as an American in my life—I shouted at her as if I were chucking dirty washing water in her face and couldn't give a damn about the consequences: "I'm going. I'm going to protest against those sons of bitches and what they're doing to us!"

She trembled slightly as I shouted at her, but then she moved closer and held me. She patted me on the back, as if I were a fitful child, and whispered, "This war's awful. People are dying and being tortured every day. When are people going to stop acting like animals and learn to get along?"

She reminded me of the composition classes I'd taken as a child and taught after graduation. Her empty words disgusted me. I didn't feel like eating or drinking. I chewed Julia the maid out because she was too slow about bringing my cigarettes to me in the bedroom. Marcia followed me inside after she'd got rid of Julia, who'd been standing by the door, frozen by my anger. Marcia lay beside me, watching television. I said, "Good night," and turned my back to her and when she asked me if the sound of the television would bother me, I said yes and she shut it off. She didn't dare touch me; she respected the airy border that separated us. We lay in the same bed, her burning breath flowing over my body, reaching my nose. I could feel her heartbeat and I pictured her chest as it rose and fell in the time between breathing in and out until she was entirely still and asleep. I couldn't believe she trusted me so much. *Marcia, do you have any idea what I'm thinking about right now? Have you any idea what I might do? Any idea what insanity might drive me to?*

25

WE WENT TO THE PROTEST Karim had warned us against going to and Marcia photographed as much as she could before the police broke up the crowd. I saw Karim and his friends, hovering around the protesters, but as soon as he saw me, he ducked his head in shame and I lost sight of him. When the police started getting rough with the protesters, I pulled Marcia away so she'd stop provoking them with the lens she was pointing at them. She obeyed grudgingly and followed me, taking a step backward for every two she took forward, as I slipped down one of the alleys. When we stopped to catch our breath at a coffeehouse nearby, she started getting on my case for making her leave so soon. Her passport could've protected her, but who was going to protect me? If I got arrested, old files from when I got arrested as a student would be passed around along with notes on my relationships with foreigners, and pictures and footage they'd taken showing my participation in the protest, and copies of petitions I'd signed; they might have even accused me of being a spy. Sometimes, I thought that would've been the best of all outcomes and, at other times, I felt that fate was expecting something of more consequence out of me. All the contradictory traits were one in me: bravery and cowardice, timidity and audacity, romance and realism, love of life and its pleasures and nihilism. But I was the master of my own decisions and a thousand Marcias wouldn't have been able to get me in line behind her. She was pissed that I wasn't saying anything so she finished her anise tea and said, "I'm going back." I smiled and told her to sit down, but she stayed standing. I pointed to the end of the street near Talaat Harb Square and the stragglers, those fleeing and those pursuing, all moving toward us. She sat back down, sullen. I picked up the camera she'd set on the table as if she were trying to advertise our participation in the protest. She didn't object; she held her bag out and I calmly put the camera inside. "I told you yesterday not to come," she said.

I sipped my coffee for a long time. "What do you think's more important: our movie or chasing after protests with our cameras out?"

She realized I had a point, but she was torn and didn't know how to respond. Then she went on and on justifying her attendance at every manifestation of Egyptian political life. She said she was ecstatic about social activism in Egypt, moved by it, and the beginnings of freedom and democracy that were growing because of student participation, and it all reminded her of Woodstock and the student movements in Paris in the 1960s and in Beijing in the 1990s, and that she was here as a witness to these events, incapable of looking away. She topped it all off with even more blather and I couldn't disguise a mocking grin as I listened to her.

When Marcia's rant came to its pathetic end, I asked her the same question a second time: "What's more important, the movie or this farce?" She lowered her head, yielding like an old, barren woman when her husband tells her he's taken a fertile, young girl for a second wife. But I didn't let up until I heard proof that she'd made a choice.

"Our movie." It was tense for a little while, but then she regained her poise, and whispered, "I'm not going to any more protests with you." She sounded like a child whose father has taken away her game and it made me laugh out loud.

"You'll come, but you'll listen," I said. She smiled, her eyes twinkling.

My Passion Week started that night when I went to Karim's hangout and his mates told me he was in jail for a few different things. I didn't dare stay over at the villa without his protection, so I turned around and left. Though the girl who'd said, at first, that Karim was running a little errand and that he'd be back soon was still waving and trying to get me to go upstairs. Karim had told them to look after me, she said. I didn't know how long the jail would have the pleasure of Karim's company so the only thing I could do was wait; wait and try to fool Marcia into thinking I was still on the job.

On the next day of Passion Week, I had a long phone conversation with Awad, who sprung the news on me that Essam was back in Egypt and that he'd divorced Samantha. Awad had bumped into him by accident at the Mashrabiya Gallery where Essam had been negotiating to book the gallery again since he'd backed out of his old agreement when he took off and went to Singapore. Awad added that Essam looked like he was in a good frame of mind, that he'd got over the shock of it all and returned a new man. When I hung up the phone, I knew I didn't trust Awad's description of Essam's state of mind. I knew Essam better than he did. Essam was good at coming across like a floating iceberg a lot of the time, like a dormant volcano, but then he knew me as well as I knew him and he hadn't thought to call me or ask for his spare keys back or even call Awad. If Awad hadn't bumped into him by accident, we would've probably still thought he was back in Singapore. He wouldn't have been able to appear wounded in front of the people closest to him; I was one of those people. I was going to go to him; I was going to face him and see if there was any Samantha left in him, or whether she'd left him in pieces.

I embraced Essam and he stayed in my arms for a bit. He told me to sit and as he collected himself, he asked me about work and how things were going with Marcia. We both laughed about Awad and how giddy he was about his unborn child. Essam didn't make any sarcastic comments about my not stopping by his apartment while he'd been away. And I didn't want to disturb the turtle shell he was hiding under. I was going to be there for him. I cooked dinner and then I brought in a bottle of whisky from the kitchen and we started to drink. I watched him as he sipped from his glass, holding the liquid in his mouth for a few moments as if he were gargling, slowly soaking it up. That was how the experts did it so they could get drunk quickly. His eyes turned the color of dark earth. "I divorced her," he said. I didn't say anything so he went on, and it was as if he could barely see me, "I got there and I couldn't find her in any of the places she'd taken me to. She refused to see me. For ten days, we talked only over the phone. The only thing she said was 'I can't bear to see you. Please divorce me.' I kept sending her messages through her friends that I just wanted to see her the once, but she wouldn't budge." There was a long silence that I didn't want to break. Suddenly, Essam looked at me like he was seeing me for the first time and smiled feebly. "I offered to stay in Singapore and work for her, or work at the landfill. I told her we could have children and I'd look after them like a nanny. I'd have watched her friends' kids, too. I told her I'd work in her company's cafeteria. I'd clean her toilets."

Essam started to cry. I was scared I'd say something stupid or that I was so angry at her that I'd blurt something out that would hurt him more or that he'd be mad at me for insulting Samantha the slut. Essam came back from Singapore to deliver the dagger that he was stabbing me with: "Over the phone, I told her I wasn't going to leave Singapore until I saw her and I wasn't going to divorce her until she explained to me what her reasons were. Two days later, her close friend Amanda came to see me and said that Samantha had fallen in love with a fellow Singaporean, and that she wanted to put an end to her life with me. I didn't believe her. Samantha used to call me in Cairo every day. She never worried about the time or the cost: an hour, two hours, those stretches when we'd just say sweet nothings to each other. Those daily calls ended just two months before I went to see her: Samantha told me she was really busy with work and she had no spare time, but she said not to worry about her. Amanda said Samantha had met someone else that same day, the day she cut off contact with me. He entered her life lightning-fast and was never going to leave was what Samantha told her."

Essam turned to me, hot tears running down his face, "How could this other guy have already given her what I gave her over the past two years?" I didn't say anything; I wanted to let him get everything that was festering inside him out. "I was determined to see her face to face. I threatened to kill myself. I made Amanda think that I was capable of doing something crazy. We negotiated through her friends, mostly Amanda; she was sitting with me when she finally called Samantha and told her that I'd agreed to divorce her on one condition: that she ask me for it in person. Samantha picked a time at the weekend. It infuriated me that she picked a day off to talk to me about getting a divorce, as if nothing's as important as work. But I went along with it and I was there right on time. I don't know how I got there. I don't know how I spent those days before we saw each other. She came a few minutes late, looking harried. Her assistant took her coat and helped her sit down. Amanda had done Samantha's eye shadow, and it was as if they'd been trying to kill me. I thought she looked pale because she was regretting what she'd done to me, but then I remembered that Amanda was a makeup expert and that the setting and the dim lighting were definitely her choice. Samantha's makeup had Amanda's touch. It was all to create this sad, dark mood to make it easier to get me to go along with what she wanted. Samantha didn't shake my hand or look at me for very long. The stupid lighting made her look like a ghost. I wouldn't have known for sure whether it was actually her or someone else if it hadn't been for the delicate finger she trained on me or her lips, which quaked as they uttered heavy words the least of which were, 'I want a divorce now.' I stormed out and Amanda ran after me. She didn't let me go until I promised to meet her at the Egyptian Embassy the next morning to finalize the divorce. It was the next day in the blink of an eye, and there I was surrendering to her lawyer completely. I ended what we'd had together without any conditions or delay."

Essam was crying and I was holding him. His mouth was pressed against my chest so I could barely hear his choked voice. I let go of him so he'd settle down. Sadly, I was almost happy to see him distraught, gleeful that his relationship with Samantha had failed, and yet—at the same time—I was almost out of my head with worry for him in that state. Then he said something that really made me angry. "Her attorney told me she'd relinquished any claims she had under our law and was offering to split her assets with me according to her law. Her friends and the legal adviser at the Embassy were all telling me to take her money as if I deserved it, but I didn't listen to them."

"Are you an idiot? Her money's better than she is."

He downed the rest of the bottle and was gasping violently and whimpering. He had tears in his eyes. "I'm alright. I'll be all right. No Samantha, no woman's going to be able to break me. My country means more to me than anything else and I'm going to make it up to her for betraying her."

Essam wasn't making any sense. "Who betrayed who?"

Sounding deeply determined, he said, "My country . . . I betrayed her and left her for another. I deserve everything I'm getting."

I didn't need any more clarification; I didn't need him to walk me through the deep corridors of his mind, all of it pouring out like when a patient comes out of sedation. I got up to leave. "I'll see you soon," I said, and I could hear him muttering behind me as I shut the door.

The crowning touch, or what was left of Passion Week, was cruel and horrible. We were out one night at the Greek Club when one of us got a call from Switzerland saying there'd been an awful accident at one of the theaters in Beni Suef. We asked the bartender to turn on the television and we flipped through all the local and satellite channels, but we couldn't find any mention of it. We knew the theater festival was taking place there; a lot of our theater-critic, actor, and director friends were participating so we tried to call them, but either the lines were busy or they weren't picking up. We took that as reassurance and carried on with our evening as usual.

Usually after a night out like that, I sleep in and don't answer the phone, but Marcia shook me awake and told me there'd been a fire at the theater in Beni Suef. The phone lines weren't down, but my friends weren't answering their mobiles. The phone was ringing constantly with calls from friends in Cairo telling me about the tragedy and where people were gathering to receive the casualties. I went to the Academy of Arts with Marcia and we stood in the courtyard of the Theater Institute. They brought the coffins in on trucks. The coffins were uncovered, but they threw some tattered old carpets and tablecloths over them. The bodies were stuck in the positions they'd been in when the fire reached them. Most of them were squatting and you could almost see their disgusting burns under the filthy veils that covered them. We were in the center of a huge crowd of mourners; Marcia was crying like a waterfall, but I couldn't. There were more than fifty victims and I knew most of them. I'd worked with them, writing the occasional operetta or poem, or I'd met them in intellectual circles. Frightened by our collective agitation, the biers set off for the Umraniya Mosque. We prayed over the bodies at the mosque, and then we left. Each one of us had our memories of them and we also heard the wrenching story of their death: they'd kept them out in the street for hours; the private hospital across from the theater had refused to take them in. We heard about how when His Excellency the Minister of Health went to visit them at seven in the morning after their night of burning, the nurses had tipped them onto the floor so they could change the sheets before the Minister's visit. The coffins went off to their final resting place in those tattered covers. And as the Minister of Culture stood there next to us, perfumed and dressed in his bespoke Armani suit, waiting to receive the bodies, his aides didn't even think to get some appropriate winding-sheets and decent covers to dignify those martyrs.

Those were tense days: I threw myself into sit-ins at the High Court, protesting, signing petitions. For the first time in years, I was active, standing up for those theater lovers, who'd gone to bring contemporary theater to life, to find new artists, to enlighten, all in return for pennies. They'd gone—like they always did—because the theater was their first and last love, their first and last passion. The Minister of Culture concluded the investigation summarily: the producer of the festival had been responsible for the tragedy. May God keep you, O Minister!

26

KARIM WAS STILL IN JAIL and Marcia had started to worry that production was falling behind. I had to tell her about it so that she'd see there was nothing I could do. She did all she could to convince me to go back and stay with the kids without Karim, bribing them with money and clothes so that they'd let me do my work in peace, but I shouted at her. I reminded her about things she seemed to have forgotten: the jugs full of acid, the alcohol and kerosene Molotov cocktails they were ready to use if anyone, or any group, ever threatened their safety. They had every type of what the government likes to call 'white weapons,' not to mention a lack of fear and a lack of conscience that could drive them to kill. I told her about how they'd quarrel over the pettiest things and settle their disagreements in blood. *Money won't stop them, Marcia, it'll just make them kill the goose who's laying the golden eggs.* I'd wake up, if I woke up at all, stripped of my money and my memories. Without Karim there, I wouldn't dare go upstairs to retrieve the things I'd stowed away. Thank God I hadn't left the camera or my notes there. Everything I'd left behind could be replaced.

Marcia finally conceded. She looked worried and as she kissed me she told me I should've mentioned it all before. Actually, she went overboard trying to show me how much she cared and begged me not to finish the film since it was so dangerous; the hell with the movie and the money we were going to make. I laughed so hard it pissed her off. I told her we'd finish the movie, but she just had to be patient. She understood.

I'd seen Essam once or twice in the tent where we paid our condolences to the families of the victims of Beni Suef, but we didn't talk. The tragedy had taken our minds off of everything else. I didn't need the al-Talabiya house anymore—I didn't need anything in this squalid world—so I decided to sell it. I'd sell the furniture, the pillars that were never built over, and the roof that was never laid. I needed Essam to get all his stuff out of there. I also needed Hagg Hamid al-Helu to find me a buyer who was going to pay what he wanted to pay without any haggling or dragging of feet.

Hagg Hamid al-Helu greeted me warmly and asked me inane questions like "Are you married yet?" and "You're still a bachelor?" "Shame on you, son," he said. "Marriage is half your religion." I was choking on the stream of admonition and advice pouring out of him, being jackhammered into my head. I really wanted to hear about Ahmad but there was no news about him except that he'd finally been dismissed from the petroleum company and now he had all the time in the world to sell bassbousa, kunafa, and tapes of prayers and Qur'an recitation. The only news was that Shahinaz had started teaching at an Islamic daycare near their house.

When we ran out of small talk, I told him I wanted to sell the al-Talabiya house as soon as possible. He surprised me by saying he was prepared to loan me whatever I needed so that I wouldn't have to sell the house. I could see the fatherly good in him, but I simply smiled and told him that the house didn't belong to the family anymore: I'd bought it from my sisters a long time ago so it belonged to me alone. I didn't need any financial help, praise be to God. I was doing fine; I just didn't have any need for the house anymore. He nodded and told me to give him two weeks so he could find the right buyer at the right price. When he asked me how much I wanted to sell the house for, I quickly answered: same as the other houses in the area, no more, no less.

When I left, I knew for certain that my house would soon belong to Hagg Hamid, and that he would pass it down to his son, Ahmad al-Helu, and his wife, Shahinaz, and that her old dream would be realized: Ahmad al-Helu would make love to her on my bed. The thought of that must have put me at ease because I walked along, whistling. I was as happy as a loon; it was as if I were the one Ahmad al-Helu was going to be making love to on that bed.

The receptionist told me that Essam was almost done with his yoga class and she handed me one of the magazines the Center published. She asked me to write an article or poem for them and said that it'd be an honor for the magazine and things along those lines. I thanked her and slipped away to thumb through the magazine. I had to smile at Essam's tricks: he'd complicated things for me with the receptionist who was now going to ask me, "Where's the article?" "Where's the poem?" every time I came to see Essam, and so I'd decide never to go there again and thus Essam would be free of me. He knew I was lazy and that I had very specific writing rituals. And he knew that I got annoyed when people pestered me and it killed me whenever someone asked me to do something I wasn't going to do.

Essam came out. He didn't seem happy or unhappy to see me. He hugged me neutrally, the way you hug an old classmate who looks familiar, but whose name you can't remember. That greeting really upset me. To make up for it, he said he'd been really busy getting ready for his exhibition and following the recent tragedies (by which he meant the events in Beni Suef), just like I'd been busy with the movie Marcia and I were making. I didn't know what to do: here was Essam, my only friend, and he knew nothing about the movie. I hadn't told him about it, not because I was afraid of what he'd say or that he'd spill the beans about what Marcia and I were doing—plus, back when the film was still just an idea, I'd asked Marcia to keep a lid on it. Maybe I hadn't told him because, deep down, I knew I wasn't going to go through with it; so that he wouldn't ask me how it was coming along every time I saw him. But Essam had found out and maybe that was why he was upset. I started to explain and justify, irritated that his smile grew the more I spoke. I stopped talking. I demanded to know how he'd heard about it. He was grinning. Awad had told him. I knew then that the damage was more widespread than I'd thought: in addition to Awad also being upset that I hadn't told him what I was working on and feeling that I wasn't treating him like a friend, that meant that Marcia had told him along with Evelyn, Diana, and all her foreigner friends. She'd made me look like an idiot because I'd never said a word about it when I saw them. Marcia had violated our secret. She didn't give a damn about the consequences; she had the protection of her American passport. All those thoughts crashing around in my head must have made me look thoroughly annoyed and angry because Essam tried to calm me down and swore he wasn't mad. He said it was perfectly normal, something between me and Marcia that no one had any right to know about until it was finished. I shouted for him to stop. The reassuring phrases he was serving me were more sarcastic than they were sincere. Essam watched me silently as I looked at his sprouting, unpruned beard. I didn't say anything about it. I asked him to set a time to come by the al-Talabiya house to pick up his stuff before I vacated it. He didn't bother to ask why I was giving it up. Instead, he asked me to store his sketches and paintings at my apartment downtown or else to sell them off to some rag-and-bone man because they represented an artistic phase he'd since outgrown. Plus they weren't worth anything; the frames were cheap and couldn't be reused.

Just as I'd expected, Hagg Hamid al-Helu bought the al-Talabiya house. He gave me part of the money and held onto the rest until after he'd taken possession of it. I offered to sell him the furniture, too, but he didn't seem interested. I wasn't in the mood for haggling back and forth so I left him the furniture as a gift. He took on the expression of a pious sheikh and refused to take it for nothing. He added a little extra to the money he still owed me. A week later, I moved my stuff and Essam's to my apartment downtown.

When I saw Marcia, we had a huge fight. She couldn't come up with any explanation for what she'd done. After all, we'd explicitly agreed. She said most of the people she'd told were friends outside

Egypt and she'd assumed I'd told Awad because he was my friend. None of those excuses placated me. I was shouting and swearing so much that Julia the maid came in more than once and Marcia had to tell her to get out. I'd latched on to Marcia's screw-up and couldn't let it go. She didn't know what to say. She tried to get me to stay, but she just got steadily more confounded until I walked out the door.

On my way home, I knew full well I'd overreacted. For the first time in my relationship with Marcia, I felt like I didn't care what the consequences of my behavior would be. When I got home, I turned out all the lights to help me relax. I could still smell Zaynab's scent; I missed her. The slut hadn't called me since she left, hadn't sent me a text or an email. It was as if I'd never plowed her. As if she hadn't ever seen me, hadn't touched me, hadn't entered my life at all. Then I started to worry about her. What'd happened to her? What'd Julio done to her? Had he left her to beg for her food? Was he a weirdo? Did he murder her and make an abaya out of her skin? Or had she genuinely fallen in love with him and forgotten about her family? Forgotten about me? Had he discovered the secrets of her body and gone mad and locked her up in his house forever? Had she discovered the men of Mexico and decided to pleasure every last one of them? And had yet to complete her mission?

Thinking of Zaynab only made me more depressed. And running away from thoughts of Marcia only added to my worry. When I thought about Karim and his gang, I grew more distraught. And when I thought about myself, I was filled only with sorrow.

27

I FINISHED MOVING my things out of the al-Talabiya house around the time of the most recent Israeli aggression against Lebanon. I switched the television to a news station, letting the sound fill the room as I packed my bags and sifted through my papers—drowning in the details of each sheet, as the stream of news only stirred my blood up more. I packed up Essam's stuff and gathered up my old poems, with Hind's beautifully handwritten comments. And other things of hers: a broken earring I hadn't been able to repair at the time, leftover pins that she'd used to post my poems at my first exhibition at university, some copies of my first collection of poetry, and other things. Every time a memory scattered my thoughts and I plunged down in its wake, the monsters' bombs brought me back to the bitter, squalid reality.

Hagg Hamid al-Helu arrived in a rush, with the driver of a pick-up truck and some movers. He was full of energy, scolding the workers and yelling for them to hurry it up. It was as if he couldn't wait to get rid of me. He pulled me aside and gave me the rest of the money. He counted it out for me, carefully so the workers wouldn't see. Then he whispered to me that they weren't from al-Talabiya, but that they were trustworthy and he took full responsibility for them, but you still had to be careful. He said it'd be better if I didn't ride with them. I should just give them my address and they could deliver my belongings. I smiled and, just to piss him off, I said I'd never dream of riding with them in the pick-up truck; I'd call for a taxi. He grumbled to himself and that made me happy. I imagined him cursing me under his breath for my arrogance. I didn't need his money, but at the same time I couldn't get over how angry I was that he was getting his hands on everything my father had sweated and toiled for. It was as if laughing at that man and the handcart he used to push around was my backhanded way of taking revenge.

Marcia called to invite me to a concert at the Cairo Jazz Club. She wanted to go support Diana's friend who was singing there. I told her I was busy following the developments in the Zionist attack against Lebanon on the satellite channels. She was quiet for a while and then she said, "What's going on is so unfortunate." I didn't say anything. She said she'd skip the concert and stay at home. She said I should come over so we could watch the news together at her place. I turned her down; I made an excuse about being exhausted from moving my stuff out of the al-Talabiya house and being in a bad mood and needing to be alone. She said she'd call again to check on me. I told her there was no point: I was dozing off as I watched the news.

I wasn't sleepy, but I turned off the TV. I was heartsick. I flipped through my first book of poems, the one I put together after Hind's death. I hadn't been able to find a publisher in Egypt so Essam told me to send it to a publishing house in Beirut. I sent copies to three Beiruti publishers, two of them replied, and one printed and published it and sent me a nominal sum and fifty copies. That collection gave me my calling card and helped gain me a little bit of fame early in life. It made the critics take notice of me. That collection was published with a dedication to Hind. It was printed in Beirut, which the bastards were now bombing. Beirut, which had offered Hind a lovely flower, was currently being shattered, being invaded by savages in armored vehicles and on warships. Beirut, which hadn't asked me whether I'd written poems or published a collection before, its residents were sleeping out in the open that night. And Marcia wanted me next to her so she could fill my ears with her bullshit like she'd done before. *What happened to all the good you predicted, Marcia?*

Here's Olmert, "the liberal opposition," as you and your friends used to brag, with his enlightened attitude, capable of solving the crisis and pleasing both sides. Here are Israel's first civilian prime minister and the first civilian minister of defense. The two of them didn't stop the violent crimes when they took power. Now, he's leading a genocidal war against the Palestinians, the Lebanese, the Syrians, and Hezbollah, and whoever else. Every argument I have with Marcia about this brutal group brings us back to the starting point: the only solution is to chuck them all down the nearest sewer. Don't be offended. You yourself used to crow that America only won its true independence after the Civil War between the North and South, which went on for more than four years and resulted in nearly a million casualties and a lake of blood. That was what you called "the price of freedom." So we, too, must sacrifice oceans of blood for our eternal freedom. We don't want a dream that shackles us, or leaders who excel at realist politics and espouse the theory of "a bird in the hand." There's a solution to the problem that'll suit us and everybody else: let's leave that contaminated place for the two of them, Israel and America. Let's leave it all to them, no exceptions. We'll leave voluntarily or compulsorily; carted off or at sword-point, and we'll go to the farthest ends of the earth, to the harshest climate: Siberia, for example, where the temperature reaches minus fifty Celsius in winter. Tell them we'd rather struggle against nature. There, life at its most basic is a struggle to survive: a struggle for warmth; a struggle for food; a struggle to find shelter, four walls and a roof. There might not be many of us left after a few years, but nature will definitely be kinder to us than they are. Nature won't defile our corpses. Nature won't abandon them to savage beasts.

Let them enjoy our land, our climate, our oil, our beliefs. Let them cut us out of history and geography. Let them cut off our supply lines and leave us to face nature. Let them eradicate every one of our genes and keep them out of their so-called civilization. It's no problem if they want to keep a few of us around to play important parts in natural history museums and freak shows and zoos. (Like the picture I found in my things from the al-Talabiya house that's in front of me now. It's a rare picture, published in the magazine *Amazing Photographs* in 1943, of the grand opening of the Berlin Zoo in 1840. The photo, if anyone cares, is of an iron cage at the zoo, surrounded by spectators throwing bananas and peanuts to an African family, who are completely naked but for a few leaves covering their genitals. The family is made up of an old man in his seventies, a father in his late twenties, his wife, and a nursing baby and the sign on the cage reads: "A Family of Savages Captured in the Jungles of Black Africa.")

I got a text message telling me about a protest against the enemy at al-Azhar Mosque after the Friday prayer. I immediately decided I was going to go to the prayer and the march afterward. Marcia was eager to come with me, but I was against it as I'd have had to leave her alone while I prayed. I told her that if she wanted to come, she should meet me there afterward.

The elevator and my chest were almost one; my heart was falling with every floor we passed. Even though I was sure the residential tower was well built, no question about it, it did nothing to ease my anxiety. The lobby was empty but for the security guards, who stood around making jokes. They stopped laughing and greeted me, staring and smiling. I thought for a moment about what they'd say about me when I left: That's the foreign chick's boyfriend . . . her friend . . . her teacher . . . spy . . . tourist-sponger . . . embassy employee . . . whatever.

After the Friday prayer, the masses of security forces were arrayed around us on all sides, but they were keeping out of it. We started marching behind all the slogans and banners announcing the partici-pation of all the political organizations, out-in-the-open ones and underground ones. We repeated the slogans of the Nasserites, the Islamists, and the Communists, and then each one of us started singing his own tune. The supporters of the different groups congregated

225

in different sections of the march. Among the Nasserites, I spotted some of the leftist faces who'd organized us in the past, walking beside those who'd betrayed us and were now cashing in on our struggle. I couldn't find a place for myself among all those different groupings. Then, I found myself walking behind the Islamists. I examined their faces from a short distance away; maybe I'd see Ahmad al-Helu or Shahinaz. I'd have recognized her even if she were hiding behind a thousand veils.

I'd never been angrier about the assaults against the Palestinians and Lebanese; and against us from all those hypocrites. All the accusations they trafficked in, poisoning our opinions of the government and the other opposition groups, became counterfeit once they became leaders and higher-ups in the Muslim Brotherhood or the Nasserites, or leading businessmen. Anyone who'd ever been locked up, even if it were only for a day, tended to his investment on the satellite channels and became a hero.

As the chants grew louder, the harassment from the security forces and the rented thugs, who'd infiltrated the march, increased. At first, the provocations weren't violent, but when a female protester was shoved and a camera was torn out of a journalist's hand, I quickly slipped away down a side street; I didn't bother to search for Marcia. Later when I looked at my mobile, I saw I'd missed three calls from her. I called her back, but she didn't pick up.

I decided to surprise Essam at his studio and get him to give me a straight answer about what to do with the paintings I'd stored at my place. I wasn't going to hold onto anything since I'd decided to put things in order and pretty soon I'd have a whole list of things I wanted to get rid of. If damned Samantha had still been in Egypt, she'd have been at the top of it. I wasn't going to leave Essam's things with Marcia, or at my house where they'd fall into the hands of people who didn't appreciate art. He had first call on them or else he should've told me who to leave them with. I decided not to take his things along with me: they were heavy and I probably wouldn't find him, or else he'd just give them back to me like an idiot.

I went to see him, but I found far less than what I'd been expecting. I didn't find any sketches, any canvasses, any clay, any brushes, any paints scattered all over the place like normal. The walls were no longer decorated with the work of other artists in expensive frames. There were no Mashrabiya or Nubian baskets hanging from the ceiling. The walls were smooth; it looked like they'd recently been done over in a white that nearly shone. It reminded me of a hospital. The floor was cleared of the old Shirazi rug, speckled and stained with dripping paint, and there was a new handmade mat, free of any images or decoration, in its place. After he'd opened the door for me, Essam sat down on the mat like a Qur'an reader, leaning back on a pillow covered in beautiful Arabic calligraphy. Ignoring me, he recited his prayers with relish. He'd shaved off all his hair and he looked like a Buddhist monk, except for his beard, which had grown long, and his mustache, which was as thick as savannah brush. He went on ignoring me, repeating his prayers, but I was busy checking the place out. He still wasn't finished. I was intimidated by him; the gray hairs, which had started to show in his beard, made him look even more dignified and serious. Out of curiosity, I stood up and went to look around the rest of the apartment. I went into the bedroom and saw that he'd exchanged all his expensive furniture for an old, iron bed and a sad, colorless, plain dresser made of green wood. He'd traded his bookcase for one made of the same wood and replaced the books with works on Sufism and Sufipoetry. The bathroom was as I'd expected: he'd smashed the Western toilet and put a squat toilet, with a hole about as wide as a big watermelon, in its place. He'd also set up a large copper basin for bathing and a beautiful copper ewer that an antique shop would've been proud to have. I'd seen enough. I didn't go into his studio so as to save myself the shock of seeing that he'd used his paintings as an ironing board and as shutters to keep the dust out. Essam had successfully transformed the apartment of a lifetime and his lovely studio, which he'd acquired with his entire life's labor into an apartment like you'd find in the ninth ward of Duwayqa, one of Cairo's most repugnant neighborhoods, as global surveys point out.

227

Essam finally finished reciting his prayers and looked at me and smiled. "It's the first time you've visited since I made all these changes," he said with an enviable grace. I didn't say anything. "You don't like it?"

"Do you want the truth?"

He waved his hand and said, "It's alright. I just want you to know that I like it a lot more this way. You have no idea how comfortable it makes me. The old furniture was so stifling. This is so spacious. I'm thinking about opening all the rooms up."

"Where are the paintings?"

"Don't worry. I took some of them to Catacomb and some to Stefania at Mashrabiya and to some other galleries. The thing is, I really haven't got any time since I'm going to be traveling a lot. You should stop by the galleries every once in a while and settle up with them as if you were me."

"What about the exhibit you were getting ready for?"

"I told them I couldn't do it." His eyes wandered for a moment. "I don't think I'm going to paint anymore." He could see how annoyed I was. "Are you mad about the paintings? Or are you mad that I'm giving it up?"

"Well, thank God you didn't throw the paintings away. Now, can you explain to me why you want to give up painting? And what are these trips you're going to be going on?"

He smiled again that smile that paralyzed me and said, "I'm going on trips to visit God's saints with the guides. Don't think I'm giving up painting because I think it's a sin like some of them. I'm giving it up because it takes up all my time and I don't have much time left. I thought I'd better give it up before it gives me up. I'll be too busy for it and I don't want it to busy my thoughts."

He was looking at me probingly, as if he'd been telling me riddles and was expecting an answer. "Tell me about these trips, or are you not allowed to?"

He was stung. He stretched out his hand. "This knowledge is reserved for a select few and a supposedly educated non-initiate like yourself, with your limited vision and superficial knowledge, can never grasp it."

I stood up quickly and pulled his hand off his knee, bending down theatrically and kissing it. "Fare thee well, O Sheikh!"

"I don't go around acting like a sheikh. I'm a student."

I left, convinced that he wasn't the Essam I knew and that this was the beginning of our falling out. I got even angrier at Samantha. She'd fed him a deadly, poisonous brew that took effect ever so slowly, every second killing just one of the millions of cells that makes up the human body. What I saw today would be nothing compared to what I'd see in the future; that is, if God ever willed us to meet again.

Marcia told me she was angry that I hadn't called her back, but I could already hear it in her voice. She was going to go to the protest organized by the feminist groups in the garden at Tahrir Square that night. She was going to film the whole thing, too, she added defiantly. She didn't ask me whether I was planning to come. But Marcia's anger was nothing compared to how angry I was at Essam. I took my medicine, anticipating potential crises, and went to the movies and ate in a fancy restaurant. But in the end, I was still drawn to the protest.

The protest was mythical. I was facing three hundred women, leaders of feminist groups and civil society, who were standing in the garden, holding candles. The security forces had turned off all the lights in the square to derail the protest, but it only ended up making it more beautiful. The candles lit the garden up like starlight. The soldiers and officers watched in awe and kept their distance. I saw Marcia and the others filming and taking pictures. Then all the women sat down on the ground, in interlocking circles, and sang Fairuz songs. The place was full of wandering vendors, selling bottles of water, cookies, and stickers proclaiming Egyptian solidarity with the Lebanese. I bought a few stickers, and then, suddenly, I spotted Yasmeen among the protestors. That was a surprise: I never knew she was political. I found myself quickly withdrawing so that Yasmeen wouldn't see me and Marcia wouldn't catch up with me. I got out of there, but I myself didn't know why I was running away.

28

SO MANY DOORS SHUTTING in my face one after the other. Essam shut his door and was carried away. Zaynab tore her door out and flew away. Marcia's door was still open a crack. Yasmeen, now that she'd been stripped of her halo and become human again, was standing in the short distance between her door and emptiness. I didn't need to see my psychiatrist as much as I needed to be alone. But with the way things were, would that wish ever come true? There were a lot of calls from numbers I didn't know on my mobile, but I couldn't be bothered to pick up. They could've been from anyone, or from Karim; most likely, they wouldn't be from Zaynab. No, she was in Mexico adding new positions to her sexual dictionary, her lusty adventures.

The ringtone I'd assigned to Yasmeen stirred me and I pounced on my mobile. I'd forgotten, or pretended to forget, that I'd made my mind up about her, and answered anxiously. She asked me to meet her at the Atelier. I had no objection to the time or the place. My mood brightened and I began listening to her intently. Her voice seemed familiar, as if it were Hind's voice, or else that was how I, in my prodigious lunacy, imagined it. I held it all in and pulled myself together. After showering and putting on cologne, I dressed in clothes nicer than a lover would wear as Fairuz songs played in the background. The fine arts students, who were standing at the entrance to their group exhibition—it was opening night—made way for me, thinking I was some official sent by the Ministry to look at their work. The young poets and writers, who didn't know me, sat up on the couches where they'd been sprawling and studied my face and checked out my clothes. Even the worker there, who knew me well, followed me to my table and whispered, "Congratulations," in my ear. I was in the wrong place, in the wrong clothes, waiting for a girl who was the incarnation of another girl who was dead. How about all this insanity taking human form before my eyes!

She showed up right on time. She walked over, her long skirt sweeping the ground, hiding the men's sneakers she liked to wear. Eyes followed her as she walked in and came over to where I was sitting. A green silk ribbon was wrapped around her forehead with "Jerusalem is Ours!" written on it in crimson and beneath the ribbon there were two headscarves, one black, the other red, strikingly layered, and wrapped tightly around her face. She didn't put her hand out, as usual, but she did ask me, awkwardly as she pointed to the ribbon, if it was too much. I nodded. She bowed her head and she began to look slowly over her shoulder. After making sure no one was still looking, she slipped the ribbon off and threw it in her big cloth bag, which looked like the bags that women take to the market. She explained that she'd bought the ribbon at the university and had worn it to an event at the Journalists' Syndicate, which had just ended. I was pondering women's enthusiasm for the struggle: do they get it with the first pains of menses or does it appear overnight like a boil? When we were alone, we used to laugh about Shahinaz the Guerilla and how she used to dream about Kalashnikovs and RPGs and taking down the enemies and exploiters of the homeland. We used to tease her, asking her what she'd do if she were holding her nursing child when she heard the roar of a protest in the street below. "If he's going to keep me from my patriotic duty, I'll stomp on him with my own two feet or I'll sit on him and flatten him," she said. Then there was Marcia, sticking her nose into every opposition or

231

anti-government movement. And now, finally, Yasmeen had rebelled against the world she was living in and started going to protests. She asked me what I was thinking about.

"You."

"Why?"

I told her I'd been surprised to see her at the feminist groups' protest the day before; she'd never told me she had those kinds of leanings.

"You think you're the only one who can fight back and get locked up?"

I hadn't told her I'd been in prison. I asked her where she got her information. "From the Internet. As soon as I put your name in, a long list of no-nos started coming up: detention, imprisonment, petitions signed."

"Ah, so that's why you've taken up the struggle."

"I've been going to protests for a long time, I just never said anything."

I didn't want to drag that pointless conversation out, so I asked her about her trip. "We didn't go to very many places, just Hurghada and Sharm al-Sheikh. But I'm planning to go see the rest of it, God willing. Even if I have to go by myself."

I realized that her voice, during our entire conversation, had been Yasmeen's voice, not—as I'd imagined—Hind's voice. Doubt lured me into wondering whether there was such a thing as Yasmeen to begin with and the deceitful part deep down in my brain was urging me to touch her, to prove whether or not she were a figment of my imagination. All my delusions and hallucinations came back again and battered my mind until I could see the panic on her face. She stared at me and whispered to me anxiously that my face was very pale. I was breathing heavily, as loudly as an asthmatic. Yasmeen quickly ran and brought me a lemonade. She held it up to my mouth. I took the glass feebly and sipped. To my surprise, many of the diners were standing by our table, offering to help. Her face was white with fear. Despite how I was feeling, I couldn't help but be sorry for her. I told the people standing around I was alright. I told them I was just exhausted from lack of sleep and they left. She wasn't convinced, not even after I told her I was overtired and that it was all merely exhaustion. She was genuinely frightened. The tears filling her eyes were real tears. Seeing her so concerned made me feel a bit better, and for a moment I was myself again. She reached into her bag and brought out a ball of papers covered in her ugly hand-writing. She handed them to me and I corrected a few miswordings and wrote down some comments, trying to give the impression that I was fine. She kept asking me how I was feeling, like a mother who keeps feeding her child past the point of being full. I barked at her to stop. Startled, her small face continued to tremble for a while afterward. And then I smiled and she smiled. Oh, if only I'd left earlier. If only she hadn't coddled me, hadn't cared for me. If only she hadn't said what she'd said; if only she'd taken it easy on me.

I gave her back the papers, satisfied with some of what I'd read. She said she was going to be putting together a collection soon and that she was going to dedicate it to me. I hid my anxiety, my discomfort. Did I mind? I shook my head. She told me she'd written a poem about how I'd taken an interest in her and helped her, but that she wasn't going to let me read it until the collection was published. Changing the subject to something less upsetting, I asked her to tell me about her new life in politics. She laughed and said her close friends had warned her off it, but she'd heard about it all by following my work and the work of some of my friends she'd heard about, and she'd been drawn in. She started getting into political discussions on blogs. She was attacked and fought back and that made her want to do it more. I came to realize that my habitat was polluted, that the air around me was mixed with toxic gases, that anyone who knew me or had ever met me was going to have bad luck. What was politics and standing in the ranks of the opposition to this little girl! She should've joined the ruling party; maybe she could've found a job, or a husband. Even if I left this life, voluntarily or against my will, my sins would live on after me and their curses would reach me in the grave.

With a father's exasperation, I told her to relax, to simmer down. She was still only a university student; she had plenty of time until she graduated and then she could do whatever she wanted. She looked at me dejectedly and whispered, "Didn't you get locked up when you were a student?" I didn't say anything. I didn't argue. "I even got hit with a

233

club at the protest on Friday. I thought my eyes were going to pop out."
I looked at her face and smirked: there was no trace. My smile irked her
so she pulled the headscarf aside with her thin fingers, revealing a
faded-blue bruise above a birthmark the size of a grape seed—exactly
like the one Hind had and in the same spot. My eyes leaped from their
sockets and words stammered about in my mouth. I bolted out of my
chair so I could get closer to her, so I could touch that birthmark. And
the expression on my face must've alarmed her because she began to
retreat. She rushed to grab her bag as I called her by Hind's name.
I was determined to touch her. The world around me was falling apart.

29

I woke up to find myself in a fancy room in a luxury hospital where I'd been for two days. From the first moment on, everything frightened me. And though the IVs hanging above my head were attached to my arm and the monitor was graphically tracking the movement of my living organs, I still felt that the only thing connecting me to this earthly life were a few thin strings. I wished they'd be cut and I'd be sent floating out into space. I wasn't exactly sure what'd happened. My memory sent no visions to point me toward a recollection. When the nurse told me it was my foreign wife who'd brought me in, I didn't correct her. Trying to curry favor, she said that my wife had been crying the entire time, but that didn't work on me: I knew Marcia better than she did. At the most, Marcia would've shed a few tears. The wretched nurse said that Marcia had stayed up at my bedside for the past two nights and that she'd only left that morning after the doctor had told her that my condition was stable. Nurse Busybody left and returned a few minutes later with the doctor on call. He told me I was okay, that I'd just been exhausted and that my immune system, already weakened by anemia owing to my innutritious diet, had suffered a sudden shock; to say nothing of my anxiety and high blood pressure. Thank God he hadn't noticed my psychiatric condition or the pills I had to take to maintain a level head. As she fed me, the nurse asked if I had any kids. I shook my head. "What a shame," she said, sighing, as if she were blaming me: it was my responsibility as an Egyptian with a beautiful foreign wife to impregnate her and thereby improve the race.

You miserable, stupid woman! On any fair scale, you'd beat Marcia and her ilk on all counts: you're naturally pretty, you've got character, you're tender and flirtatious, you take care of your body. I said nothing to her. I kept it in, but then I abruptly asked her to leave me alone and she left bewildered.

After a little while, she came back in, looking confused, with Awad in tow. I figured the only people who'd been into see me, both while I'd been unconscious and now that I was awake, were blond and light-eyed. Awad seemed moved by the sight of me and he said he was sorry but he'd only heard that morning that I was in the hospital, and then he apologized on behalf of his wife, Aisha, who couldn't come because she was pregnant. I whispered to him that it was no big deal he hadn't come the day before or the day before that since I'd been in a coma and I'd only come out of it a little while ago; Marcia didn't even know I was awake. He nodded as if he believed me, but then he smiled and corrected my error: Marcia did know, he said. She called the hospital every hour to check on me and the doctor had her phone number so he could call her and give her updates. Before I could ask why she hadn't called or come to see me yet, he winked and said she was planning to get in touch with Essam, Evelyn, Diana, and the rest of our friends so they could all come celebrate my recovery at the hospital that evening. My blood boiled. That lunatic was planning to turn the hospital into a nightclub? To hell with her and her brilliant ideas. She was acting exactly like a miserable third-world government: throwing a party for every occasion, even for defeats. I was exhausted, and I knew that if I were to call her, I'd go right back into a coma so I begged Awad to call her and put an end to her idiotic behavior. I told him to tell her I was pissed off and completely opposed to the idea. He was stroking my hand. I insisted he call her immediately, and that he tell her I'd fallen asleep so she wouldn't demand to talk to me to try to pressure me into agreeing. After saying a pleasant, "Yes, sir" in that accent of his, he did exactly as I'd asked. I liked Awad; out of all the Westerners I'd met, he was the one I picked to be my friend. When I asked him what was new, he said, "Just waiting for my heir," with a smile. I laughed. "Do you think Essam'll visit you?" he asked after some thought, his brow furrowed. I didn't say anything. "I went to see him before I came, but he was on his way to al-Hussein Mosque. He's on a mission," he said, sarcastically.

"On a mission to find his sheikh and teacher."

"You know about that?"

I couldn't help but smile. "Yeah, I know. And I know he's got to find him. It's one of the major steps in becoming a Sufi. Sufis have to search for their teachers, their guides. The teacher could be a sheikh in a mosque, or a shoe shiner, or a bileela seller, or a doctor in a government hospital, or a janitor in a public bathroom, but when they meet, they'll recognize each other without having to say a word."

Awad was listening raptly. "Did you study Sufism, too?"

I shook my head. "Essam taught me a little a long time ago when we went abroad together, but I wasn't into it."

"It seems really exciting and cool and I'm starting to get into it. Next time I see Essam, I'm going to borrow a few books from him."

After I told him several times not to give in to Marcia and that I refused to have people come celebrate my recovery as if I were a baby on circumcision day, Awad left. After Awad left, I smiled as I thought about how after he read the books Essam was going to lend him, he'd become an obedient soldier, a submissive initiate of our sheikh, Essam al-Sharif.

My mind cleared a little after I napped for a few hours in the afternoon. I fell in and out of sleep; when I woke up, I didn't tax my mind trying to remember what had happened. Mostly, I needed the forced rest. A few moments after I'd woken up, Marcia burst in loudly, followed by the doctor and the nurse. She kissed me quickly on the cheeks and forehead and then she started to examine the monitor and the IVs as if she were a doctor. She settled down. The doctor assured her, in English to show off how worldly he was, that everything was fine. "Thanks. Thank you, Doctor," she said back to him in Arabic and then she asked him when I could leave. The next morning, he said, and then he told the nurse to stop the IVs. He wrote out a long list of instructions for me: avoid stress, overexertion, and anxiety and then the doctor and the nurse left. Before Marcia could start making plans for when I got out of the hospital, I told her, in no uncertain terms, that I wasn't going to spend the whole prescribed recovery period in Cairo. Marcia interrupted me: "We'll go to Switzerland for a month and you'll come back like new."

I raised my voice a little and over-enunciated, "I'm going to go to Alexandria, or Mersa Matruh, or Hurghada, by myself. I'll work on something, a collection, a play, my memoirs. I'll play in the dirt if I feel like it."

She didn't protest; she simply lowered her gaze. Then, in a loving whisper, she said, "Okay. Good. We still have time to finish the film." I said nothing. "How come you didn't want us to throw a party for you?"

"This is a hospital, not a foreigner's apartment. It's full of sick people."

She was quiet for a second. "So we can have a party for you tomorrow at our apartment before you leave town?"

I picked my words out as carefully as if I'd been walking through filthy mire. "Tomorrow we'll celebrate, just me and you, and then I'll be off," I said with a smile I made sure she saw. The look on her face was transformed: pleasant and relaxed and her mouth turned up into a lovely smile unlike any I'd ever seen from her before.

As she took my mobile phone out of her bag and handed it to me, she sprung a worrying question: "Who's Yasmeen?"

Her question caught me off guard, but I regrouped and said, "She's a young poet I've been helping."

She didn't buy it. "She called two days in a row to ask how you were doing. I told her you were better today." Marcia just looked at me, but I was silent, worried that if I changed the subject, she'd only get more suspicious. "Actually, when I was bringing you to the hospital, the guy at the Atelier said you'd been sitting with Yasmeen when you got mad at her and passed out, and that's when she ran off," she said, her tone neutral, her face turned away from me. My mind started to pick up the scattered strands. So I hadn't dreamt it. I'd been with Yasmeen at the Atelier. But what had me so upset? And how did the employee at the Atelier know her name? She wasn't a regular. Ideas and questions were at war in my head and I had to think of some quick excuse to quieten Marcia's suspicions.

"I guess we were talking about what's been going on in Palestine and she said something that made me angry."

"Mustafa, you shouldn't talk to anyone you don't trust about how you really feel."

That made me angry, but to throw her off the scent, I said, "But Yasmeen's not just anybody, and anyway I trust my students."

"Well, look what happened. Anyway, your student's a young girl. Her brain hasn't finished developing yet. Of course she's not going to understand you." I told myself that Marcia wouldn't have let the employee at the Atelier go before interrogating him like a hardened detective. She'd found out every detail of Yasmeen's description, which backed up my story about us disagreeing.

To double-check, I asked, "Did the guy at the Atelier say it was Yasmeen for sure, not someone else?"

"He didn't know her name, but he went through the guestbook and found it." It was definite then; I'd been with Yasmeen. Marcia had found out I'd been with Yasmeen and Yasmeen had spoken to her twice, but what about? Marcia seemed to have guessed what was swirling around in my head and said with a Westerner's nonchalance, "Just so you know, I didn't talk to the girl about anything. I didn't want to give her the time of day. I told her you were fine, that's all. When she calls, you can tell her how you're doing yourself."

Was she being jealous? Or possessive? Or just nosy? What had I been talking to Yasmeen about? What had upset me so much? God knows.

I pretended I was feeling weak and drowsy so Marcia stood up and hugged me tenderly. I found myself kissing her hand, thanking her for everything. When she was at the door, she smiled and said, "Evelyn and Diana will be at my place tomorrow to welcome you home. Or should I have them come visit you today?"

"No that sounds good, but don't let them stay too long. We want to have some time alone together." She beamed, her eyes twinkling. Blowing me a kiss, she rushed off.

Then the cat-and-mouse game started. As soon as Marcia left, Yasmeen called my mobile. She breathlessly asked how I was feeling and what did the doctor say. Her voice trembled and her words flowed in an uninterrupted stream, letters dropping out and colliding. But, at the same time, she tried to avoid the subject of our meeting and what had taken place. Had I actually lost my temper? Why? She pretended she didn't know what I was talking about, but her denial, mixed as it was with concern, scared me. I was dead set on getting her to tell me exactly what had happened. She mumbled for a while, her voice quavering, and then, in a hoarse whisper, she said, "You really don't remember?"

"No!"

She was quiet for a few moments. "It's no big deal. Nothing bad. Ordinary stuff like with any two people."

"Tell me! What did we talk about that made me so upset?" She started sobbing and as the sound of her weeping grew louder and louder, all I could do was beg. "Please, Yasmeen. I'm still not feeling well, don't make it worse. What happened?"

When she stopped crying, she said, "I swear to God nothing happened. I could tell you weren't feeling well from the moment I got there. You said yourself you were exhausted."

"I'm sure we talked about the protests at al-Azhar and the university," I said to ease her along, but I got no answer. So I continued, "You were probably in the library or at the movies, clueless about what was going on, so I got mad at you, right?"

"Right."

"So if you saw I was in bad shape when you got there, why did you argue with me and get my blood up?"

"I'm really sorry." She started to cry; another crescendo of sobs. I told her to knock it off. She said she was sorry that she couldn't come see me. She couldn't stand seeing me ill again, she said. She got very excited when I told her I was going to go to Mersa Matruh for at least a couple of weeks because I was gearing up for a writing project I hoped to finish while I was there. "Email me what you write every day. Don't forget."

It was nice to hear her so happy, but I stood my ground. "Yasmeen, I'm going to cut myself off completely. I won't have my mobile with me and I'm not going to tell anyone where I am. It's the best way for me to get better. I'll call you as soon as I get back."

She was quiet for a second. "Who had your mobile when you were in the hospital? Your sister?"

"Yeah." I laughed.

"Fine. You don't want to tell me. Fine." Then she told me to feel better and said goodbye. All her fretting about my health didn't strike me as genuine emotion; it seemed more like a symptom of fatherlessness. That bothered me, sure, but what really got under my skin was the image I'd had of her ever since I'd first laid eyes on her: a sad little puppy, scurrying around. She hadn't thought to check on me, except by phone, as Marcia had pointed out. She didn't visit me. She didn't even bother to ask the name of the hospital I was at so she could send flowers, so that they'd be there among all those bouquets bearing cards signed in Latin letters.

That eternal day wouldn't end. The nurse had a surprise: my sisters, their husbands, and their children were waiting out in the hall. She asked me whether she should bring them in in two batches or if it'd be better if I went out in the hall to see them. I was furious with Marcia, who'd taken my mobile so she could tell whoever called how I was doing. For one thing, my sisters rarely called, and when they did, it was either to complain about their husbands or their kids, or to tell me some aggravating bit of news. Why would one of them have called me in those embarrassing circumstances? And why hadn't Marcia told me she'd called? The nurse was still jabbering away, but I was too angry to listen. "Out in the hall!" She gave me a seething look and stormed out. Even though I was freed up since they'd removed the needles and tubes

241

from my body, I was still weak. I took a few steps, but it was like learning how to walk all over again. I stopped and sat down on a chair. The nurse came in again and found me sitting. Before she could open her mouth, I stood up, and she supported me as I made my way toward them. My two sisters hugged me, crying with simultaneous sobs and identical wrenching of faces as if they were twins. The children said hello as they stared at me, wide-eyed; perhaps because I was wearing a gallabiya, and they'd only ever seen me dressed nicely on those few occasions I visited them at home. My eldest sister Mahasin's husband practiced his paternal instinct on me, but his patting me on the knee and giving me stupid advice got on my nerves. My younger sister Rida's husband seemed bored. He was squirming nervously in the plastic chair, which screeched against the marble floor. I figured he was dying to get out of there so he could go keep an eye on the fishmonger's shop he'd bought with my father's money. His fidgeting was making me nervous so I told him to quit moving the chair.

"What's the matter? You look jumpy. I thought they said your shop's doing well because of the bird flu." He glared at his wife, as if to blame her for bringing him there, or for being the one who'd told me. My sister lowered her head, cowering, while he explained that he couldn't breathe from the smell of Dettol and rubbing alcohol and he was always uncomfortable in hospitals. My eldest sister's husband stood up before I could tease him about his activities in the stock market. He had his two kids kiss me and made an excuse about having to go pay his condolences to someone. My sister stood up after him meekly. "If you don't like the hospital food, I can bring you something to eat tomorrow," she said.

"I'm getting out tomorrow."

My younger sister's husband, who was afraid of catching something, stood up. He was carrying his two kids in front of him so he wouldn't have to hug me or shake with both hands. He held his palm out and I grazed it slackly. My sisters, on the other hand, kissed me like homeless kids kissing a TV presenter in front of the cameras. When they'd finally left, I went back to cursing Marcia. When I reckoned that maybe it wasn't one of my sisters who'd called, that maybe Marcia had gone through my phone to get their numbers and called them, thinking that it'd cheer me up, I became irate. That was likely, for there was more awkwardness and anger in my relationship with my sisters than there was blood and intimacy.

I'd thrown my eldest sister and her husband and their two kids out of my house a few months earlier. Her husband had been insolent, stupidly asking what I did and how I made my money, but I put up with it. I saw how servile my sister was and how she fawned over him pathetically, but I bit my tongue. And when I'd given her eldest son, who was ten years old, a comic book to look at, he asked me, out of the blue, "Uncle, are we going to get all these books, too, when we inherit the apartment?" No, it wasn't a hallucination, it wasn't paranoia. Their whole family was already making plans for what they were going to inherit from me. And this was after each of those two losers had already got his hands on my sisters' inheritances, plus large sums for selling their shares in the apartment downtown and the house in al-Talabiya. What else could these hangers-on have asked for? To inherit from me while I was still alive? And they were making plans in front of their young children. I suddenly found myself chasing after my eldest sister's husband with a shoe as the children fled in terror. The coward disappeared from my sight while my sister stood in the stairwell, gathering up the things that had spilled out of her handbag when I threw it and her headscarf at her. They said I'd lost my mind and they told my younger sister about it, but when she called to scold me, I gave her her serving over the phone. Then I calmed down. I was rid of them. Neither one of them dared to visit me after that. They'd call occasionally; sometimes I answered, but mostly I ignored their calls. Well-intentioned Marcia had brought them back into my life after I'd nearly forgotten about them, imagining myself an only child. But, now, they were really here and they had to be taken into account.

Marcia had told our friends who'd gathered to celebrate my recovery that they'd have to leave early. At the high point of the party, I could see they were getting ready to leave. I tried to get Awad to stay, but Marcia was giving me looks, and then finally she leaned down and whispered that it wouldn't do: "Either everybody stays or everybody goes." As he was leaving, Awad told me he was angry at Essam because he'd refused to come. I smiled.

"Don't worry." I said. "I know what Essam's going through."

"What he's going through . . . . What he's going through? He said, 'May God have mercy on all of you.' What's that supposed to mean?"

I laughed. "May God grant us mercy from him." I patted him on the back and told him to forget about it. Essam, the old Essam, would be back with us soon.

Awad looked at me closely. "You think?"

30

In spite of all the reasons I gave Marcia for why I had to cut myself off from the rest of the world, and though she seemed convinced, she made sure to keep me in the loop just like before. She insisted I take what I'd written of the script so that if I got bored while I was away, as she expected I would, I could entertain myself by working on the film. That way, I'd be ready to give the signal to start as soon as I got back from Mersa Matruh. I complied, especially since she'd agreed not to visit me in Mersa Matruh and let me get away with not telling her where I was planning to stay. I even warned her about trying to get in touch with me. I took the SIM card out of my cell phone in front of her and told her I was going to be completely off the grid. I asked her to respect my wishes.

The ocean cleansed me with its virginal stones, its high tide and low, its seductive seaweed, its silver froth. In it, I forgot about the rest of the world. I didn't read a single newspaper, or listen to or watch any news reports. I didn't stay in a hotel or pension as Marcia would've expected me to. I didn't stay in town either. I stayed on the outskirts. I told Marcia I was going to Mersa Matruh because I knew how her mind worked: if she did try to look for me, she'd look everywhere but Mersa Matruh, certain that I'd mentioned it to her as a red herring. I spent twenty days in a delicious vacuum, reclining outside of time. I didn't think about the things that upset me. I was too wary even to recall a happy memory in case the tragedies came trailing in its wake. It was very difficult at first, but my brain got used to it and began ejecting those kinds of thoughts. I immersed myself in playing games with regular folks, cycling for long distances on the main road, picking out fruit and vegetables—which I could barely cook—like a housewife, catching fish and women I'd meet at the nightclub or in the market. I'd wake up to find myself bent over their sweaty bodies of all shapes, sizes, and colors. A foot near my mouth, an arm on my chest, a leg against my behind, a woman's stocking wrapped around my head. Chubby ones and thin ones. Pretty ones and plain ones. Surprised to find them there when I woke up, I'd kick them out and instantly forget about them, only reminded if a girl scurried away from me as I walked on the Corniche at night. I'd give up following her, then, because I'd know that she'd already spent the night with me.

There I was on the way back to Cairo, a solid, contented young man returning to meet all of life's surprises head on, no matter what they were. I went back ten days ahead of schedule to get my life in Cairo in order. I holed up in my apartment fixing the script, comparing it to the footage I'd shot and what I was planning to shoot, and I sketched out some other shooting locations, too, to get Marcia thinking I'd worked on our project while I'd been away. I was like a student, underlining my book just to make the teacher think I'd been studying.

The first house I visited after my seclusion in Mersa Matruh, besides my apartment, was Marcia's. Her face lit up as soon as she saw me, and she said she was feeling better again. She'd been really annoyed at her maid, Julia, who'd been ignoring her orders recently and pleading absent-mindedness. I told her, loudly and in English so Julia could hear me in the kitchen, to send her back to the church, or to lend her to a friend, or to let me deal with her. Marcia smiled and tickled my knee and then glumly explained, in a whisper, that the number of refugees had gone up of late and that the United Nations wasn't planning to send the refugees to Canada, America, or Europe anymore. After the peace agreement, the agenda had shifted to repatriating them to Southern Sudan. That was what had Julia and her cousin so bothered. "Well then, you should just use your connections to help her and her fiancé immigrate to America," I said maliciously. She looked at me silently for a long time and I could tell that I'd gone right up to a red line; beyond it there were mines poised to explode. I didn't want to take it back, or pretend I'd been kidding so I was silent, too, until she had to say something.

She trained her gaze on me. "Mustafa, don't ever think I'm going to leave you and go back to the States. Either you come back with me or I'm going to live here with you forever." Marcia was moving near territory I'd long been avoiding. Ever since we'd outlined our relationship at the beginning, I'd never asked her where it was going. I didn't care. And she was equally careful to give the impression that our relationship was no more serious than a surface wound, but a scratch.

It was the first time she'd brought up settling down and although it made me nervous, it also made me proud. It meant that out relationship wasn't just a game as I'd often imagined. It was love. And maybe it was the rut we'd fallen into that had something to do with why the passion had dwindled.

We stayed up late together and Marcia insisted I spend the night. I promised her I'd get in touch with Karim and his crew the next day so we could start wrapping up the film as the funding organizations had started asking what the holdup was. The sheaf of emails she'd thrust into my hand added credence to what she was saying.

I was near the shrine of al-Hussein at noon and guided by my curiosity: I was taken up in a spiritual, mystical state and it made me squeeze in with all the visitors: the pious, the needy, the Sufiinitiates, Westerner voyeurs. As I was absorbed into the crowd, I looked for Essam in the faces next to me, around me, behind me, as we slowly revolved in

247

never-ending circles. Maybe he was searching for his sheikh at the same time in the same place. Maybe he'd found what he'd been searching for for so long, found the one who'd command him in the simple words that would go right over the heads of the ordinary and close-minded— like when Essam had tried to teach me the Sufiranks. Maybe I'd wept with those who wept, or gone with them into the Barzakh, the land where the dead wait for either heaven or hell. Maybe I'd lost consciousness or found inner peace. Maybe I'd died and been reborn. Maybe I hadn't even gone into the courtyard of the mosque. Maybe I'd never left the spot where I was sitting, waiting for Awad.

He'd asked Marcia for some means of getting in touch with me while I was out of town because he had something very important to tell me. When Marcia put him in touch with me, he asked me, his voice trembling over the phone, to meet him the next day near al-Hussein. When I asked him why al-Hussein, he gave me what sounded like a scripted answer about going to the market near al-Hussein in the afternoon because his mother-in-law had asked him to get a bunch of different oriental herbs and she told him he could get them all at the famous herbalist shop near al-Hussein. We set a time to meet, but I wasn't convinced that he was telling the truth. And then it occurred to me why Awad had brought me there: Essam, of course. I was sure Essam had gone nuts and started wearing filthy rags and loitering around with beggars and lunatics and miracle workers. Maybe Awad was going to surprise me by taking me to Essam's refuge, his hiding place, his lair.

Awad put two big bags brimming with herbs on the ground, which really threw me for a loop because I knew he hadn't bought all those herbs just to fool me. He undid the string around the middle of a little parcel and took out an ivory mouthpiece, which he stuck into the hose of the water pipe the waiter had brought over. He started breathing in the smoke and exhaling the sickening scent of artificial apple. He looked at me for a long time and then asked whether Marcia had mentioned anything to me about Essam. I shook my head, suppressing a smirk. It seemed like Awad the German, who'd left Berlin to settle in

248

Egypt, worked here, got married here, and was about to have a half-Egyptian, half-Western baby here, had come to Egypt for just one reason: to tell me astonishing stories about Essam every time he saw me. He'd gone quiet. He exhaled smoke and looked at me as if he were reluctant to talk. "What about Essam, Awad?" I asked.

He took the pipe out of his mouth and sighed. "Essam's in real danger, Mustafa." I smiled, thinking about the Westerners who lived in the Middle East, but who never lost their ability to be amazed and how the littlest things excited and bewildered and frightened them. Awad loved Essam so much that it had filled his heart with worry. What was he going to tell me about Essam? Was there anything more to say? He'd say that Essam had become a dervish and about lost his mind and walked naked through the streets? It wouldn't surprise me. He'd say he'd fallen in with the saints, the crazies, the people who hold zikrs, and the Rafaaiya Sufis? That was to be expected. It was perfectly normal. He'd say he'd gone mad and proclaimed himself a great leader and that he had followers of his own? Or that he'd become a prognosticating prophet? That wouldn't get me riled up either. Awad didn't say anything. He reckoned my curiosity would get the better of me and I'd eventually have to ask, but I was playing it cool. He shouted at me, "Mustafa, Essam's your friend. Why don't you care about what's happening to him?"

I smiled and tried to calm him down. "It's simple, Awad. I've known Essam for a long time and I've come to expect just about anything out of him."

Awad was quiet for a few moments. "Did you know he went back to Singapore?"

I was stunned and the words came out before I could stop them, "God damn him! He went back to her?"

"He came back a week ago."

"He deserves everything he's getting," I said. "I thought he was stronger than that."

Awad raised his hand so I wouldn't go on. "Samantha's dead, Mustafa." I didn't process what he said at first, so he had to repeat it twice.

"When?" He said she'd died two days after I'd left for Mersa Matruh. "She died just like that?"

"She was very sick," he said. "She had advanced brain cancer and the doctors had told her she wasn't going to live more than six months. That's why she broke up with Essam. She didn't want him to go through the pain of finding out she was sick."

"Where'd you hear all this?"

"I saw Essam when he came back," he said. "He was trying to keep it together, but he was a wreck. He told me she left him everything. The money, the company, plus a letter and a videotape she'd recorded telling him not to be upset with her."

"Where's Essam now?" I asked, getting to my feet.

"No one's heard from him for a week. He doesn't answer his phone, he's not at home. I'm guessing he went back to Singapore for the reading of the will and stuff."

I left Awad without saying anything and went straight over to Marcia's. I yelled at her for not telling me what had happened to Essam. She was visibly taken aback, but she started kissing up to me to try to get me to calm down. She said she hadn't wanted to upset me after I'd come back from my vacation; she'd been waiting for the right moment to tell me. She said she'd gone to pay her respects to Essam with Awad and the rest of our friends. He was lost, numb, she said, walking around like a drunk; he didn't care who'd come or who hadn't. Her weak explanation didn't work on me. She should've told me the moment she'd heard about it, not waited until I came back, or until even after that. She could've got in touch with me if I'd been in the belly of a whale. And even if she hadn't been able to find me, I'd have thanked her for trying. The old wounds reopened and I accused her (bringing up the past, as they say) of telling my sisters I was ill without asking my permission. Caught off guard for a second time, she reverted to that American accent of hers, "You're impossible. Unbelievable. How was I supposed to get your permission when you were unconscious?" I ignored her and began calling some of my friends and Essam's friends and colleagues to try to get some information. I failed. They didn't add anything to what Awad had said. Essam wasn't answering his home phone or his mobile. I was angry at myself for not getting his number in Singapore when he'd tried to give it to me back when he'd first started traveling there. When he saw I wasn't that excited to have it, he stuck the card back in his pocket and never offered it to me again. The only thing left was to go down to the embassy and ask them for Essam's number there. It was certain to be in their records. But what could I have said to get them to give it to me just like that? Marcia wanted to help so she made a show of searching on her laptop. I ignored her and left.

The girl at the Indian Cultural Center assured me that Essam hadn't been in for a long time. I left when she started going through her register so she could tell me exactly how long. At the coffeehouse, they said they hadn't seen him for a while. The waiter told me Karim was out of prison and that he'd asked after me twice. I didn't say anything. I ran around to Essam's house and his studio, but the doorman just said he was out of town. At Bar Estoril, no one was any help. At the Greek Club, one of Essam's old artist-friends told me he'd seen him buying paints, dyes, and brushes at the Kida Lown store on Mahmoud Bassiouni Street. He said Essam had looked like he was busy getting ready for a new exhibition. Essam had been cold toward him, the old friend said. He figured Essam had forgotten his old friends, that he had no class; after a surly Essam had outright ignored the old friend's attempt to make conversation, he backed off. But when I explained the tragic circumstances Essam was going through, he appeared sympathetic and his anger melted away.

When I got home, the riddles and puzzles started to pile up. Awad thought that Essam had left town and most of Essam's acquaintances agreed with him, but there was this one friend, unimportant as far as Essam was concerned, who'd said he'd seen him two days ago buying art supplies. There was no way Essam could've been thinking about putting on a new exhibition while he was grieving, but there was no proof that this acquaintance was lying just to lie. He had nothing to gain from lying. My mind still hadn't processed that Samantha was dead; it was as if it'd simply rejected the idea. The only thing I could think about then was finding Essam, no matter what I had to do. I didn't drink much that night and I woke up right after dawn. I walked around downtown and Abdeen, following Essam's jogging route, but I didn't see him. I couldn't find anyone—an office-worker, mechanic, or coffeehouse boy, who might've seen him running, or out shopping even, in the past few days.

I sent the cab driver away when I got to Essam's house and studio. The doorman intercepted me angrily. He looked anxious. I could sense something was up. I sat with him though he didn't want me to and while my threats got him to listen, he still wasn't answering my questions. When he did give an answer, it was delivered with absolute contempt. Temptations were what worked with that doorman: his eyes lit up when he saw a hundred-dollar bill, which he knew all about, but he was embarrassed and he kept on pretending he had no information about Essam. When I threw in another bill and told him that if he didn't tell me, I'd go to the police and report Essam as missing and accuse him of hiding him, he smiled and took the money. He told me Essam was in his apartment, but he wouldn't open the door for anyone. He said that Essam had told him not to tell anyone he was there the last time he saw him, which was when he'd brought him the stockpile of groceries and cigarettes Essam had asked for. When the doorman saw that I meant to go in, he begged me not to tell Essam what'd transpired between us. I nodded.

It was a little after noon and the apartment was completely dark. No artificial light, bright or faint, nor any sunlight, creeping into the room, showed on the glass of the door. No movement. Not a sound. No evidence of human life. I rang the doorbell over and over. I kept my finger pressed on the doorbell, like Zaynab used to do. No one stirred. I grabbed the lion-faced doorknocker and pounded on the door. No answer. I bloodied my hand knocking on the door. It was no use. When I started up again, the neighbors came out in the hall to complain and yell at me: "No one's home. We're going to call the police," so I went down the stairs, my head bowed.

But I didn't despair. I waited on the floor below until they shut their doors and then I snuck back up on tiptoe. I leaned back against Essam's door and sat, resigned, pondering what to do. If only I hadn't given him back his key. If only I'd had a copy made; it would've come in handy. I sat there for a while, anxiously watching the doors of the neighboring apartments, worried that one of them would suddenly swing open and the neighbors would see me and make trouble. At the same time, my ear was listening for the slightest movement in Essam's apartment; even if it were only the sound of his brush passing through the surface of water. I called his apartment from my mobile and listened as the phone inside rang incessantly. It was a waiting game between the two of us. The nights I'd spent with Karim's crew had made me more patient and better prepared for when things went wrong. I was sure that Essam, if he were inside the apartment, knew full well that the pain-in-the-ass who was determined to get into his apartment could only be me. And that he also knew I could've waited for days and weeks at his door until he opened up. I amused myself by calling his apartment from my mobile and I knew that if the same stupid, persistent thing were happening to me, I'd have gone out and killed whoever was doing it.

Finally, I heard faint footsteps disconnecting the phone and I knew he was inside. I leaped up to my feet, propelled by fury and nerves. My left hand was pressing on the doorbell and my right hand was slamming, with all the force I had, the iron knocker against the door. I didn't give a damn about the neighbors and their threats. I made a hell of a racket; the patients at Abbasiya Mental Hospital couldn't have done any better. The doors of the neighboring apartments opened just as Essam was opening his door. The neighbors poured out, man, woman, and child, like bloodthirsty monsters, but as Essam opened the door they were terrified by what they saw. They retreated when they saw Essam's face, his bald head, his matted beard, his linen gallabiya stained with paints and ink, mostly red which made him look like a butcher who'd been frantically slitting throats on the morning of the Feast of the Sacrifice.

Essam's apartment was drowned in darkness. The neighbors' apartments were lit up. He turned his back on me and withdrew into the apartment. The darkness drew him toward the deep. I went in and shut the door behind me. I couldn't make anything out in the pitch-dark. I began to turn on the lights as I walked around. I nearly fell more than once, stumbling over the paint cans stuck in every corner of the apartment. It was an astonishing sight. Throughout the entire apartment, the floor was stained with splotches of paint, kerosene, and oils; it looked like the rooms the glue-huffing kids lived in. But the walls and ceiling had all been covered in beautiful murals. I admired them for a while and then I went to look for Essam. I found him lying on a mat in the kitchen. He'd cleared the kitchen out completely except for a kerosene stove, a sibirtaya, some wooden dishes and other essentials like spoons, forks, and chopsticks. He'd replaced the big refrigerator with an office mini-fridge, which he kept his cups and dishes on top of. He'd torn out all the ceramic and glazed tiles and replaced them with terracotta. He'd carved and painted on the kitchen walls and ceiling. He stood up then to finish, I guess, what he'd been working on, paying me no mind. He was putting the final touches on Samantha's clothes, having already painted her cooking on her immense stove. There was a table in front of her laid with spicy fried chicken, grilled fish, and a bunch of platters she'd filled with green salad and seafood. Next to these, there were some grilled crabs and a whole array of sea creatures I didn't know the names of. There were pineapples, mangoes, bananas, and apples strewn along the table. There was Samantha with her back to us and her short black hair that nearly shone. In the other corner, she was smiling bigger than the whole world as she served the food. She looked proud, showing off what she'd made. She fed you with a fork, smiling affectionately. Her lips were almost moving, wishing you bon appétit.

All of this was painted on the walls and ceiling with such precision and skill. It was as if Essam had hired dozens of artisans from Singapore to come and sketch all those amazing details. He watched me through eyes strained from insomnia and painting fine details. I was blown away, but there wasn't a single muscle in his face that showed he was proud or happy about what he'd created. It was as if what he'd done was only the beginning of a duty he'd been born to carry out. I hadn't said anything to him since I'd come in. I didn't need to say anything to him. I pulled up one side of the mat to reveal miniatures of Samantha's shoes; Samantha cooking, wearing latex gloves; her pollution masks; her small socks in gaudy colors with tiny details. I went to look through all the rooms, Essam following me and turning out the lights of each room as I left. I couldn't remember what the rooms were called, what Essam used to use them for; I just saw Samantha. She was everywhere, beside you, above you, getting dressed to go out, or getting ready to go to bed. In winter clothes and summer clothes. Sweeping the floor. Watching the washing machine. Eating. Making food. Sitting in front of a huge TV. Sitting at her desk working on the computer. Playing with dolls. In the small room Essam had planned to use as a nursery, Samantha was a child, younger than ten, playing with Asian toys. Studying as a teenager. Going out with her friends as a twenty-year-old. Marrying Essam in her late thirties. There were paintings of them in there, too, touring around Cairo and Singapore and in the bars there. In Essam's bedroom, on the wall directly in front of him when he lay in bed, there was Samantha, wrapped in a shroud, waiting to be cremated. On the ceiling, Samantha and Essam were lying in bed together. On the nightstand beside his metal bed, there was a ceramic urn that held Samantha's ashes. Essam was planning to keep it beside his bed forever.

I couldn't get him to tell me any more about the tragedy than what I'd heard from Awad. I couldn't get him to leave that museum place either. I don't think anyone could've moved him a single centimeter away from there. Essam was reliving his life with Samantha moment by moment. That place would astound anyone seeing it for the first time, but you could never go back there, not after you'd been filled with all that tragic energy. The tragic energy that had depressed and frightened me, that had made me try to erase Essam and Samantha from my memory as fast as I could.

What I did barely get out of him was that he'd refused to take any of her money, or her company, or any of her things. For her, he'd put an end to his own life. Essam had failed to find his sheikh, his teacher, whom he was going to apprentice to and who was going to help him to the end of his journey, because his greatest leader—ever since the beginning—had been Samantha, yet he hadn't known it. Those aren't my words: that was what he'd said as I kissed him and hugged him. Afterward, I felt as if I'd hugged and kissed a gelatinous phantom, as if I'd talked to air, as if I'd told the light I'd come back and visit. I knew I was lying. We both knew we'd never see each other again.

31

I NEVER GOT OVER WHAT HAD HAPPENED to Essam. I avoided the places where our friends went because I didn't want anyone to ask me about him; I wouldn't have known what to say. I didn't want to call him or visit him because I didn't want to be faced with any unexpected news. I didn't want to be the first person to find his body. I didn't want to be the one to identify his corpse. His obliteration was imminent; he was moored to the earth by only a few unraveling threads. I didn't listen to Marcia, or Awad, or Diana, or Evelyn, or anybody else no matter how close they were to Essam, when they tried to get me to go visit him, either with them or on my own. To me, Essam was like a swan in its final days: when it spies death on the horizon and heads toward the seashore to dance its last dance, and to sing its one dirge, and to die. I could see that Essam had made his apartment into a tomb for Samantha and himself; that he'd raised his anchor and sailed off with his memories. I knew he was working to free his soul from his bones and decaying flesh. I wasn't going to let them use me to get to him, not after he'd shut them out and sworn he'd never open up.

Even though I'd forced myself to stay away, Awad and Marcia were constantly bringing me any news they heard about Essam. The latest was that some of the neighbors had reported an awful smell coming from Essam's apartment so the police, accompanied by the neighbors and some of Essam's relatives, forced him to open up and stormed into the apartment. They looked all over for the source of the rotten stench, but all they found was some food that'd gone bad. They got a harangue from Essam and then they left. The officer told Essam's relatives that they should take him to see a psychiatrist, but they resisted as he might've taken it badly and broken ties with them. They were content to have the doorman keep an eye on him for them since he saw Essam twice a week when he went to take him his groceries. Marcia would tell me what she'd heard, but I had nothing to say. Awad would beg me to do something, but I didn't care. I didn't even react when Diana shot me a scornful look and stormed off, though Marcia was furious with her.

I went to see Karim when he got out of jail, but I didn't bring the camera or anything to write with. On my first night back at the crumbling villa, I packed up my things in a bag I'd brought with me and gave him back the lock and key. He was surprised, but he knew better than to ask any questions. He left for a little while and came back with two hash cigarettes. He handed one to me and started smoking the other. I took a couple of drags and asked him if he was switching over to hashish. He denied it as though it were an insult. He grinned as he explained he'd bought them for me. I asked him what his most recent lockup had been about. "A few begging and assault charges from way back. I'm taking care of 'em one by one," he said, cheerfully. "You're not going to film today?"

"Not today. Not tomorrow. Not ever."

"You're already done with the movie?" he asked. "Did you film while I was in jail?" I shook my head. "But back before I got arrested, you told me there was still some left to do. Why're you quitting?" I kept my counsel, but his curiosity got the better of him. Thinking carefully about his words so as not to make me angry, he said, "Don't take this the wrong way, but is it the foreign lady?" Sensing I wasn't going to say anything and that I didn't look angry, he said, "It's a good thing you got rid of her, Mr. Mustafa. She's just like Warda, I mean, no offense, but if you can't keep up with her, she goes and gets someone else." I couldn't help but laugh. Karim—even though he had the whole wide world as his playground and he went around claiming to be his own man—was still prisoner to that mangy girl; as if there were no one else in the entire world but her, as if she were the star he'd use to find his way. My laughter was making Karim uncomfortable so I stopped, but he just kept on looking at me, waiting for an explanation.

"Me and the foreign lady are as close as ever. Don't you forget it."

I could tell he was embarrassed. "Then why aren't you going to finish the movie?"

"Let's drop it for now and I'll tell you later," I said. "Maybe in a few days." He didn't pry; he respected my silence. Maybe he could tell I was in a bad mood and that was why he seemed friendlier and told me he was happy to help in any way he could. He shouted at the kids to leave me alone and quit their racket, but—for the first time since I'd started going there—I wanted Karim to leave me be so I could go and sleep in the arms of one of those girls, wanted him to ignore how they flirted and tried to seduce me. I was hoping he'd go out to make some money and leave me to face their abuse, their delights, their tragedies even. I wanted to spy on their sexual debauchery, their brawls, the crimson blood that sprayed out of their wounds. I needed something to take my mind off everything that was happening around me, but that's wishing for you: neither of us was bold enough to understand the other. The bridge between us buckled under him—too filthy, his reality too crushing—and me—too pretentious, too cerebral. *Karim, if you only knew how badly I want to dive into the mire right now. I want to die dirty . . . I want to purify myself in squalor. Maybe the squalor won't put me off, maybe it won't turn my stomach. The science, the theorizing, the melting pot we live in, that we hide behind, has cut us off from the real world. We've built another parallel world; it's not beautiful, it can't be compared. It's a trivial, stuck-up, soulless world.* What had I done for Karim besides ruin him with the vain manners he'd learned from me during the few days we'd spent together? He kept himself from spitting or snorting when he was around me. He got embarrassed when the others would ask him for their share of food or money in front of me. He bore their blunders patiently because he didn't want to do anything unseemly while I was around. If one of the girls tried to settle up with him, he dismissed her with a glance. When I told him I was worried his newfound manners would ruin our movie, he grinned and said, "Don't worry, Boss, I won't hold back in front of the camera."

I gave up wishing that he'd leave me the space to escape from my cocoon and I begged him to let me turn in. He went to lock my bag up in the drawer, but I stopped him; I said I was going to take all my stuff with me in the morning. "You're not going to come back, Boss?" I promised I'd come back and told him not to get up to anything illegal in the next few days because I was going to need him more than ever. His face lit up.

"Yes, sir. Anything you want."

I left the villa in the morning and caught up with Awad at his place a few seconds before he left for the hospital where his wife Aisha was about to give birth. I told him I wouldn't keep him long, but it was very important. His ears pricked up; his whole body seemed alert. He was watching my mouth as if he were expecting a vicious snake to come out. I told him I'd taken all Essam's paintings and sketches to the Catacomb Gallery and I'd told them to send them all to him—with his permission, of course—so he could look after them until Essam got better or until God carried out what's been predetermined. Frigid European that he was, he said, "Why don't you hold on to them? You've been his friend longer than I have." I didn't want to keep him long since he was on his way to welcome his first son. I didn't feel like arguing with him either.

"Will you hold on to them or should I have them sent to Evelyn in Fayoum?"

Hearing the threat in my voice, he became sensible. "Are you going on a trip?" I stood up and said goodbye. I said I'd stop by some other day to fill him in on all the details.

I was happy that Awad was going to take the paintings and sketches. They were destined for Western houses and American mansions; that was what they deserved. We didn't deserve them. I didn't give them to Marcia because we had a common fate whether I liked it or not. I wasn't planning to sell the apartment downtown, not even to Misr Insurance, even though I knew I'd never come back once I'd decided to leave. I also decided I wouldn't put the apartment in anyone's name. I'd rather let the inheritance process grind them up, rather they fought it out among themselves until the wiliest, the biggest thug of all took the biggest share; except for the bookcase, that I left to my nephew who'd had his eye on it. That just left my money. The money for which I'd worked, suffered, and abased myself. I faced the moment that strikes us all sometimes: when they tell you you've been killing yourself to amass a surplus you won't get to enjoy, for a profit that some unworthy person will get to cash in on. I wasn't going to leave part of it to Karim and his crew; that would've confirmed that I was completely nuts—granted, that was to be expected—but it also would've meant I was naive and stupid, and that was going too far. No matter how much I gave them, or put in a trust for them, the glue would've wiped it out in a few months. They'd have gone to jail over it, and dirty rumors about my motives would've followed after me. All the same, I wasn't going to leave my money for bankers, moneylenders, heirs, and taxmen to steal. That would've tortured me till the Day of Resurrection. It would've made everything I'd worked for in my life—if I'd ever done anything worthwhile—no more than a handful of air. That was what was plaguing my mind, what was making me fight to find a satisfactory solution.

I told Karim to find a stand or a small shop I could buy him so he could use it to earn a living. "Shame on you, Mr. Mustafa. Do you want 'em to kill me?"

"Who's going to kill you?"

"The kids. My friends." He couldn't believe I was so dense. "They'll say I got the money from their hard work or I cheated them out of their shares and stole it behind their back."

"You idiot!" I shouted. "Are you go on living like this till the glue kills you? Think! One day, you're going to get locked up for a long time and when you get out these kids'll be grown up, they'll be bosses themselves. You won't be able to control them. They'll chase you away like a dog."

My words seemed to affect him. "You think so?"

"Yeah, and worse. Let me buy you a shop and you can do whatever you want with it. Open a paint shop, if you want. You can sell paint to the builders and glue to your friends." I smiled, trying to convince him.

He laughed and rubbed my hand; he was stoned. "Now, that's a good idea. I'm down with selling glue." He came closer and whispered, "What do you want me to do for you?"

I didn't understand him, but he play-punched me as if I were his best friend and said, "What do you want me to do for you to buy me the shop?"

I laughed and an idea flashed across my mind. "I'll tell you later."

Before I left, I told him to get cracking and to call me as soon as he'd found a place. Then something occurred to me: "Do you have an ID card?" He pulled his ID out of his pocket to show me. He held the plank from upstairs so I could get down and insisted on carrying my bag down for me. For the first time since I'd started going to the villa, he walked me out.

At the lawyer's office, we took care of the contracts and my will and we agreed to meet the next morning at the notary office to enter them in the record. I also told the lawyer to write a watertight contract so the seller couldn't use any loopholes to get the shop back, not even if Karim were executed or imprisoned for life. My thoughts were all over the place; there were wide outlines, but nothing lucid that I could see. I'd decided not to take my medicine. I told Marcia I was up to my ears in work, but I was actually busy trying to take care of everything as quickly as I could. I bought some high-denomination fifteen-year savings bonds for my sisters' kids and I put them in a small, lockable briefcase along with a large sum of money and Awad and I went to a bank to put it in a safe deposit box. I left him two envelopes: one had the savings bonds in it and the other had a letter for Zaynab; on the outside, I'd written instructions for getting in touch with her if she ever came back to Egypt. Awad was to give her the briefcase as soon as she returned. He was nervous and spooked, but I tried my hardest to calm him down. I even told him I was going on a secret overseas trip and pleaded with him not to tell anyone, especially not Marcia, until after I'd left. He didn't believe me until I swore on his infant son that I was telling the truth. He tried to get me to tell him why I was leaving— "Why? What's the point?"—but he couldn't get anything out of me. He didn't shut up about it until I swore he'd be the first person I called and that I'd tell him where I was even if I were in hell. I left Awad, feeling like I'd actually sent him down to hell. I was like the old imperialists, who used to draw borders between their colonies with landmines, and after they'd left, the borders remained like festering wounds, dividing a single people or neighbors, refusing to scar over. I left Awad a mined, radioactive envelope; if he ever did meet Zaynab and give her the envelope, she'd undoubtedly take him to the real hell and then there'd be no need for me to get in touch.

I rose through the highest ranks of spiritual certainty and I started seeing celestial visions and image after image of hell. Mornings, afternoons, and evenings all blended together. I was being knocked back and forth between visions, foggy and distorted, and thoughts as pure as milk. I don't know how many days I'd spent hiding in my cave until Marcia brought me out. She phoned me, irate, screaming that her apartment had been robbed. I didn't get her point at first. "Call the police," I said.

"I'm not calling anybody. I know who did it. Are you going to let me face them by myself or are you going to come over?" she said and slammed the phone down. I put on whatever clothes I could find and went over to her apartment. I hadn't appreciated her tone and I wasn't happy about obeying her once more so to take my mind off it I asked myself: who was this thief whom she knew, what could've been stolen, how valuable might it be? I was worried that Marcia was going to finger Karim or Warda and claim the burglar was someone they'd sent. If the police got involved, all hell would've broken loose. I was racing against time to get to her before she could set off a disaster. She'd said she wasn't going to tell anyone, but I knew her better than that. If I didn't get there fast enough, she'd call her embassy and Interpol straight away—maybe even before she called the local cops.

Marcia yanked the door open and shut it behind me without uttering a single word. Julia the maid was sitting, bound to a chair and trembling, her face puffy from Marcia's slapping. Seeing her, I groaned, and seeing me, she nearly died of fright. Her eyes were completely red, as red as blood, but there was no sign of tears, not even as she adamantly denied that she was the thief. I dragged a chair over and sat down across from her, like detectives do in American movies. I sat there silently, examining her face. Her dark skin was almost shining and her braids made her head look like the globe. Her thick lips were quivering and her delicate nose was a little swollen from Marcia's abuse. Every time I moved my chair forward an inch, the girl screamed and shivered as if I were the devil. That seemed to be how she'd always thought of me, and Marcia had only made it worse by using me to threaten her, telling her I was a monster and on my way over. I didn't lay a hand on her; I merely asked her where she'd hidden the stuff she'd stolen. She was rabidly denying she'd done anything so I let her be and took Marcia into the kitchen to find out what exactly had been stolen. Ten thousand dollars, Marcia said, the first installment of the Dutch funding. She'd withdrawn it from the bank in order to put a deposit down on the raw film stock she was going to order from Kodak and to pay for some other production costs, but then it'd been stolen. I didn't say anything about her feeble justification for keeping such a large amount of money in her apartment. "You're sure you've searched the entire apartment?" I asked. She said she'd searched every corner of the place.

She pointed to a big bag beside the stove and said, "That's Julia's bag. She packed all her clothes and stuff. She was planning to run away." I went to look through the bag, but she said, "You won't find anything in there." It was obvious that Julia and her cousin, having lost hope of emigrating since the United Nations had stopped helping the refugees resettle on the grounds that Northern and Southern Sudan had signed a pact and the situation had stabilized, had decided to take matters in their own hands and get as far away from UN agreements as they could. If Marcia had called the police, it would've ruined everything: the money would still be lost and Julia's cousin, Sibt, would've got wind of things and fled on his own, abandoning Julia to her fate. We had to get her to talk, to tell us whether she'd given the money to Sibt or hidden it somewhere and hadn't had a chance to give him any of it yet. I could tell Marcia was angry and on edge so I spoke softly as I asked her which of her friends had been at the apartment before the robbery. She answered snappishly that no one had been over for the past three days. When I told her to calm down and not to interfere with how I was going to handle the situation, she smiled for the first time since I'd been over and kept quiet. I undid Julia's restraints and apologized for Marcia's behavior. I told her I'd make Marcia forget all about the robbery and help them go to America. All Julia could do was gasp for air like someone on their deathbed and pass out repeatedly for a few seconds at a time. Her chest was heaving. It was as if she were prepared to put up with insults, abuse, and prison in exchange for the money. When she realized I wasn't going to lay a hand on her, she raised her voice and started accusing us of cruelty and slander. She said it was racist of us to accuse her and not accuse the friend Marcia had had over the night before. What Julia had said caught me off guard, but when I turned to look at Marcia, she simply said, "She means Diana. The retard wants me to think Diana did it."

As if Diana were merely air and it was perfectly ordinary for her not to tell me she'd been there. When Julia brought Diana up a second time, Marcia totally lost it and charged at her, but I held her back. I took my belt off and pulled Julia down to the floor. I chased her around every corner of that apartment, the belt making a terrible sound every time it hit a wall or table. Marcia helped me chase her, but the girl was besting us, leaping acrobatically over sofas and chairs; that was until she

265

ran out onto the balcony. Julia stood in the corner of the balcony and Marcia shut the door behind me so she wouldn't be able to slip past; she even shut the door to the adjacent room. I leaned back against the glass sliding door, struggling to hide my fear of heights. Julia was looking all around her like a cornered cat and I was trying to calm her down, but then when it looked to her like I was going to come closer and grab her, an indomitable fear seized her and she jumped off the balcony, fourteen stories to the ground.

32

MARCIA PULLED ME BACK INSIDE and pounded on my chest until I came to my senses. She was talking frantically, and though I heard the various languages, I couldn't understand her as the words had lost any meaning to me. I can remember her opening the front door, as steady as a professional killer, and telling me to go hide in Diana's apartment downstairs. Terrified, I scurried down eleven flights of stairs to Diana's apartment on the third floor. Diana was standing behind her half-open door and she quickly pulled me inside. I felt like I was in a science fiction movie, or a Hitchcock thriller. She sat me down on the sofa and brought me a glass of cold lemonade. She told me Marcia had explained to her what had happened and that I had to pull it together. With pity in her eyes, Diana laid me down on her bed like a feverish child. I was soaked with sweat and shivering as though I were possessed. She was concerned about my condition so she ran to bring me a glass of whiskey. I drank it down in a few seconds. She massaged my face with her fingers, behind my ears, pushing on my temples. I felt so calm. Her fingers roamed all over my body and I began to be bathed in a green light. And then I disconnected from the world. Hours later, at twilight, I woke to voices arguing: Marcia, Diana, and Sophie. Marcia, sensing I'd stirred, burst into the room, and Diana and Sophie were right behind her. She hugged me and wept and asked them to leave us. They left; we were alone. She told me everything had been taken care of smoothly, that the police understood what motives Julia would've had for committing suicide and that they were looking for her cousin, Sibt, to get Marcia's money back. I was enveloped in her embrace and her voice was booming in my ears. She also mentioned that the policemen were polite and respectful and they hadn't involved the embassy in the matter. I raised my head and looked at her; I asked her about Julia.

"Julia's dead, Mustafa. Did you think she was going to jump from that high up and not die? You think she's Batman or something?" She smiled. We'd worked in concert to murder the poor girl and now Marcia was smiling.

She thought I was making a joke, something to smile at. I said nothing. Suddenly, Diana was taking Marcia to sleep with her in the living room across from the bedroom where I was sleeping; Sophie had gone home. I offered to trade places with them, but they refused. Diana wanted to give me another massage to help me fall asleep, but I wasn't having it. She had to give me a sleeping pill before she left me alone though. All I heard them talking about in the other room was the disciplined policemen and the decent security guards from the building, who'd backed up Marcia's story. They didn't talk about the crimson blood that poured out of Julia, her brain smeared across the ground, not even about the cars out in front of the building that were dented by Julia's fall. They didn't talk about Julia's dreams of moving to the West, to the promised paradise, the stuff Marcia used to fill my head with. They didn't talk about human beings or humanity. The thing Marcia had really cared most about was making sure her money would be returned to her in good time so we could start filming. I fell asleep, the pillow belonging to Diana's boyfriend, Sharif the Singer, held tightly in my arms. I could smell his sweat over every inch of it. I fell asleep, facing the picture of Diana's two daughters, who watched what their mother did on that bed every day.

That long day had finally come to an end. In the morning, I was greeted by the security guards as I left the building. There were some doormen and workers from the garage standing around in the middle of the street where there was a chalk outline of a small body. They were talking about what'd happened, pointing upward, mimicking the sound of impact. I walked right past them, but they didn't pay the slightest attention to me. They didn't look at me. None of them had a flash of insight; no one pointed at me and shouted to the others that I was the killer so they could take their revenge.

Julia had immigrated to the afterlife and her cousin was going to immigrate to prison, and I didn't know whether Marcia had put a necklace around my neck or a noose. I was responsible for the death of a girl who wasn't even twenty years old. Her destiny had driven her out of her faraway country and she'd barely been able to shoulder the dreams she'd had for herself, and for her children after her, and for her entire line; the dreams that'd nearly broken her back: the dream of freedom, the dream of living like a human being. As far as she was concerned, nothing had changed. She became a maid, then a thief, and finally a suicide. And her dreams were buried alive. What price was Marcia expecting me to pay in exchange for protecting me? What secret deal had we struck without exchanging a single word? Was she going to use me to get money, or a promotion from the high-level organization she was working for, or was she going to get a scolding because of me instead? Would I give a damn? Or would I be like Goha, who, whenever they said to him, "There's someone screwing in your house," replied, "So long as it's not in my ass"; "There's someone screwing in your bed," they said, and he said, "So long as it's not in my ass," and as the screwing made its way closer and closer to his own ass he just went on bragging about his personal safety?

Things between Marcia and me changed after the accident. I heard from her less and she started being curt with me. I couldn't stand to be at her apartment anymore; I fled from it in fear and took refuge inside my own shell once again. I was doing complex, disorganized calculations, but every result was a disastrous loss. I had to try to figure out

269

which was worst. The lawyer called to tell me that Karim had picked out a shop, but it needed to be fixed up, painted, and furnished. I told him to buy the place and have it done up. I didn't answer any of the calls I got from Karim or from unknown numbers until the grand opening of his shop. He'd surprised me by choosing a spot in al-Wayli, but I was even more surprised when I heard he was planning to make it into an offalery.

Karim had put on a clean outfit and he and the lawyer were waiting for me outside my house. He greeted me warmly, but when he tried to kiss me on the cheeks, I leaned away. The lawyer drove us to the offalery, which Karim had put his older brother in charge of. I really enjoyed the food; I got my appetite back. I asked Karim why he'd changed his mind about opening a paint shop and opened up that place so far away from his crew instead. He smiled confidently and said that this was the family trade and that his brother wasn't going to cheat him, and even if he did cheat him, "At least the money'll stay inside the family." Then he winked at me and said he'd tell me the rest in private.

When we finished eating, he went over to the sink ahead of me and stood there holding the towel as I washed my hands and rinsed my mouth. He tried to dry my hands for me, but I wouldn't let him so he handed me the towel. I could tell he wanted to get me alone so he could tell me something and I braced myself, expecting him to ask for more money and thereby ruin my opinion of him. If he had, I might have given up on him completely as I don't like being extorted. I looked him in the eye. "What is it you wanted to tell me?" I asked. He smiled and motioned for me to lean down so he could whisper in my ear. That only made me more apprehensive, but he surprised me: he explained that he'd picked this far-off place and left it to his two brothers to run so it'd be at a safe distance from the suspicions of his crew who'd have wondered how he'd got his hands on the money; plus he was getting himself ready for a long trip.

"What trip?"

He laughed. "The trip you're going to send me on!" That wily dog always blew me away. With that incredible, unexpected, innate intelligence of his, he always seemed to know what was going on in my head. Yet, in my agitation, I couldn't tell whether he'd said it in proper Arabic or in dialect, or whether my mind had started translating everything it heard into Arabic since it was used to hearing so many different languages. There was no way Karim could've put it like that: he was a street kid. The really astonishing thing was that I actually was preparing to send Karim on a long trip—though I didn't know if he'd survive it—and I'd been trying to figure out how I was going to bring it up, but now he'd cut to the chase and told me he was ready.

As I was leaving, Karim came up to me beside the car. He whispered that he was ready at any time and his body language said the same thing. The lawyer leaned over and asked me what Karim had been talking to me about, but I didn't tell him. He didn't get the hint and kept on talking, as if he were tutoring me about the dangers of street kids and how you can never tell how they'll react, so I told him to mind his own business. I'd made it clear from the beginning that if he didn't ask too many questions, didn't act too surprised, and didn't proffer his own opinions, I'd reward him handsomely, so I gave him another warning and told him how easy it'd be for me to fire him and find another law firm. He shut up. I returned home, feeling like I'd laid out a fail-safe script for the coming days, and so I stretched out and fell into a deep sleep.

As soon as I woke up, I went to take a shower, but then I was suddenly set upon by my mobile, whose ringing reached me all the way in the bathroom. It wouldn't stop. The only thing that came to mind was that it was Zaynab so I ran over to it, imagining that she'd escaped from under Julio's surveillance and was calling me for help, calling to tell me Julio hadn't let her phone me. But it was Yasmeen. She was calling to take me to task for not getting in touch since I got back. Why hadn't I sent her what I'd written day by day as I'd promised I would? She was like a bratty child, smothering her parents with requests for holiday presents. She didn't even give me a chance to come up with an excuse. Mostly she was mad that I'd ignored her constant phone calls. I couldn't think of anything to say. I wasn't going to level with her and tell her I was disappointed that she'd abandoned me, lying on the floor of the Atelier. She was really letting me have it, but then she remembered I'd been ill so she sounded concerned and asked about my health. Her resentment came back shortly after. She said she wasn't going to call me anymore and that if I wanted to talk to her, her line was always open. She said goodbye and hung up.

That girl bewildered me. Most of the time, I treated her like a mature woman and had respect for her mind, but she'd often shock me with her childish behavior. When we talked, she used to listen to me as if I were her teacher and occasionally we'd argue gingerly. Sometimes, she'd revert to being a child and want me to take her to the amusement park and push her on the swings. I'd heave the thread of my memories up from the depths and think back to the days at university, the tumult of it, and my mood would come in line with hers. But then she'd pull on her memories even more and she'd take us back to secondary school and middle school and what all the teachers had hoped for her and the notes her friends had written to her in her notebooks. Those were the times I was closest to sending her away, or cursing her, or telling her never to come to see me again. Yet soon enough she'd address me seriously and intelligently and I'd back off. That girl always amazed me, so much so that I almost wouldn't have been surprised if she'd come up to me dressed in her school clothes, two ribbons in her hair, a scratch on her knee from a fall during a schoolyard fight; like when she'd showed up with the ribbon that had "Jerusalem is Ours" written on it. Sure, that rebellious child had turned the heads of the people at the Atelier, but I was mortified. A child who told me all about how she'd taken part in the protest and about the nightsticks she'd faced and the blow to her temple, right beside her eye. My mind cleared in an instant and I could remember everything. I had no idea what to think; my heartbeat rose alongside her voice in a desperate attempt to muddle my thoughts. I could see how she'd lifted up a corner of her headscarf so I could see the pale blue bruise just above her birthmark, which looked exactly like Hind's birthmark. That was the sign. My unconscious had been determined to hide it from me, to distract me so I wouldn't remember. God! It'd been so many days since we'd met at the Atelier and I'd been unable to remember. How unjust, how powerful and omnipotent you are, stubborn mind! Hind came to me and revealed her sign like a bolt of lightning and you erased it from my memory for all those days. I didn't need a spiritual apparition of Hind's entire body to know she'd returned. She'd made me a promise after she left and then faded away like scent from a flower, like light from the moon, like soul from body.

I got up, jumped into my clothes, and rushed out the door in the direction of her house, which I'd never been to before; I'd never intended to visit her house, but I'd often walked her back to the street corner nearby. Her old grandmother opened the door. I didn't ask for her by either name: the earthly or the heavenly, the old one or the new one. I simply told the woman: "I'm Mustafa." She greeted me anxiously and let me into the ancient apartment. She led me to a seat in the cramped living room as she repeated her greeting in a metallic tone. Out of habit, she asked me why it'd been so long since I last called the house. When I told her I'd been sick, she softened a bit and said she hoped I was feeling better. She was looking at me, annoyed; not moving, nor wishing to move. I was looking around and it got on her nerves so she asked me what I'd like to drink. I insisted I wouldn't have anything so she got up and went to call for her. I got distracted, trying to compare the place to what I'd pictured. I could see they were identical: what was in my head and what was real at that moment. A narrow doorway off the small sitting room leading to a hallway, on the right side of which there were two small bedrooms facing the kitchen and the bathroom. I was sitting directly in front of the hallway. The woman went into the first room on the right; the door was ajar so I could see a big banner with some drawings, which I couldn't make out, over the National Pledge, which was written out in marker: "I swear to God that I shall be loyal to the Arab Republic of Egypt and, as God as my witness, I will do the utmost to lift her up and defend her against all enemies and usurpers and that I shall be a good model in both my character and my deeds." I knew for sure that room was hers, but as soon as I'd made certain, the door shut behind the woman; as if it'd been enough just to show me its sign. The grandmother came out first, followed by Hind, wearing a headscarf and a winter nightgown, in the body of a very young girl, exactly as her own body had been back when we used to study together. Hind, or Yasmeen, or whatever purely terrestrial name, was looking at me, terrified, and her grandmother was insisting I drink some orange juice. I took a sip. I didn't show her any mercy by explaining the reason for my surprise visit. I was waiting for a chance to get her alone and she was clinging to her grandmother's side as if she were afraid of being raped. I pulled out a cigarette and went to light it, but the stern grandmother stopped me, saying the smoke hurt her chest. My plan to get the grandmother to bring me an ashtray so I could be alone with the girl had failed. I'd have traded the entire world: everything I'd won, everything I'd gained, all that was left of my life, for a glimpse of the sign. The bloody grandmother never gave me a chance and the girl was much too withdrawn and frightened; her eyes nearly screamed, "What the hell problem is this you've brought with you?" I was torn between the shadow of my mind, which was drawing me toward Yasmeen, and the transcendental world, which was pulling me toward Hind. The old woman squirmed in her chair. "Would you like to stay for dinner, Mr. Mustafa?" she asked as if trying to make me leave.

I caught her off guard with a decisive blow: I instantly said yes. She looked at me, stunned, and then she sullenly got to her feet and grabbed onto the girl's hand. The girl said, "I'll come help you, Granny." The sounds of clattering pots, water pouring out of the faucet, and the scraping of dishes and forks and knives began to emerge. The noise was getting louder and it was as if they were doing some communal ritual to drive out the evil spirits. The awful noise was making me nervous, but I held it together. The kitchen was on the left-hand side of the hallway. Steam and smoke emerged from it along with clouds of anger, displeasure, and astonishment rising from the old woman's mouth. All those vapors reached me in the living room where I was sitting. It was like torture by unconventional methods. I lost it completely and made the most lunatic decision of my life that day. I tiptoed over to the kitchen and popped in on them as they were caught up in the fuss I'd made them go to. I'd assumed that the girl would've taken off her headscarf so I could've caught another peek of the sign, but the headscarf was still there. The knife fell from the girl's hand and the tomato she'd been dicing fell to the floor. When the old woman saw me, she left her frying to rush over, with more energy than she seemed to possess, and stood between me and the girl. She looked at me in horror. I couldn't understand what they were so afraid of so I smiled and pretended that I didn't want them to go to too much trouble making the food. I told them I was happy to eat whatever was already prepared. The girl begged me with her eyes to leave off all that madness, but I didn't care; I was determined to see through what I'd come to do. When the old woman turned around, I asked Yasmeen to stop what she was doing for a moment because there was something I needed to talk to her about and then I turned around and walked back to the living room. The girl came in. She was irate, her jaw clenched. "What is it, Mr. Mustafa?" she shouted under her breath.

I whispered back, trying to sound balanced, "I want to talk to you about something important. It won't take more than five minutes, but, please, make sure your grandmother doesn't come in so we can talk."

"What's so important? You're scaring me."

I nodded toward the kitchen for her to go check to make sure her grandmother was distracted. She obeyed and went to look in on her grandmother. When she came back in, she anxiously rushed me to get talking. Her headscarf was wrapped tightly around her head. The beads of sweat on her forehead almost shone. Her dark eyes and lashes brought out her beautiful white skin. I moved closer to her as if I were going to tell her a secret and begged her to show me the bruise. She inched backward in fear as I continued to beg and plead. She was terrified. She hunched her shoulders against the sides of her head as if to protect the sight of it from me. The kitchen had suddenly gone quiet so I knew her grandmother was coming. The more I pleaded, the more terrified she got. She stood up as if to escape, but I put my hand out to sit her back down. She screamed, but her scream only made me more determined and I grabbed her face and tried to pull the headscarf away to get a look at the sign. No matter how she screamed or trembled I wouldn't stop, not until I saw the sign and touched it and made certain this was Hind. The old woman was pummeling my back with her bony arms. The girl's body had fully transformed into Hind's body. And, then, when I saw the tomato smeared across the apron she was wearing over her gallabiya, it reminded me of the blood and it drove me into a frenzy. I started matching every one of her screams with a louder scream until the neighbors broke into the apartment.

Subsequent investigations determined that I'd been strangling the girl and shouting for her to let Hind's soul out of her body.

33

IN HER COMPLAINT, the old woman maintained that I'd broken into the apartment and attempted to rape her granddaughter. She also enlisted the help of some of the other tenants and the people from the street who'd roughed me up. They claimed that they'd seen me assaulting the girl and were using the opportunity of my standing in front of the investigating officer to smack me as if the injuries they'd inflicted over every inch of my body hadn't been enough. They weren't satisfied with the damage they'd already caused. I didn't feel like defending myself; I'd seen what I needed to see. I was ready for something crueler than death. The investigator seemed pleased at the sight of my injuries and his assistants were like hyenas, sniffing my blood and getting ready to finish me off. The girl was as white as a corpse, shivering and sobbing. The fear beyond which there is no greater fear showed on her face. But I didn't care about any of those people, or the investigator sitting there, or the other officers walking around, or the assistants, or the old woman. The girl and I were off in our own world. I was examining her, trying to distinguish Hind's features from Yasmeen's. It was difficult, nearly impossible, like trying to separate the colors of a rainbow, but then suddenly I saw her face transform. Hind appeared to me clearly and vividly, wearing a stern look like when she wanted something.

She had drafted Yasmeen into service and made her bawl and scream at the investigator and then weep in front of them all, denying everything they'd accused me of. The old woman was bristling with anger and she was about to smack the girl, but then she started pretending that she was going to have a heart attack. The neighbors bowed their heads and muttered as the investigator asked his questions again, skeptically this time, looking back and forth at me and the girl. Then he went through my papers, which were spread out in front of him: my ID card, my National ID number, my Visa card, my American University in Cairo library card, membership cards for a bunch of news organizations, and a few hundred dollar bills. The officer shuffled the notes with his finger and then he said, "What do you do for a living?"

I nodded toward the notes. "I'm Hind's classmate from university."

The woman was shaking again and shouting, "He's crazy! He's crazy!"

The girl went up to the investigator and leaned down to talk in his ear. She looked at me sweetly. "I'm Hind, Officer," she said in a voice everyone could hear. Then she whispered to him in a voice only the two of them could hear. From time to time, the investigator would look at me and smile. Then he made me sign some papers. He gathered up my possessions and as he handed them back to me, he told me to go see my doctor. I would've cursed him if the old woman hadn't started screaming at him for letting me go. The girl turned to her with daggers in her eyes and shouted at her to be quiet. The old woman was shocked into silence by the girl's outburst. Before the investigator could dismiss me, the girl walked over to me. The old woman tried to stop her from going near me, but the girl pushed the old woman's hand away and looked at her angrily. She started moving toward me once more and gestured for me to walk to the far corner of the room. As we stood there, she leaned forward and, to everyone's amazement, whispered in my ear. "I'm not going to come back anymore. It's enough what I did just now." It was Hind's voice. I swear she said those words; it wasn't a hallucination. I couldn't have wished for more. I smiled and the blood returned to my face. As

I stood there in front of the investigator, I felt intoxicated, felt taller than everyone there. The investigator yelled for everyone to leave, but he held me back. He waved a restraining order in my face and warned me not to try anything again. A few minutes later, the girl came back in, alone. The investigator didn't know what to think, but he was too curious to intervene. She stopped a half a meter away from me and bowed her head.

"I'm sorry," she said and the voice was Yasmeen's. Then she said, "Goodbye," and the voice was Hind's. She turned her back on me almost as if she were asking permission to leave Yasmeen's body. I could only imagine how Hind would return to me the next time. What form would she come in? Or maybe, as she'd had Yasmeen say, she'd never appear again. The investigator had tried to get his head around it all, but I guess I must have stumped him because he ordered his assistant to take me to the nearest bus stop.

I kept myself under house arrest for more than five days so my wounds could heal over and my bruises recede. Marcia called me once a day. She checked up on me and told me she was staying with Diana because she couldn't stay in her apartment by herself and she was thinking about giving it up. She said she'd tell me when she found a new place. I told her to wait for a couple months until the yearly lease was up and not to renew it, but, for once, I wasn't able to convince her.

Those days were all about the lawyer: I had to send for him several times so we could take care of all the necessary arrangements. He was upset, or he pretended to be, when he saw the sorry state I was in two days after the police station incident. He was mad that I hadn't called him: he'd have liked to have given the investigator and the detectives a lesson they'd never forget. I thanked God that I hadn't been stupid enough to call him. If I had, we'd have both been in jail till Kingdom come.

I had some of Marcia's things in my possession, most importantly the professional-quality camera, the notes I'd taken, and what I'd recorded of the film. I called Awad, who came over right away, and told him I wasn't going to finish the movie with Marcia. To my surprise, he lowered his gaze as if he understood perfectly well. I hadn't wanted to

279

get into a whole discussion about it as it would've distracted me from what I'd had planned for him, but he threw me a curveball. He told me Marcia had sent him to get the camera and tapes from me, but he'd have been too embarrassed to come see me if I hadn't called. Then he consoled me, saying it was all because of Diana; she'd scared Marcia by telling her that she'd seen a thirst for blood in my eyes after Julia's tragic accident. Seeing how distraught I was, Awad tried to calm me down. He said Marcia was going through difficult circumstances and that soon it'd all be water under the bridge—as if I cared whether I ever saw her again. I told him to stop talking about it and gave him the camera. I took the bag of my clothes he'd brought, but I told him I wasn't going to turn over a single tape that I'd shot and Marcia could do her worst. He said he'd act as an intermediary and clear up the mis-understanding. He said it'd all pass, like a cloud in the summer sky; Marcia had just fallen under Diana's influence. I told him to get out.

I own a 9mm Beretta pistol given to me by the producer Yusuf Hilmi with the blessing of his martyred son, Said. I've had the gun for years and I've never used it for its intended purpose. Yusuf Hilmi told me that his martyred son had come to him in a dream and told him how happy he was that he'd given me the gun. Obviously, Yusuf Hilmi had been gripped by a horrible nightmare and taken it for a dream. A loaded revolver has been by my side for years, but it hasn't fired a single bullet. An obsolete grenade lay in the Expedition Club office watching as the students changed year after year: they'd start university, they'd graduate and all the while it waited for its chance to tear Hind's body apart.

Karim finally called to tell me he was ready. I told him to come over to my apartment; he knew where it was because the lawyer had brought him by before the grand opening of his new offalery. I was waiting for him. I didn't want to see anyone: not Essam, not Ahmad al-Helu, not Shahinaz, not Zaynab, not Yasmeen, not Evelyn or Awad. I was no longer the master of my fate. I'd been a wretched servant to moneymaking. My end was musk, poison, and madness. I'd lived stupidly, like a coward; I'd hidden my feelings in my breast. The few months I'd spent locked up when I was younger had turned me into a receptacle for the filth of the whole world. After that, I didn't even risk sitting with political types at the coffeehouse. I escaped overseas and when I came back I disappeared behind an American woman's camera. What's the difference between me and the people who hock human rights and anti-discrimination and feminism? Our old friends gave up secrets and cashed in on their weeks in prison. They've filled the satellite channels, boasting of their struggle. I heard them screech with my own ears, heard them weep, heard them beg. I can see what little they've gained by giving up our secrets. Who among us has remained stoic until today? They sold out and got their price and called the rest of us cowards. I thanked God we were no longer in the same trench so that we couldn't be wiped out by the fluctuating ideals and world transformations no one ever saw coming.

The nineteenth day of Israel's demolishing of Lebanon. Lebanon, where my first book of poems was published. Lebanon, the smallest Arab country, the country charged with defending all Arabs. The butchers committed a new slaughter yesterday in Qana and Olmert asked Condoleezza Rice for an additional fifteen days to wrap up the attack on Lebanon. Pictures of dead children in newspapers are thrust under the door. I gathered their pictures and their stories and pasted them onto poster board next to the pictures of Israeli children kissing the missiles that were going to explode in Lebanon and take Hind away all over again. I put the poster up on the wall of my bedroom; the bedroom Zaynab had walked out of. The person responsible for the grenade that killed Hind has become a leader who wades through our blood. I still own a 9mm Beretta pistol. Said the martyr forgot to take it with him when he flew his plane up into the sky of war. Said, did you burn up with your plane so quickly you couldn't feel it? Or did you eject with your parachute after a missile hit your wing? And when they surrounded you, did you reach for your weapon and find it wasn't there?

I put all the digital videotapes, the detailed scenario, and plans for the work and the idea—how I'd got interested in it and got Marcia excited about it—into a locked briefcase and wrote the name of a director friend of mine, who worked at the National Film Center, on the outside of it; I couldn't remember his address. I also left him a letter explaining what I thought he should do with the tapes. Karim came over and I told him how to get to Cinema City and to put the briefcase in my director friend's hand, to give it only to him in the flesh and not to anyone else. Karim listened to me very closely. When I finished giving him instructions, he fretfully asked what'd happened to me and then he asked about Marcia and whether I'd ended things with her. I started telling him stories about foreigners and the kinds of things they expected from us and the kinds of things they forced us to do. I told him to do everything in his power to keep them from finishing the film. I lied and said that I'd exposed what they were up to only after they'd got me to start filming. Karim seemed slow, like he didn't understand what I was saying. I felt like I was never going to get away from failure. I gave up all hope for him, but even so I gave him the gun. His eyes lit up as soon as he saw it, but he seemed reluctant to take it. Then he asked me what he should do with it. I didn't say anything, but when he'd eagerly taken it in his hand and his face lit up, I told him to keep it somewhere safe and not to let anyone else see him with it. Then I told him the story of Julia and how she'd jumped from the balcony and it seemed to affect him.

He wrapped the gun in a cloth and stuck it in his trousers. He took the briefcase and the envelope with the key and the letter for my director friend and headed toward the door, but then he set the briefcase on the floor and returned. He'd remembered about me. He hugged me affectionately and told me not to worry and then he was gone.

I didn't need all those medicines any more. Not the ones that level me out, or the ones that rescue me from insomnia, or the anti-depressants, or the ones that make me sluggish, or control my mania, or make me at peace with myself. I emptied all the pills out in front of me: the yellow ones, the reds, the blues: navy and sky, the oranges, the pinks and crimsons, the greens and whites, the ivorys, the capsules, the round pills, the square pills, the triangles, the cylinders. I made cities out of them and shacks, trees fruiting colors of the rainbow, a colored iron cell, trains blowing orange smoke, a big soccer pitch where I chased the pill around with my cocked finger, flicking it with my fingernail and making it fly over the heads of the spectators. I drank glass after glass and then I began savoring those soccer balls, sucking on them. The sweet mixed with the bitter mixed with the acrid mixed with the tasteless.

I could see nothing but a long, endless street then. No clouds in the sky, no fog, no cars, no traffic. Only legions of people coming toward me: some wearing headscarves, some not, office workers and school kids, tissue peddlers and street magicians. Wandering vendors, carrying their goods like coffins. Topless streetwalkers smiling and welcoming me with open arms. Sullen men of religion. Cats riding dogs. Pigeons with falcon beaks and trees bearing devil heads.

The street stretches as far as I can see, spitting humans and animals and rocks up out of its depths. I listen to the sound of their breathing, the roar as they clear the way for me. They don't look at me. They don't come toward me. And then I catch sight of an utterly white, empty expanse behind them. The wind is still. I can see so many people waving to me from behind that expanse: Yusuf Hilmi and his martyred son, my mother and Julia, Hind and Samantha, and when I enter into that space everything ceases. I can't hear anything, I can't see anything. There's nothing, only the utter emptiness.

Glossary

Abdel-Halim Hafez (1929–77): an Egyptian singer and, along with Umm Kulthum, one of the most important Arab recording artists of the twentieth century.

Ahmad ibn Hanbal (780–855): a theologian and founder of one of the four canonical Sunni schools of law.

Amal Donqol (1940–83): an Egyptian poet who rose to fame in the 1960s. His poems often dealt with political topics through allegory.

Asar al-Hakim (1958–): an Egyptian actress.

Fairuz (1935–): the most famous Lebanese singer, her career has spanned the most turbulent decades of Lebanese history.

Fatiha: the opening sura (chapter) of the Qur'an.

al-Ghazali (1058–1111): a religious scholar, philosopher, Sufi, and mystic. His *Deliverance from Error* is an account of his development as a religious thinker and mystic.

Hamza Alaa al-Din (1929–2006): a Nubian musician from southern-most Egypt. In the 1960s he settled in America.

Ibn al-Arabi (1165–1240): a Sufi poet and philosopher, regarded as one of the most important Islamic mystics in history.

Kamil al-Shennawi (1908–65): an Egyptian poet and journalist.

kanaka and sibirtaya: a kanaka is a small pot for making tea and coffee that is heated over a sibirtaya, a small alcohol burner. One advantage of the kanaka and sibirtaya combination is that hosts can make coffee or tea in the sitting room in the presence of their guests.

al-Mutanabbi (915–955): traditionally considered the greatest classical Arab poet.

Nagat al-Sagheera (1939–): an Egyptian singer and actress.

Salah Jahin (1930–86): an Egyptian poet notable for writing in colloquial Arabic. He wrote many famous songs for Abdel-Halim Hafez (see above). His famous operetta, *The Great Night*, was written for the puppet theater.

Sultan Abd al-Hamid II (r. 1876–1918): the last Ottoman sultan to rule, he was deposed by the Young Turks in 1909 and later reinstated as a puppet ruler until his death in 1918.

Umm Kulthum (1904–75): the most famous Arab singer of the twentieth century.

Zaki Naguib Mahmoud (1905–93): an Egyptian philosopher and intellectual. He was a proponent of logical positivism and later turned his attention to attempting to reconcile the Islamic cultural heritage with modernism.